*Only he can make all of
your dreams come true.*

"Are you afraid?" he asked.

"Of course not. I just don't want to kiss you."

"Not at all?"

"Not one little bit. Not an iota."

"No curiosity about what it might be like to kiss the man Queen Victoria said was most certainly the worst rake in all of London?"

"No."

"You're fibbing, Minerva."

"I'm not."

He lowered his head, brushed his lips over her heated cheek. To his surprise, she didn't move away. Slowly, he traced a path to her lips, breathing against them before placing his mouth on hers.

A kiss should be an appetizer. A kiss was a prelude, strings being tuned in an orchestra pit, dawn on an important day.

A kiss was not a feast. A kiss was not an explosion of the senses. But this one was.

He could smell her, that hint of earthiness mixed with her new perfume. Her skin was warm against his fingertips, her cheek heating as he inclined his head to deepen the kiss.

Her mouth opened slightly on a gasp.

He wanted to banish her sorrow, the pain Neville had caused her. He wanted to change the tenor of her thoughts, give her something to replace her dread.

He could give Minerva passion. That's the gift he could give her.

KAREN RANNEY

Scotsman
of My Dreams

AVONBOOKS

An Imprint of HarperCollinsPublishers

AVON BOOKS
An Imprint of HarperCollins*Publishers*
195 Broadway
New York, New York 10007

Copyright © 2015 by Karen Ranney LLC
ISBN 978-0-06-233750-4
www.avonromance.com

First Avon Books mass market printing: September 2015

Avon Trademark Reg. U.S. Pat. Off. and in Other Countries, Marca Registrada, Hecho en U.S.A.
HarperCollins® is a registered trademark of HarperCollins Publishers.

Printed in the U.S.A.

10 9 8 7 6 5 4 3 2 1

To Jeff Stutsman: a classy, witty guy

Scotsman
of My Dreams

Chapter 1

London
July, 1862

$\mathcal{F}$our hours past noon on a muggy July day, Minerva Todd got into her carriage, jerked her gloves on, retied her bonnet ribbons, and stared straight ahead as if to speed the vehicle to its destination.

The day, although already well advanced, was shy on sunlight. Pewter-colored clouds moved in from the east, bringing with them a sodden breeze and the scent of rain.

She inserted a gloved finger between her cheek and the bonnet ribbon, wishing the fabric wasn't irritating. Anything new was bound to chafe, at least until a certain familiarity had been achieved.

The dress was not new, however. Instead, she wore one of her serviceable dark blue day dresses. She'd had half a dozen of them made so she could detach the white collar and cuffs when she was working. Otherwise, she wore her most favorite garment, a divided skirt much like trousers.

Today she had to appear garbed like a proper woman of London, at least until this ghastly errand was finished.

As much as she would have liked to be on an expedition, the wet spring and early summer weather had prevented it. Yet even had she been blessed with sunshine in Scotland she wouldn't have left London. Not until she had an answer about Neville.

Where was her brother?

The Earl of Rathsmere must know, but the man hadn't answered her five letters, the latest only three days ago. She had no choice but to call on him.

She'd heard stories about Rathsmere, of course. The man had a foolish soubriquet—the Rake of London—and was rumored to have once had a royal lover, one of the cousins of the Queen herself.

The fact that he'd broken off the arrangement was scandalous enough, but he'd also recounted certain personal facts to a gathering of men no better than himself. Namely, that the woman in question liked the color red. To please her, he'd had his undergarments dyed crimson. He'd flaunted his Scottish heritage by parading around her rooms attired in nothing more than a swath of crimson and black tartan.

The Queen had not been pleased by the tales of her cousin's licentiousness. The poor woman had been shipped off to Australia to tour sheep farms. No doubt she'd been told to mend her ways if she ever wanted to appear at court again.

Wayward women were never applauded in society.

The Rake of London, however, was a perennial darling. People laughed at his escapades. They excused his excesses. They allowed—no, encouraged—his complete disregard of the most basic tenets of civilization.

He was, in a word, a reprobate, a miscreant, and a libertine. And now he was an earl. A complete and total waste of a proper title.

When the carriage stopped in front of the large town house belonging to the man, she stared through the window at the broad steps, her eyes traveling upward to encompass the three stories of the structure. How like MacIain not to simply live in a fashionable square, but in a house that took up one whole corner of it. The structure seemed to proclaim itself a royal residence. At the very least it was a home for someone filled with his own consequence.

From what she'd heard, the man was attractive. Looks faded. Intelligence didn't. The earl was, from his actions, a very stupid man. What did she care how attractive the apple if the fruit within was rotten?

She had quite a wealth of correspondence from various men across the continent. The topic had not been as important as her missives to the Earl of Rathsmere, but each man had been kind enough to answer her letters.

Yet the earl had not seen fit to respond to her inquiries, and he was the only one with the information she was desperate to obtain.

Her driver dismounted, came around, and opened the door for her.

"Are you very certain you wish to do this, Minerva?"

She bit back her sigh. Hugh was the perfect example of attractiveness, intelligence, and character. Unfortunately, he was also too curious. She was to blame for that. By her actions, she'd led him to believe he had the right to be so intrusive.

"I see no other recourse," she said. "He hasn't answered my letters. What else can I do?"

"He may refuse to see you."

She nodded, placing her hand on Hugh's arm, allowing him to assist her from the carriage.

"He may," she said. "If he won't see me today, he'll see me tomorrow. If he won't see me tomorrow, he'll see me the day after. And a thousand days if necessary, Hugh."

He raised one eyebrow.

Very well, perhaps she was a tiny bit stubborn in certain situations. She was a woman who toiled in a man's world. She couldn't afford to be perceived as soft and demure. That was for women who rarely left their parlors or used fans, for the love of all that was holy. She couldn't imagine using a fan to flirt with a man. She'd feel like a fool.

Shaking her skirts free, she did a quick perusal of herself. Of course she looked nothing like the scores of women who'd probably made their way up these broad white steps.

She was simply Minerva Todd, whose assets were not those of figure or face.

Before she made it to the door, she felt the first droplets of rain. In moments it felt like a full bucket had been upended over her head.

At the top of the steps she took a deep breath, squared her shoulders, and stared at the black painted door with its whimsical brass knocker. Why a mushroom, of all things?

She raised the knocker and let it fall, hearing the soft echo in the foyer. Her heart galloped in her chest, tightening her breath. Inside her gloves her fingertips were cold.

He must see her. He must tell her. Even if it was the worst possible news, she must know.

When no one answered the door, she let the knocker fall twice more.

The front windows were clean and sparkling. The stoop had been swept. No debris of any sort was on the steps. Yet she had the feeling the house was deserted.

Taking a step back, she looked up at the windows through the rain. All of them were shielded by curtains. No one stood there watching her.

She turned, calling out to Hugh standing beside the carriage.

"Would you go to the stables, Hugh? See if there's a carriage there."

If the earl wasn't home, it would be the reason he hadn't answered. Did he have a country house? How would she find out where it was?

Hugh nodded and began walking to the corner and around to the back of the town house as she stood there waiting. The steps had no place where a visitor might stand and be shielded from the elements, and it felt almost like a personal affront.

She let the knocker fall again.

The rain smelled of dust and the London streets. London seemed to be a city that contained odors, holding them in as if jealous they might escape. Now she picked out the scent of honeysuckle and roses, old buildings, manure, dust, and the ever-present and pungent smell of the Thames.

The door opened so suddenly she nearly fell forward.

A tall, thin man greeted her. The sleeves of his shirt were rolled up, revealing muscular arms. His hair was brushed back from a face made stern by a prominent nose and pointed chin.

Sweat dotted his brow and above his lip.

His look of irritation was a little off-putting, but she ventured a smile anyway.

"Yes?" he said.

She had the strangest urge to apologize. No, that would never do. She was there for a reason.

"I'm here to see the earl."

"Are you?"

How very odd to be questioned by a major domo.

She pulled a calling card from her reticule and held it out until he took it. A good thing, since she was becoming drenched and the card was decidedly soggy.

Why hadn't she brought her umbrella?

"Will you tell him that Minerva Todd is here to see him, please, on account of her brother, Neville."

"He isn't receiving visitors."

She ignored that comment.

"Please tell the earl I shall not take up much of his time. I only have one question to ask."

Had the majordomo begun as a footman? His height was impressive. She truly disliked having to look up at him. The stony expression on his hawkish face would have been daunting if she weren't determined to see the earl.

"That won't be possible."

He moved to stand half behind the door, edging it closed with his foot. Minerva deliberately inserted her leg in the opening. She wasn't as tall as the majordomo, but she was not excessively short either. She and Neville were of a height.

"Please, I really must see him."

His brown eyes remained flat and unmoved.

"I regret, Miss Todd, that His Lordship is not receiving visitors," he said.

"Can you take him a message, then? I need to know where my brother is. Neville hasn't returned to London."

"I'm afraid I couldn't."

"I've never met a more insolent majordomo," she said, annoyed beyond measure.

The man startled her by smiling, such a transformative expression that his entire face softened. The hooked nose lost prominence, the jutting chin didn't seem as sharp. Even his brown eyes bore a twinkle.

"I'm the earl's secretary, Miss Todd," he said, making a small bow. "Stanley Howington. I suppose I act as majordomo as well."

"Do you have no other staff?"

"Is that any of your concern?"

"It is if you leave a visitor standing in the rain."

"It's the housekeeper's half day off and the maids

are engaged in other tasks, Miss Todd, not that it's any of your business."

"Did you go to America with the earl, Mr. Howington?"

He shook his head, placed his hand on the latch and started to slowly close the door again.

"Will you ask him about Neville?" she asked, putting her own hand on the edge of the door. In order to completely close it, he was going to have to shove her out of the way.

Mr. Howington, for all his rudeness, didn't look the type to brutalize a woman.

"Will you, sir?"

"His Lordship doesn't like to discuss America, Miss Todd."

She told herself that she could be excused her bad manners because of worry. Attempting to get the Earl of Rathsmere to answer her was frustrating to the extreme, and having Mr. Howington say he wouldn't see her now was enough of an incitement for rudeness.

She pushed the door inward.

"I am not talking about America," she said, her voice this side of a shout. "I am talking about my brother. Where is Neville?"

Since the door was advancing on her knuckles and was already pressing against the toe of her shoe, she had every expectation that the Earl of Rathsmere's secretary would toss her from the stoop. So much for not brutalizing a woman.

"Do not force me to be ungentlemanly, Miss Todd. You are getting very wet. Would it not be best for you to retreat to your carriage?"

"At least tell me you will ask the earl."

He considered her for a moment. She had the feeling whatever he said next would be a lie, anything to get rid of her.

"Very well," she said, taking a step back.

Sometimes it was necessary to retreat in order to fight again another day. Besides, he was correct. She was drenched. Rain had permeated her dress until even her shift was wet. Droplets slid down her spine, leaving an icy trail.

Her bonnet emitted a peculiar smell, something reminding her of their neighbor's dog. Frederick loved water and sought it out at every opportunity. At the moment a wet Frederick and her bonnet smelled the same.

She turned, grabbed the wrought-iron railing and descended the steps with hard won dignity. Hugh stepped in front of her, his hair wetly plastered to his skull.

"The carriage is there," he said. "I think the earl must be in residence."

Nodding to him, she entered the carriage, more determined than ever to succeed in her task. She had to find Neville, and no secretary, diligent as he was, was going to stop her.

She would see the Earl of Rathsmere. She would.

Chapter 2

$\mathcal{D}$alton MacIain, Earl of Rathsmere, stood in the doorway of his library, listening to Howington argue with a harridan. Were there peddlers in Tarkington Square now? He couldn't hear their words, only the tone. Howington was maintaining his usual calm demeanor. The woman wasn't, her voice growing louder, vying with the thunder growling overhead for dominance.

Turning back to the room, he dismissed the two of them. Howington would get rid of her, whoever she was.

He shouldn't have sent his majordomo to Gledfield. If Samuels had remained here he would have opened the door, thereby sparing Howington the duty. Samuels would have also been a buffer between him and Howington. Pity that he hadn't considered that earlier. Now Howington was always present, forever hovering in that obsequious way of his.

He moved unerringly to the window, reached up and closed the drapes against the storm. He remembered their shade, an emerald color he favored. Everything else about the room was as he recalled it: two wing chairs upholstered in a dark green fabric sat before the fireplace with a small table between them; enough books in the shelves that he gave the appearance of being a well-read man. His onetime companions would have been genuinely shocked to know that he had read most of them, a good thing now.

Thunder rumbled, the windows shivering in response. The drumming of rain on the street outside sounded like muffled artillery.

He made his way to the sideboard on the opposite wall, a distance of exactly ten feet.

Removing the stopper from the cut glass decanter, he reached for a glass and tried to hold it steady. Another roar of thunder, this one sounding too much like cannon fire, made him put down the decanter and the glass, hearing the chink as they landed on the tray.

He stood with his fingers braced against the sideboard, staring straight ahead and willing his hands to stop their trembling.

On the wall in front of him was a painting in a gilded frame, a scene of Gledfield, the MacIain country house. A talented artist had created an image he'd always remember. The great house, constructed of yellowish brick, seemed to attract the sun from its perch on a rolling hill. Dozens of massive oaks dotted the landscape. He'd climbed each one of them, had hidden among their branches and used their trunks as a backrest when he sat and contemplated his home.

Of course, boy that he'd been, he hadn't seen the pastoral serenity. He'd only been wishing for excitement and adventure.

He'd gotten that, hadn't he?

From long practice he calmed himself, taking one deep breath after another. A technique he had learned, strangely enough, in the hospital in Washington. A doctor there had been an aficionado of Oriental principles.

Evidently, if you were getting your leg sawn off, it was helpful to be calm. Helpful for whom: the patient or the doctor?

Luckily, he had kept all his limbs.

He thought about the scene in the painting: the house on the hill, the rolling green lawn, pale blue skies, and a radiance that spoke more of man's wish for heaven than the actuality of Gledfield. He remembered the house as a place of chaos, of laughter, he and Arthur—the two older brothers—getting into mischief, fishing and swimming in the nearby Deton River. They had often talked their tutor into giving them lessons beneath the sprawling oak at the bottom left of the painting. His youngest brother, Lewis, was five years younger, while he and Arthur were only a year apart. Most of his memories of Lewis were of the boy whining that he and Arthur wouldn't play with him. Lewis had been right; they'd spent a good deal of time hiding from him or making his life miserable.

Hidden from view in the painting were the stables, his favorite place at Gledfield. He could ride almost before he could walk. He and Arthur challenged each other on a daily basis. Who could take the fence higher and faster? Who could race from Gledfield to the village and back? The prize was never anything important. The one and only time he'd lost to his older brother, he'd had to muck out the bay where Arthur's horse was stabled.

Arthur's forfeits weren't physical. No, he insisted Arthur memorize one of Burns's poems when he lost. Arthur didn't prize their Scottish heritage as much as he did. Lewis was the same. They considered themselves English first and foremost, while something in the Scottish spirit called to Dalton. He'd relished the idea that their ancestors had been Highlanders and wanted to emulate their daring and courage.

Wind rattled the window panes as the storm grew. The floorboards trembled with the grumbling thunder.

He returned to his task of pouring himself a glass of whiskey. What a pity his ancestors hadn't invested in the whiskey trade. No, they'd chosen coal instead, thanks to the Welsh heiress his great-grandfather had married.

Cautious not to fill the glass to the top, he carried it carefully back to his desk, one he'd had especially built for him to resemble his great-grandfather's at the family home in London. This was his house, bought with his inheritance, filled with his choice of furniture. A home he'd packed with his friends, sounds of merriment, and parties to all hours of the night.

Arthur wasn't here and neither was his father. They were gone, packed tightly away in the mausoleum at Gledfield.

He took a sip of whiskey, anticipating the first sting in his throat.

Thunder rumbled again and he held out his glass in salute to nature itself.

I'm not afraid.

He wasn't foolish enough to say the words out loud. If he had, Howington would have come to the door, knocked softly, and called out, "Is anything wrong, Your Lordship?"

Then he would be forced to clear his throat, put some modicum of humor into his voice, and answer with a lie. "Nothing's wrong, Howington."

He wondered if his secretary had gotten rid of the woman yet. Better for Howington that he be occupied with the visitor than with him. Regardless of how long it took, when it was done, Howington would come to the door to inquire as to his health, mentally or physically.

When would this damnable storm be over?

His imagination made it sound like warfare, he knew that. That wasn't the only reaction to his environment lately. When anything fell to the floor, he jerked, startled. And the nightmares? He didn't even want to consider the nightmares.

He placed the glass on the surface of the desk and forced himself to lean back against the chair. All he needed was enough time. Or maybe time would be his worst enemy. Perhaps after a few more months of this, he would grow so tired of pretending that nothing was wrong that he'd do something dishonorable, something to stain the MacIain name forever.

He could just imagine the conversations now.

Did you hear about Rathsmere?

Damnable thing, wasn't it?

Expected it ever since he went off to war. Damn fool.

He always was rash like that. Strange thing for him to come into the title, though. Don't imagine he expected it.

If he'd known, he would probably have remained in America.

No, he damn well wouldn't have.

Just as he expected, Howington knocked on the door.

"Is there anything I can get for you, Your Lordship?"

A little less toadying, but he didn't make that remark. Howington was immersed in a bubble of propriety. God forbid should he try to burst it.

His mother had hired Howington for him, back in his wilder days. Not that he wouldn't have been as wild now had circumstances been different.

Interesting what a bullet could do.

"Who was that at the door?"

That he'd asked surprised him. Normally, he didn't have any interest in the comings and goings of tradesmen and the like. Still, they shouldn't come to the front entrance, but the back one instead.

Howington didn't say anything for a moment, but Dalton knew the secretary was studying him. He recognized the man's considering silence, having encountered it often since returning home.

Now, instead of answering his question, Howington said, "The doctor is coming today, Your Lordship. What with the weather, he'll probably be late."

"Is that a gentle hint, Howington, not to get myself soused before he arrives?"

"I wouldn't say such a thing, Your Lordship."

No, but you'd be thinking it.

"Did you report to my mother when she was alive?"

"I beg your pardon?"

He knew a stalling tactic when he heard one.

"Was it your duty to write her once a week? Once a month? Did she want to know what I was doing?"

"The dowager countess expressed an interest in you, sir, but she did so for Arthur and Lewis as well."

"Good God, did you spy on all of us?"

"When the countess asked, I responded."

Howington's voice had taken on a decidedly frosty tone. Had he offended the man? It wouldn't be the first time, and doubtless it wouldn't be the last.

He'd once been quite urbane, known for his charm. Had he left that behind in America?

He waved his hand in Howington's direction.

"I will attempt to remain sober until I'm examined again. Not that it makes any damn difference. There, are you happy?"

"Have you eaten, sir?" Howington asked, the words still coated with a chill.

"God, man, you're not my nanny. Stop hovering."

"Of course, sir." Howington didn't leave, however, only continued that considering silence.

"What is it?"

"The woman at the door, sir, she wanted to know about America."

How many times had he told Howington that America wasn't a topic of conversation he would allow? How many times had he cut off the man when he would have asked or commented about something striking his fancy? The fact that Howington mentioned it now was punishment, a little goad for his being an ass.

Maybe he deserved it.

He finished the whiskey, let the glass fall too heavily onto the surface of the desk. The sound was like a slap, one that made him aware the storm was finally passing.

"I'll let you know when the doctor arrives, Your Lordship."

"You do that," he said, straightening and walking to the sideboard again. What did it matter if he was drunk when the damn physician arrived?

Chapter 3

*T*he moment Minerva entered her kitchen, Mrs. Beauchamp advanced on her. The housekeeper, a tall woman with a slender build, possessed a long face that regretfully reminded Minerva of a horse. Her large mouth was often arranged in a smile, however, which gave one the feeling that you were in the presence of a genuinely caring soul.

If Mrs. Beauchamp had any flaws at all, it was that she was too concerned about others.

"Oh, dear, Miss Minerva," she said now, helping Minerva remove her sodden bonnet. "The poor thing's ruined."

Since her hands had turned blue from the dye in the ribbon, she could only agree with the older woman.

"It was such a pretty shade," Mrs. Beauchamp said. "But not if it bleeds so profusely."

Minerva glanced at herself in the mirror above the sideboard and bit back a yelp. Her cheeks were blue and there were two blue streaks running down her forehead. She wasn't a vain woman, but she didn't want to go through London looking like one of the early Picts, either.

Had she faced Rathsmere's secretary looking the same? She sincerely hoped not. Why hadn't Hugh said something to her?

She fluttered her fingers toward the offending bonnet, now in the housekeeper's hands.

"There's nothing to do but dispose of it, Mrs. Beauchamp. Toss it away in the rubbish. I shall keep to my older bonnets. They've never disappointed me."

"You need a few furbelows, Miss Minerva. One or two flowers would not be amiss. A touch of color here or there."

She removed her gloves, wondering what she could say to this comment, a version of which she'd heard every day for the last two years. For some reason, Mrs. Beauchamp had it in her mind to have her dress in pastels with silly little things in her hair. The housekeeper would have her go to dances and soirees, dinners and balls, as if she had anyone to take her to those places. As if anyone wished to.

A change of clothing wouldn't alter who she was. Fine feathers make fine birds, but she was neither fine-feathered nor a bird. Her wardrobe was more than adequate for what she needed. Most of the time she forgot what she was wearing anyway.

What did it matter?

She truly didn't need to be cosseted, but she often found herself the object of Mrs. Beauchamp's not inconsiderable attention.

Each one of her bureau drawers was sprinkled with a spicy potpourri. While it was an agreeable scent, it was strangely strong, reminding her of the scones she ate every morning.

Mrs. Beauchamp was evidently a seamstress of great talent. A week after the housekeeper arrived, two years ago, Minerva's unmentionables suddenly began boasting lace. She truly didn't need lace or ribbons on her pantaloons or her corset covers, but she didn't have a choice. One day she opened her bureau and a favorite shift had been adorned. Over the next weeks every single one of her undergarments had been altered.

There was a direct correlation between the number of Mrs. Beauchamp's tasks and the amount of lace appearing on Minerva's undergarments, which is why she tried to keep the estimable woman busy at all times.

Still, the woman hovered. When Minerva wasn't hungry, it was as if she had insulted Mrs. Beauchamp's menu selection on purpose. That led to at least a quarter hour of the housekeeper offering a selection of other foods that might tempt her appetite. On more than one occasion Minerva had attempted to explain to the older woman that she wasn't an invalid and that the lack of one meal was not going to alter her health in any regard.

Mrs. Beauchamp was a tyrant with good intentions.

Minerva had the thought that it was a good thing the woman never accompanied her on one of her expeditions. She would have been horrified at the lack of proper meals, not to mention the primitive conditions.

The housekeeper had recently taken on a new role—guardian of Minerva's virtue.

"It's not at all proper the way he looks at you," Mrs. Beauchamp said one day after Hugh left the kitchen. "It's too familiar." The housekeeper leaned over the table and whispered, "It's as if he's lusting after you."

For a moment Minerva actually considered feigning shock, then realized that if she did so she'd have to continue that faux emotion in the future. Better to simply be herself.

"Hugh and I are old friends," she said, deciding to leave it at that.

Before Mrs. Beauchamp's employ, she and Hugh had been a great deal more than that. The affair hadn't lasted more than a month, but if Hugh had his way, it might still be ongoing. Passion, however, was a dangerous addiction, especially when it wasn't accompanied by any other emotion.

She had made him her lover. She had taken him to her bed, and it had been a worthwhile and laudable decision at the time. At twenty-eight, she was certain no one would ever want her and even more certain that she would never marry.

She didn't want a husband; she just wanted to feel passion.

Hugh was a very attractive man, tall with broad shoulders and a handsome face. His green eyes often sparkled at her mischievously.

If she was to be faulted, it wasn't for inviting him to her bed, but for not ending the affair before Hugh got the wrong idea.

She hadn't wanted a permanent liaison.

He had been a most admirable lover and brought her more pleasure than she'd expected. Her body had trembled and shivered and erupted in delight. Unfortunately, her emotions had not been engaged.

In all good conscience, she could not bring herself to take advantage of Hugh. When she tried to explain it to him, he'd only smiled and said that it wasn't a hardship for her to feel nothing. He would be more than happy to come to her bed for the physical enjoyment if nothing else.

Was she a fool to want some emotion? A simple liking was not enough. She felt there was something missing every time they loved, and she couldn't explain it either to him or to herself. She longed for something more.

Her parents had it. So did some people she encountered day to day. The neighbors on the far side of the square, the Hamptons, were both young and so bliss-

fully in love it hurt to look at them. The wife rushed
out every morning to give him a kiss on the front
steps, and the husband raced up the same steps at the
end of day.

She told herself she wasn't the only person who
would do without love for the rest of her life. She
would manage.

"Was your errand successful, then?" Mrs. Beauchamp asked now.

Minerva shook her head. "I'm afraid not."

Mrs. Beauchamp's look of disappointment no doubt
mirrored her own. Neville was a favorite of hers.

"I have not given up, however," she said. "There
must be a way to reach him. I must find a way."

"And if you cannot?"

"There is no allowance for failure, Mrs. Beauchamp.
There must be a way to see the earl, even if I have to
masquerade as a maid."

The housekeeper's eyes widened and her mouth
opened. Twin spots of color bloomed high on her
cheeks.

"Tell me you are only jesting, Miss Minerva. You
cannot think of going into service."

She reached over and patted Mrs. Beauchamp on
the shoulder.

"No, of course not," she said. But she wasn't going to
rule out anything at this point.

She smiled at the housekeeper, took a plate of biscuits with her and left the kitchen for the comfort of
her room. She needed to change her clothes, dry off,
and take some time to plan her next move.

At the top of the steps she hesitated at Neville's old
room.

When she was eighteen, their parents died. First, her
father of a failing heart, and then her darling mother
of influenza a few months later. Neville had been ten,

and she'd become his parent, responsible for rearing him.

He was a delight, a treasure, the sweetest, most intelligent boy. He'd wanted to learn, to absorb every bit of knowledge his tutor could provide him.

If he'd only stayed as innocent.

She couldn't keep him in short pants forever, tucked away under her arm as if she were a mother hen and he one of her chicks.

More's the pity.

Ever since Neville had assumed his majority and come into his inheritance, he'd begun acting rashly and quite unlike himself. He frequented gaming and music halls, was seen escorting women of ill repute to their lodgings, and boasted of being in a cadre of young men with too much time on their hands and little common sense. All of them led by Dalton MacIain, now the Earl of Rathsmere.

Over the last two years, her brother had changed. To her horror, he became wild. His friends were not those of salubrious character, no matter that a great many of them had titles. Neville had too much money, too much kindness, and too little knowledge.

Perhaps the world needed followers, good soldiers who marched behind great generals. The problem was, Dalton MacIain was not a leader to emulate. Yet he'd taken his hangers-on, those young men who worshipped his air of daring, and gone into battle all the same.

The fool had gone to fight in the American Civil War as if war were a game.

Neville had followed Rathsmere to America with a smile on his lips and some idiotic notion it would be a lark, a great experience through which they would drink whiskey, wench, and tell themselves how heroic they were being.

Rathsmere had returned a few months ago. Neville

hadn't. Somewhere along the way the earl had managed to lose her brother.

"*Are your* headaches still as bad, Your Lordship?" the physician asked.

"They are tolerable," Dalton said. One lie to add to the many he would utter by the time the fool man left.

"If they're still bad, take the laudanum I gave you."

"No doubt it would help, but I've no intention of going the rest of my life with hallucinations, Doctor. If you have any other tonic you could give me that would otherwise leave me with my sanity and my senses, I might take it. But I'm not going to imbibe opium."

"If you don't, the headaches will persist."

"Then persist they must, I suppose," he said.

If they got much worse, he could always put a bullet in his brain, a match to the one that had hit his right eye and ricocheted over the bridge of his nose.

"Any change in the vision in your left eye, Your Lordship?"

"No."

"Still only a sensation of light and dark?"

"Yes." Another truth.

He'd better watch himself. The way he was going, he might become known for his honesty.

The doctor cleared his throat and said in a sepulchral tone, "Your right eye is gone, Your Lordship. It's a miracle you have any sight left at all."

He wouldn't exactly give the credit to the Almighty. Instead, it was due to him turning at the last moment when he saw the pistol aimed at his head.

He was an expert at not revealing his emotions. Not because he was the Earl of Rathsmere, but because he had years of practice being the second son. Any sign of weakness was an excuse for the earl's disapproval or his tutor's punishment.

The trait had come in handy in the last several years, especially when he was faced with unbelievable stupidity or great duress. Now he allowed a small smile to curve his lips.

He saw and yet he didn't see. All he could discern was light, if the day was bright enough. Sometimes, if someone stood close to him, he could see a darker shape.

That was all.

"Perhaps one day I'll be able to see the faces of angels."

He could sense the physician's affront.

"Have you any other complaints, sir?"

"In other words, something you could cure? Like a stomachache, perhaps?"

"Is there anything, Your Lordship?"

"Otherwise I am a picture of great health, Dr. Marshall. I am hail and hearty and shall, no doubt, live fifty years or more."

If I wish it.

The unspoken words hung in the air between them.

He lifted the glass to his lips. He had changed from whiskey to wine in the last hour. He could feel the glass, knew the shape of it from countless times he'd held a wineglass in his hand. He couldn't see the glint of light from the lamp on the crystal or the deep claret of the wine. Nor could he see the doctor's face, and had no idea of his appearance, having never met the man before returning to London.

What use did he have for a physician prior to leaving for America? He'd rarely been sick. His good health was as much a part of him as his height or the blue eyes now damaged beyond repair.

"I still hold out hope for your recovery, Your Lordship. In some fashion."

"Hope is a foolish thing to cling to, Dr. Marshall.

I've found it's much better to look at life with realism than with hope."

The doctor did not respond, which surprised him. He'd expected a lecture. Something along the lines of: *Anyone with your fortune and your title, Your Lordship, should possess hope above all things.*

Instead, the doctor remained silent.

What good was a blind earl?

RETREATING TO her suite, Minerva removed her clothes, dried herself and, because the day was well advanced, donned her wrapper and walked into the sitting room.

She had equipped the room to resemble a library, something that might be found in any man's establishment. A large marble fireplace occupied one wall, a window the next. An archway led to the bedroom, but the fourth wall was filled with a wide mahogany bookcase holding hundreds of books, each of them handpicked and read and, in some cases, reread. There were a few novels among them, but most of the books were on subjects dear to her heart: anything dealing with antiquity, Scotland, and archeology.

In front of the bookcase, and occupying the middle of the room, was the desk she'd found in a secondhand furniture shop. Three men had struggled for hours to bring it up the stairs and into the sitting room, but it was worth the cost once they were done.

Here was where she wrote letters to learned men all over the Continent, asking for them to expound on their discoveries or give her advice. None of them were shy about doing either. For some reason, men felt compelled to give her direction. Most of the time she just nodded, filed away the important bits mentally, and ignored the rest.

Her father had never felt the need to have a library.

But then, he went off to work each day. Being wealthy was never an excuse for sloth, he would say. Her great-grandfather had been a minority owner in one ship. He'd made his fortune by always reinvesting his wealth. By the time he died, he owned ten ships, a fleet her grandfather had only expanded. When her father died, the Todd family had either a minority interest in over a hundred ships or owned them outright.

She'd never felt wealthy, only because such an attitude would have been discouraged. Money was a subject rarely discussed in their house. But she'd never had to worry about the cost of things or her future. She was able to pursue any interest she wished. Nor did she have to marry in order to provide for herself.

What would her parents say to see her life now?

Her father would have been more direct than her mother. Her dearest papa would have put his arm around her shoulders, drawn her in, and smiled down at her.

"Minerva, my dear, I'm afraid you're becoming an independent woman. What some might call a spinster."

She might be a spinster, but she wasn't a maiden, but of course she would have never made that confession to her father. Nor would it have been possible to discuss the matter with her mother, even in a roundabout way.

Nora Todd had been a sweet woman, one who gave the appearance of being too delicate for life. Things had to be polished and brushed and perfumed, tied up in a bow, before they were presented to her. Everyone around her mother seemed to accept her fragility and never tested the limits of her strength. Instead, all of them—even the child Neville had been—were more gentle with Nora than they were with anyone else.

Strange, how she had never been considered delicate like her mother. A good thing, as it turned out. Otherwise, she would have been unable to manage Neville. Or meet with their solicitors. Or endured this last year.

If she ever married, it would be because of her parents.

They had been a couple, partners in truth. Where one was, the other could be easily found. Even during the difficult birth of her brother, her father would not be relegated to another room, but insisted on sitting beside his wife's bed and holding her hand during the travail.

Minerva had been eight years old the day Neville was born. Eight years and two weeks. From that moment on, their birthdays were celebrated together. When she held him, Neville never fussed. Instead, he gnawed on one fist and looked up at her with bright blue eyes as if he trusted her completely.

Her heart was engaged from the first moment she saw him. What a darling little boy he'd been. What a precocious youngster and fine intelligent young man.

Until he'd met Rathsmere. Then Neville changed, had become someone she didn't know, couldn't understand, and didn't like all that much.

That was the worst of it, wasn't it? She wanted to like him. She loved him. She couldn't erase the love. Yet she found as time progressed she didn't admire the man he was becoming. Neville had no plans to work at the Todd Shipyards, preferring to let others run the company their great-grandfather had founded. Nor was he using his fortune in a good way.

Was it because of her that he'd become so wild? That was a question she couldn't banish, especially at night when loneliness was her only companion.

Had she been responsible for Neville's descent

into hedonism? Had he wanted to escape her—or her rules—to the extent that he'd done everything just the opposite? Or was it the money that altered him to such a degree?

From the rumors, Rathsmere was fantastically wealthy, but that didn't mean his hangers-on were as well-funded. Neville might be the only one who had any degree of income. Had the others depended on Rathsmere's largesse for their very existence?

She should've taken Neville with her on her last expedition, regardless of his reluctance. She should've found a way, somehow, to make him come with her to Scotland. If she had, she wouldn't have returned to London to discover he'd gone off to war. If she had, he wouldn't have written her the letter she retrieved from her desk now.

My dear sister,

> *I hope this letter finds you in good health and your expedition to Scotland pleasurable and worth your while.*
> *Occasionally, I have envied you your single-minded pursuit of history. I have often wondered why you pursue such a path. I have no interest in the subject myself.*

She knew that. Neville had never expressed any curiosity about her expeditions to Scotland. She pushed that thought to the back of her mind and continued reading, even though she didn't need to. She knew the letter by heart. How many times had she read it? A hundred? Five times that? Each time, she was filled with shame.

Somehow, somehow, she should have been able to stop him.

*You go to seek the remains of those who've passed,
Minerva, while I seek to live in the present day.
Perhaps one day people will look down on my grave
with the same admiration you extend your long
buried Scots and say, "Neville Todd, now there was
a man of adventure."*

*I have gone to America to fight in their war. I
know my decision will not meet your approval.
Sometimes women must simply accept a man's path
in life. This is mine, to seek adventure where it is. To
test my own mettle. To see if I am as brave as I think
I am.*

Yours in fondness, your brother, Neville

She didn't know what part of the letter made her
angrier, the fact that he had gone off to see if he was
brave, or his thought that women should simply agree
to anything a man suggested.

What poppycock.

Sitting at her desk, she calmly folded the letter and
held it against her chest.

She would not cry. Tears did nothing but make her
eyes and nose red and congest her breathing. They
didn't solve the situation. They didn't make her feel
less guilty.

He had never mentioned America to her. What did
he know about their war? Did he simply want to go
into battle to see if he could survive it?

Dear God, had he survived it?

That was the one question no one could answer.

She replaced the letter in the drawer of her desk
and sat quietly, thinking of her next move. If she wrote
the earl again, he would probably ignore her, as he'd
already done five times. If she returned to his house
tomorrow, encountered his secretary again, and mar-

shaled her arguments better, was there any guarantee Mr. Howington would listen?

She had only been jesting when she was talking to Mrs. Beauchamp, but perhaps she should engage in a little subterfuge. Every house needed servants, and the earl's large home must require quite a number of them in order to run smoothly.

The plan being born in her imagination died a swift death. Mr. Howington had seen her. Perhaps she could attempt to engage the housekeeper's help. Or bribe one of the servants to turn the other way when she gained entrance to the house.

She had to find a way in to see the Earl of Rathsmere. She had to find out what happened to Neville.

How could she live another day without knowing?

Chapter 4

$\mathcal{D}$alton dreamed he was standing on a hill above the battlefield, staring out at what had once been a field of corn. Now the crop was death, ready to be harvested, the sight of the sprawling bodies so hideous that his mind shied from it even in his dream. He stopped counting at thirty-three. The death toll had to be in the thousands.

The question came from his left, uttered by a voice as booming as God's. He couldn't see the speaker. Perhaps it was the voice of his conscience or the whispers of his soul.

What was the reason for the slaughter of these men? Was it political necessity? Pride or arrogance? Had it all been a horrible mistake? What was won by the winning of this battle? What was lost, other than the lives of all these men?

He struggled to wake up, knowing it wasn't a dream but a memory. On that day, after that battle, he'd been staggered by the death toll, unable to answer the questions that still haunted him. Perhaps that was the beginning of his disillusionment. Or simply the day he grew up.

Coming awake, he blinked up at the ceiling, only to find himself swimming in a vast black pool.

He hated nights.

The pattern was relentless. He drank enough to

ensure himself an easy descent into slumber. Two hours later with the precision of a timepiece, he woke. For those first few seconds, staring up at the ceiling, he was disoriented. He expected to see faint moonlight or the gradual graying of the sky through the open window. Ever since he was a boy he'd disliked sleeping with the curtains closed, but now it didn't matter.

First came the panic, then the realization that he couldn't see.

He sat up as he did every night, pushing the pillows around him, creating a cocoon of safety in his large bed.

His darkness then was absolute. Like being on the ocean on a moonless night, he was unable to tell what was water and what was sky. The sheer formlessness of night terrified him, but it was a confession he'd never made to another soul. Nor would he, as long as his courage lasted.

There were times when he wondered just how long that would be. Would he be like one of those poor men so traumatized by battle he could only sit in a corner at the hospital, back against the wall, rocking and staring out at the patients with terror in his eyes? Would he lose his senses one night? Would they find the new and reluctant Earl of Rathsmere running down the road stark naked, screaming wildly and pulling out his hair? Not that, then. He couldn't see the road, let alone run down it. He'd probably slam into a fence or a carriage.

Self-pity was not one of his greater virtues. But then, the longer he endured being blind, the more he found himself saturated with it. Would he, as the years passed, become so disgusted by his own wallowing that he did himself in?

He rose from the bed, donned his robe, and moved to the sitting room. He found his way to a wing chair beside a round mahogany table and sat there, staring at a cold fireplace, hearing the wind whistle down the chimney until it sounded like a far off train.

At least, having acquired an earldom he didn't want, he hadn't had to move from his own home. Lewis was the only occupant of the MacIain family town house, located a half mile away. He would have to solve the problem of Lewis one day, but not tonight.

The silk robe was cool against Dalton's skin even though the night was muggy. He wished he'd had the foresight to bring the decanter of whiskey to his room. He would not ring for one of the servants. First of all, it was after midnight. Secondly, he didn't want one of the maids or, God forbid, Mrs. Thompson, wondering about his drinking habits.

On another night, before America, if he'd been alone and without companionship and unable to sleep, he would have read to pass the hours. He didn't even have that ability now.

To occupy himself, he conjured up the pattern of the upholstery, the exact hue of the mahogany table. He knew, unless it had been changed for some odd reason, that the bed coverings were made of a particular color of dark blue he liked, matching the curtains. The windows on both sides of the bed were tall, looking out over his garden.

Alexandra MacIain had been able to coax any growing thing into flourishing, even here in London. His mother had insisted on supervising the construction of his garden. If he opened the windows now, he would smell an assortment of blowzy flowers no doubt bobbing their heads listlessly in anticipation of her return.

The MacIain clan was decimated. First, his father of a stroke, and then his darling mother. He had heard more than one person at Gledfield say something to the extent that the countess simply didn't want to do without her husband.

He had never acknowledged hearing the remarks. Secretly, however, he wondered if they weren't correct.

His father and mother adored each other, a singular achievement in the society that was London. Maybe such affection was possible because they didn't spend much time in the city, choosing, instead, to live most of the year at Gledfield.

His father enjoyed serving in the House of Lords, a function Arthur had taken to as well. But then, Arthur was gone now, too, the victim of an idiotic hunting accident.

That left Lewis and him, the lesser of the MacIains, according to almost anyone.

He had spent most of his life enjoying himself, and it looked like Lewis was ably following in his footsteps.

Once more he pushed the problem of Lewis to the back of his mind, concentrating on his memories of his sitting room.

He knew the pattern of the carpet beneath his bare feet, could feel the worn parts directly in front of the chair. He hadn't often sat here in front of the fireplace in solitary contemplation. If anything, the chair had been the scene of a few trysts.

Without much difficulty, he could envision the last woman who'd occupied his bedroom. Cassandra, that was her name, the wife of a baronet. Her husband, she'd said, was supremely uninterested in her. She'd retaliated by bedding any man she could.

In the time before America, when he was adrift in hedonistic impulses, he told himself she was besotted with him. Cassandra would not have looked for another lover once she'd come to his bed. The truth, likely as not, the minute he was gone she'd found someone to take his place. And the other women? No doubt they'd done the same. Hadn't he?

Yet he'd been remarkably celibate since America.

First of all, when you were fighting for your life, one of the last things you thought about was bed sport. Then there was the fact that he was surrounded by a sea of men but very few women. The few hardy feminine souls who appeared on the battlefield were either nurses or wives.

None of the females he'd known would be interested in coming to his bedroom now unless it was out of a misguided sense of pity or as a lark. Perhaps it might be considered something novel to bed a blind man.

He needed to become accustomed to this new way of life, this monastic existence. He didn't fool himself by thinking he offered anything to the opposite sex at the moment. Of course, there was the money. His family was wealthy, and according to his solicitor, under Arthur's able handling the estate had only grown in size.

Perhaps he should send out a notice that he was in the market for a female companion, one whose greed would have her overlook his damaged face and blindness.

He hadn't yet descended to that state. His pride dictated that he remain alone for the time being. Besides, as long as Lewis was alive and well, he saw no need to marry. He had his heir.

Who the hell cared if he remained a bachelor?

The idea of a wife, especially one who was solicitous, charming, and eternally underfoot, was hideous. He could barely tolerate his own pity, let alone that rendered by someone else.

Dalton placed his hands on the ends of the chair arms, feeling the edge of the upholstery and the piping there. He wondered what color the piping was and knew that before America he wouldn't have even noticed it.

Some poor benighted fool had told him that his other senses would be heightened because of the loss of his sight. On hearing that, he'd remained silent, finding a curious power in remaining mute. People couldn't argue with him if they didn't know what he thought. Nor could they seize on a certain sentence or a comment and recall it to death.

No, silence was the best recourse. Somehow, though, he had to find a way to endure these nights. He would bring the decanter of whiskey into his bedroom from now on.

He eased back against the chair, digging the balls of his feet into the carpet. The potpourri Mrs. Thompson distributed throughout the house was even more pungent here. Something citrusy with hints of flowers. She was not unlike his mother in her love of growing things, perfuming things, or in finding things about which to be joyous each and every day.

He should send her to Gledfield, like Samuels. The fewer servants around, the better. The fewer people to meet in the hall and have to greet. The fewer with which to pretend that all was well, that life was worth living, and weren't they all fortunate?

Bollocks.

He didn't hear any carriages, although they weren't forbidden in Tarkington Square after midnight. God knows he and his friends had made a racket often enough returning to his home. But it seemed as if he were the only rake living here. The others went to bed with the sun and no doubt rose with dawn, farmers in their blood.

A good thing he didn't need a light. Otherwise he might give the other residents something about which to be curious. What on earth was the Earl of Rathsmere doing up at this hour? Did his conscience bother him?

The silence was absolute, deep enough that he could

hear the pounding of his heart. He was, despite his blindness, healthy and would no doubt live to an old age. Perhaps he would be known as the curmudgeonly earl.

Oh, him. He was a rake when he was younger. Cut a wide swath through London society. Was even reprimanded by the Queen. Then he went off to war. It's said it changed him. At least he needn't stand on a street corner with an outstretched cup. No, the MacIain wealth shelters that blind beggar.

He might unbend to be a doting uncle to Lewis's children when he had them. A little niece might clamber up onto his lap, requesting a horsey ride. A nephew might whisper questions about the war.

Did you kill anyone, Uncle Dalton?

What would he say to his imaginary nephew, born only in his imagination?

Would the child understand? Probably not, any more than anyone else.

Yes, but the whole experience was anticlimactic, he might say. *I was surprised there weren't angels singing and trumpets bellowing. Just a look of surprise as a cloud of red bloomed on the man's chest. His legs crumpled beneath him and he rested on the cold ground, his eyes staring sightlessly at a gray sky.*

No, that wasn't a tale he would tell any child. Or anyone else, for that matter. He would leave his confusion about war and death unvoiced.

A sound made him turn, staring at the door that led to the hall. Was one of the servants awake? Had he somehow alerted them to his sleeplessness? Was someone going to knock on his door and be solicitous?

No one in all of London had a more eager-to-please staff than he, and no one wanted it less.

He should banish them all to Gledfield and live here

alone. That was an amusing idea, since he had no idea how to feed himself or even deal with the stove. Perhaps he could subsist on vegetables from the market, brought to him by some charitable soul and left on his doorstep each morning. Dammit all, he really liked beef from time to time. Or Cook's fish stew. No, perhaps he wouldn't banish Cook to Gledfield.

Maybe he should make the hallway outside his suite off limits. No one was to come and be kind. Only once a week, when he was in his library, could they enter to straighten up the room and change the sheets. But no trays and no midnight knocking on his door.

Leave him alone, dammit.

He wanted the whiskey even more now.

"*I DON'T* think this is wise, Minerva."

She didn't bother to look at Hugh. He'd said the same thing at least five times since they left the carriage behind the earl's town house.

"Perhaps you can visit your solicitor," he said. "Apply to him. Perhaps the man has some ability to make the earl listen."

She truly detested when someone suggested a man might be able to handle a situation better than she could. Granted, there were times when she needed a man's help. Although she was strong, for example, Hugh was stronger. But to imply that a man might have more persuasive powers—especially when right was on her side—was the most insulting thing Hugh could have said.

Therefore, when he reached out and grabbed her shoulder, she shook him off and strode on ahead.

If she hadn't been able to get past the Earl of Rathsmere's secretary, she was simply going to circumvent the man. If that required doing something shocking, she would do it.

If Hugh didn't want to participate, that was fine with her. She would prefer it, in fact.

She wasn't given to breaking the law. Perhaps there were times when she bent it a little. As for society's edicts, she didn't give a barleycorn for them.

Society said she should wear a cumbersome hoop and lace herself to within an inch of her life, thereby ensuring she could barely breathe. Clothes, according to society, were not for the purpose of shielding her nakedness, but to render her miserable.

Nor was she, according to society, to say anything remotely intelligent. She wasn't to venture her opinion, most especially in a group of men. She was to be demure and defer to their greater experience and wisdom.

What balderdash.

The earl's town house was on the end, at the south side of Tarkington Square. She squeezed between a line of healthy looking hedges and the wall, grateful that she'd worn her split skirt. The outfit was eminently practical, especially on an expedition. One had to look closely to ascertain that the garment was nothing more than a full set of trousers. However, the skirt was shocking enough that she normally didn't wear it in London. She eschewed society and most of its rules, but she wasn't altogether comfortable with the disapproving looks from the women who were her neighbors.

Although she and Hugh had left her home after midnight, it was entirely possible that one of the three Covington sisters had been awake and peering intently from a window for just such an occasion as this.

"Please," Hugh said, adding a comment in Italian.

Hugh came from Cornwall, but he had an uncanny ability to sound Italian or French or the inhabitant of any country whose males were great lovers. He'd often teased her with romantic phrases. At one time, she'd been delighted. Now it was only annoying.

She turned and frowned at him in the darkness.

"You know I've asked you to stop saying such things," she said.

"It's the only way you listen to me."

There was a kernel of truth in that comment, enough that she didn't offer a rebuttal.

"Do you think we can gain access through this window?" she asked, making her way to two very tall windows spaced six feet apart.

Because of the bushes, she didn't think they could be seen. The streetlamps were dim, indicating their globes needed to be cleaned. In her own square, the Covington sisters ensured the watchman cleaned the lamps once a month.

"I don't think we should gain access at all," Hugh said. "Send him another letter."

"I've wasted months sending him letters. I doubt he's even opened them, let alone read them."

"There has to be a better way than waking the man, Minerva."

Was Hugh now the voice of her conscience? She truly didn't need him to be. Gaining admittance to the Earl of Rathsmere's home was a small act in light of his greater sin.

The man had lost her brother.

All she was going to do was find his bedchamber and talk to him. In the middle of the night, surprised out of slumber, he would certainly tell her the truth.

Whether he wished to do so or not.

Chapter 5

Standing, Dalton made his way to the door of his sitting room. He'd had time, since returning home in May, to reacquaint himself with the furniture in the room. The maids were under strict orders not to re-arrange anything. If an ottoman was moved to brush the carpet beneath, it must be returned to its exact position. Otherwise he would go flying over it as he walked from one side of the room to the other.

He opened the door, stood listening as he tightened the belt of his robe. He had no idea the color of the gar-ment, so he imagined it burgundy with black lapels and a black belt. It could be pink or chartreuse for all he knew.

Perhaps he should hire a valet, but the idea of having to be dressed or even asking advice was so repugnant that he hadn't yet.

He could just imagine their conversation every morning.

Are you certain this is brown? Or is it blue?

Brown as a horse's droppings, sir.

That's why he'd ordered only white shirts and black suits. Otherwise he would probably wander through his home dressed in a mishmash of colors and patterns. None of his very kind servants would ever indicate that he clashed, however. But he paid them very well, enough to be loyally silent before he'd left for America, and they were doing the same now.

Life, in those days, had been one enjoyable interlude after another. Was he desirous of bed sport? There was the Countess of this or the Duchess of that or the daughter of a merchant who'd made her way in society by dint of her talented tongue. There was Amanda and Jane and Mary, and not to forget Diane or Alice, all girls in the marriage mart who were willing to do almost anything to snare a husband, even a rich rake.

His father had once been a younger son and was determined to treat his three boys more equitably. Although Arthur had always been reared to understand that he would be earl, responsible for all the duties inheriting the title required, both Dalton and Lewis were gifted with an enormous sum when each turned twenty-one.

Dalton had taken his father's advice and employed a banker with extensive financial acumen to manage his money. Therefore, his individual wealth was increasing each year. He would never need to go to Arthur for additional funds. He'd even been incredibly lucky in his wagers. His horses had won most of their races. He found cards boring and rarely played, but when he did he was fortunate there, too.

His luck had run out in America.

He stepped out into the hallway, a small smile pasted on his face in case he encountered a servant.

Thankfully, no one was there.

He counted the steps from his door to the end of the hall. Fear surrounded him like a cloud as he approached the head of the stairs. He felt the hollow space around him, stretched out his hand and gripped the banister. He slid his right foot forward, grateful that he hadn't put on slippers. His toes felt the edge of the step and he took the first one, then the second.

The painful tightening around his chest eased, the more steps he took. Descending was much harder than climbing up the steps.

He hesitated at the bottom of the stairs, then pushed off, crossing the foyer. At the end of seventeen steps he came to a wall. If he turned right and went ten more steps, he would hit the front door. If he turned slightly left, he would enter the hall that led to his library.

Once past the cold marble flooring, he turned left and pressed his fingers against the wall, feeling the rail and below to the wainscoting. Above it was a very pleasant blue-and-white-pattern wallpaper. His mother had chosen it. In addition to supervising his garden, she'd overseen the redecoration of the house when he first purchased it.

Alexandra MacIain had been a generous and loving soul. He could still hear her laughter echoing throughout the house.

"Dalton, my love, you simply must choose the fixtures you prefer. If I chose them, the house would reflect my taste, but it's your home, not mine."

He remembered her comment whenever he went to Gledfield. The great house was hundreds of years old, but his mother had managed to put her stamp on it.

He'd only been there twice since her death, finding it difficult to believe that she wouldn't suddenly appear, grab his shoulders, and pull him down for a kiss.

"You can't be growing more, surely, my darling child. I must be shrinking."

To his eyes she was eternally beautiful, her blond hair always kept in an upswing style. She liked long dangling earrings and she never left her bedroom unless fully dressed, down to her ear bobs.

He knew she was dying the day he was summoned to Gledfield and entered his mother's bedroom to find her in bed, no jewelry in sight. Her hair had been brushed until it shone, spread on the pillow in a cloud of pale yellow. Curiously, her face was not as lined as other women of her age. Only her eyes betrayed her wisdom and the sure and certain awareness of that moment.

Words had stuck in his throat. Grief had been given talons and was clawing at his flesh. He found it impossible to swallow. Slowly, he walked to her bedside, sank down to his knees on the floor like he was eight years old, frightened of a storm or nightmare and seeking her out.

He held her frail hand between both his hands and forced himself to look into her eyes. With all his soul he'd repudiated what he saw there.

Her time was done. She wanted to leave him, and he didn't want her to go.

He had lowered his head, his forehead touching the mattress. He supposed he prayed, but it wasn't a normal prayer. Not a solicitation to the Almighty, but an oath, a curse, an imprecation to spare her despite her wishes.

With the hindsight of several years, he wished he hadn't been so selfish that day. He should have sat at her side, holding her hand and telling her he understood. In some way, he should have eased her passing. Instead, it was up to Arthur to be the man of the family, despite the fact they were only a year apart.

They'd all congregated outside her bedroom door, and in the morning their vigil was over. She'd smiled at them the night before, patted his cheek, and then never woke up.

She, more than his father, had been his lodestone. When he was a boy, he wanted to please her the most, knowing that his father's praise was always egalitarian. Arthur might have been the heir but wasn't singled out above Lewis or himself. But his mother's approbation was always accompanied by a smile, a soft laugh, and a gleam in her eyes that made him certain she truly thought he was special.

What would she have said to his adventure in America? Would she have castigated him for even wishing to go? It had been a fool's journey, hadn't it? He had been repaid a dozen times over for his stupidity.

He heard another noise. Had he summoned up ghosts? Here, Arthur had only been a visitor. Here, his mother had flitted it in and out, rarely remaining more than a few hours. He purchased the house after his father's death, so it came with no taint or tinge of Harland MacIain.

Perhaps it should have. God knows, his father's shade would have acted as a calming influence. Perhaps the ghost of the fifth Earl of Rathsmere could have curbed some of his more licentious impulses.

He could just imagine some of his conquests encountering his father in the hall.

Until he returned from America, he'd thought that society held no surprises for him. He'd been startled to discover that wasn't entirely true. Instead of being besieged by visitors who'd learned of his return to London, not one person had come to his home.

He opened the door to his library, entered the room, and shut the door softly behind him. He would probably never become accustomed to the thought that he should light a lamp, before remembering it wasn't necessary.

Stepping a few feet away from the door, he folded his arms, staring into the darkness as if to will it to part, revealing a room shrouded in shadows and only faintly illuminated by the moon.

He didn't even know if the moon was full. Nor did he know if it was truly night. His only clue was the absence of sound and activity. The world was hunkered down to sleep, and he felt like the only solitary soul awake.

Stretching out one hand, he walked toward where he thought the sideboard was located. He hated the feeling of disorientation, but he would probably have to get used to it, just like all the other things accompanying blindness. Being unable to tell how large a room was, if he was alone or not. Being unable to gauge the distance to his mouth with a soup spoon or fork. He was not only annoyed at being a blind toddler, he was enraged.

He was, though, becoming adept at pouring whiskey into a glass without spilling it all over the surface of the sideboard. That little trick was accomplished by sticking his finger in the tumbler. When his second knuckle was wet, he had poured enough.

A sound made him hesitate.

With his damnable luck, he had probably roused one of the servants.

No, that wasn't one of the servants.

The noise was so peculiar that he left his glass beside the decanter and made his way back to the library door. He opened it slowly, then stood in the doorway for a moment, trying to trace the origin of the sound, a grating noise, like something rubbing against wood.

He left the library, trailing his hand over the wainscoting as he walked through the hall toward the parlor. This room was not often used and had been designed by his mother for formal occasions. His own life had not been marked by formal occasions, only revelries, jaunts, and carousing. Consequently, he'd rarely been in the parlor.

The pocket doors were halfway closed. Placing two fingers in the recessed handle, he slowly opened one side.

A man with less pride would have summoned someone else. He knew that even as he stood there without raising an alarm. He might be wrong and he didn't want to appear the fool.

Did you hear? The earl was screaming for help in the middle of the night because of a mouse.

No, that wasn't an image he wanted other people to have of him.

He had almost convinced himself that he'd been mistaken when he heard the noise again. This time it was accompanied by whispers.

The thieves weren't accomplished at their task, evidently.

He had not been in this room for months, and hoped the furniture hadn't been moved. He slid around the edge of the door, his back to the wall. To his right was a secretary, and perched on the top a globe lamp with a glass shade. Slowly, his right hand reached out and found the edge of the desk, his fingers sliding over the wood until he located the lamp.

His heart was pounding so hard he was almost breathless with it. The least he could have done was taken a sip of the whiskey for a little Dutch courage.

Ahead of him was a fireplace with windows on either side. The thieves were trying to enter through the window to his right.

Common sense said that all he really had to do was announce his presence for them to scatter. A thief didn't want to be revealed; otherwise, why come to his home after midnight?

It was a thought he had just as he heard the sound of the window being raised.

Dalton grabbed the lamp with his right hand and moved sideways in front of the secretary.

His mother had installed ferns by the window in copper pots set into iron stands. He transferred the lamp into his left hand, reaching out with his right. When he felt the delicate touch of fronds on his fingertips, he smiled. Thank God his staff hadn't changed anything in his absence.

He was trying to remember what kind of window was installed in the parlor. He'd never been interested in such things before, so he didn't have an answer. Whatever the thieves were doing was probably designed to jimmy the lock.

He heard the sash raised slowly and stepped behind a chair. To his right was the potted fern. He held the lamp in his left hand.

Timing would be everything.

He heard whispers and swore mentally. Two against one didn't seem fair. His only advantage was the darkness.

"Minerva, truly, will you not reconsider?"

What the hell?

"Yes, Minerva, won't you reconsider?" he said as he pushed on the brass pot, sending the fern toppling.

A woman cried out.

"You almost coshed me over the head with that thing," she said a moment later, her voice surprisingly educated.

"That's what happens when you rob a house, madam."

"Don't be ridiculous," she said. Her voice changed, as if she had picked herself up and was now standing. "I'm not a thief."

"Then why are you gaining entrance through a window, madam?"

"Miss," she said. "Miss Minerva Todd. I need to speak with the earl."

That was a strange request, one that had him lowering the lamp in his hand. It was easier to place it on the floor than to find the secretary again.

"Why?"

"I'd prefer to speak to the earl. If you're another one of the earl's overbearing servants, I warn you, I shan't take no for an answer. If I can't see him tonight, I'll just come back tomorrow."

She was the most outlandish female. She offered no apologies for breaking into his home, but was announcing that she would continue to be obnoxious.

IT WAS so dark that she could barely see him, only a darker shadow in the absence of light. He moved toward her as if he had cat's eyes. She would've backed away but was already standing with her back against the window.

"Who are you?" she asked.

It wasn't Howington. She remembered his voice. It hadn't been as low or as intriguing as this man's. Was he the Earl of Rathsmere's bodyguard? Did the man require one? His valet? Certainly not a majordomo, or he would have sounded more officious.

She felt him come closer. She stretched out her hand, startled when she encountered a soft, almost filmy garment. Silk, if she wasn't mistaken. She jerked back her hand just as quickly.

He took another step. This man was taller than most men she knew. She had never been so conscious of a man's size before or of his potential strength.

He bent his head until his face was only inches from hers.

"You smell of cinnamon," he said. "Are you some sort of errant baker who breaks into homes to make biscuits and scones?"

The question summoned her smile.

"Unfortunately," she said, "I've never had any talent in cooking. Even when I attempt to toast bread, I burn it."

"If you aren't a thief, then who are you and what are you doing in my house?"

The surge of relief she felt was almost enough to knock her to her knees.

"You're the Earl of Rathsmere, then," she said. "Just the man I want to see."

"And you've come to see me at midnight?" His voice held a tinge of astonishment.

"Your secretary wouldn't let me see you."

"At midnight?"

She truly couldn't blame him for being annoyed, but she'd been desperate.

"Where is my brother?"

"I beg your pardon?"

"My brother, Neville Todd. He went with you to America, but he hasn't returned."

"And you think I know where he is?"

She frowned at him. "Who better?"

To her surprise, he turned away from her.

"*You could* have injured me dreadfully with that pot," she said.

"Next time you break into my house after midnight I'll have to remember that. Are you going to exit by the window or do you want me to escort you to the front door?"

"I want you to tell me where my brother is."

"I haven't the slightest idea," he said, making his way to the fireplace. To his relief, there was nothing in his way. He jerked on the bellpull before turning back in the woman's direction.

He could hear her moving toward him. He stretched out his hand to stop her and encountered a female arm. Instead of pulling back, he allowed his hand to trail up to her shoulder.

She didn't move. Was it pity that froze her in place?

Had he fooled himself and there wasn't a Stygian darkness in the room?

He splayed his fingers, thumb touching her chin. Her skin was incredibly soft. He wanted to cup his hand over her cheek, keep her still to better measure the shape of her face. He wanted to stroke his fingers over her, marvel at the differences women offered from men. He wanted, in an odd and disturbing way, to tell her it had been a great many months since he'd touched anyone willingly, and never a woman in all that time.

"They depended on you to be their leader," she said.

The words, said in a dark parlor in the middle of the night, held a tone he couldn't decipher. Perhaps it was condemnation. Or partly regret. Something lingered there, just below the surface, an emotion that warned him not to examine it too closely.

He finally pulled back his hand, wanted to apologize for his effrontery. Or question hers. Who was more at blame here? Her, for breaking into his house to demand answers? Or him, for daring to touch her?

"Aren't you going to light a lamp?"

"No, I'm not. Nor am I going to discuss America," he said. Nor would he talk about Neville Todd.

"I don't give a flying fig for America. Or MacIain's Marauders or whatever you called ourselves. All I care about is my brother. Where is he?"

He should have expected the next question. In fact, it probably should've been the first one she asked.

"Is he dead?"

"I don't know," he said, "but I sincerely hope he is."

"I beg your pardon?"

"Your Lordship?"

He turned, grateful to hear Mrs. Thompson's voice. "We have an unexpected guest," he said to her.

"Show her to the door. If you have any trouble, summon one of the stable boys."

He retraced his steps with more speed than sense. Thankfully, he didn't encounter any wayward otto- mans or misplaced chairs.

At the door, he stopped. "If you return, Miss Todd, I'll notify the authorities."

"What do you mean, you hope Neville is dead?"

"Did you hear me?" he asked.

"And me, Rathsmere? Did you hear me?"

Mrs. Thompson said something calming, but he was already out the door and heading for the stairs, his whiskey be damned.

Chapter 6

$\mathcal{D}$alton was seated in his library, in front of the cold fireplace. He'd taken the right-hand chair, leaving the other one vacant for his soon-to-be arriving guest. James Wilson would be the first person who saw him outside of his servants and medical attendees.

He had traveled from America with two people, Duane Abernathy and his wife, Constance. Expatriates, they had been convinced to return to Scotland by way of London first. Mrs. Abernathy had proved to be a skilled nurse, and her husband was a general oddsbody, a man of all work and a capable protector.

Once they brought him home, he had offered them both positions either in London or Gledfield. They had, to his surprise, refused, saying they were all for seeing their homeland again.

"If you change your mind," he said, feeling a warmth for the couple who had made it possible for him to return to London, "the offer is always open."

They had thanked him again, Mrs. Abernathy startling Dalton by kissing him on the cheek.

"And I can't think of anyone I would rather work for," she said, further surprising him.

He was fortunate in his London servants as well.

Mrs. Thompson had been selected by his mother from a phalanx of candidates. She'd been more maternal toward him ever since he returned. No doubt it was his blindness that prompted her attitude. Howington had been with him for years before he left for America. The man had opted to stay behind in England to oversee his affairs. A good thing, as it turned out, since Arthur had gone and gotten himself killed. Between Howington and Arthur's staff, nothing had fallen by the wayside.

The MacIain fortune was well served and growing by the day, he was told. His solicitor, however, had been hinting that Dalton should be like his older brother, overseeing it all. Pulling strings here, opening a factory there, hiring and firing and being an observant puppet master.

He couldn't imagine a worse steward for the MacIain wealth. He'd never before been responsible for anything other than himself, and look how well he'd handled that task.

What would James Wilson think to see him? He'd never had to question whether his appearance scared another human being and it irked him to do so now.

Should he tell James the entire truth or hold back certain details of his expedition to America, the better to appear less of an idiot?

No, the whole truth must be told. Nothing less would suffice. And his full measure of arrogance must be revealed as well.

Howington announced his visitor in his usual abrupt manner. His secretary crept on soundless feet to the door, never even seeming to breathe to give his position away. Then, when Dalton was lulled into thinking he was alone, Howington burst into speech.

"Mr. Wilson is here, sir," the secretary said in an unnecessarily loud voice.

He'd lost his sight, not his hearing.

A second later he felt Wilson's hand clamp down on the shoulder.

"James," he said smiling. "I would say it was good to see you, but I can't quite manage that right now."

"I hadn't heard, Dalton," James said. "What the hell happened?"

He waved toward the chair then turned his head slightly, not having heard Howington leave the room. It was possible the man had slithered out as soundlessly as he entered.

Bells—that was most definitely the answer. A necklace of bells if Howington refused to wear them on his shoes. Either that or the man had to be told to announce his arrivals and departures.

"We'll have refreshments now," Dalton said, hoping the secretary hadn't left. Otherwise, he was going to look the fool.

"Very well, Your Lordship."

Another thing about Howington. He didn't use that officious tone unless someone else was with him. When they were alone, his secretary behaved normally. Only when there were guests did he act as if Dalton were king.

Ever since returning from America, he'd been annoyed by his secretary, whereas before, the man had rarely disturbed him. Did the man miss the old Dalton?

His guest settled next to him.

James Wilson had been his roommate in school and was the fifth son of a duke. They had found in each other not kindred spirits as much as boys with similar backgrounds. He'd been a hell-raiser even back then, while James always urged caution. He'd called James his conscience more than once.

But whenever he had succeeded in one of his routs, James was more than willing to share the proceeds, such as those times he'd raided the school's larder. Together, the two boys often shared a jar of brambleberry jelly slathered on a loaf of bread.

Dalton had always been hungry back then, and as he grew, his appetites hadn't diminished as much as changed direction. James had been as prudent and celibate as a monk.

They hadn't seen each other for a number of years and, in that time, James had acquired a reputation as an adept investigator, one with not only talent but tact. If a man suspected his wife was seeing another man, he went to James Wilson. If a member of the peerage was disturbed about his heir's habits, he too went to James. Whatever sin was unearthed was never spoken about or revealed to another soul.

Dalton had even recommended James to Arthur. His brother hadn't mentioned the subject of the investigation or pried, but Dalton had his suspicions. Alice, his sister-in-law, had defied society and remarried shortly after Arthur's death.

While James spent the intervening years adding to his good name, Dalton had done the opposite, a thought that kept him silent for a few moments.

Despite their differences, he and James had been true friends. When had friendship ceased to be important to him? He'd cultivated hangers-on, boys turning to men, men with little to do but carouse and drink. None of them offered him anything in the way of intellectual challenge. Nor had their characters been such that he was compelled to emulate their better behavior. They were all like him, adrift in the world, with no greater thought than the next night's woman, drink, or bet.

Two years ago he'd been at the center of a popular group in society. They shocked, amused, horrified, and fascinated all of London. Yet not one person had called on him on his return. Not one of them sent him a note or letter. They vanished in a puff of smoke as if they'd only been figments of his drunken, hazy memories.

"I'm going to tell you a story," he said now, before he lost his nerve. "I wish I could tell you it's all fiction, but unfortunately none of it is. I also wish I could tell you that it paints me in a good light, but almost none of it does."

"I've heard tales of your exploits," James said.

He wasn't the least surprised. "I'm sure you have," he said.

He hesitated when Mrs. Thompson announced herself at the door. At least his housekeeper knew the proper way to comport herself around a blind man. Perhaps she could give lessons to Howington.

She bustled about, ensuring that James had tea, scones, and oatmeal biscuits.

"I've soaked the raisins in whiskey, sir," she said.

To Dalton's surprise, she didn't urge him to partake. Maybe she knew how much he liked oatmeal biscuits, or perhaps she thought it was worthless to urge him to do anything he didn't want to do. Or perhaps she was trying to restrict his intake of whiskey.

He settled back on the chair, more than willing to wait until James had eaten his fill. Perhaps he would change his mind about revealing everything. They spoke for a few moments of the past, of the school they had attended, and of people they both knew, most of whom had gone on to marry and beget an impressive number of children.

"You're not married?" he asked James.

"I am," his friend said, to his surprise. "Happily so, I might add, but we've no children yet."

He hadn't heard and the oversight disturbed him. He'd have Howington send a belated wedding present.

They sat in silence for a few moments while Dalton ratcheted up his nerve again.

"In May of last year I left England with eleven friends," he said. "Or perhaps the word 'friends' isn't right. Call them acquaintances." Probably even less than that. Parasites? Maybe a dozen different names, but not friends.

Not someone like James, who, despite the fact that he hadn't seen him in years, came when he needed him.

"Someone once called us Dalton's Dozen. MacIain's Marauders was the name that stuck. I wanted to go to war and maybe the others did, too. Or maybe they simply followed me because it was something they did."

"MacIain's Marauders?" James said.

"I know. An idiotic name." One so childish it might have dated back to his days at school.

Still, he had been their leader, their colonel, their general-at-war. *Follow me, boys, into the breech, and we'll show those damn Americans how a real man goes to war.*

"We got to Washington in June. My first battle was in July."

He reached over to the tray, picked up an oatmeal biscuit and held it lightly. He wasn't hungry as much as he was hesitating.

"Why, Dalton?"

The question was voiced with genuine curiosity. Because of that, he answered as honestly as he could.

"Boredom. Ennui. Stupidity. I lean toward the latter myself. War was an adventure, something none of us had ever experienced. We read about it in books; we heard tales, but we wanted to know what it was like firsthand. So we went off to war, the twelve of us."

Thankfully, James didn't comment.

"Once in Washington, we flipped a coin to see on which side we would fight. I got the North along with four other men. The others got the South."

To his credit, James still didn't say a word, but Dalton could imagine his friend's incredulous stare.

Within a week the peaceful serenity of the Virginia countryside was clawed open by screams and yells, the cloud of smoke from the rifles and cannon, and the shocking crimson of too much blood.

His first taste of war had been at Manassas, a battle the Union lost. They'd lost the second, too, at Big Bethel. They'd won a few skirmishes before the last battle he was in.

"Tom died in the second week. Lawrence in the third."

By that time he was reevaluating his idiotic decision to come to America and was all for making for the British Legation in Washington.

"I realized that war wasn't a game or an adventure. It was bloody and smelly, terrifying and horrible. I hope never to see as many dead men in one place again." He laughed mercilessly. "But I can't see at all, which is probably divine justice."

"What happened to the men who fought for the South?"

"I don't know," he said, the admission grating on him.

He'd written the families of the men who'd died, but he hadn't contacted them once he returned to London. He should have, though, to ensure they'd gotten word. Another regret for his pile.

Virginia was not unlike England in its topography and lush vegetation. The summer had been too damn hot, but he'd thought of it with fondness as they made their way through the bitterly cold November day. Sleet bit at his face with icy teeth.

On that gray day when the lowering sky masked any hint of sun and made it feel like nightfall at noon, he made the decision to return home. He'd been a damn fool to think war was a lark, that it would add meaning to the bland sameness of his life. Shame sat on his shoulders like one of the Union blankets he'd been issued, scratchy and irritating.

In the intervening months, he'd obeyed orders and given some. He'd kept the men with him safe while respecting General Patterson, the man under whose command he served. The Rake of London had transformed himself into a soldier, and the metamorphosis surprised even him.

"We were licking our wounds after the defeat at Leesburg and were headed toward Washington. I remember thinking how serene the terrain was. Not very far away thousands of men still lay on the ground, either dead or dying. All I could smell was the cold and a hint of snow, not blood and smoke."

He reached toward the table to pour himself a cup of tea.

"Here," James said grabbing his hand, then settling a saucer with a teacup on it.

He would much rather have had whiskey, but he would settle for tea until his friend left.

Never let it be said he wasn't aware of his vices. What he chose to do about them, however, was his business. He might not be a womanizer any longer. He might not stay out all night. He might not even smoke a cheroot.

Whiskey was still a friend, God help him.

"Then what happened?"

He almost smiled at James's curiosity. His friend had always been there at school, whispering cautions, then desperate to know, exactly, what he had done. As if there were two parts of James's character, the angel and the angel who wished he could be more devilish.

"There were still three of us left," he said. "From the original five who went with the Union army. William Harris, Neville Todd, and me."

A clearing to the left of the track they were following made him turn and direct his mount through the trees. Near a creek, the space was large enough for their encampment.

"I turned to call out to the other men and saw Neville raising his pistol and aiming at me."

That moment was firmly fixed in his memory, replaying slowly every time he thought of it. He felt himself frown as he stared at Neville, then recalled starting to ask what he was doing. He saw the other man raise the pistol, aiming down the sight, and a puff of smoke as Neville pulled the trigger. Everything after that was black and red until he'd awakened in a hospital. Neville and William had both disappeared.

"I told myself I must have been mistaken. I couldn't have been right. I hadn't seen what I'd seen. After Neville disappeared, I didn't have any other choice but to think he'd tried to kill me."

He took a sip of his tea, again wishing it were whiskey.

"I wondered if he'd been a casualty of war, but I was assured that neither he nor William were on any of the lists. Then I thought they must have given me up for dead and come back to England."

"Had they?"

He shook his head. The gesture always made him slightly dizzy. Another sign of the change in his life— even simple movements had to be rethought.

"I don't know," he said.

"And you want me to find him?"

"Yes," he said, a decision only hours old.

He'd thought himself insulated and isolated in his London house. He'd spent his time recuperating, not worrying whether he was going to be a target again. Neville's sister had proved that he'd been foolish to forget. She'd broken into his house. Neville could do the same.

"I dislike the idea of being a target, especially since I don't know why the man tried to kill me."

"I think I have a dual role, Dalton."

He was grateful James didn't launch into that *Your Lordship* business. His friend's next words, however, weren't as welcome.

"I'll find him," he said. "At the same time, I think you need a guard."

"I don't need a nursemaid, James."

"No, just another set of eyes."

He was silenced by the other man's frankness.

"Your sight, is there nothing they can do?" James asked.

"I've been told that if I'm a good little boy, I might regain some sight in my left eye. Right now I can sometimes see a little light, but that's all. The right eye is completely gone, of course."

"You're damn lucky. You could have died."

He started to nod, stopped himself and said, "Yes, I could have." He didn't mention that there were several days when he wished he had.

Life, however, had relentlessly dragged him upward from despair. He lived despite himself.

What the hell had he ever done to Todd to deserve the man shooting him?

When he first met Neville, he'd been amused by him. He was like a boy reveling in his freedom, testing his boundaries in a way that made Dalton feel avuncular toward him. Over the months, however, Neville's boyishness hadn't matured, but his ability to whine certainly had.

"Well, what do you think?"

He was dragged back to the question of a guard. "I don't like the idea, but I dislike the idea of Neville gunning for me even less."

"You don't know why he tried to kill you?"

"Not one idea. I've spent hours trying to figure it out."

"He might not be in London, but we won't know until I make inquiries."

"His sister is here, so he'll probably return."

What did she look like? Was she tall or short? Did she have blue eyes or brown? Was her hair blond or a darker shade? Or was she, perhaps, a redhead?

Last night she'd smelled of cinnamon. Why?

"I'll find him, Dalton, and keep you safe as well."

He wasn't all that fond of the idea of having a shadow, but he didn't want to be murdered, either. His life might not be what it had been, but it was still his. Therefore, he claimed ownership of his present and his future, whatever that was.

Chapter 7

"You say there's a garden in the back of Rathsmere's house?" Minerva asked.

Hugh nodded. "I don't think you should go back there, Minerva."

She really wished Hugh weren't so overprotective. Her driver remained standing at the door of the parlor. She'd given up trying to assure him that it was fine if he took a seat. Perhaps it was all well and good. Their relationship was not what it had once been and she didn't want to give him an indication it had changed.

She finished the rest of her tea and placed the cup back on the tray.

"I understand your reservations, Hugh," she said. "Truly, I do."

"If you did, you wouldn't insist on going back to the man's house. He could have called the authorities last night and what would you have done then?"

Without giving her a chance to respond, Hugh turned on his heel and left. She hoped he was going to ready the carriage.

She retreated to her bedroom, planning her strategy for today.

The earl had startled her the night before. She hadn't meant for their first meeting to go so badly. Of course he'd walked away. He'd just found her breaking into his house.

All she needed was a few minutes in his company. That's all. Enough time that she could convince him to tell her what he knew.

She would begin by apologizing for last night. Then he would tell her what he meant about hoping Neville was dead.

Today she was dressed in her serviceable blue again, this time without the cuffs and collar. Since she'd returned her new bonnets to the milliners, she was going to wear an older serviceable one. After pinning her brooch watch to the right side of her bodice, she surveyed herself in the pier glass.

Yes, she looked plain and unassuming. Her mother had always said she had strong bones, which meant she was built like her father with broad shoulders, long legs and arms, and wide hands. Her hands were tools and she used them in that fashion, to the extent she had calluses on her fingertips. Her palms, too, were hardened by years of digging in the dirt.

She looked as dependable and work worn as a scullery maid. If she fixed her hair in a different manner, would it make her more attractive? Her face was just her face. Perhaps there was something she could do there, too.

Reaching into the top drawer of her bureau, she moved aside the small jar of pomade she never used and grabbed the salve for her lips. The delicate pink shade made her mouth seem even larger. Rather than wiping it off, she did something she'd never done before and placed a little on her cheeks, surprised when the color made her brown eyes sparkle.

The earl was used to women who were known for their beauty and charm. She had little hope of impressing him with her appearance. No, she would have to marshal her arguments and appeal to his conscience.

If he had one.

Bidding Mrs. Beauchamp good-bye at the door, she ignored the woman's look of interest—surely wearing lip color was not such an egregious fault—and pulled on her gloves.

This morning's rain had cleared the air, bringing the scent of summer to her in the form of heated, fragrant blossoms and wafts of odor from the Thames.

She descended the steps, heading toward the carriage, carefully not looking in the direction of the Covington home. She knew, even without seeing them, that all three sisters were watching her enter the vehicle.

As they pulled into the road behind the Earl of Rathsmere's house, birds roosting in the nearby trees greeted her arrival with alarm. She stepped out of the carriage before Hugh could dismount and walked to the driver's seat.

"I'll only be a little while."

"I wish you wouldn't do this."

He could be the most stubborn man sometimes, rivaling Neville in his obstinacy.

"I'll be fine."

The wall enclosing Rathsmere's garden was built of the same red brick as the house. Every few feet there was a wide pillar topped with white stone and a curious winged creature made of black iron. She studied the statue for a moment before deciding it must be something mythical created by the MacIain family. Wide wings were tucked behind its body. Its talons gave the appearance of being dug into the white stone, while a beaklike protuberance looked down with a supercilious air. The breast of the bird—or the eagle, if that's what it was—was inscribed with a crest she couldn't read from there.

The stable was to her right, separated from the alley by a wide strip of grass. Several men were working there and more than one glanced in her direction. She ignored their looks as if she belonged in the lane.

At the gate, she hesitated, her hand on the latch. What would she do if it was locked?

To her relief, the gate swung open easily. She peered behind the wooden door to find herself in a lush overgrown English garden, complete with birdbaths, feeders, and hedges bordering the paths.

An assortment of trees, some of them large and leafy, shaded the area, giving her the impression of an isolated, almost secret, place. She took a few steps inside and slowly closed the gate, careful to make no noise. This enchanted garden looked to be the scene from a child's fairy tale, the home of fairies and woodland nymphs who rarely visited London.

She'd never had an interest in the names of foliage and flowers, but now she wished she had. She wanted to know what that orange and yellow striped blossom growing in the corner was, or the red and pink dotted flowers blooming in such abundance along the path. She bent to sniff one bright blossom, thinking the scent reminded her of her mother's perfume from Paris.

She appreciated nature; she just didn't revel in it. Here, however, she might change her mind. The gravel paths were wide, encouraging two people to stroll side by side, hands or arms interlocked. A stone bench sat at an angle to another grouping of flowers and was shaded by the branches of a tree. Was it an oak or an elm? She wasn't sure. She reached up and inspected a limb, studying a grouping of shiny light green leaves. She was no expert on trees, either.

"Who's there?"

She let go of the limb and it sprung back into place. Turning, she grabbed her skirts with both hands and stared.

A man sat on a stone bench with his back to her.

Even though he was attired only in a white linen shirt and black trousers, it had to be the earl. Who else would sit in a private garden, his posture ramrod straight as if he sat on a throne?

She took a few hesitant steps toward him. This meeting could not end like the night before.

"What are you doing here, Miss Todd?"

"How did you know it was me?" she asked, surprised.

"You smell of cinnamon."

"I do?"

He nodded but didn't turn.

His right arm rose, fingers waving her toward the garden gate.

"Get out of my garden. Leave the same way you entered."

She circled the bench, intent on addressing him.

And froze.

Taking a few steps back, she wrapped her arms around her waist and tried to understand exactly what she was seeing. From the rumors, Dalton MacIain was a handsome man. This man was still handsome, but a pink and white scar twisted from his temple across one eye to end above the bridge of his nose. White cloudy fluid filled his right eye, the lid half closed, while the other, a cerulean blue, stared at her in disdain.

The lower half of his face was untouched, his full mouth thinned in obvious irritation.

"Have you taken a backward step? Is your hand over your mouth to silence your shrieks of terror? Are you nauseated?"

She should turn around and follow the path back to the gate, leaving him in peace. But he was the only one who knew what had happened to Neville. The only one who could tell her where her brother was.

"What happened to you?"

He didn't stand and face her. He didn't frown. Instead, his expression froze and his shoulders stiffened as if he were turning to stone. He might have been a statue in the garden. An image of a Greek god slightly damaged by war.

"Get out," he said, the words slowly enunciated.

She gathered her skirts in her hands, came and sat down at the end of the bench only a foot or so away from him.

"Are you completely blind?"

"Are you completely daft?" he asked.

"That means you are."

"Miss Todd, if you do not leave my garden now, I will be forced to bodily remove you."

"I doubt you'll do so," she said, inclining her head to study him. "You'd have to call for someone to help you."

He clenched his hand on the edge of the bench so tightly she could see his white knuckles. Did he wish to strike her? She had never heard people speak about his penchant for violence, but perhaps going to war had changed him.

"Have you always been so obnoxious? I don't remember Neville being the same. A good thing your brother didn't take after you."

"If he had," she said, "perhaps he could have protected himself a little better around you. He wouldn't have been led like a rat following the Pied Piper off to war. Who on earth goes to fight another country's battles? Only an arrogant fool."

"They weren't rats, Miss Todd, but grown men."

"Who saw you as their leader."

"Are you done?"

"No," she said. "I have no intention of leaving until I find out what happened to my brother. You can call the authorities. You can call Mr. Howington. You can summon your entire staff to carry me from this place, but I refuse to leave."

"What do you look like?"

"I beg your pardon?"

"Are you ugly? I found that women without an iota of appeal often appear strident. As if they think they need to face the world as a combatant. Are you ugly, Miss Todd?"

"I have never measured myself by my appearance."

"That's a lie. Every woman has."

"Perhaps women of your acquaintance. No doubt they've nothing better to do all day but stare into a mirror."

"I would think that a woman as acerbic as you would defend her sex."

"I doubt beautiful women require my defense," she said.

"Which is an answer. So you aren't beautiful, Miss Todd. Are you acceptable looking? Or do you have a mole at the end of your nose? A squint, perhaps? Do you wear a lorgnette? Is your skin sallow? Is there gray in your hair? I seem to remember that you're much older than your brother. Are you aged?"

He really was the most terrible person.

"I'm only eight years older than Neville," she said.

He smiled.

With her words, she'd fallen into his trap. What did she care what he thought of her?

"Should you care so much about the appearance of other people?" she asked. "Especially since your own appearance has been so grievously altered by your stupidity?"

"Get out of my garden."

She studied him. At closer inspection, his scars weren't that onerous. The worst of the scarring was on his right temple, the bridge of his nose, and the damage to his right eye.

"What did you mean, you hope my brother is dead? Where is Neville?"

"I know why Neville came with me. To get away from you."

"I don't like you very much," she said.

"I find I don't care very much."

"Where is Neville?" she asked.

"I don't know where your brother is."

"He was in your charge."

"He wasn't in nappies, Miss Todd. He's a grown man. A fact you evidently find difficult to accept."

"Oh, Your Lordship, I didn't know you were having guests."

Minerva turned her head to see a plump woman in a severe black dress approaching them. On her head was a poufy white ruffled cap edged in black. Her face was round yet lined with a web of delicate wrinkles, making Minerva wonder at her age. Her smile was as bright and charming as a child's, her round cheeks lightly dusted with pink. Eyes of sparkling blue gazed on them with a surprising look of delight.

He'd summoned his housekeeper to escort her to the front door last night, but Minerva had simply left the same way she arrived, by means of the window.

The tray the woman carried held a small white teapot, one cup, and a selection of pastries.

"She isn't staying, Mrs. Thompson. In fact, I would appreciate it if you would summon Mr. Howington and a few of the footmen as well. Someone to escort the woman from my garden."

"Oh, sir, I couldn't do that, could I? Not without a cup of tea, surely."

"Mrs. Thompson, she isn't a guest. She's an interloper."

"I've never been called an interloper before," Minerva said. "But he's quite right. I haven't been invited. But I have no intention of leaving until he tells me what he's done with my brother."

"With your brother, miss?"

"He has absconded with him."

"Surely he wouldn't do such a thing." Mrs. Thompson glanced at the earl.

"She is looking at you chidingly," Minerva said. "What a pity you can't see it."

The housekeeper drew a breath in sharply.

Minerva glanced at the older woman. "I know, I should apologize for my rudeness. But the earl is sufficiently arrogant that I doubt anything I say to him would matter."

"Then take yourself off, Miss Todd."

"Not until you tell me exactly where my brother is and why you wish him dead."

"Should I bring another cup, sir?" the housekeeper said, still standing there holding the tray. Minerva felt pity for the woman who had unconsciously walked into a war.

Standing, she took the tray from the housekeeper and put it on the bench between them.

She didn't have an iota of sympathy for the Earl of Rathsmere. The man positively oozed arrogance and wasn't pitiable in the least.

Instead, she was rather disconcerted to realize that he was still handsome. What did his looks matter, when it was clear his character was abominable?

Chapter 8

"*D*o you take sugar?" she asked, pouring the tea.

When the earl didn't answer, she dispensed with the sugar and held the cup up in front of him.

"You need to reach up with your right hand," she said. "I have no intention of feeding you. Quickly now. I'm not your nursemaid."

His look was no doubt designed to quell her. She had the feeling that he would like to throw the cup at her, but he took it, nonetheless.

"Thank you, Mrs. Thompson," he said. "That will be all."

"Would you like me to summon Mr. Howington?" she asked, looking from Minerva to the earl and back again.

"Give us five minutes," he said. "After that, if you would ask Mr. Howington to attend me."

She nodded, a gesture that sent her odd poufy cap bouncing on top of her head.

Once the housekeeper left the garden, Minerva turned to the earl. "You can remove me bodily," she said. "I'll only return."

He didn't say anything for a moment, only brought the cup to his lips, sipping from it.

"I don't doubt you will. What would it take for you to leave me alone?"

"The truth. It's all I want."

"I don't know where Neville is. I've told you the truth. Here's more truth for you, Miss Todd. I don't care."

"That is only too obvious."

She stared at the tray that she'd placed on the space between them. What a pretty little teapot. Royal Dorchester, she thought. Her mother had a similar pattern in her best china. When was the last time she had used it? She didn't entertain, especially since Neville had been gone. There were no friends of his to arrive at the house unexpectedly. No one to attend a dinner party. She had few friends, and those she might call more than acquaintances were involved in her work and as separated or aloof as she herself was.

He took another sip of his tea, then placed the cup back on the saucer with a delicate chink of sound.

"Did you ever think that your blindness is some kind of divine justice for what you've done?"

"I doubt God gives a flying farthing for me, Miss Todd."

"Did you lose them all? Don't you care what happened to them? Don't you feel any sort of responsibility?"

"I didn't lose them on purpose, Miss Todd. We were separated because I was in the hospital for a number of weeks."

"And now? Do you feel nothing now? Or only pity for yourself? I can't be the only relative who wonders, who waits. What do you say to the others?"

"The others haven't bothered me."

"No, no doubt they're in awe of your consequence. The great Dalton MacIain. The powerful and wealthy Earl of Rathsmere, who can do anything he wishes without having to explain to a soul. Well, I want an explanation. I want to know how you can turn your back on men who looked up to you. You're not only blind with your eyes, but with your soul."

"Are you finished castigating me now? Who the hell are you, Miss Todd, to come marching into my home and lecture me?"

"Who the hell are you, to lose my brother and not be concerned about it?"

She didn't use profanity often but she found it was called for from time to time. This was one of those occasions.

His brow furled and the corner of his lip twitched. Had she shocked him? Good. The Earl of Rathsmere needed a little shocking.

"Where is my brother?"

"Where are your manners?"

"No doubt in the same place my brother is," she said. "Where is he?"

When he remained silent, she frowned at him.

"I have every intention of finding my brother," she said. "If you could just provide the information I need, I shan't bother you again. What ship did you travel on?"

He still didn't speak, and she wondered if he was going to hold back all the details of his trip. How would she be able to find Neville if he did?

"The *Honoria*," he finally said. "I had a double cabin. Unfortunately, I was alone. I believe a companion of the female sort would have made the voyage more interesting."

She felt herself warm. Must he be licentious even now?

"Where did you disembark?"

"Maryland. Baltimore, to be exact."

She took a notebook and pencil from her pocket and made a notation.

"I need the names of MacIain's Marauders," she said.

"An idiotic name."

"I agree."

"So is this meeting, Miss Todd."

She looked over at him. His face was turned toward his house, presenting his left side.

Her breath caught. How shallow was she to be caught up in a man's appearance? Beauty was revealed in character, not in the symmetry of cheekbones and a chiseled jaw.

How many women had stared at him in the past, more than content to simply look at him as if he were a work of art?

"I've engaged an investigator. If your brother is hiding in London, James Wilson will find him."

She made a notation of the name, biting back the quick nausea at his announcement.

"What are you going to do once you find him?"

He smiled, and she felt her stomach flutter. Did snakes smile?

"I'm going to attempt to have justice done."

"What does that mean?"

"Your brother tried to kill me, Miss Todd. He only managed to blind me." He held up one hand, waving it in front of his face. "Yes, I got this in America, courtesy of your brother."

"I don't believe you. You're wrong." She held both hands tightly together to keep them from shaking.

"Hardly something I would lie about, Miss Todd."

"However you arrived at that conclusion, it's an incorrect one."

"Your brother leveled a pistol at me. He fired that pistol."

"You must be mistaken."

"Your inability to accept the truth doesn't negate it. Are you one of those women given to hysteria and emotionality to the exclusion of all reason?"

"You're autocratic," she said, knowing that as insults go, hers weren't nearly as damaging as his. She would have to try harder. "You're a self-pitying twit."

He didn't say anything for a moment, which made her wonder if she'd scored a direct hit.

"You smell of whiskey," she added. "It's barely noon. Are you a drunkard, too?"

"You've allowed your loyalty to blind you, Miss Todd."

His words were sharp, his voice soft. She had the sudden feeling that Dalton MacIain was at his most dangerous in moments like this. Another man might raise his voice or posture. The earl would be quiet, deadly, and determined.

"He's my brother," she said.

"Does that mean he's incapable of wrongdoing? That he couldn't possibly be homicidal?"

"I'm his only relative," she said.

"So, in your eyes, he's perfect, even when it's obvious he's not?"

"You would have him hang, before giving him an opportunity to explain himself."

His laughter startled her.

"There is no explanation that would induce me to forgive him."

"YOU'VE BROKEN into my house. And now my garden. Where can I expect you next, Miss Todd? If I swear on something holy that I don't know where your brother is, will you be satisfied?"

"No."

The stark answer didn't surprise him. He had the feeling that she was abrupt at times but almost always direct.

He could be as direct.

"I think it's time you left, don't you? You've come to see the beast in his den. Now it's time to go."

He tried to bank down his rage, but it was building. She wanted to know where Neville Todd was? With any luck, at the bottom of some deep ocean. Or buried in the fertile Virginia earth. Or in hell.

She stood and walked away. A moment later the garden gate opened and she was gone. Either that or she was still there and being silent like Howington.

Neville had a strong advocate, someone who evidently loved him enough to make a complete ass of herself.

Now that his mother was dead, was there anyone else on the face of the earth who felt that way about him? An uncomfortable question and one he didn't want to examine too much at the moment.

He didn't want to think about America. It had been a suicidal venture, one filled with hubris and arrogance. He'd been an idiot, an opinion Miss Todd shared.

Why did he care what the woman thought? He'd lived his life remarkably free of caring about the opinions of others.

The sun warmed his shoulders and back. The interlude in the garden had been a pleasant one before Miss Todd arrived.

He wished he knew what the woman looked like. He could always ask Mrs. Thompson or Howington.

How many years would it take before he accepted what had happened? He would never see again, no matter how much he wished and bargained and railed against his fate. He would never look at his own reflection, gauge the weather by scanning the clouds in the sky. He'd never ride again, never see a smile on his lover's face.

For that matter, what woman would want a blind man?

A greedy one, who chose a fortune over affection.

On that depressing thought he stood and slowly

made his way into the house, both hands outstretched a little for balance. He'd never considered that blindness would make him feel wobbly. Perhaps he should acquire a walking stick or a paid companion whose only task would be to lead him from one place to another like a child in short pants.

That image was enough for him to wish that Neville had been a better marksman.

MINERVA STOMPED to her carriage, nodded at Hugh and said, "Let's go home."

"Did you see him?"

She nodded.

Hugh didn't approve of her actions. He hadn't approved of Neville, either, taking issue with her brother's demeanor and speech. She had listened to his comments because she had no other choice. Hugh was loquacious when he was annoyed.

"After this, I hope we won't come back here," Hugh said now as he stood in the open door of the carriage.

She didn't answer.

When one does something out of the norm, one must be prepared for all the ramifications. That was not a lesson she had learned at her mother's knee, but from her own experience.

She was paying for her mistake with Hugh now. He evidently felt he had the right to make comments about her behavior when she neither solicited nor appreciated his opinion.

She must solve that situation somehow, as soon as she found Neville.

Sitting back against the seat, she closed her eyes. She would not cry. Tears didn't bring about any resolution of the problem and only made her eyes swell. She looked then like a rabbit with her pink nose and pink eyes.

Perhaps if she'd been more understanding, Neville would never have left for America. If she had been gentle and sweet like their mother, he might have listened to her counsel once or twice.

Neville had been going through some difficult times, learning who he was, how he fit into the world. He would have been better served by going into the family business, but he'd been led to believe that only the lower classes worked for a living—another fault she lay at Dalton MacIain's feet.

But he wasn't a murderer.

How dare that irritating man say such a thing.

She was not going to feel anything for him, and certainly not pity. The war had damaged him, but wars killed people. What had he expected, that he could blithely sail into battle without it affecting him in any way? Or did he think he would return to England with a rakish scar that would make women swoon at his feet?

He was blind. That must ruin his plans for a hedonistic life. Yet his scars hadn't altered his appearance all that much. The man was still a handsome devil, no doubt still capable of charm if he chose to exert it. Evidently, he hadn't around her. Of course, she had trespassed in his garden. Nor was she his type. She possessed too much intelligence to be charmed by Rathsmere.

She deliberately blocked out the memory of him sitting alone on the bench. She would feel nothing but irritation and annoyance for the man, which was all he deserved.

How dare he imply that Neville tried to kill him?

Once home, she dismounted from the carriage, escaping before Hugh could question her further.

The fact that she felt so weepy was disturbing. So, too, that she recalled Dalton MacIain's words too well. He'd as much as called her ugly.

Who was the Rake of London to criticize her?

As she walked from the stables to the back of her house, she saw a glint in one of the upper windows of the Covington house.

For the last few years, armed with their nephew's spyglass, the Covington sisters kept a lookout on all her activities, just like she was a ship at sea. She wouldn't have been surprised if they knew when she left the house and when she returned, down to the exact minute.

She was in no mood to endure their endless prying.

Stopping on the path, she folded her arms and frowned up at the window on the second floor. A moment later the curtain twitched closed.

Nodding, she made her way to the house.

Somehow, she would have to prove the Earl of Rathsmere wrong. The idea of Neville trying to kill anyone was ridiculous. Secondly, she was going to find her brother, even if she had to stay glued to Rathsmere's side.

Chapter 9

"*W*hat are you doing?" Dalton asked. He sat at the desk in his library with a tumbler of whiskey at his right hand.

He heard something heavy slide along the floor. He guessed it was Howington, since the man hadn't announced himself, only entered the room as he had for months, silently and with little regard for the fact that Dalton had to guess who the hell it was.

"Your brother's solicitor has sent over the last of his papers, sir. "

He'd already informed Arthur's firm that he was making other arrangements and using his own solicitor. Evidently, the decision hadn't inspired them to haste, since it had taken them nearly three months to provide all of his brother's documents.

"There's also a pouch, sir, containing letters. Would you like me to go through them?"

"Leave it on the desk for now."

He felt something land near his right hand. Had the man thrown the pouch at him?

The easiest solution was to allow Howington to go through the letters. Then why was he balking? Because they were Arthur's personal papers and he disliked the idea of anyone prying through his brother's private life, especially Howington.

Perhaps he should have his solicitor send over a

dozen applicants for the position, someone he could trust more than Howington.

The thought startled him.

He'd trusted the man well enough before America, enough to leave him in charge of his household while he played soldier. When had that changed? Was it because of Howington's refusal to announce himself? Or the fact that he felt his secretary was standing there watching—and judging—him?

He wasn't certain. The only thing he did know was that his antipathy to the man had begun on his return and was growing each day.

"Go away, Howington. Go find some other chore to do."

"If you're certain, sir." A vague snideness licked Howington's words. "There are two trunks beside the door, sir. Set side by side."

"I will endeavor not to trip over them, then."

He could feel the man standing at the door watching him. He'd hated being stared at even during his sighted days.

"Go away, Howington."

"Sir."

With that, he was gone.

At least the man didn't live here. Most of his servants had quarters on the third floor, except for the stablemaster and the lads who slept in the stable. Mrs. Thompson had the most luxurious quarters, having taken the majordomo's rooms when he sent Samuels to Gledfield. Samuels was ecstatic to reign over Gledfield's servants rather than a small London staff.

Dalton stared at the doorway, wondering what he should do about the trunks. Did he really want to go through Arthur's papers?

Ever since his meeting with James a few days ago, he'd been in a reflective mood, one that didn't suit him at all. He didn't like measuring himself against a more perfect person, the one his mother always considered him to be.

Arthur had been nearly perfect. He wasn't anything like Arthur, and from what he'd heard, Lewis wasn't emulating Arthur, either.

He abruptly missed his older brother's counsel. Arthur was down to earth, a pragmatist, stolid and stable. What would Arthur have said about his current dilemma?

You're still thinking too much about yourself.

The words were so strong in his mind that he could have sworn Arthur spoke them.

So what would he be in the future? There wasn't a role model in his mind, someone to fashion himself after unless it was an ancient uncle relegated to an attic somewhere. Or a raving lunatic kept in chains. Surely the MacIain family boasted one or two of those.

Standing, he made his way to the fireplace and rang the bellpull. When it was answered in only minutes by a young-voiced thing, he asked her to summon Mrs. Thompson.

Returning to his desk, he waited for the arrival of his housekeeper.

"You wanted to see me, sir?"

Her voice was tremulous with enough hesitancy that he wondered if she'd grown afraid of him. If so, he needed to change her opinion.

"Mrs. Thompson, I have a favor to ask of you."

"Of course, sir. Anything."

He wondered if she was wringing her hands. She'd had a habit of doing that, he remembered, especially when she was awaiting his judgment on a dish, the arrangements for a party, or the accommodations for one of his frequent guests.

"I haven't told you, have I, Mrs. Thompson, how much I appreciate your efforts?"

"My efforts, sir?"

He was botching this, wasn't he?

"I would be miserable without you," he said, determined in this comment, at least. "I appreciate all your efforts on my behalf."

"Thank you, sir."

Her surprise irritated him. Why should she be surprised at his thanks? Hadn't he thanked her enough in the past? To his discredit, he couldn't recall one instance.

Shame slithered up his body, hissing at him before heating the back of his neck.

"What favor is that, sir?" she asked, returning to his initial remark.

He gestured in the direction of the trunks with one hand. "I've received my brother's things. I need someone to help me go through them."

"Of course, sir," she said, but she didn't move.

Had he somehow offended her with the request?

"Sir." That one word was laden with hesitation.

"What is it, Mrs. Thompson?"

Was she going to tell him she couldn't read? Surely not. How could she perform her job? Should he excuse her now rather than cause her further embarrassment?

"I've made something for you, sir. I thought it was a good idea at the time, but I don't know if you'll be offended or if I've overstepped. You're such a handsome man, Your Lordship, even with the scars. But I thought you might feel a little more comfortable with it, rather than not."

He hadn't the slightest idea what she was talking about.

"What is it, Mrs. Thompson?"

He heard her skirts brush against the desk. She

leaned forward and gave him something that he felt with both hands. He was able to discern that it was a disk of fabric stitched so it had a certain dimension with a length of string attached on either side.

"It's an eye patch, sir. It will hide the worst of your scars. And your eye, of course."

He didn't know what to say.

"Forgive me, sir. I shouldn't have."

"No," he said. He cleared his throat. "No, Mrs. Thompson. Thank you. I appreciate the gesture."

"If you don't mind, sir, I'll help you."

In the next moment, she'd taken the eye patch from him and fixed it over his right eye.

"Hold it here, sir," she said.

He found himself obeying her instructions.

"If you tie it like this, it will stay on." She moved his other hand to the back of his head where he felt her tie the string into a bow.

"Well, Mrs. Thompson?" he asked when she was done and had stepped back. "What do I look like?"

"Oh, sir, you are even more handsome now."

He didn't know what to say. With her gift, he could shield the worst of his scars from people. Perhaps he could even pretend a rakish air, a don't-give-a-damn attitude toward anyone who might happen to see him.

She'd thought about him, considered how to help him, and in a gesture filled with generosity, had reduced him to silence.

"Well, sir, would you like me to begin with the parcel?"

He nodded, grateful for her tact and her kindness.

"The first seems to be a letter from the solicitor."

She began to read.

Forgive my delay in sending these to you, Your Lordship. On being notified that you've selected your

*own firm to handle matters, we have gathered all
remaining correspondence to forward to you.*

*Some of these documents are of a personal nature,
as you will note. However, I did not feel it within my
province to destroy them without being instructed to
do so. Your brother left no provisions for them.*

The housekeeper suddenly made a quashed sound
of distress.

"What is it, Mrs. Thompson?"

"Well, sir . . ." she began, only to stumble to a halt.

He waited, but when she didn't say anything further, he spoke. "You are my eyes, Mrs. Thompson. I
don't know what disturbs you until you tell me."

"It seems to be letters, sir. Love letters."

He hadn't known much about Arthur's marriage.
He'd only his suspicions that it hadn't been a happy
one. He wasn't around Arthur and Alice often enough
in the last few years to know. Arthur made his home at
Gledfield while he remained mostly in London. When
his brother did come to London to sit at Parliament, he
stayed in the family home.

They hadn't socialized together; they didn't have
friends in common. As close as they had been as boys
were as distant as they were as adults. How had that
happened?

Arthur hadn't approved of him, he knew that well
enough. Still, they were only a year apart and had
grown up together. You would think all those years
of childhood would mean something more than they
had.

What had happened with Arthur's marriage?

He held out his hand and a moment later Mrs.
Thompson handed him the letters. The stack was
thick, tied with a leather string. Up until this moment,
he hadn't realized that Arthur had a strong core of sen-

timentality. He pulled a letter free from the middle of the stack, handing it to Mrs. Thompson.

"Would you read it?" he asked.

He couldn't explain his curiosity. Maybe it had something to do with suddenly missing Arthur, more than he had before. Or regretting that they had each allowed their relationship to disintegrate into nothing more than acquaintances, strangers who had once known each other.

"Are you certain, sir?"

"Please."

" 'My dearest Arthur,' " she began, her voice taking on a soft tone. " 'Our child brings me so much joy I feel I must be smiling all day. He looks so much like you, even down to the little dimple on the right side.' "

For a moment Mrs. Thompson didn't speak. Nor did one word find its way to his lips.

Alice had never borne a child.

"Is the letter signed, Mrs. Thompson?"

She cleared her throat. "Yes, Your Lordship. Sarah."

Who the hell was Sarah?

He was more than a little shocked. Evidently, his stuffy, pedantic, authoritarian brother was more like him than appearance would dictate. Arthur had an illegitimate child.

He sat there, growing more conscious of Mrs. Thompson's silence. Was his housekeeper embarrassed?

"There's a last name, sir," Mrs. Thompson finally said, her voice reedy. "Westchester. And an address on the envelope."

He handed her the pack of letters, curious. "Where did she send them?"

The address she repeated was that of Arthur's solicitor. How convenient—and tactful—of them, Dalton reflected. And ironic: if he hadn't decided to change solicitors, instead of using the same firm his brother had employed for years, he would never have known about Arthur's child.

Had Alice known? He suspected she had.

"What's the date of the last one?"

He heard her fumble through the letters, then open an envelope.

"March fifth."

Two days after Arthur had been killed.

"Will you read it, Mrs. Thompson?"

She drew a quivering breath, sighed, and began to read.

My dearest darling,

I can't wait to see you again. The weeks have not passed gently since I saw you last. I want to show you how much little Arthur has grown, but most of all, I want your arms to enfold me, and make me feel that there is no other place on earth I would rather be.

My dearest, the days cannot pass quickly enough until I see you again. Until then, know that you have my love.

For the first time since he'd been blinded, he was grateful for it. He needn't see Mrs. Thompson wipe away her tears, tears that were audible as she closed up the letter and put it back in the stack. He needn't witness her sorrow, slathered as it was on top of her embarrassment.

"I can count on your discretion, Mrs. Thompson." It wasn't a question.

"Of course, Your Lordship."

He sat there silently for a moment, trapped in his blindness, and Mrs. Thompson no doubt ensconced in propriety. Had he shocked her with all the goings-on in this house years earlier? He'd had his share of women coming in and out. More than once, the maid had served him and a woman breakfast in bed. If he was forced to do so, he didn't think he could list the names of all the women he'd brought here.

Had she been scandalized? It was suddenly important to know. An odd impulse and one on which he didn't act.

"Shall we go through the rest, sir?"

"I find I don't have the heart to do so, Mrs. Thompson."

How much more about Arthur did he need to know? How strange to miss him now, to wish he'd taken the time to visit with his brother before time was gone.

What would Arthur have said to his adventures in America? He suspected that his brother wouldn't have castigated him for his foolishness, reasoning that being blind was punishment enough. He also suspected that Arthur would have been his greatest champion.

He put the letters in his desk drawer. He would either destroy them or put them in a safe place so they wouldn't be read by anyone else. He could at least do that for Arthur.

One other thing he could do—visit with Sarah and see if there was anything she needed.

But his visiting anyone was not a sentiment shared by James when he met with him the next day.

"I must insist, Your Lordship."

When the hell had James started calling him *Your Lordship*? What was there about a title that rendered everyone a little foolish? He was the same man he had always been, replete with faults and flaws. Inheriting a title hadn't made him better.

"I think it would be best if you remain inside your house. It would be easier to watch you here."

"And I've decided I need to go somewhere."

"Surely your errand can be delegated to someone."

"No, it can't," he said.

Besides, he hadn't been out of his house for three months. Didn't he deserve an outing?

That thought startled him to a stop.

Had he really been a recluse that long?

That couldn't be right, but it was. He'd been blinded in November of last year, spent months healing in Washington before beginning the voyage home. He'd arrived in London in May and had been a hermit ever since.

He'd never needed to leave his house. All his creature comforts were provided. His home was large enough that it hadn't seemed confining. No more than blindness was. A good thing he'd never been bothered by tight spaces. Being surrounded by blackness meant that he was forever in a dark closet.

"I need you to expend your efforts on finding Neville Todd," he said to his old friend.

"I need to ensure you're protected," James repeated. "Besides, I have some of my operatives working on Neville's location."

"And William Harris?"

"Him, too."

"I can fire you," Dalton said.

"Then I would consider it an act of charity to follow you anyway and ensure you're protected. Let's just say a pro bono exercise."

"I don't remember you being so intransigent."

James laughed. "That's amusing, coming from you, Dalton."

At least James had stopped calling him *Your Lordship*.

"Very well. If I can't stop you, at least keep some distance between your carriage and mine."

He gave the address to James, not explaining who Sarah Westchester was or her relationship to Arthur. Some things were better confined to the family, a thought that drew him up short. He had no intention of telling Lewis, either. He felt like he owed Arthur some privacy.

His brother had been an icon of respectability. The fact that Arthur had a mistress shocked him. Strangely enough, it also made his brother more approachable, essentially more human. His older brother hadn't been perfect after all.

He wished he'd understood Arthur better, and regretted that they had grown apart. He also wanted to be certain that Arthur's son—his nephew—was being cared for.

He owed it to Arthur and to the child.

Once James left the room, Dalton walked to the bellpull and jerked it once. When Mrs. Thompson answered his summons, he forced himself to face her.

"Have I dressed myself correctly, Mrs. Thompson?"

All of his shirts were white, while his suits were black. The chances of him mixing colors was nil, but there was always the possibility that he'd stained himself. He might've gotten ink on his silk cravat. His shoes hadn't felt dusty, but he was unused to leaving the house without performing a final inspection.

He wore his eye patch in the hopes of not scaring Sarah of the letters with his appearance. He'd taken his time shaving, too. A few mornings, he hadn't known he'd cut himself until Mrs. Thompson said something to him in her usual cheerful air.

Now, sir, let me get some sticking plaster for you. Sit right there and we'll get you set to rights.

He'd always been an independent sort, wanting to do for himself rather than rely on others. Yet here he was, waiting on Mrs. Thompson to be his mirror.

"Oh, Your Lordship, it's a sight you are," she said now. "If you don't mind my saying so, sir, you're still as handsome as ever."

He wanted to grab the older woman, hug her, and give her a kiss on the cheek in thanks for her kindness. She might be lying to him, but at least she'd done it well.

"No spots? No stains?"

"You're quite the sartorial gentlemen, Your Lordship."

"Thank you, Mrs. Thompson."

To his surprise, she reached out and grabbed his arm. "Would you allow me to accompany you to the stable, Your Lordship?"

Damned if she hadn't done it again. If he were the weeping kind, she might've brought a tear to his eye. Still, he felt his chest expand a little at her kindness. He had worried about navigating the path from the kitchen to the stable. With one simple gesture, she'd taken that fear from him.

"I would be honored, Mrs. Thompson."

Before he left the house, he grabbed one of the walking sticks in the umbrella stand. He'd never used one before and he didn't know who they belonged to, but over the years he'd accumulated at least a dozen of them. He thought they might aid his balance.

The journey across the garden and the alley was done without incident. Mrs. Thompson alerted him to a step down or up by simply saying so, without drama or exhortation.

"You'll need to turn left here, sir," she said.

He could tell by the smells that they'd entered one of the bays. The odor of horses, manure, and the pungent chemicals used to polish the carriage assaulted him all at once.

"And here is Daniels, your driver," she said. "All ready for you."

For the life of him, he hadn't remembered his driver's name, but she eased him past that barrier as well. Still, it bothered him that he couldn't recall the man's face. For that matter, none of the rest of the servants were memorable to him.

"Mrs. Thompson," he said, prompted by a sudden impulse, "would you provide me with a list of everyone employed here?"

"A list, sir?"

"Yes, and their occupations as well." He'd get Howington to repeat it to him often enough that he could memorize it. "How many people work here?"

"Twelve, sir. It really should be thirteen what with needing another upper maid, but I've always thought thirteen an unlucky number, don't you?"

"I never would have considered you superstitious, Mrs. Thompson."

"Well, there's no sense in taking chances, is there, sir?"

He didn't have an answer for that remark. He'd taken chances all his life and look where it had gotten him.

Chapter 10

"*L*et me follow the earl on my own," Hugh said. "I'll make note of where he goes and let you know."

Minerva shook her head, unwilling to continue arguing with him.

"Isn't it time for you to go on an expedition?" he asked her. "Don't they have ruins in Scotland anymore?"

Hugh didn't understand her work even though he assisted her. He called it digging for a bunch of bones, but he didn't know how much it meant to her.

She'd never found anyone who truly understood. Sir Francis's widow, Lady Terry, bless her, was the only person who did.

She had grown accustomed to being considered slightly odd, even by people who were close to her. Neville called it her hobby. It wasn't a hobby but a genuine desire to learn, to know, to take what she suspected was true and have it proven.

Besides, what would she do with herself all day if she didn't pursue her interests? She had absolutely no talent in needlework. She found those women who involved themselves in good works for the poor annoying in the extreme. Affluence didn't give you the right to tell anyone else how to live or raise their children.

If Neville hadn't been missing, she would have been in Scotland by now. In her last letter, Lady Terry had written asking when she was going to return. She hadn't known how to answer.

After climbing into the carriage, Minerva settled her skirt. She couldn't abide some of the new styles that made skirts so wide it was difficult to go through a doorway. Consequently, she rarely wore as many petticoats as was proper, which made her hem drag a little. She would much rather have worn her trousers skirt, but it was daylight and people would notice.

She turned and looked through the carriage window at the Covington house. She didn't see the glint of the spyglass but knew better than to assume she was free of curious eyes. One or more of the sisters was bound to be standing at a window, just out of sight.

Would she be the same as she aged? Would she find delight in the happenings of her neighbors? Would she live vicariously through other people? Good heavens, she hoped not. At least let her get a cat or dog or some kind of companion, four-legged or two, to keep her company.

When the carriage began to move, she reached for her journal. She had notes to make of new equipment to purchase before she traveled to Scotland again. In addition, she had several lists she needed to compile to give to Mrs. Beauchamp. Though not exceptionally frugal by nature, she was very conscious of the fact that the money she'd been left by her parents had to last her lifetime. Therefore, she practiced economies where she could, surveying the household accounts every month.

Hugh parked not far from MacIain's home, close enough to see if the man left the house but far enough away not to be obvious. They might be sitting here for the entire day. She didn't care. Tomorrow she would do the very same thing. She was not going to allow the Earl of Rathsmere to find Neville without her knowledge.

Her brother wouldn't stand a chance against a peer of the realm. Nobody would want to know Neville's side of the story. That could be the very reason Neville hadn't come home. He didn't want to involve her in his troubles with the earl.

Something had happened in America. She just didn't know what. It certainly wasn't Neville trying to kill the earl.

THIS NEW world terrified Dalton, alone as he was. He dared himself, therefore, in the same spirit he had challenged himself on countless occasions in the past.

He knew that James was somewhere in a carriage behind him. If he had invited James to share the carriage, he wouldn't be as lonely. Nor would he be beset by introspection. Instead, they could've talked about their school days, the weather, a dozen different topics to get his mind off his fear.

But that would hardly be courageous, would it? At least this way he faced down the terror himself.

He knew what the inside of his carriage looked like. Yet he had never felt the space before as he did now. He could recollect some of the scenery outside the window. London truly didn't change. Yet he wasn't knowledgeable about the way to their destination. Nor did he know what Sarah looked like or where she lived.

Almost everything outside him was amorphous, unformed and only speculation. That's what terrified him. He couldn't see a smile or danger, a pretty girl's face or figure, or something amusing. The world was black, as if it had ceased to be, and yet he heard it, smelled it, and sensed it.

Traffic was as it had always been in London—congested. The stops and starts of the carriage made him uncomfortable at first. Gradually he became used to the rhythm, leaning forward when he anticipated a sudden stop, allowing himself to rest against the squabs when the carriage took off again. He smelled the horses, the odor of manure that always accompanied his memories of London streets. The occasional scent of straw laid down on an adjoining street indicated a quiet zone. The stench of the Thames meant they were close to the river.

The sounds were the same, recollections assembled from years of living in London. The jangle of harness, the rumble of wheels on cobblestones, hawkers and tradesmen either shouting their wares or arguing with each other. He could almost pinpoint where they were now, near the center of the city.

At least if someone recognized his carriage or noticed him, he wouldn't know. He'd be unable to see pointing fingers or incredulous glances.

No doubt there were a goodly number of people in London who wouldn't be displeased should they hear of his condition. All the straying wives and widows of England were safe.

He would become known as the Celibate Earl, an appellation that would've made him laugh in the past. Or perhaps he would just become an object of horror for the neighborhood children. *Eat your porridge, little Jimmy, or I'll tell Rathsmere.* Would his name become a verb? To *Rathsmere* someone would be to render them sightless and scarred.

The carriage slowed to a stop, but this time it wasn't traffic. He felt Daniels dismount from the driver's seat. A few moments later the door opened.

"We're here, sir."

"Would you mind walking me to the door?" he asked after he left the carriage.

"Right you are, sir." Daniels grabbed his arm and directed him over the cobbles to a set of steps. "It's eight steps up to the door."

Whatever he paid the man wasn't enough. He made a mental note to tell Howington to raise Daniels's salary plus an extra stipend for tact.

He held onto the rail, trying to assume a nonchalance he didn't feel.

Perhaps he should have sent Sarah a note to warn her he was coming. Or even asked her to come to his home? No, that wouldn't have been right. But what if she didn't want to see him? What if anything that reminded her of Arthur was disturbing and disconcerting?

Yes, he most definitely should have sent her a note to prepare her for this moment.

Why had he overlooked such a simple polite gesture? Because simple and polite gestures were beyond him of late? Or perhaps they'd been beyond him for a great many years. A hellish thing to realize as he climbed the final step and stood before her door.

What if she were greedy and grasping and he'd made a huge error in judgment by appearing on her doorstep?

"Would you like me to knock, sir?"

"I presume the door is right in front of me," he said.

"Right you are."

He placed his hands flat on the door, fingers splayed. Reaching up a little, he found the knocker and let it fall twice.

"It's all right, Daniels, you can wait for me at the carriage."

He didn't want an audience if Sarah refused to see him. Some of his pride was still intact.

"Right you are, sir."

The door opened and he was suddenly wishing he had forgotten all about Sarah.

THEY FOLLOWED the earl for ten minutes, their destination unknown. Fascinated by the journey, Minerva didn't bother opening her journal again. Just when she thought they were going into the city proper, they turned and entered another square. Not as prosperous as Tarkington Square or her own home, but a pleasant place with older town homes and a park protected by a tall wrought-iron gate topped with spikes.

The trees there were full grown and lush, home to a bevy of squirrels running from the upper branches to the ground and back.

Once Hugh parked at the curb, she opened the door, making no secret of the fact she was watching the other carriage. The earl's driver dismounted, opened the door, and the Earl of Rathsmere emerged.

Dalton stood, his shoulders straightening, his head lifting as if to scent the air. He kept his head level as if he could see in front of him.

Who lived here? she wondered.

Chapter 11

"Yes?"

The woman who answered the door smelled of yeast, flour, and strawberry jam. He was suddenly eight years old and scrambling to sit on a stool in the kitchen and savor cook's newest batch of scones.

"Is this Miss Sarah Westchester's home?"

"It is."

Dalton pulled out one of his calling cards, trusting that Howington hadn't lied. His new title was inscribed on it as well as his given name. For all he knew, Howington could have made them read Dalton MacIain, King of All the Fools.

"I'm Arthur MacIain's brother," he said.

He held the card out, relieved when she took it. He had no idea if she was the housekeeper, the cook, or one of the maids.

"I will tell her you're here, Your Lordship," she said, answering one question. Howington had gotten his calling cards right. "If you'll wait in the parlor, it won't be a moment."

Since he didn't have the slightest idea in hell where the parlor was, let alone how to get there, he simply stood where he was.

Very well, if he must be blunt about it, he would be.

"I'm afraid I'm blind," he said.

Her indrawn breath was enough of a comment. He

wanted to ensure her that in all other ways he was in perfect health. But all he did was smile or at least attempt to do so. He was afraid the expression was perfunctory, the same wisp of a smile that indicated to a society hostess that he was utterly bored or completely annoyed. Fortunately, the woman at the door didn't seem to take it as such.

She grabbed his left hand and pulled him with her. He had no choice but to go along, a dinghy in the wake of a steamship.

The room they entered was hideously cluttered and his guide wasn't the least helpful. He ran into at least two tables by the time he nearly toppled into an overstuffed chair.

Once the woman at the door had deposited him in the parlor, she left without another word, leaving him adrift in an ocean of smells.

The most overpowering scent was oranges, followed by something heavy like French perfume made of old roses. The odor of tobacco was layered over that, one lingering like a memory. He had never considered it, but was Sarah married? Had she married soon after Arthur's death just like Alice? Or was there a male relative in the household, someone who might take umbrage to his suddenly showing up today?

He really should have written the woman a note.

What would he have said?

Dear Sarah,

You seem to have loved my brother, enough to bear him a child. May I call on you one day to discuss the relationship, you, and the child's future?

No, he doubted the woman would've answered that letter.

Nor had he wanted to go through Howington to write it, either. There was his pride again.

As he sat waiting, he had no idea how much time had passed. Another thing about blindness. Time could pass with alarming speed or tick along with arthritic slowness.

He heard a clock whirr then strike the hour. He hadn't made note of the time when he left his house, so it didn't matter what the time was now. Besides, he had nowhere else to be.

Due to the silence in the room and the lack of traffic outside, he heard her footsteps. First, she came down the stairs. Then, she hesitated and walked down the carpeted hall. He sensed that she stood at the open door of the parlor. Did she take a deep breath? Or say a prayer before she entered?

Why had he come?

For Arthur. He mustn't forget that. He was here for Arthur.

"Dalton?"

His smile was more natural now. He placed his hands on the arms of the chair and stood.

"Miss Westchester."

"Sarah," she said softly. "I feel as if I know you. Arthur spoke of you often."

He spoke of you not at all. Words he wouldn't say.

"You look so much like him."

"Do I? Arthur was always so much more dignified," he said, for lack of anything else to say.

She came and sat not far away. Was there a settee opposite him? He sat again as well.

"My housekeeper said the most distressing thing. Pardon me, but I must ask. What do you mean, you're blind?"

He'd already endured Minerva Todd's bluntness. Answering Sarah seemed so much easier.

"I was wounded in America," he said.

"How utterly terrible for you."

Her voice held a note of sadness he suspected was not just for him.

"Thank you," he said, and because he wanted to ease her in some way, he added, "it could have been worse, I suppose."

Could it have been?

You could have died, you bloody fool.

Suddenly, Arthur seemed to be in the room with them.

"I'm so sorry that happened to you, Dalton. You do not mind if I call you Dalton, do you?"

"No," he said, and it was the truth.

He had the impression she was delicate, fragile in her beauty, a sylph of a woman with grace in each of her movements. He pictured her with blond hair, soft blue eyes, and perfect features. She would be of average height, slender with a willowy way of moving that managed to be both serene and seductive at the same time.

"What color are your eyes?"

She hesitated for just a second, but answered him. "Brown," she said.

He mentally replaced her soft blue eyes with brown, nodding when the portrait of her was complete.

"I didn't know about you," he said, deciding to be honest with her. A curious sentiment and one he'd rarely had in the past. But he'd found that the truth was easier than a succession of lies. "Arthur's solicitor sent me the rest of his documents and your letters were there."

When she didn't respond, he cursed himself for saying something that obviously embarrassed her.

"He saved them?" she asked, her voice holding tears.

"Yes," he said. "Would you like them back?"

"Would that be possible?"

"Of course," he said. "They're not mine to read. I apologize for intruding on your privacy."

"Oh, but if you hadn't, you wouldn't be here now, would you?"

He suddenly wished Arthur had told him about her. Or that he'd seen the two of them together. He knew, even without her telling him, that his brother had been happy. Perhaps with Sarah, Arthur had allowed himself to relax a little, to laugh, and to not take the responsibilities of being the Earl of Rathsmere so seriously.

"You have a son," he said.

Her answer was interrupted by the housekeeper who bustled into the room. The aroma of something delicious wafted over to him, and like a little boy who had been deprived, he wanted some.

"We've toffee biscuits," she said. "Chocolate cake and toffee biscuits, which Arthur loved, and tea, of course. Can I serve you?"

"Please," he said. "I'd like one of the toffee biscuits."

To his surprise, she came and sat on the ottoman in front of him.

"Stretch out your left hand," she said, "and I'll hand you the tea."

He did and she did, their movements so perfectly orchestrated it was as if they had practiced them before now. He heard her set down a plate on the table to his right.

"The biscuits are there."

"You're very adept at dealing with a blind man," he said. "Have you had much practice in it?"

"None," she said. The hint of tears had disappeared in her voice, replaced by gentle amusement. "But I have a little boy, and I suspect it's much the same."

He didn't know whether to be amused or insulted. A moment later he chose amusement.

"Can I meet him?"

She stood, returning to her place on the settee. Had he disturbed her with his request?

"Why?"

"He's my nephew," he said. "Arthur's son."

"And mine," she said.

He inclined his head in agreement of her comment.

"I'm very careful about the people who come in contact with my son. It's bad enough he lost his father before he got to know him. I don't want him to meet an uncle who would never again reappear in his life."

He replaced the tea with a biscuit. Normally, he didn't eat in front of other people. He didn't like the idea of them watching him drop his food or having to guide a fork to his mouth with studied precision.

The toffee biscuit was an explosion of taste and flavor. He wasn't certain what all the spices were called, but one thing he knew was that he'd never tasted them all in one confection.

"May I have the recipe for my cook?"

"I'll ask again, but every time I have, my cook hasn't divulged it. It's a family thing, I believe. Her great-grandmother's recipe, and one she refuses to part with, I'm afraid."

"Pity," he said, finishing up the biscuit. "It's wonderful."

"I'll tell her what you said."

"What makes you think I would never reappear in little Arthur's life again?"

"Your brother spoke about you often."

"Am I to infer that Arthur was not, shall we say, complimentary?"

"On the contrary," she said. "I thought he was very

fair. He merely related your adventures. He didn't comment on them."

"So if anyone is to be blamed for my reputation of inconstancy, it's me, is that it?"

She didn't answer him, which was a response.

What could he say to her? That he no longer discarded people with the alacrity he once did? That wasn't altogether the truth, was it? Just ask Minerva Todd. She would have a mouthful to say about his attitude toward the men he'd taken to America.

He sat with both hands gripping the saucer, wishing he knew if there was space on the table. Wishing he could put the damn thing down somewhere.

"Fair enough," he said.

He had discovered the child's existence only a day ago. Learning that he was too flawed to see Arthur's son was something he'd just have to accept.

"I came, mostly, to make sure that he was taken care of," he said, feeling his way through the words. "I don't know if Arthur made allowances for him."

Her voice, when it came, was low and soft, but instead of tears it held a steely resolve. He had the impression that Sarah Westchester had her own share of pride and it was being trotted out right now for him to experience.

"No," she said. "Arthur didn't make provisions, but then he didn't expect to be murdered."

The cup in his hand jumped against the saucer, the clinking noise startling him almost as much as her words.

"What are you talking about? It was a hunting accident."

That's what Arthur's solicitor had said on meeting him at the ship. He hadn't even gotten off the vessel before he'd been informed that his brother was dead and he was now the Earl of Rathsmere.

Welcome home.

"How many hunting accidents do you know of that take place in full view of a house? And when the victim isn't even carrying a gun?"

Stunned, he could only stare in her direction.

"Arthur wasn't hunting the day he was killed, Dalton."

The cup shook again. This time she reached out and took it from him.

"How do you know that?"

"I asked questions, which is something you evidently didn't do," she said.

She was right. He hadn't. He'd merely assumed that the information he'd been given was correct. His brother had been an avid hunter and the grounds of Gledfield were rife with partridge and pheasant.

"Who told you he was murdered?" he asked, wishing his voice didn't sound so thin. He cleared his throat, asked again. "Who told you that?"

"Does it matter?"

Yes, damn it, it does.

"Who told you that?" he asked for the third time.

"Edmonson."

"Edmonson's dead."

The poor man had been ancient when he'd expired a few months ago. He'd sent Samuels to Gledfield to replace him.

"He came to see me," she said.

The man had been ninety if he was a day, and kept in his position by Dalton's mother, who prized loyalty. Besides, as she often said, pensioning Edmondson off would have been destructive to the man's pride, not to mention hurting his feelings.

They'd grown used to Edmondson tottering around Gledfield in his black suit, but he'd never known the man to leave the house.

"Mrs. MacNeal accompanied him," she said, heaping another surprise on top of the first two.

The housekeeper at Gledfield was an exceedingly proper woman. His mother had often said that Mrs. MacNeal was the conscience of the house. If Mrs. MacNeal had shown up on Sarah's doorstep, what exactly did that mean?

"Why didn't she go to the authorities?"

"Perhaps she did. Perhaps they both did. Perhaps nothing was ever made of it."

"But you think they were right."

He wished he could see her. Did she shrug? Did she look away? Did she blot at her eyes with a handkerchief? He didn't know, dammit, and the silence didn't give him any clues.

"I think they were right," she finally said.

"You think Arthur was murdered."

"Yes," she said softly.

"I'll make investigations," he said.

He'd give James another job, that of determining if Arthur was murdered or not. He'd be better served in that task than guarding him.

"In the meantime, I've settled an amount on little Arthur." He withdrew the draft from his inner jacket pocket. Howington had made a sound of alarm at the amount, but his secretary had filled in the draft nonetheless and he had signed it.

"I'd like to come and see him, if you would allow it. But in the meantime, take this, please."

She didn't, as he half expected, argue with him or demur. A sign, then, that Sarah was imminently practical. Or that she would do anything for her child, even bury her pride.

His mother would've liked her.

A few minutes later, having taken out his manners, dusted them off, and utilized them in thanking her for the refreshments and apologizing for his arrival without notice, he found himself at the front door again.

He was prepared to call for Daniels, but Sarah startled him by taking his arm and leading him down the steps and across the cobbles to the door of his carriage.

She had to be wrong. It had to have been simple negligence or an idiotic hunter who thought Arthur a grouse. She had to be wrong, because otherwise, there was an implication there he couldn't ignore. Two brothers—one killed and the other shot in an attempt to kill him?

She surprised him by placing her lips against his cheek.

"I'll have the letters delivered to you," he said. "Will you let me see your son one day?"

His insistence startled him. He had never been responsible for another soul. Until this moment he had never wanted to be responsible for anyone else. But he felt an obligation to the child he'd never seen. Even if Sarah didn't think him good enough to meet him.

"Perhaps," she said. "One day. Will you really do something? Will you look into Arthur's death?"

He nodded, surprised when the gesture didn't nauseate him.

"I hope you're wrong," he said.

"I know I'm right."

He almost asked her if she knew Minerva Todd. The two women were alike in their stubborn insistence. Sarah, in her insistence that Arthur had been murdered, and the Todd woman, in believing that Neville wasn't a would-be murderer.

He hoped Sarah wasn't right. As far as Neville, he knew he couldn't be wrong. There, a little stubborn insistence of his own.

OF COURSE the Earl of Rathsmere would make a visit to his mistress.

A beautiful woman at that, with blond hair and a face borrowed from the angels. She was petite and delicate, one of those creatures written about in the papers and labeled a London treasure.

Minerva was suddenly more than irritated. Her emotions tumbled into anger. She was trying to find her brother and he had the temerity to think only of his loins.

He had hardly been inside long enough for a tryst, unless, of course, the man had performance issues. Minerva wouldn't put it past him to be an exceedingly selfish lover. As long as he received satisfaction, no doubt that was all that was important to Dalton MacIain.

The woman was very solicitous of him, patting his arm, walking him down the steps. Had she broken off their liaison? Did a blind man disturb her? Were Dalton's scars off-putting?

If so, the woman was a fool and Dalton was better off without her in his life. Or had he come to terminate the relationship? Was it an impulse born of martyrdom? He didn't want to inflict his horrible self on a beautiful woman, was that it?

What rubbish.

She doubted the Earl of Rathsmere was that generous a soul. Besides, his scars gave him a rakish air; they didn't detract from his overall handsomeness. Any woman could see that.

As Dalton got into his carriage, the woman turned and walked up the steps slowly. Suddenly, a child barreled out of the door, only to be caught up in the woman's arms. She laughed as she grabbed him, turning to watch as the carriage moved away, the child resting on one hip.

As they drew abreast, she wanted to look away, but Minerva glanced at the woman and the child. The

little boy had black hair and Dalton's features. The re-
semblance was unmistakable.

The reason for the visit was suddenly clear. He'd
come to see his son.

She grabbed her journal and held it close to her
chest.

What did she care that the earl had a child? All that
she cared about was Neville's whereabouts. When
it was obvious they were returning to Tarkington
Square, she bit back her disappointment.

Perhaps nothing would come of today's adventures.
There was always tomorrow and every day after that.

She would be the earl's shadow for as long as it took.

Chapter 12

*D*alton made his way to his library, thinking about what he'd learned. Not only about Sarah's thoughts of Arthur's death but about himself.

Venturing outside of his house had been more upsetting than he'd expected. The world wasn't a playground anymore. It wasn't filled with potential adventures, beautiful women to be loved, places to go, and people to meet.

His environment had narrowed to only those things he could feel, hear, smell, or sense in the space around his body.

He was no longer Dalton MacIain, brother of the Earl of Rathsmere and wealthy in his own right. He wasn't shocking, a rake, or up for a good time. He was limited, a disability, and more than a little unsettled by his blindness.

He entered the library, casting the walking stick in the direction of the trunks so he didn't trip. When he was done going through Arthur's papers, he'd have them sent off to Benny Carlton, his solicitor.

Benny Carlton was another of Dalton's old school friends. The runt of the litter, Benny hadn't grown much until later. Added to that unfortunate school-boy circumstance was his pudgy appearance. Benny was round all over. He had a protuberant nose with a round tip, a round face, and wide, round brown eyes.

He looked perpetually startled and had been the target for one bully or another.

Once, giving some thought to having his own children, Dalton decided he would never send them off to school. Instead, he would see to it they were educated at home. His school memories included being cold and hungry much of the time, and like Benny Carlton, terrorized until he started to grow. By the time he was thirteen, he was as tall as an adult. Plus he had filled out—not due to the school's cooking but to his mother's parcels from home.

Arthur had attended the same school, his father's alma mater, and in some ways Dalton was grateful to his older brother for sparing him from the worst of the torment. But those boys who couldn't join Arthur's wide circle of friends took it out on him. Over the years, he'd gathered up his own contingent. The sad, the lonely, the small, and the defenseless all clustered around him as if he were the only one who could protect them.

Dalton's adult friends were the same, those who came in from the storm, so to speak. Men who were finding their way in a treacherous social environment. As boys, like Neville, they were newly wealthy and didn't know how to handle either their money or life itself.

Recently, Benny Carlton had been badgering him to become more involved in handling the MacIain interests. The ghost of his father was providing an impetus as well.

"It only takes three generations to lose a fortune," Harland MacIain had often said. "One to make it, the next to invest it, and the third to squander it. I'll be damned if we follow that example. You'll know how to administer and grow what we've given you."

The words had been directed to Arthur, but Dalton

felt as if the shade of his father was turning in his direction and pointing a bony finger at him.

The MacIain wealth was seven generations old. If he were going to step into Arthur's shoes, he'd have to make decisions he had never considered before. He'd have to learn a damn sight more than he knew about all their ventures.

He was blind, damn it. An excuse that didn't seem to have an effect on his father's ghost.

Maybe he should make a visit to Arthur's solicitor and query him on his brother's death. Why hadn't the authorities been involved? If there was any doubt, any suspicion about Arthur's death, shouldn't someone have talked to them?

Or was Sarah just a grief-stricken woman, trying to find a reason why Arthur had been taken from her?

He heard James in the corridor speaking to Mrs. Thompson. He smelled something chocolate baking and smiled. In several ways, his staff treated him as if he were a child, bringing him treats to ease the day. At the moment he felt as insecure as a child, wanting reassurance that his world hadn't changed.

But it had, hadn't it?

He had to convince Sarah to let him see Arthur's son. Or perhaps she would come here and allow Mrs. Thompson to dote on the child. His house had never known the sounds of childhood, a thought that both amused and disturbed Dalton.

"You were followed," James said, entering the room and stripping every thought from his mind.

"What?" The idea was so preposterous, he could only stare in the direction of the doorway.

Mrs. Thompson bustled about, putting a tea tray on the table between the two wing chairs. She said something about serving him and he nodded as James sat in the adjoining chair.

"Thank you, Mrs. Thompson," he said finally, wishing her gone. The minute she was, he put down his cup and saucer and turned to James.

"What do you mean I was followed? By whom?"

His initial thought was that it was Neville, and coldness seeped through to his bones. The man had almost been successful at killing him in America. How did he face an enemy he couldn't see now?

"A woman," James said.

"It was Miss Todd, Your Lordship," Howington said.

When the hell was his secretary going to learn to announce himself? Had the man been listening at the door?

"She's outside now, sir."

Dammit all, would the woman not go away?

"Do you want me to talk to her?" James asked. "If nothing else, I can arrange for her not to trouble you again."

"How are you going to accomplish that? Break one of her carriage wheels? Assault her driver? Anything short of violence won't convince Minerva Todd to leave me alone. No doubt she's one of those women who marches and shouts and holds up placards." He'd witnessed demonstrations before he left for America, something to do with women wanting the vote. "She's obnoxious. She goes wherever she wants to go with no thought about anyone. She does what she wants, without a by your leave. She says whatever the hell she wants."

"She sounds a great deal like you, Dalton."

Even a blind man could detect amusement in James's voice.

"I was never that arrogant." The minute the words left his mouth he knew they were wrong. He waved his hand in the air. "But she's a woman, for the love of all that's sacred, James."

"And women are not supposed to be anything like men, is that it?"

"No, they're not. They're supposed to be better." His own comment startled him. "There's a certain class of women who are supposed to be better," he said slowly, reasoning it out as he continued. "Women like my mother, for example." He would've added Alice to that list but wasn't sure she fit the label. "Women you marry, who are supposed to keep men honest and decent."

"Is that why you never married, because you didn't want to be kept honest and decent?"

He would've said something scalding to James, but he had a feeling his friend was right.

"What about the other kind of woman? The kind you've associated with all these years?"

"They weren't innocents, that's for sure."

Most of his bed partners had been bored wives or lonely widows. He'd never once seduced a chit right out of the schoolroom.

"So which class is Miss Todd in?"

Damned if he wasn't stymied again.

"I don't have a clue," he said. "Maybe she's in her own class, with a total of one. The class of Minerva Todd."

He had a feeling he was close to the truth.

"You've let her get under your skin," James said, his words coated with humor.

"No," he said. "She's burrowed there all on her own."

James laughed.

"What does she look like?" he asked.

"She's an arresting woman," James said. "She isn't beautiful in the traditional sense, but she does have a fascinating face. Her eyes are very expressive. So, too, her mouth."

He heard the clink of the cup and wanted to offer James something stronger than tea, but he wasn't about to become a drunken sot simply because he couldn't see a damn thing.

Before he solved the problem of Minerva Todd, there was another matter he needed to present to James.

"Thank you, Howington," he said. "That will be all."

Would the man leave? Or did he have to be rude?

"Is he gone?" he asked James a moment later.

"He is."

"I think Arthur was murdered."

He told James about Sarah and what she'd said.

"Why does she have any credence with you, Dalton? You didn't meet the woman until today."

He didn't know if he could explain it. He'd never known Arthur to be sentimental sort. His brother was rooted in practicality and pragmatism.

Once, when one of their horses needed to be put down, Arthur had done the deed without emotion. Afterward, he'd accused Arthur of having no feelings.

"It's not that I don't care," his brother had said. "But I can't see making an animal suffer because I'm selfish. I didn't want Monty to die, either, Dalton, but he was in pain and he wasn't going to get better."

The discovery of the letters, however, had startled Dalton because his brother had kept them, a sentimental gesture unlike Arthur.

Arthur cared for Sarah. Whoever Arthur cared for, he was going to extend the benefit of the doubt.

"I trust her," he said. "You're just going to have to accept that."

"Then I shall as well. I'll go to Gledfield," James said. "But I'm still going to leave one of my operatives here."

"A waste of resources, James."

"Let me be the judge of that, Dalton."

When had James become so damn stubborn?

"In the meantime, what are you going to do with Miss Todd?"

"Will you go ask her to come inside? I'd like to speak with her."

"Are you certain, Dalton?"

"Yes," he said.

"Then I'll go, but I'm not sure this is the wisest course."

He only smiled and settled back against the chair, thinking about the upcoming battle with the woman.

Minerva Todd was annoying to the extreme. Words meant nothing to her. Circumstances meant little as well. She didn't care that he'd seen her brother firing at him. She simply refused to believe it. And if Minerva Todd refused to believe something, ergo, it couldn't possibly be true.

How did he deal with obstinacy of that magnitude?

How did he deal with a woman like Minerva Todd?

For the first time in his life he was without any charm whatsoever. He couldn't flirt. He couldn't flatter. He couldn't seduce.

His reasoned approach had made absolutely no difference to her. She hadn't wanted to hear what he had to say. She had labeled him by his behavior, putting him into a box he resented.

The very same box Sarah Westchester had put him in.

He wasn't a satyr. He might have done some things that embarrassed him to this day, but he wasn't the youth he had been. Granted, perhaps some of his maturity had been foisted upon him by his blindness, but that was no reason to negate it completely.

Chapter 13

"*I* really do not like being fetched, Your Lordship. I am not a parcel you left in a shop. I am not a book from a shelf. I am a living, breathing, human being. I am not to be summoned."

Miss Todd stood in front of his desk. She really was quite good at upbraiding him. She reminded him of a cross between his nurse and his first tutor.

"My apologies, Miss Todd. It was easier asking you to attend me than finding my way to your carriage."

There, a bit of pathos that silenced the woman. Only for a second, however.

"You're wearing an eye patch," she said.

"Dare I hope it meets with your approval?"

"Are you expecting me to compliment you on your appearance? I shan't. No doubt there are many other women who would be delighted to do so."

"Ah, but you're here and they aren't. In fact, you seem to be everywhere. I really do not like being followed, Miss Todd."

"A pity, Your Lordship. I intend to be everywhere you are."

"James, could I prevail upon you to ask Mrs. Thompson for another cup?" he asked. "Miss Todd, how do you like your tea?"

"Nonexistent at the moment," she said, her voice very precise.

"James, do you mind leaving us alone?"

"Dalton—"

"I can assure you, I have no intention of ravaging Miss Todd." He inclined his head in her direction. "Do I have your guarantee that I am as safe from you?"

"Your virtue is safe, Your Lordship. That is, if you retain any virtue."

"I shall not make any assumptions in regards to you, Miss Todd. No doubt you are as virginal as heaven's angels."

"Are heaven's angels virginal? I might ask how you know such a thing. Did one of them confide in you?"

He heard the door close softly.

"In my case, you would be wrong," she said.

He had committed the cardinal sin by referring to her virtue. Instead of calling him on it or acting shocked, she'd turned the tables on him.

He hoped he managed to keep the surprise from his features. Revealing what he felt would give her an advantage in this meeting.

"I saw absolutely no reason to remain virginal," she added. "It was not an attribute in my case."

"Why not? Don't you wish to be married one day, Miss Todd?"

"Good heavens, no. Why should I? It seems to me that it would be like yoking myself to an ox. When I want to turn left or right, I'd have to prod him in the rump."

What an absolutely astounding woman.

"You have no intention of having a family?"

"I have a family, Your Lordship, or have you forgotten Neville?"

"Oh, the estimable Neville. The perfect Neville. I can tell you that I don't remember him being quite the epitome of all that was good and holy."

"No doubt because you led him down the path of sin."

He laughed, genuinely amused. "It has been my experience, Miss Todd, that most men don't require a great deal of urging to race down the path of sin."

"Neville was a very nice young man until he met you."

She could truly push a man toward exasperation.

"You have one vision of your brother, and that's from a viewpoint of being his sister. You see what you want to see, Miss Todd. That doesn't necessarily translate to the truth."

"My brother is not an elephant, your lordship."

"I beg your pardon?"

"The poem by John Godfrey Sachs. The blind men and the elephant."

"You have me at a disadvantage," he said. "I've never read it. I don't, for the most part, choose to read poetry." Nor did he want to read about blind men.

"Pity," she said. "You might find yourself learning something."

To his surprise, she began to quote.

"It was six men of Indostan
To learning much inclined,
Who went to see the Elephant
(Though all of them were blind),
That each by observation
Might satisfy his mind."

She then explained, "Each of the six had a different impression of the beast. The first fell against the side and decided that the elephant was like a wall. The second felt the tusk and thought that the elephant was very round and smooth and sharp like a spear. The third grabbed the trunk and declared that the el-

ephant was like a snake. The fourth felt the elephant
leg and stated that the animal was like a tree. The fifth,
who grabbed the ear, said that even a blind man could
tell that an elephant was like a fan. But it was the sixth
man, grabbing the elephant's swinging tail, who re-
marked that the beast was very like a rope."

"So am I, like a blind man, measuring Neville?" he
asked.

"Yes, and your version of him is only a small part
of who he is."

"What can I do to get you out of my life?"

"In all honesty, Your Lordship, if you'd given me the
information I wanted, I would have left you alone. But
then you told me that Neville tried to kill you. Now I
am as determined to clear my brother's name as I am
to find him."

"I don't think I'm out of bounds in saying that you
are perhaps the most obnoxious, the most irritating,
the most . . ." His words trailed off. Startling. Amazing.
Incredible. What other words were there to describe
Minerva Todd?

"Should I weep, Your Lordship, because you don't
like me?"

"Do you always say exactly what you think?"

"Why should I not? I believe you do the same, do
you not?" she asked.

"I have. At least in the past. I believe, in the last few
months, that I have learned some restraint."

"How awful for you. It seems to me that losing your
sight should give you something in recompense. Some
daring in words, perhaps. People can talk about you.
'Did you hear what that scandalous Earl of Rathsmere
said now?' Aren't you familiar enough with gossip as
it is? I believe your reputation was shocking before you
left for America. Don't you wish to continue in that
vein?"

"Now should I be the one who weeps? Or should I be embarrassed? Or feel some measure of shame?"

"I doubt you've ever felt shame about anything, Your Lordship."

That's where she was wrong, but he'd didn't illuminate her.

"Do you miss it?" she asked.

"I'm assuming you're speaking of my life of debauchery?"

If she nodded, he didn't know, but she followed it up with a comment that surprised him, as it appeared she was one of the few people he'd been around who understood. He couldn't bloody well see them, after all.

"Of course, your life of debauchery," she said. "And the reputation you've gained. I always had the impression that you were very proud of it. Even your upbraiding by the Queen. Not very many people could boast of having Her Majesty say something bracing to them."

He felt the tips of his ears grow hot.

"I can't exactly say that it was a bracing conversation, Miss Todd. I can tell you without equivocation, that Her Majesty has a particular way of bringing down all sorts of trouble about your ears if she disapproves of you."

"Is that why you went to America?"

He had never been asked that question before, and the fact that it was Minerva Todd who figured it out startled him. He gave her the truth, a compliment, if she but knew it.

"Partly," he said.

"Was another part because you were bored?"

"Again, partly."

"No unrequited love? No disappointment in your conquests?"

"Perhaps a surfeit of them."

Why was he being so honest with her? Why was his

heart beating so rapidly, and why, most of all, did he have the most incredible urge to smile?

There was something about her that enlivened him, that made him want to goad her into saying something even more provocative or outrageous.

"I suspect that Her Majesty would not approve of you, either, Miss Todd."

"I'm not entirely certain you're correct," she said in a clipped way.

Had he insulted her? Had she taken umbrage to his comment? If so, it was the first time she'd indicated it.

"Although she's a great deal more traditional than I, there's something brave about Her Majesty, something that makes me think she would not hesitate if someone she loved needed her."

"You mean she would be just as tenacious as you?"

"I believe she would be."

"So," he said, "I should now attribute royal behavior to you, is that it?"

"No, I doubt I should like to be royal. Or even of the peerage. All those people expecting you to be a certain way."

To his surprise, he agreed with her.

"Did people expect you to act in a certain way," she asked, "being the son of an earl?"

Another question no one had ever asked him.

"I'm not sure it was people who expected it as much as my family," he said.

"So you left no doubt in their mind that you weren't going to be their person as much as your own."

How the hell did she know that?

"I think Neville was the same. But instead of a family, he only had me. I became an object of his rebellion. Who did you rebel against?"

She really was the most amazing woman.

"If I tell you, will you tell me who you rebel against?"

"Why do you think I'm a rebel?"

"Because, Miss Todd, you're like no other woman I've ever met. You will have to take my word for it that I know a great many women."

"Oh, I don't really have to take your word for it, do I? The gossips all say the same. You have cut a very wide swath through London society, Your Lordship."

"Arthur," he said.

"I beg your pardon?"

"Arthur is the one I rebelled against. He was perfect. He could do no wrong. He was gracious in every circumstance. He married well. He made my father proud, and when my father died, Arthur made the rest of us proud."

"The Covington sisters."

"The Covington sisters?"

"The three of them. That's who I rebel against. Why is it that bad things always seem to happen in threes?"

He bit back his smile.

"They live next to me and have been observing me from the day I was born. When my mother was alive, they were the first to inform her of every infraction. 'Minerva was running down the street. We could see her petticoats. Your daughter picked up a toad in her bare hands. She was studying the creature. Minerva was playing with the boys again. She hasn't a feminine bone in her body.' Later, they began to complain about my deportment, the way I walked, my posture, and anything else that they noticed from their windows."

When he didn't say anything, she continued. "Their nephew is at sea. He sent them a spyglass, of all things. Their eyes are failing, so this way they don't have to strain to see what I'm doing."

"So you find yourself being more disreputable just to annoy them?"

She chuckled, such a surprising sound that he wanted to make her laugh more often.

"I'm not truly disreputable. Perhaps in certain ways I am, but they do make be want to do things like stick my tongue out at them or raise my skirts and show my petticoats. They have made it perfectly clear to me how idiotic it is to listen to other people in society. Society is just like the Covington sisters, always waiting for you to make a mistake."

"So you make mistakes on purpose."

"I do not need to try to make mistakes. I make enough of them naturally."

Her candor surprised him.

"The one thing about the Covington sisters that annoyed me the most was that they never seemed to notice my mother loved me. She always took my side against theirs. They seemed to think that all they had to do was say something scathing about me and she would immediately believe them. She never did, of course, even when she probably should have."

"Did you disappoint her?"

She didn't speak for so long that he nearly apologized for the question.

"I think, in a way, I disappointed both my mother and my father. Not in who I was," she added, "but in who I didn't want to be. I was always interested in things that surprised them. I wanted to know about people who had lived centuries earlier. I wanted to dig in the ground and find things that other people had discarded generations ago. I wanted to imagine their lives. I didn't want to go to dances or balls. I didn't want to dress up. I wanted to go find something."

The longer he talked to her, the more fascinating he found her. That in itself was a danger sign. He didn't want to be interested in Minerva Todd.

"So, other than Neville, you have no other relatives? No doting aunts or uncles? No insidious cousins?"

"I have two insidious cousins," she said. Her voice sounded as if she were smiling. "We don't see much of each other. My female cousin is married and has three children. My male cousin is a banker. He, too, is married, and has four children. The two of them are trying to repopulate Surrey all by themselves."

"They don't live in London?"

"No."

"Then, in London, you have no other family."

"I don't. Is that of particular interest to you?"

He found himself curiously interested in everything about her, no doubt an indication of his boredom. In previous days, a woman like Minerva Todd would not have garnered his attention. She didn't flatter. She didn't flirt. She was too direct. She used none of her feminine wiles, if she even had any. She was the most obstinate woman he'd ever met. In addition, she had opinions on everything.

She repeated gossip directly to his face, which no one had ever done. She assaulted him with tales of himself. Everyone else had merely ignored the stories or, if they were pressed, alluded to them. She didn't. She came right out and called him a hedonist. He had been, but he didn't go around admitting it.

"I have a brother," he said. "A younger brother. His name is Lewis."

"Are you close?"

"I'm not," he said. "Although it seems to me that Lewis is attempting to emulate certain parts of my life."

His brother was well on his way to being a hedonist, too. Perhaps a profligate one.

"Are you protective of him?"

"No, I find no reason to be. Lewis is his own man. He'll make his mistakes on his own. He's grown."

"And you would have me treat Neville the same, wouldn't you?"

"Why not? Neville has reached his majority. He's a grown man to the eyes of the world. He's no longer in nappies."

"Maybe it's different with sisters and brothers. He was only ten when our parents died."

"So you raised him, basically. And now you're treating him like an overprotective mother."

"If I am, I see nothing wrong with that. Especially if Neville is in trouble."

He allowed himself a smile at that comment.

"I would say that he is in trouble, Miss Todd. Trying to kill someone is trouble enough."

"I don't believe you. I don't care if you swear on the Bible. I don't believe you. I won't believe you. I'll never believe you. There must be some explanation."

"And if there isn't?"

She didn't answer.

"What would it take for you to simply retreat to your house, Miss Todd? When I find your brother, I will inform you of that fact."

"After you've ensured he's in jail," she said.

He couldn't argue about that. What he didn't tell her was that he wasn't sure he could have Neville arrested. The crime hadn't taken place on English soil. Granted, it would be his word against Neville's, but he had the advantage of being a peer of the realm. He was the Earl of Rathsmere, and coming from a long established and well-respected family gave him more credence.

"I'm more than willing to give you a certain sum of money," he said, and named an amount. Her indrawn breath was indication enough that he had been generous.

"I don't have the wealth of the MacIains," she said. "But I don't need your money."

That was a surprise. People could always do with money. So Minerva Todd was independently wealthy. That explained a great deal. Women who didn't have to depend on others for an income had a certain freedom that the rest of women in society did not.

"What do you want, then? An introduction to someone? What can I do to make your life easier?"

"Cease your search for my brother. I will find Neville on my own."

"What do you want me to do, Miss Todd? Simply accept that I'm blind without being angry about it? You ascribe to me feelings of a saint, and I'll be the first one to tell you I'm not the forgiving type. Especially about this."

"Why didn't you look for him before?"

She'd managed to startle him again.

"Why didn't you try to find him before I showed up?"

"How do you know I didn't?"

"You didn't, did you?" she asked.

He should lie to her, but he found himself loath to do so. The truth, however, didn't put him in a good light.

"I was healing."

"You were feeling sorry for yourself," she countered.

He resented her ability to see through his defenses and spear him to the wall with her words.

"I regret that I am not able to walk you to your carriage, Miss Todd."

"Who walks you?" she asked.

"I am not a dog, Miss Todd."

"Pardon me," she said. "I should rephrase that better. Who helps you get from place to place? Your driver?"

"Would you like the position?" he asked.

"I beg your pardon?"

"You've already indicated that you intend to be a burr on my arse, if you'll forgive the plain speaking. Perhaps if you accompany me you can also act as my eyes."

What the hell was he doing, inviting the woman into his life? Had he lost his reason?

"Are you jesting?"

"I don't joke about my blindness, Miss Todd."

"I didn't mean that," she said, her tone acerbic. "I meant, why me and not Mr. Wilson, for example?"

"James has better things to do than to follow me."

"Why is he following you?"

"Because he has an idea that your brother might try to kill me again."

She made a sound he interpreted as derision. His imagination furnished her expression: brows drawn together, eyes fiery, mouth pursed.

"I thought the man had some sense," she said. "We don't even know if Neville is in London, in England, let alone that he would ever do something like you stated."

"I'm not going to argue about Neville's saintliness at the moment," he said. "Would you like to accompany me?"

It might be interesting to be around Minerva Todd for a little while. She might cease to be astounding and be boring, instead.

"I am planning a visit with my brother's solicitor," he told her. "Shall I send a note around to you when the meeting has been arranged?"

"Would you really do that?"

"I would."

She didn't answer, long enough for him to question his sanity again. But better to keep the woman close than have her follow him all over London.

When she gave him her address, he nodded.

James had a more important job than to keep him company. He had to determine whether Arthur had been murdered.

In the meantime, he'd keep Minerva Todd close. Which of the two of them had the harder task?

Chapter 14

$\mathcal{D}$alton decided, as he made his way to his library the next day, that the walking stick might become a permanent accessory. Using one seemed to help his balance.

He stopped in the middle of the hallway and sniffed. Even here he could smell the cinnamon that seemed to waft around the Todd woman. As if that weren't unusual enough, he could still hear her voice.

How odd that voices had begun to replace faces in his mind. Mrs. Thompson's voice was pleasing and soft, like the woman herself. Howington's voice held an edge and was grating. Again, like the man.

Miss Todd's didn't sound like it should. Instead of being caustic and thin, her voice was low and throaty, as if the words were rounded as they left her lips. He might even call it a seductive voice if it belonged to another woman.

Using the walking stick, he swept the doorway of his library in case that fool Howington was standing there.

"I'm here, Your Lordship," Mrs. Thompson said when he entered the room.

Was that so hard? Why couldn't Howington accommodate him to that degree? He banished thoughts of his secretary in favor of the task he'd set himself today: going through Arthur's papers.

"What would you like me to do first, sir?"

Dalton bent slightly, put his hand out and found the arched top of one of the trunks.

"If you'll help me," he said, "we'll move this over to the chairs in front of the fireplace. To create a base of operations, so to speak."

"If you push, sir, I'll pull."

They managed admirably, if he did say so. Well enough that they went back and got the second trunk and moved it beside the first.

He sat in one chair and Mrs. Thompson in another.

His hands fumbled with the lock. He hadn't thought to ask if they needed a key. A moment later he found the hasp, lifted it, and was able to push the top open.

"Oh dear," Mrs. Thompson said. "It's filled with papers, sir."

"My brother liked to keep records," he said. "And journals."

She didn't say anything for a moment. Was she inspecting the trunks' contents?

"Everything is in stacks, sir. It all seems to be well marked."

She handed him a large envelope. "Those are marked Mill and Mine Revenue."

He nodded and put the envelope on the floor.

"I see the journals," she said, and began to hand them to him one by one. By the time they were finished, he counted twenty. He knew Arthur liked to record things; he just hadn't known to what extent his brother had done so.

Once the journals were unearthed from the trunk, it was empty, so they began on the second trunk. This one seemed to be filled with envelopes, all having to do with annual receipts from the various MacIain enterprises. He had no idea they owned property in

India and Ireland. He had always known about the coal mines, but not about the silver mines.

For the next hour they burrowed down to the bottom of the trunk. Nothing more was forthcoming about Arthur's personal life, but he was driven to respect his brother's organizational ability.

Arthur documented everything about Gledfield, from the dry rot at one end of the stable to the mold that showed up ten years ago in the upper gallery. With his records, he ensured that future generations knew what care had been taken and what repairs were made.

Arthur had left a legacy a damn sight better than the one he himself had left. In his case, tales of debauchery and daring.

A hell of a thing, to be outclassed by a dead man.

LEWIS MACIAIN rolled over, stared up at the ceiling, and wished his mistress wasn't a chatterbox first thing in the morning.

He had a blazing headache, which he always got when he smoked too many cheroots. Of course, the cognac didn't help. It tasted so damn good going down and he liked the feeling he got after a few snifters. But there was always hell to pay the next morning.

They'd had a wonderful time in bed together, a fact Susan had to mention more than once. In fact, she liked going over all the details, as if doing so would incite him to grab her for another round.

He might have, if the headache hadn't nearly incapacitated him.

Now he closed his eyes, took a few deep breaths, and tried to ignore her.

"I don't know what got into you last night, Lewis, my love. You were a beast."

"Was I?"

"I was very impressed."

He opened one eye, turned his head slightly and stared at the screen behind which she was dressing. Since he couldn't remember most of last night, he was going to have to take her word for it.

Had he vowed his undying love? He wasn't going to ask. Doing so would only bring up the subject again and he had already tired of it.

"You were quite vigorous."

He closed his eyes and relaxed a little.

"I'm so glad you're pleased," he said.

All he had to do was wait until she was dressed. She would soon go home, give some excuse to her housekeeper, and return to her outwardly proper life as a widow of three years. The fact that her husband had been a wealthy merchant meant that she didn't need to marry, which was a relief to him.

What a pity he didn't feel comfortable asking her for money. He'd not yet descended into being supported by a woman. Perhaps he needed to readjust his thinking, however. It would be a damn sight easier asking her for money than to ask his brother.

"What have you got planned for today?" she asked.

He opened his eyes to find her coming out from behind the screen. She still wore mourning, although the proscribed time for proper mourning had passed. She was simply one of those women who looked exceedingly beautiful in black.

"I'm off to see my brother," he said.

A planned visit, given the state of his finances. He'd waited long enough. Following Arthur's death, the stodgy solicitor refused to give him any more money, pending Dalton's ascendance to the title.

So he'd done the only practical thing: he moved into the family's London home. It was bigger than his lodgings, and free. The only problem was money. He didn't have any. There were no servants to speak of, but the tradesmen would no longer take credit, and he couldn't make the solicitor budge when it came to paying for his food, drink, or clothing.

"I'm no longer just the third son," he said to Susan. "I'm the spare to the heir. From what I hear, my brother isn't doing well. Poor boy might just end his suffering one day."

"Haven't you seen him since he's come home?"

"Only once," he said. Long enough to be horrified at the ruin of Dalton's face and grateful he hadn't been foolish enough to accompany his brother to America.

"Not a loss to you, then."

He shrugged.

But for an accident of birth, he might have been the Earl of Rathsmere. If so, he wouldn't have had to beg anyone for the funds necessary to live.

His father had been hopelessly old-fashioned, unaware of the money necessary for a man to make a life in London nowadays. He could always live at Gledfield, if he wanted to be buried out in the country. With Arthur gone and his widow already remarried, there was no one to refuse him. He doubted Dalton would give up London for their country house. The stipend he'd been given on his majority would have lasted his lifetime if he'd rented a cottage on the moors, refused to see anyone, and eschewed any of the creature comforts.

But he wasn't about to withdraw from society.

This last year, however, had been difficult. He had a dislike of gambling, of tossing away his money on the off chance that he might win against luck. His experience had been that luck—or the gambling establishment—won most of the time. The problem was, unless he occupied himself with Friday to Monday house parties, he was doomed to be bored to death. No, he had to find a way to stay in London and be able to afford it. Ergo, a visit to dear Dalton.

With any luck, his brother wouldn't be as tight-fisted as Arthur.

AFTER MRS. Thompson left, with his thanks, Dalton sat in the wing chair staring in the direction of the fire-place. He had often sat there in the past, listening to conversations swirling around him. The topics were never serious: the size of a mistress's breasts, boasting of a man's stamina, tales of horse races, outlandish bets. He couldn't recall one time when he was impressed by a man's intellect or spurred to thought by a comment someone had made.

Arthur's life, in contrast, had been filled with meaning. He'd been a fine steward for Gledfield, for the MacIain fortune. Their father was proud of him; their mother never once glanced at Arthur and shook her head in mute fondness.

Arthur mattered; his life counted for something.

Dalton knew that in ten, fifteen years, he'd recall his brother to someone and the comments would be lau-datory. "Oh, yes, the sixth earl. A fine man, yes, a fine man."

What about him? Would anyone be able to say the same about the seventh earl?

A recluse, I've heard. Damn fellow went off to play soldier and managed to lose his sight.

He was suddenly blazingly angry. Not at his blind-ness this time, but Death itself.

Arthur shouldn't have died, and he shouldn't have ascended to the title. What the hell did he know about being the Earl of Rathsmere? Who in blazes thought he could replace Arthur? Or even wanted to try?

Standing, he made his way to the sideboard and the whiskey decanter. His left hand reached for the tumbler; his right was on the stopper of the decanter when Minerva Todd spoke in his mind.

Are you a drunkard, too?

Damn the woman.

He made his way to his desk, leaving the whiskey untouched.

In his charmed life before America, in his days of hedonism, he'd never considered Death an enemy. It was just there, like a shadow before dusk. An event that would one day happen to him, that had already visited his family, but had crawled back into the beyond, patiently waiting.

After America, he knew Death was more cunning and greedy. Not content with waiting, it often reached out a bony hand and plucked the unwary from life.

He couldn't forget the sight of men strewn over a battlefield, most of them dead, some of them dying. Those who were unlucky enough to come down with disease barely stood a chance, spending their last minutes adrift in hallucinations in a hot, foul-smelling tent adorned by barrels of legs and arms at the entrance.

Yet through it all, he'd survived. Not because of any skill on his part, although he'd been taught to shoot at a young age by his father. Not because of any cowardice on his part, either.

He'd just been damn lucky.

As a British citizen, he was initially viewed with suspicion by the men in his regiment. He couldn't blame them. When he was done playing at war, he could go home, sail away from the sound of incessant gunfire, scavenging for food, and the paralyzing fear of standing there watching as waves of men kept coming and coming despite volleys of gunfire.

The fields on which they marched belonged to someone. The crops they trampled had been grown to be food, not mattresses for thousands of men.

Death had won in most instances.

Nor was Death content with simple victory. Instead, it seemed to chortle with delight, rubbing bony hands together with glee until Dalton could swear he heard the clicking sound.

In those months in America, life had seemed something special, to be cherished and noted each passing minute. When he woke at dawn, he appreciated the air, heavy with dew. On some mornings there was fog, the low lying cloud of it obscuring his feet. Hunger was something he'd rarely experienced before leaving London. In America he grew to appreciate any food he received, no longer the epicure who demanded perfection from his cook.

He found himself interested in the stories of the men with whom he fought. Some of them had surprising ties to England: a niece here, a second cousin there. They all seemed intertwined somehow, members of long lost families.

There was nothing like knowing he might die tomorrow to make him appreciate every day. He should have taken up Arthur's habit of writing in a journal. Sometimes he wanted to share ideas, but the men around him were a laconic sort, exchanging tales of battles with more ease than they discussed their own lives or philosophies.

The euphoria abruptly left him the day he was shot. Several times since, he'd considered doing himself in. His anger had stopped him. He was damn well going to win this undeclared war: Death vs. Dalton.

Now he had another battle to join: Dalton vs. Todd. Minerva Todd, to be exact. Strange, that this one filled him with anticipation.

Chapter 15

"*J* beg your pardon, sir," Howington suddenly said.

Dalton turned toward the door. At last, Howington was announcing himself. Was the man out of sorts because he'd asked Mrs. Thompson for help the other day?

"Your brother is here."

For a fleeting second his mind produced the image of Arthur standing there, tall, thoroughly English, with that slight frown above his nose. Arthur, forever solemn . . . and dead.

"You mean Lewis," he said.

"Yes, sir."

He decided not to try to interpret Howington's tone, but he hoped he was mistaken about the note of humor he detected.

"Shall I show him in?"

"No," he said. "To the parlor, if you don't mind."

"Of course, sir."

He could almost feel Howington's confusion. He wasn't about to explain it.

This room was his sanctuary, where he went to hole up. Here he brooded. He knew every inch of the space and could walk without stumbling from one side to the other. It was, like his suite, private.

He didn't want Lewis in his library.

Standing, he made his way to the door.

Lewis had called on him when he first returned to London. His brother had expressed horror at the tragedy that had befallen him, a sentiment Dalton didn't believe. Lewis had never cared about anyone but Lewis.

He let his fingers trail over the wainscoting, counting his steps to the parlor door. He'd never considered, before being blinded, that he could sense the size of an area simply by the feel and sound of it. He wondered if he'd now be able to tell whether a room was occupied or empty.

Ahead of him were voices. Mrs. Thompson offering refreshments, no doubt. He would have to thank her for her constant hospitality. She made up for his deficits in being a host.

He hesitated at the door to the parlor, the sound of Lewis's chuckle immediately alerting him to his brother's location. Lewis was seated on the chair to the right of the fireplace, near the fern he'd toppled the night Minerva Todd had broken into his house.

"Do I amuse you?" he asked.

"On the contrary," Lewis said. "I approve of the patch. It hints at a foreign appearance. But other than that, you look well. I'm glad to see it."

He knew condescension when he heard it. He allowed a small smile to curve his lips. He had no doubt that Arthur would've come up to him, clapped his hand on his upper arm and said something like, "Damn, Dalton. What the hell have you gone and done to yourself?"

Lewis, however, buried himself in false flattery.

"If I had known I was so attractive, I would've had a tintype taken."

Five small steps. He reached out and grabbed the back of the chair, his hand trailing down to the arm. A moment later he sat, facing the direction of Lewis's voice.

Another chuckle from his brother. "You haven't lost your wit, I'm glad to see."

"Are you here to check on my appearance, Lewis?"

"I only came to see you. You're my only relative, after all."

I'm his only relative.

Minerva Todd was loyal to a fault to her brother, while he felt only irritation toward his. Neville Todd didn't deserve his sister's fidelity, but could he say the same about Lewis? His brother was his mirror, which meant he was the embodiment of a wastrel, a man whose only occupation was to find pleasure.

Shame drifted down on him like a soft blanket.

"Thank you," he said, trying to be more gracious. "I'm fine."

He made a wager with himself, though, one he hoped he lost. Lewis would ask him for money before he left, thus revealing the reason for his sudden brotherly affection.

"Are you still having headaches?"

He was surprised Lewis remembered that.

"No," he said, realizing it was true. He hadn't had a headache for a week now.

"Have you seen any of your old friends?"

"No." No one had visited him. Nor had he sent anyone an invitation to do so. He'd realized that they belonged to a time that existed before America, one that he couldn't replicate now. "Is that why you've come? To make sure I don't shame the family name by venturing out into society, exposing my *foreignness*?"

"I haven't seen you for three months, Dalton. Do you begrudge me caring about you?"

Had he ever been as clever with words? No doubt he had or was even more talented in the easy quip, the meaningless assortment of syllables. Words meant more now than they ever had. Words had flavor, something he'd never mentioned to anyone else. A certain tone, a way of speaking, could coat a word with sarcasm, derision, a mean amusement. Just as easily, a word could connote compassion, understanding, even friendship.

But Lewis wasn't his friend.

He'd never been as close to Lewis as with Arthur. He was five when Lewis was born. Arthur had been six. The years stretching between them had been an eternity to them as boys. They'd never wanted Lewis to tag along or participate. When he'd done so, it was solely at their mother's urging.

Even back then, Lewis had been whiny and grasping, taking credit for accomplishments he'd never done.

Although they both lived in London, and had some common acquaintances, they didn't travel in the same circles, just like himself and Arthur. But he would occasionally see Lewis at an establishment or encounter him at a ball or dinner. When they spoke, their conversations were shallow. When his mother was alive, they spoke of her or Arthur or Gledfield. Rarely did they talk about anything deeper. Perhaps there hadn't been anything deeper to speak about then.

"Thank you for coming," he said.

Silence met that remark. Lewis was one of those people, like Howington, who hadn't yet figured out that he couldn't see visual clues.

Half of conversation, he'd realized since being blinded, wasn't comprised of words at all, but expressions and gestures. Without being able to see, he participated in only half the conversation. Unless the person was like Mrs. Thompson, who seemed to understand.

He realized, with a measure of surprise, that Minerva Todd was another woman who made it easy to converse.

When Lewis still didn't speak, he smiled. "You need money, is that it?"

"If I do?" Lewis asked. "Are you disposed to loan me a little?"

"Have you applied yourself to an occupation, brother? Some way of earning money?"

"Damned if you don't sound like Arthur."

"Did you solicit funds from him as well?"

When their mother was alive, Alexandra had funded her youngest son. If she lectured him as well, Dalton wouldn't have been surprised, but she never said no to Lewis. It must have been a shock to Lewis after her death not to have a ready source of cash.

"From time to time," Lewis said. Each of his words was tinged with anger. What had it taken Lewis to come here today? He must be desperate indeed.

Luckily for Lewis, he knew something about pride and its loss.

"How much do you need?"

Lewis named an amount, one that knocked the smile off his face.

"How long will that last you?"

"Long enough."

"Make sure it does," he said.

"You're going to give it to me?" Lewis's words were coated with surprise.

"What's a brother for?" he said, smiling. "Just don't come to the well again. You'll find it's dried up."

"You're more like Arthur than you know," Lewis said.

Once, he might have considered his brother's remark an insult. Now, oddly, it felt like a compliment.

"MISS MINERVA," Mrs. Beauchamp said, after knocking on the storeroom door. "This just came for you."

The housekeeper held out a note.

She thanked the woman, took it and opened it, conscious that Mrs. Beauchamp hadn't moved. She didn't often get notes. In fact, this might be the very first, and the fact it was hand delivered was even more unusual.

I am visiting my brother's solicitor this afternoon at one. If you would like to accompany me, I will pick you up at twelve. Please don't make me wait.

What an absolutely arrogant note. But at least he had made good on his promise. If she wanted to accompany him she would have to hurry.

She glanced up at Mrs. Beauchamp, stood up from behind the table, and explained as quickly as she could.

"It's from the earl," she said. "He wants me to accompany him to his brother's solicitor."

The housekeeper looked as if she wanted to ask a question, but she didn't give the woman a chance. She raced up the stairs thinking to change, but realized she didn't have the time.

She grabbed her bonnet from the dresser, wishing she didn't have to wear the blasted thing. When she was on an expedition, she wore a wide straw hat fastened to her head with a broad, soft ribbon. By the end of the day, when the ribbon was damp with sweat, she either replaced it or did without the hat.

At exactly twelve o'clock she went to the front door. To her surprise, the carriage was already there.

She glanced toward the Covington sisters' house and almost waved. One of them was sure to see the earl's carriage. Quite an equipage it was. This carriage wasn't the one he used the day before. This one was a larger vehicle, a shiny onyx and pulled by two beautiful matched horses.

Wasn't he doing it up a bit too much?

She greeted him with that question when the driver opened the door for her.

"I can't imagine who you're trying to impress," she said. "Do we really need as large a carriage? Are we going to Cornwall?"

"Do you have a yen to go to Cornwall, Miss Todd?"

"I've never been," she said. "Is it lovely?"

"Windy," he said. "But the views are magnificent, especially if you like the ocean."

"Do you like the ocean?"

"I'm rather ambivalent about it, Miss Todd. I think of the ocean as the ground, something to travel over. Although, I will have to admit that a storm on the ocean is something that should be experienced. But only when you can see it. Otherwise, it's intensely frightening."

That surprised her, that he would admit to being afraid.

"Is it very frightening being blind?"

"I am growing accustomed to your pointed questions, Miss Todd."

"While I am growing accustomed to the fact that you deflect most of them."

He smiled.

"On the contrary. I've probably been more honest with you than with most people."

She wanted to say something cutting to that remark, but for the life of her the words would not form on her lips. She wasn't sure she believed him. Nor was she sure she should.

He was dressed as he had been the last time she saw him, in a black jacket and trousers with a snowy white shirt. His shoes were polished to a shine and his appearance impeccable. The man was impossibly handsome, and the black eye patch only added a certain dangerous appeal.

"Why are you going to see your brother's solicitor?"

"I agreed to allow you to accompany me, Miss Todd, only because you seem determined to do so. No part of that agreement stated that you were to be privy to private matters."

She felt her face flame. He was a master of the put down, wasn't he?

"Does it have anything to do with Neville?"

"I can assure you that the conversation will not touch upon your brother in any way."

"Are you sad about the meeting to come? Your voice sounds different."

He laughed, surprising her. "I've confessed to feeling fear, Miss Todd. Do you want the entire gamut of emotions from me?"

"If you did tell me anything, I wouldn't share it with a soul."

"So you want me to consider you my father confessor."

"I'm wearing trousers," she said.

"I beg your pardon?"

"I feel you should know. It isn't fair to take advantage of your blindness. You don't know what I look like, but you should at least know what I'm wearing."

"Should I?"

"It started off as a skirt," she said. "I have two seams stitched down the middle, sewing it together. After that, the seamstress cut it. So it's like a voluminous pair of trousers."

"Is it?"

"It's quite shocking. I'm sure I shocked the seamstress by requesting it. If I'm seen by anyone, they would no doubt make a notation of it, but I didn't want to be late so I didn't change."

"It might be an article in the *Times* tomorrow, is that it? The blinded Earl of Rathsmere was seen in the company of a scandalous woman who took advantage of his affliction to parade about in a pair of trousers. Something like that?"

"Exactly," she said.

"Most people don't notice things unless it's forced on them. They're mainly concerned with themselves."

"I think you're entirely wrong when it comes to you," she said. "I suspect all of London is still curious. They want to know if you can see anything at all, and why you carry that walking stick with you. How is it that you still manage to be handsome? Are you even more of a rake now than you were before? How has America changed you?"

"All that? Do you feel the same curiosity, Miss Todd?"

Oh dear. Should she tell him the truth or hide behind some deflection of her own?

"I think you carry the walking stick to maintain your balance. I blindfolded myself the other night and the first thing I noticed was that I kept wanting to topple over."

"Did you?"

His voice had taken on a strange note and his features were still, as if he commanded them to be like stone.

"I quite hated it," she said. "But I sat in the middle of the parlor and I heard the most amazing things, things I didn't pay any attention to before."

"Unlike you, Miss Todd, I don't hear amazing things."

"Was your hearing damaged? Or are you simply not trying?"

He turned his head and stared at the carriage window as if he could see through it.

"I can see light with my left eye. A few shapes. For example, in the garden, I could see your shape but nothing else."

"Will your vision ever improve?"

"I don't know. I have a physician who is entirely too optimistic. I suspect it won't."

"You must be more positive, Your Lordship."

"Why must I be?"

"Because you simply must believe that tomorrow will be better. If it's raining today, it will be sunny tomorrow. If your mood is foul today, you will be happy tomorrow. You must always have hope. I think living without hope would be the most terrible thing in the world."

He didn't answer her. But at least, she reflected, he hadn't disparaged her beliefs like Neville had. Her brother made fun of her sometimes, saying nobody could be as innocent or naive as she. She wasn't, either, but did believe it was important to look forward to things.

When their parents died, it had been the most terrible time in the world for her. Neville was the one who made it possible to wake every morning, to go about the business of living. She never knew what he was going to say or do. His laughter charmed her down to her toes. His smile banished her despair. How very strange that he should later ridicule what he himself had taught her.

The carriage slowed, and she thought it best that they didn't continue this conversation. She always said too much around him.

"Where are we going after your brother's solicitor?"

"Why should we be going anywhere else?"

"Aren't you going to look for Neville? Or have you set Mr. Wilson on that task?"

"Perhaps we could visit a few places," he said. "What would the Covington sisters say?"

She was surprised he remembered what she'd told him. "No doubt they saw me leave the house today, so I'm already being discussed in horrified tones."

"Saw you in your trousers."

"In my trousers. You could take me home and I'll change. I would be more respectable."

"I'm the Rake of London, Miss Todd. In my company you'll never be respectable."

There was that, of course. She really shouldn't be so excited.

Chapter 16

To Dalton's surprise, the carriage slowed. Were they at their destination so quickly? The time had passed faster than he'd expected. Perhaps it was talking to Miss Todd that made the time fly by.

She reached over, unlatched the door and pushed it open.

"I'm going to be very impolite right now," she said in a businesslike manner. "I'm going to exit the carriage first. Then, if you don't mind, I will take your hand once you've disembarked. We will stroll like lovers up to your solicitor's office."

He didn't know whether she had planned it or not, but her comment took away any of the awkwardness of the moment.

"I think you try to be shocking, don't you, Miss Todd?"

"If I do, Your Lordship, you are the only person who thinks so. No doubt it is due to your own nature."

He heard her leave the carriage, then felt the slight rocking as she placed her feet on the step before descending to the cobblestones.

Just as she promised, once he was in the doorway, she reached up and grabbed his hand. To his surprise, her fingers were callused.

"You aren't wearing gloves."

"I forgot them in the carriage. Would you like me to retrieve them now?"

"No," he said.

He wouldn't tell her how long it'd been since he touched a woman's hand. However, he'd never felt a woman grip him with such strength.

Why did she have calluses on her fingers?

"I'm going to put my other hand on your arm," she said. "If I direct you to the left, you must walk to the left. If I direct you to the right, you must walk to the right. The thoroughfare is slightly crowded, and I don't want you to crash into another person."

"I have a feeling I'm a dog being walked."

"Nonsense," she said. "You're a fine thoroughbred. Very well trained."

He couldn't help but laugh.

Dalton knew he was probably going to have trouble with Arthur's solicitor. It would all be very pleasant, aboveboard, and professional, but he'd withdrawn the MacIain account from Paul Doherty's law firm and it had to have been a very big part of the firm's business.

Therefore, he was unprepared for Paul's garrulous greeting.

"Come in, come in," he said. Evidently, the solicitor had been waiting for him at the door, and now escorted him down the hall and into his office.

Where had Minerva gone? She'd dropped his arm, extricated her hand from his and suddenly disappeared.

He couldn't smell cinnamon anymore.

"How have you been?" Paul asked, gripping his arm with both hands.

He recognized that he needed help moving from one place to another, but it didn't require someone acting as if they were saving him from drowning.

Once he was seated in Paul's office, the man released him. From the sound of his voice, he must have circled a desk to sit on the other side.

He had never been here before, so he had no range of reference, no memory of rooms or locations. Paul, who met his ship when he arrived, had been one of Arthur's classmates in addition to his solicitor. He now had the same difficulty as earlier, trying to place the boyish face on a grown man.

"Of course, I understand completely why you moved your business from our firm," Paul said. "We're very conservative, but it's your account, after all."

Before he had a chance to speak, the solicitor continued. "I am willing to keep a portion of the business, if you will. Anything that would make you comfortable, of course. If you would like to transfer the majority of your account back to us, we would be overjoyed."

He opened his mouth, but Paul wasn't finished. "I hope that everything has been smooth for you. I trust the transition has been easy?"

"Exceedingly." There, he got one word out.

"I'm pleased. Truly pleased. If your solicitor or his firm have any questions, I hope that you convey to them that we stand ready to assist."

"I'll tell them," he said.

Finally, it seemed Paul ran out of words.

"I didn't come here to discuss the MacIain account, Paul. I came here to ask what you know of Arthur's death."

"A tragedy. A true tragedy. A loss of a great man. A great friend. A great, great friend. Life will not be the same without Arthur."

"How did my brother die?"

"But I told you myself, Dalton. I know I did."

How had Arthur tolerated the man?

"Who told you how Arthur had died?"

"Why the countess, of course. By way of a messenger. No one would have expected her to call on me in person."

"And you just accepted her word?"

This question was met by silence, an indication of Paul's shock.

"I don't understand what you're saying, Dalton."

"Did you believe her?"

He heard the creak of the chair. Had Doherty stood? Or had he simply leaned back in his chair, regarding him with disbelief? His imagination conjured up a dozen expressions Arthur's solicitor might be wearing.

Perhaps he should have brought Miss Todd along, if only to tell him what he couldn't see. Being blind was grating on him.

"Why would I not? Perhaps it's best if you plainly state what you think, Dalton."

"I have recently received information that Arthur wasn't hunting the day he was killed. Also, that the accident took place within view of Gledfield. Is that correct?"

He heard the chair creak again. Was Doherty squirming?

"When I reached Gledfield," Doherty said, "Arthur was laid out in the grand parlor. Alice was barely able to converse, she was so distraught."

So upset that she married another man in a matter of months.

He remained silent, using it as a weapon. He had never realized, until he was blinded, how much people say when they were nervous. Or how uncomfortable people were with silence.

It seemed a minute passed before Doherty spoke again.

"I didn't learn until after the funeral that the accident had taken place within sight of the house. But until you came today, your Lordship, I didn't know that Arthur hadn't been hunting. How certain are you of your information?"

He believed Sarah, perhaps more than he should. The woman had no reason to lie.

"Very certain."

Had Alice had a hand in Arthur's death? Or someone else in the family? He pushed that suspicion to the back of his mind.

"What do you want me to do, Your Lordship?"

"Nothing, for the moment. No, that's not true. Tell me why Arthur didn't make any provisions for his mistress or his child."

He half expected the other man to claim ignorance about the situation, but the letters had been addressed to Paul's office. To Doherty's credit, he didn't try to lie.

"He had mentioned it on two previous occasions and I believe that he intended to do so in a matter of weeks. He didn't expect to die, of course. None of us do."

Instantly, the picture of Neville Todd raising a pistol in his direction penetrated his blindness.

"No, we don't. Did you not suggest anything to Alice?"

"Of course not," Paul said, sounding horrified. "I would never have mentioned the existence of Miss Westchester to Her Ladyship under any circumstances, let alone at such a mournful time."

He didn't like the idea of Sarah being left to fend for herself. Arthur, his well-organized, well-planned, exceedingly dutiful brother, had left a woman who loved him without a cent. If a man was going to engage in a relationship, especially one that resulted in a child, he should go out of his way to ensure that the woman was protected.

Evidently there was one thing he had learned before his brother: the meaning of mortality. He'd had that thrust upon him by the sight of thousands of men dead in a single day.

After the Battle of Manassas, he discovered the bodies of several men he knew strewn along the ground like fallen leaves. He sat in the middle of them, his hands clenched on the rifle across his lap, and stared at a lone tree not too far away, the only tall object on the horizon. The tree became a lodestone, a beacon for his eyes as he sat there quietly among the dead. He, who had prided himself on never revealing a soft emotion, who considered a man who disclosed too much of himself to be an idiot, found himself sitting cross-legged on the earth, tears falling soundlessly down his face.

The memory startled him, coming as it did without being summoned.

"Thank you," he said, standing.

"Are you certain there is nothing you want me to do?"

There was nothing to do, was there? He had no information to take to the authorities, other than his suspicion that Arthur hadn't died because of an accident. He had no proof, only his thoughts.

To his surprise, Minerva stood outside the office, announcing her presence in a way that made him wonder if she'd had experience dealing with people who'd lost their sight.

"I'm here, Your Lordship," she said, placing her hand on his sleeve and winding it around his arm.

"Where did you go?" he asked.

"You told me the meeting was private."

"I would never have guessed you to be tactful."

She didn't respond, only sighed.

"I'm sorry," he said. "I'm in a foul mood and I'm taking it out on you."

His memories grated on him, as well as the fact that the meeting had been damned annoying.

"I would ask," she said, "but I expect your mood

has something to do with your private meeting. You were very companionable earlier."

"Was I?" He hadn't been companionable for a very long time.

"There are five steps down and a bit of a bump on the first step. At least it isn't raining, although the sky is an odd gray color."

They might have been walking to the dance floor or out to the terrace.

"What are the flowers I smell?" he asked.

"Oh, I see a stall across the street. Do you have a yen for blossoms?"

He smiled. "Not today, I think."

"But we should mark where they are, just in case you wake up one night craving nasturtiums."

"Do you do that often? Wake up craving nasturtiums?"

"Ices," she said. "If I wake at midnight it's craving ices. Or chocolate in any form. Isn't it hideous that something should have a hold on your mind like that?"

Did she expect him to confess that whiskey had once held that power over him?

Before he could formulate an answer, she said, "We're at the carriage now. The door is open. I'll go first, shall I? Of course, the horses are to your right, so you'll turn right when you get inside."

"Thank you, nurse."

She stopped and turned to him. "Have I been too abrasive? I do apologize if I have."

"I haven't forgotten all my manners," he said.

"Did you have good manners before? I can't remember hearing any tales of it."

He was startled into laughter once again.

"Why do you always smell of cinnamon?" he asked as he entered the carriage after her.

"Do I?"

She sounded surprised. Good. He had a feeling that the best way to deal with Minerva Todd was to keep her slightly off center.

"I noticed it that first night in the parlor. And every occasion since then."

"My housekeeper has a penchant for potpourri," she said. "She's forever putting spicy potpourri in my dresser drawers and it contains cinnamon. Plus I eat a cinnamon scone every morning. It's my favorite."

"Then between the scone and the potpourri, I believe we have the answer to a mystery. How many of them do you eat?"

"Only one," she said. "Or perhaps two if I'm feeling gluttonous."

"No more than that? Are you given to being plump, Miss Todd?"

He could hear her sit back against the squabs and hid his smile.

"Let me smell your hair."

"I beg your pardon?"

He half raised himself, and before she could mount an objection, placed his hand on her shoulder, then on top of her head. He bent over her and sniffed.

In the next moment he sat again, smiling slightly.

"Your hair smells of lemon."

"It's in the rinse I use," she said.

She had such an expressive voice. He wondered if she knew it.

"Do you try to be rude?" she asked.

"Occasionally I do," he said.

"Like now?"

"I find it enjoyable to tease you, Miss Todd. Do you not have a sense of humor?"

"I have a wonderful sense of humor," she said. "If I didn't, I wouldn't be riding in a carriage with a man who wants to put my brother in jail."

"That denotes a certain flexibility, Miss Todd, but nothing of humor."

"Must I tell you some jests in order to prove that I do find amusement in certain things? What would be a good test?"

"Do you know any jests? Unfortunately, the only ones I know are ribald in nature."

"That does not surprise me in the least," she said.

"Very well, I will concede that you have a sense of humor."

She didn't respond, which disappointed him.

She'd already charmed him out of his bad mood, a fact that both surprised and worried him.

He hadn't expected to *like* Minerva Todd. Nor had he planned on taking her around London, but the idea had merit.

A warning bell sounded in the back of his mind and he recognized the peal of it. But the caution belonged to a different time and perhaps to a different man.

Chapter 17

"*W*here are we going now?" she asked as the carriage set off.

"Are you feeling up to being my eyes?"

"Of course," she said. "As well as your minder. We'll walk together and people will never know that I'm escorting you, instead of you escorting me."

He didn't say anything, only smiled politely.

"Do you miss your former life? The rumors made it sound very exciting. Disreputable, but exciting all the same."

"Do you listen to rumors a great deal, Miss Todd?"

"I have a very voluble housekeeper. Mrs. Beauchamp reads the most salacious kind of news. What she doesn't find out in the papers she discovers from her friends. I'm sure the Covington sisters know a great deal about you as well, for all that they're homebodies."

His smile altered character, became a little more natural.

"I quite liked Prince Albert, although most of my contemporaries did not. They chose to ridicule the man for his accent and his array of uniforms."

"But you didn't?"

"I thought him intelligent and fascinating despite his oddities."

"Which meant that you were considered odd for

enjoying the prince's company. What a pity he died so young."

"I was informed of the event by Arthur's solicitor before he informed me of my brother's death."

His tone was acerbic, but she could understand why. "He probably didn't want to tell you about Arthur," she said.

He inclined his head toward her.

"Are you feeling magnanimous toward Arthur's solicitor for some reason, Miss Todd?"

"On no account," she said easily. "I am merely putting myself in his position. I think I would've discussed the weather, the news of the day, almost anything rather than have to tell you that your brother died."

"As I recall it, he did talk about the weather to some great length."

"Do you still blame him?"

He frowned a little, an expression made even more arresting by the presence of his eye patch.

"Blame him?"

"For being the bearer of bad tidings. Sometimes we resent the people who bring us bad news."

"If I used that philosophy, Miss Todd, I would think that you resented me a great deal."

"A part of me does," she said.

He remained as still as a stone. "Only part of you?" he finally said.

"Where are we going?" she asked, changing the subject.

"I could take you to the Cave of Harmony in Covent Garden. It's a cellar establishment that's occasionally vulgar. Or the Alhambra, where there are flying trapezes. But I think, instead, that we will go to Cremore. It's a public garden and one of your brother's favorite haunts."

"And those of your friends?"

"It isn't the season, and most of my acquaintances wouldn't be caught dead in London. They were either for their country estates or guests at Friday to Monday events."

"Not friends?"

"I beg your pardon?"

"You called them acquaintances. What about your friends?"

He looked away, as if he wanted to avoid the question, or perhaps her.

"I have found, since returning to London, that I have few friends, Miss Todd. The ones I do have always been constant, but they were never my companions in my revels."

She didn't know what to say to his candor.

"Could we go to Astley's Amphitheater? I remember Neville talking about the equestrian performances. Or the elephants."

"I think it best to limit our visits to those places Neville spent the most time at, don't you?"

"Was he very well-known?"

"What you're asking is, was he disreputable, as well-known for his escapades as I. He's a man, Miss Todd. Young, yes, but he possesses all the flaws and faults of his kind. Neville enjoyed the company of his friends, laughing, and other occupations known to be enjoyed by other men."

"In other words, he was an acolyte of yours, attempting to be as licentious and dissolute."

He didn't answer, and she realized she'd probably been too acerbic again. Or honest.

She settled back against the seat, her eyes on the view out the window.

"Are we going by the river?"

The gardens had a pier on the Thames. She knew a great deal about Cremore, opened twenty years earlier, even though she'd never gone. It wasn't considered proper, for all its popularity.

"I think Kings Road would be best," he said.

"Will we be able to see all the light displays? I've been told they are magnificent."

"One of us will."

"Oh, I am sorry. How insensitive of me."

"Never mind, Miss Todd, I've seen them many times before. You mustn't miss the crystal platform. It's a study in various colored glass and iron work."

They sat in companionable silence for several minutes. It surprised her how comfortable she was in his presence.

When the carriage stopped, they repeated the same dismounting procedure as at the solicitor's office. After they left the vehicle she took the earl's arm and they walked sedately down the wide thoroughfare, her eyes taking in all the sights.

Dusk was settling over the gardens. By the time she returned home it would be dark.

The Covington sisters would be scandalized.

Should she worry about her reputation? After all, she was alone with the Earl of Rathsmere without a chaperone. None of her maids were suitable; they would have been charmed by the earl within minutes of being in his company.

She had never truly cared what people thought of her, and was now putting that philosophy to the test. Here she was, sauntering through Cremore Gardens with the Rake of London while wearing her trousers skirt.

To her surprise, Cremore was filled with plainly dressed people. Once in a while she'd see a female attired in something more fashionable, but most of the crowd seemed to be the working people of London.

The crystal platform was just as he had described.

The iron work was magnificently crafted with swirls, circles, and leaves surrounding roses that looked to be on the verge of opening. Mirrors sat in among the decorations, reflecting the emerald, garnet, and blue crystal droplets. Behind it all were gas jets, illuminating the platform in the approaching dusk. In total darkness it would be an awe inspiring sight.

But it was nothing to the pagoda and its orchestra, so brightly lit by all the gas chandeliers that it pushed back the oncoming night.

To her surprise, they were playing a waltz. The dance floor was crowded with good-natured people all smiling and looking as if they were thoroughly enjoying themselves.

She envied them their freedom and their light-hearted joy.

She didn't like to dance. She wasn't good at it. Although her mother had insisted she learn, she was well aware that she stepped on the feet of her partners. But here, with the soaring music and the coming night made day by the gas jet lights, she wanted to try again.

"Would you dance with me?"

"Are you daft?" he said.

"I don't think you need sight in order to dance. I often close my eyes when I'm dancing."

"That's because you were in your partner's arms," he said. "He was leading you, and one of the reasons he was leading you was to watch for other dancers so you didn't crash into them."

"I can lead you," she said.

"I repeat, are you daft?"

"Are you worried that it might damage your consequence? Someone might see the great Earl of Rathsmere being led about the dance floor by a woman?"

"No, I'm more afraid of the great Earl of Rathsmere being led around the dance floor like a trained monkey. I'm not that good a dancer anyway. You'll thank me for refusing."

"I don't believe you. You walk quite well."

"I beg your pardon?"

"I watch how men walk," she said. "Oh, not all the time, but when it occurs to me to do so. Men who walk with confidence often turn out to be very good dancers. You walk with confidence even now, though you can't see where you're going."

His startled laugh made her smile.

"Is there no end to what you'll say?"

"I thought you didn't mind when I was being myself," she said, inexplicably hurt. She wouldn't dance with him now even if he begged her.

She moved a few feet away, her attention directed to two very attractive women walking close to the pavilion. She knew, without being told, that they were members of the demimonde. One was blond while the other had black hair. Both were dressed in the highest fashion, even if their bodices dipped a bit low. Their makeup, however, was excessive. Their brows had been drawn in and their lips coated with bright red color.

"Miss Todd—" he began.

She interrupted him. "Exactly why are we here, Your Lordship?"

"To meet someone."

"Someone who might know my brother?"

"Exactly that. Miss Todd, I must apologize."

"You must? Why ever must you?"

Here in the gaslight he was even more attractive. His eye patch attracted some attention and then the women looked again. Did they recognize him? Or were they just remarking on his good looks?

"I hope you don't want to apologize for what you feel or say in my presence," she said. "You see, I much prefer people to be who they are. And if some things they say don't please me, I simply keep my comments to myself. I don't hold myself up as the only arbiter of taste or fashion."

"I don't bloody well think I'm the only arbiter of taste or fashion. I just have this abiding dislike of looking the fool. I didn't mean to insult you. I'm not saying that you would be the foolish one. But I'm blind, Miss Todd. I can't see the dance floor. I can't see you. I can't see the other dancers. Hell, I can't even tell if it's day or night."

"It's turning into a very lovely night, Your Lordship, and I'd appreciate it if you wouldn't ruin it."

Really, he could not bring her to tears with his words. He could not make her want to pat him on the arm and tell him it was going to be all right. It had been a silly suggestion anyway. Maybe she'd just wanted to be held in his arms for a while, and wasn't that a terrible admission?

Was she losing her mind around him, becoming one of those silly women she'd heard about?

"Dalton."

She turned to find that the blond woman she'd been watching was standing right beside her. The woman ignored her as she stretched out her hand to touch Dalton's sleeve.

"Oh, love, what happened to you?"

"War," he said.

Another surprise, that he didn't immediately excoriate Neville in public.

The blonde leaned forward and kissed him on the cheek.

"It's Lilly, isn't it?"

"Oh, you dear sweet man. Fancy that, you remembering after all this time."

"You're one of those women that is difficult to forget."

Her laughter sounded like crystal teardrops clinking together, while she, no doubt, brayed like a donkey when she laughed.

Minerva turned away, unwilling to see the blond rub all over the earl like a kitten.

She could not, however, ignore their conversation.

"I'm looking for Dorothy," he said.

"What can Dorothy do that I can't, Dalton?"

The woman was as arrogant as a lord. Was bragging about her qualifications a requirement of being a member of the demimonde?

"Dorothy was a particular friend to someone I'm looking for."

Minerva turned to stare at him. What was he implying? That Neville utilized the services of a girl here at Cremore Gardens?

"I haven't seen her tonight," the blonde said. "Would you like me to pass along a message?"

"I would."

To her surprise, he extended some pound notes to the woman. She didn't hesitate to take them and stuff them into her bosom. The bodice was so low it was a wonder her nipples weren't exposed.

"Ask Dorothy to contact me," he said, pulling out one of his cards and handing it to her. "If she sees Neville Todd."

"Neville the Devil? What a lark he was. I haven't seen him, Dalton, but I'll pass along the message."

After another kiss, some whispered exchange that caused the earl to smile, she was gone in a flurry of French perfume, ruffles, and a rustling sound like silk petticoats.

"Neville the Devil?" Minerva asked him. "What's your nickname? Other than the Rake of London?"

He didn't answer her. "Dorothy's very fond of Neville."

"Yes, well."

"Are you under the impression that your brother is celibate?"

"I haven't actually thought about it," she said. "Nor do I want to think about it now."

In her mind, Neville would always be ten years old. Of course, she knew he wasn't, but the idea that he might have engaged one of the women here was shocking.

"He might get the pox. You might get the pox."

"I can assure you, Miss Todd, I have not taken advantage of any offers here."

That made her feel a little better, and she couldn't imagine why.

"Did Neville never go to Vauxhall?"

"Vauxhall has a fashionable reputation. When one wants to be an iconoclast, one finds the venue to do it."

What on earth did she say to that?

DALTON WOULD have given a sizable chunk of his fortune to be able to see Minerva Todd's expression as they left Cremore Gardens.

As the evening advanced, she became quieter. They made six additional stops, all places he knew Neville frequented. He left his card at each one, with instructions for them to call him if Neville was seen.

When they entered the carriage for the last time, before giving Daniels instructions to return to Miss Todd's home, she spoke again.

"No one has seen him."

"No," he agreed. "They haven't, which leads me to wonder if he's returned to London at all."

"You think he's dead, don't you?"

Did she know how expressive her voice was? He could hear the grief she tried to push back, along with sorrow and regret.

Suddenly, he wanted to reassure her, to take the sadness from her voice.

"I know nothing of the sort," he said. "He might've returned to England and just not to London."

"London is his home," she said, her tone dull and nearly lifeless.

"Weren't you the one who advised me to be positive in my thoughts? Is that a case of do as I say and not as I do?"

"You're right of course," she said, a false cheer coating her words.

"We don't know where he is, Miss Todd. He might still be in America, waiting transport home. Or perhaps he's fallen in love with an American and can't bear to part from her."

"He's entirely too young to take a wife."

He couldn't help but smile.

"You think me an idiot, don't you?"

"I think a great many things about you, Miss Todd. None of them is that you're an idiot."

"You do? What do you think?"

He wasn't about to venture down that path. It wouldn't do to let the woman know he was becoming more interested then was wise. Minerva Todd had a charm all her own. He found himself smiling often and even laughing from time to time. She was most definitely her own person, and that creature was someone totally alien to his knowledge of women.

She fascinated him. She smelled of cinnamon and lemon. And her voice made him want to listen to it. She wasn't shrill, even when she was emotional. Her voice was pitched lower, almost seductively.

No, it wouldn't do to let Minerva know what he thought of her.

"What do you look like?" he asked.

"I beg your pardon?"

"Did you not hear the question or are you stalling for time?" he asked, amused.

"I've never had to describe myself before."

"James thinks you're arresting."

"Does he?"

"Your voice softens when you're pleased, do you know that?"

"No," she said.

"And it hardens when you're annoyed. You have a decidedly facile voice, Minerva."

"Why are you calling me by my given name? Are you trying to be shocking now?"

He hadn't intended to do it, but her name had slipped from his lips with ease. Now that he'd violated a tenet of polite society, he saw no reason to retract it.

"I'm tired of calling you Miss Todd."

"Are you?"

"There's that hardness again."

When she didn't respond, he smiled. He knew better than to think her feelings were hurt. No, Minerva was no doubt sitting there with her eyes slitted, thinking of some way to retaliate.

"You have to be a raving beauty for all the annoyance you summon. Only truly beautiful women are allowed to be harridans."

"Were you this rude when you could see?"

His smile broadened. He'd been right. "Occasionally, I'm afraid. What do you look like?"

"I'm arresting, of course."

"I doubt you've ever thought that of yourself. Most women bemoan their looks. They concentrate on their flaws to the exclusion of all else. A bit like not being able to see the forest for the trees."

"And men don't? Don't men have any qualms about their looks? Don't you?"

"I don't think we consider it much."

"Oh, come now," she said, her voice dripping with sarcasm. "You, the darling of the ton, never thought about your appearance? I've heard how women nearly swooned at the sight of you."

His laugh filled the corners of the carriage.

"Swooned at the sight of me? Whoever told you that tripe?"

"Never mind."

Was she embarrassed?

"I'm serious," he said. "I never considered my looks. Now I'm afraid I would frighten my previous companions."

"No doubt they are shallow people. Your scars aren't that terrible."

He really had to stop analyzing her voice. Now it seemed to be filled with compassion. Too close to pity, that.

"You've never said what you look like, which is a masterful piece of deflection, by the way."

She made a sound, and he wondered if she was gritting her teeth. He bit back his smile with an effort.

"I have brown hair," she said. "And greenish-brown eyes. Sometimes, they look almost emerald when I'm wearing a certain color green, but mostly they stay a muddy brown. They're not a very interesting color."

"And your face? What shape is it? What is your nose like?"

"My nose?"

"Is it like the prow of a ship? Or is it, perhaps, rounded at the tip and bulbous? Does it redden when you drink wine?" Before she could answer, he continued. "I'm betting you have a sharply pointed chin."

"I don't. Nor do I have a bulbous nose. It's just a nose."

"Come here."

"I beg your pardon?"

He slid to one side of the seat.

"Miss Todd, if I may prevail upon you to join me here." He patted the seat beside him.

"Why?"

"Would you deny me the ability to equalize our positions?"

"What balderdash. What do you mean, equalize our positions?"

"You already know what I look like. I have no idea of your appearance."

"Why is it so important to know what I look like?"

"Are you ashamed of your appearance?" he asked.

"Of course not."

"Then is there any reason why you wouldn't join me?"

"How is my sitting next to you going to give you an idea of my appearance?"

He heard her move, then felt the material of her skirt against his hand.

He reached up until he touched her shoulder, extending his hand farther to her neck, up her throat to her cheek. Turning slightly, he moved so that both hands were on her face.

"I can't see you. Therefore, my fingers must be my eyes."

After her first startled jerk, she remained still, almost quiescent beneath his touch. His fingertips stroked from her temples to her chin.

"Not a pointed chin after all," he said. "Perhaps your nose is, however." His fingers stroked down her nose, hesitating at the tip. "Your nose is very imperious looking. An aquiline nose." One that twitched at his touch, as if she were ticklish.

His thumbs brushed her bottom lip, then traced the upper one. Her mouth was large, the bottom lip fuller.

An intriguing mouth and one that didn't remain closed very often.

"Have you given any thought to what people will think if they see you touching me this way?"

"Why on earth should I consider the thoughts of strangers, Minerva?"

"Don't you care about what people think of you?"

He pulled his hands back and thought about the question.

He wanted to say he blithely disregarded the opinions of others, that he hadn't minded if he caused others to talk about him.

But his actions had been designed to shock, hadn't they?

Riding a horse into Malverne House on the occasion of a ball marking the opening of Parliament was the action of a man wishing to incite conversation. So was taking the Duchess of Fernleigh to his bed. She had been fifteen years older and one of the wealthiest women in England, not to mention the bawdiest.

He'd evidently wanted the attention of the very society he was about to claim to eschew.

"I think," he said, giving her the gift of the truth, "that I once cared too much about what people thought."

"And now?"

"Now I'm no longer part of that world."

Only one person had breached the moat that separated him from the rest of the world, and she was sitting beside him.

His hands returned to her face, his fingers splaying across her cheeks, thumbs resting below her lips. Her skin was soft and warm. Was Minerva blushing?

His fingers stroked her eyebrows, then closed her lids to trace the fluttery length of her lashes.

"I should scream," she said softly. "Perhaps someone would come to my aid."

"I think a scream would no doubt enhance my reputation. 'Look at MacIain, even blind he is able to capture a beauty in his carriage.'"

"I'm not a beauty."

"Ah, I think you are, Minerva Todd, but you just don't realize it."

"I think it's been a very long time since you had release."

He choked back a laugh. "Release?"

"A woman in your bed. Lovemaking. That kind of release. Women need it as well, you know."

"That's right. You're no virgin, are you? You seemed extraordinarily proud of that fact."

"I wasn't proud," she said, her voice taking on a harder tone again. "It's just that I knew I would never marry. Why should I deny myself the pleasure of passion just because of that?"

"Was it pleasurable?"

"Exceedingly," she said without a pause. "I liked it very much. I could see how one could grow accustomed to passion. Or even addicted."

"Do you?"

"You're annoyed," she said.

"Indeed I'm not."

She'd managed to surprise him again, however. Or perhaps the word was shock. He'd never met anyone who was so completely herself as Minerva Todd.

"I've enjoyed your company today, Minerva."

"You haven't been the worst of companions, Rathsmere. Even if you wouldn't dance with me."

"I find that I am in need of a set of eyes, especially in view of my new role as the Earl of Rathsmere. Would you come and work for me?"

"Don't you have a secretary? A rather officious man, as I recall."

"Howington."

"If you already have a secretary, why do you need me?"

"Howington is becoming an irritant," he said, giving her the truth again. "My solicitor has just sent me a great many problems that need solving. I want someone who would be honest with me. You have always been honest, Minerva. Bluntly so at times."

"I see no reason to lie. But I can't imagine why you would choose me. We're almost always quarreling."

"Is that what you consider it?"

"What do you think it is?"

He considered it foreplay, but he wasn't going to tell her that.

Chapter 18

Dalton awoke early the next morning, took additional time shaving and dressing, and was in his library a good hour before he expected Minerva to arrive. He'd taken the precaution of sending Daniels for her. There was no need, he'd told her, to keep her driver waiting all day. What he didn't tell her was that by sending his own carriage, she couldn't suddenly announce that she changed her mind and leave precipitously.

Even so, he half expected her to send him a note explaining that she'd reconsidered the matter and wouldn't be arriving.

If she did that, he'd be disappointed. No, the word wasn't quite disappointed, but something more. She amused him, fascinated him, and interested him for hours. He couldn't remember the last time a woman had done that without being in his bed.

When the time came for her to arrive, he sat like a puppy awaiting a treat or a child anticipating a toy.

He had the sudden feeling he wasn't alone. A moment passed, then another, but no one spoke.

"Who is it?" he finally asked when his patience had expired.

"Sir, you have a visitor," Howington said.

He bit back his impatience at Howington and moderated his tone. "Show her in."

"It's not Miss Todd, sir. It's a Scot. He says he's your cousin. Duncan MacIain."

He had met his Scottish cousin twice in his life. Once when he was five and their Scottish relatives had visited at Gledfield. He had memories of running through the grounds merrily accompanying Duncan as they chased after one of the hunting hounds. On the second occasion, he'd been pulled into the family reunion when he was eleven, already deeming himself much too sophisticated for childish games. After all, he had been sent away to school by that time and thought he knew more than his parents or any Scottish relatives.

Duncan, he recalled, had been as standoffish, as if they were fighting a war of independence between themselves. They were a few months apart in age, but where he had few responsibilities, Duncan was being trained to assume the role of the head of the MacIain Mill in Glasgow.

The families, linked as they were to a common ancestor, were independent in every other way. The Scottish MacIains had become prosperous mill owners, while the English branch of the family was awarded an earldom and possessed a fortune that continued to grow.

"Shall I show him in, sir?"

A few weeks ago he would have sent Howington back to the door, explaining that he was too ill to see anyone. A lie to spare feelings wasn't really a lie, was it? But whose feelings would he be sparing—his or Duncan's?

"Yes," he said, daring himself. "When Miss Todd arrives, tell her I've been delayed a while, but show her into the parlor and have Mrs. Thompson serve her refreshments."

Howington left. At least, he assumed the man left,

because he didn't speak again and there was a feeling a vacancy in the room. One of these days his secretary would learn that he couldn't see him, so verbal cues were important. Or he would dismiss the man and hire someone else. He was leaning toward the latter.

"Mr. MacIain, Your Lordship," Howington announced.

"I didn't know you'd been injured," Duncan said, coming toward him.

The other man's hand clamped him on the shoulder, startling him not because of the touch, but the matter-of-factness in Duncan's voice. There wasn't a shred of pity in his tone.

"Damnable thing to have happened," Duncan added. "Are both eyes affected?"

"I can't see anything in the right," he said. "In the left only bright light."

"What a hell of a thing to be blind."

His Scottish cousin had more nerve than anyone he'd met since returning home, except, possibly, Minerva Todd.

"I was sorry to hear about Arthur, too. Do you think the MacIains are just in for a run of bad luck?"

"I don't doubt the American side of the family would think that, being in the southern states, but is the Scottish side having troubles as well?"

"The Americans' Civil War has played hell with us," Duncan said. "I've no cotton to loom and unless I get some soon, I'll have to shut down the mill."

That was a piece of bad news, but it could be worse. The mill closing could be fixed by money. If money could solve a problem, it wasn't really a problem.

He suspected his cousin hadn't come to London to renew old acquaintances but to obtain a loan.

"My mother had a fondness for your sister, I believe. How is Glynis?"

"Recently returned to Glasgow," Duncan said. "Her husband was with the British Legation in America. Unfortunately, she's now a widow."

"I'm sorry to hear that."

There were thousands of widows in America, and unless the war ended soon, there would be thousands more.

"I've recently returned from America myself."

"Were you wounded there?" Duncan asked, surprise lacing his voice.

Dalton smiled. "I was. Although nothing as honorable as being wounded in battle, I'm afraid. It was an assassination attempt."

"Good God. Are you sure?"

"Unfortunately, yes."

"Who on earth would want to assassinate you? Not someone hoping to become the next earl?"

"No," he said. "Although I should make a point of remaining healthy. We don't have an excess of MacIains to take on the title. There's only my brother Lewis left. After that, no doubt the title would pass to the Scottish side of the family."

"Then I hope both you and Lewis remain healthy for a good number of years," Duncan said. "I've no intention of being an English earl. Granted, the fortune would be nice. Which is why I'm here."

He liked this Scottish cousin of his. He was growing to appreciate frankness in people. Was that an offshoot of being around Minerva?

"I've laid off a third of my workforce and I'm faced with closing the mill my great-grandfather started if I can't find a way to make it through."

"And you need a loan."

"Not a loan," Duncan said, to his surprise. "An investor in an adventure."

Now he was intrigued.

"What kind of adventure do you have in mind?"

"I want you to finance a voyage to America. In exchange, I'll give you fifty percent of the profits."

"Why the hell would you want to go to America?"

"For cotton. It seems to me the only way to get any is to go after it myself."

So many emotions came rushing in that he didn't know what to say first. He wanted to caution Duncan that his idea was foolhardy. But if someone had done that to him, would he have listened? Would he have allowed rational thought to prevail?

"I've been in contact with our American cousins," Duncan said.

That was a surprise as well.

"I had every intention of visiting them," Dalton said. Two things had stopped him. The first, the fact that the American branch of the family was located in one of the southern states and he was fighting for the Union. Secondly, his injuries had put an end to anything but returning home.

Yet he'd carried a copy of the letter his great-great-great—and probably a few more greats—grandmother had penned to her sons as way of introduction. He'd heard about the home the MacIains had created in America. He hadn't had a chance to see it and now he never would.

The idea interested him. Not the profit portion of it, which would be considerable if Duncan made it back alive with a ship's hold filled with cotton. But the adventure angle, the idea that Duncan wasn't just going to sit there and allow Fate to happen to him. He admired that. He understood it.

God knows he had the funds to finance the voyage.

"You know how dangerous it is, don't you?"

"Yes."

A simple answer on the face of it. He might've said the same.

Dalton leaned forward, bracing his forearms on his desk. Duncan sat opposite him, swathed in blackness.

He had to make his cousin understand.

"I'm not just talking about the voyage, or even the blockade you have to run. You're going to a country at war. They're tearing themselves apart, Duncan, and they don't care who gets in the way. They'll kill you just like you're the enemy."

He didn't know if he could explain what war was like to someone who hadn't experienced it, but he knew he had to try.

"There isn't one waking hour that you're free of danger. There's not one moment you feel safe. Sometimes, the enemy has a uniform on, and sometimes they don't. Sometimes, an ally sounds like a southerner, or he might have the accent of a New Yorker. You can't tell."

He took a deep breath, waiting for Duncan to interrupt him with a dozen reasons why he still had to go. When the other man didn't say anything, Dalton continued.

"There isn't enough food to eat. There's only the ground to sleep on. You drink some swill that you've heated over the fire so you don't get dysentery from the river water. What you do manage to find to eat is jerky that's a year old or hardtack that's still managed to be riddled with bugs. You make friends only to see them die the next day. You get the smell of death in your nostrils and you know it will never leave you."

Sometimes at night, he woke to smell it again.

He didn't tell Duncan the most troubling aspect of war, that you make peace with the idea that you might die at any moment. You begin to almost welcome

Death since you've been worried about it so long. Then you stop worrying about it. You know, with a deep and troubling certainty, that you will die, and it strangely doesn't bother you.

No, with any luck, his cousin wouldn't have that experience.

Duncan didn't speak for a moment.

"I don't have a choice," he finally said. "I have to try. I can't let the mill fail."

Had he ever been as idealistic? Or driven by a goal? Even going to America to fight had been more a way to break the ennui of his life than any bone deep necessity.

"I've more than five hundred people relying on me," Duncan continued, as if Dalton's silence weighed heavily on him.

Not one person had ever depended on him. Not one soul had ever said: *Your actions matter to my life.*

A curious feeling surfeited him then, one he couldn't quite recognize. Not shame, although that was a part of it. Not regret, although some of that was also present. Envy? Did he envy his Scottish cousin?

What the hell was wrong with him?

"I'll help you," he said, before he could talk himself out of it.

"I'M SORRY you have to wait, Miss Todd," Mrs. Thompson said, entering the parlor. "His Lordship's Scottish cousin appeared this morning, without a hint of notice. But I like surprises like that, don't you?"

She really didn't know how to answer that question, so she nodded and smiled.

"I do so love a Scottish brogue. There can't be any more delightful a sound. And a man in a kilt is a sight to cause a woman's heart to flutter."

"I travel to Scotland quite frequently," she said.

The older woman waved the maid off and set about preparing tea for Minerva.

"Do you now? Now that is a wondrous thing, for a young woman such as yourself to be able to travel. What freedom. Do you often encounter men in kilts?"

"I'm afraid I don't, Mrs. Thompson."

"Oh, well, we can't always have what we wish, can we?" She smiled at Minerva and brought her a cup of tea.

She took it with thanks.

"Like the earl. A shame what happened to him. I've been tending to things for His Lordship ever since he set up his own establishment. Of course, at the time, he wasn't His Lordship, you know. He was simply Dalton MacIain. That's who's with him now, another MacIain. From Glasgow, he is."

She clucked her tongue. "And here I am, gossiping away. Please forgive me."

"There's nothing to forgive," Minerva said. "Besides, it's not so much gossip as it is simply information."

Mrs. Thompson beamed at her. "How understanding you are, my dear. How lovely that the earl has employed you to help him."

She wanted to explain that she wasn't quite sure why the earl had employed her, but she was almost certain it wasn't for her understanding nature. A strange employment, since they'd never agreed on duties or salary.

"You'll find he's quite fair. He's always been that way, ever since the very beginning. He's never treated the staff with anything but respect and he's never made untoward suggestions toward the maids. Nor has he ever asked any of us to do something we wouldn't feel comfortable doing. I understand His Lordship's reputation, but you mustn't worry. He is not that way, not at home."

"Thank you," she said, hoping it would be enough of a response.

"I worry about him, I do. What with his sadness about his brother. And being blind and all. I say a prayer every day that he regains some of his sight, and if he doesn't, that he comes to accept God's will."

She couldn't see the Earl of Rathsmere placidly accepting what God had in store for him, but she didn't say that to the housekeeper.

"He's been such a recluse ever since he came home. Burying himself in his library. I think he considers himself grotesque, Miss Todd. Something that must be hidden away lest he frighten the children."

"Nonsense. Granted, he has a few scars, but the eye patch makes him look, well, rakish, if nothing else."

"Exactly," Mrs. Thompson said, smiling. "Oh, I know you're going to be good for him."

To that, she had absolutely no response at all, so she settled for a smile.

She had no business helping the Earl of Rathsmere with his reading. The very idea of being here was somewhat shocking. Heaven knows what the Covington sisters would do if they learned about the situation.

Even her mother might have looked askance at her.

She could almost hear her mother's question now. *Dearest Minerva, are you sure this is wise?*

No, it wasn't at all wise.

Dalton MacIain was both autocratic and plebeian, enigmatic and too revealing. He was an object of compassion and, strangely enough, she was growing to admire him. If that wasn't a sign of her insanity, she didn't know what was.

He was a danger to Neville, but even more than that, she suspected he was a danger to her as well.

She had never been a romantic. She had never listened to music and allowed her heart to soar or her imagination to lead her to places where she could never go in reality. She had never read a novel and wished herself the heroine. Nor had she ever sighed over a handsome man.

For her, character was what counted above all, and it was all too obvious that Dalton MacIain was lacking in character. He had refused to listen to her about Neville. He adamantly refused to believe that Neville was innocent.

By coming here, by assisting the earl, she might be able to alter his behavior and his actions. She would certainly be in a better position to protect Neville than she would be if she sat at home.

That's what she told herself.

There was no need for her pulse to spike as she waited. *Really, Minerva, mind yourself around the man.*

How, exactly, did she do that?

Chapter 19

"*W*hat you want me to do?" Minerva asked.

"What are you doing right now?"

"I'm sitting in front of your desk, looking intently at you and smiling just a little."

She amused him, and he realized he hadn't been amused for quite some time.

"I've been asked to make some decisions by my solicitor," Dalton said. "Evidently, he sent a brief, describing each situation. I need to have you read those."

"Very well," she said. "I've been told I have a quite a good reading voice."

"I enjoy listening to you speak," he said.

"Oh. Is that why you asked me to help you?"

"You have a distinctive way of speaking. As if you weigh each word and give it extra solemnity."

"I don't think I weigh my words, especially with you."

"Actually, your voice is only part of the reason. I find myself annoyed at my secretary most of the time."

"What has poor Howington done to deserve your annoyance?"

"Poor Howington? What has the man done to deserve your sympathy?"

"I can't imagine working for you is an easy occupation. No doubt you bark orders and expect people to do phenomenal things at all hours."

"I do not," he countered. "I barely ask Howington to do anything. And I never disturb him after hours."

"Never?"

"No. He doesn't live here."

"Ah," she said.

"What does that mean?"

"It means you can't belabor him because he isn't here, not that you wouldn't."

"Are you going to belabor me with all my imagined flaws and faults?"

"Imagined?" she said.

"Your voice is only one of the reasons why I asked you to help me," he said.

Perhaps he was reverting to his Scottish heritage. Or becoming more like Minerva, with her startling frankness. He had the oddest sensation that he should tell her the truth.

What would he say?

I find I like being around you. There's something about you that's refreshing.

Instead, all he said was, "You're unlike any other woman I've ever known."

"No doubt because other women fall at your feet in admiration, Your Lordship. I shall not be overcome."

"That's reassuring." He couldn't help his sarcastic tone, because he had no illusions as to his appearance. He might have once had some attraction for the opposite sex. Some of that might have been his physical appearance, his reputation, or his fortune. Now all he had was his fortune.

He reached down into the bottom drawer on the right-hand side of the desk, pulling out a sheaf of papers. His solicitor had sent him five issues that needed to be resolved. With each one, Benny had sent a single sheet explaining the situation along with a packet of information for more in-depth study.

"And I'd like it if you wouldn't 'Your Lordship' me to death," Dalton said. "Howington does that and it is grating to the extreme."

"What would you like the poor man to call you? Your Excellency? O Exalted One?"

He smiled. " 'Sir' is just fine from Howington. You can call me Dalton."

"Well that's only fair, isn't it? You already call me Minerva. Not that I gave you permission."

" 'Miss Todd' seems extraordinarily proper, and I wouldn't exactly call our relationship proper, would you?"

"Do we have a relationship?"

They had something and he wasn't sure what he would call it.

"I think we have a truce," Minerva said. "You're all for declaring my brother a murderer and I'm prepared to protect him."

"So you enter the lion's den for the express purpose of taming the beast, is that it?"

"Can I? I've never thought of myself as a lion tamer."

He pushed the first packet across the desk to her.

"What do you want me to do?"

"Begin with the summary sheet. Then, look in the packet and see if there's anything I need to know."

She took the envelope from him.

After reading it, she said, "It seems your neighbor wants to use your water. It's a petition to utilize the sluice on Deton River feeding into Gledfield Lake. What is Gledfield?"

"Our country house," he said. "It was where I was raised."

"Not in London?"

"No. What about you? Were you raised in London?"

"I was, yes. We didn't have a country house. My parents loved the city."

He sat back, placing his hands on the arms of his chair. "Do you feel the same?"

"I don't, actually. I prefer Scotland and the solitude of one of my expeditions. I have a sponsor, Lady Terry. Her husband, Sir Francis, was awarded a baronetcy for his copper mine in Portugal. The poor man died only months later. Five years ago she bought land in Scotland. There's a ruined castle on it. We've found quite a few things there."

"So you're to the past what James Wilson is to the present?

She laughed, a surprisingly lighthearted sound that made him smile as well.

"So I'm an investigator? I suppose I am. I've always thought of myself as a caretaker. I very carefully unearth what I find, examine it, catalog it, and try to protect it as much as possible while I learn everything I can."

"Have you ever worked in England? Or only Scotland?"

"There aren't that many female archaeologists," she said. "I don't know if I can even call myself an archaeologist. I have the interest. I've taught myself everything I can, but I never had any formal training. Nor have I been able to join any of the scientific communities. Therefore, without a sponsor, it would be very unusual for me to be invited to a dig. That's why I'm incredibly grateful to Lady Terry.

"Will you allow them to use your water?" she asked, changing the subject so quickly that he was startled.

"What's it for? I don't mind diverting a little of the river if it's to irrigate crops or fields. But I don't think it would be a good idea if it's just to build an ornamental lake."

"But it sounds as if you have an ornamental lake of your own."

"Gledfield Lake is a natural phenomenon."

He heard the sounds of the packet being opened.

"I have something that looks like drawings," she said. "Plus a letter from your neighbor and a selection of other documents. Should I go through them one by one?"

"Please."

For the next quarter hour, Minerva read, making few comments but asking a share of questions, all about Gledfield. He couldn't get the image of her out of his mind, waist deep in a hole in her trousers skirt, digging away with a shovel. Dirt smeared on her face and a bright smile indicated how happy she was.

What an astounding woman.

"Well?" she asked.

"Well, what?"

"Have you decided to give him the water? It's for his wife's garden. Evidently she has it in her mind to grow flowers. From what I can see of the plans, lots and lots of flowers."

"What would you do?"

"I'd give him the water, but I would only make it for a certain period of time," she said. "Perhaps a year. No more than that at first. Then, if there is no effect on Gledfield's lake or the rest of the river, perhaps you can negotiate for a longer time frame."

"An excellent outcome," he said. "Why don't you make a note to that effect on the summary sheet and we'll dispense of that one."

The next case had to do with one of the farmers who worked a plot of land belonging to Gledfield. He needed a new plow and was insistent that the irrigation gates be replaced.

"There isn't a note from the farmer," Minerva said. "But this doesn't appear to be in your solicitor's handwriting, either. Could it be your brother's?"

"Arthur?"

He stretched out his hand, not entirely certain what he wanted. When she handed him the note, he placed his right hand atop it, almost as if he wished to absorb some part of Arthur.

He handed it back to Minerva. "Do his *y*'s have strange little tails?"

"Yes," she said. "And his *j*'s, too. He doesn't sign it, but he began a sentence with an *A* and it's larger than the rest of the words."

"Then it is from Arthur. What does he say?"

"That Mr. Thornton has been at Gledfield for more than twenty years. He's never been known to be profligate and he's well-versed in irrigation."

"Tell Benny to advance him whatever funds he needs."

"I quite like working with you," she said, startling him. "It's almost as if you're the king and you have the power over all your subjects. Do you ever get to adjudicate morals, by any chance? Punish a man because he's unfaithful to his wife or admonish a maid because she made off with a silver fork?"

"Dear God, I hope not. I've never heard of any kind of moral court. I'd hardly be one to sit in judgment."

"I wouldn't be so critical of yourself, Dalton. They say reformed rakes are the most steadfast of people."

"Who says that? Besides, is there really such a thing as a reformed rake or just a rake who hasn't been, well, rakish lately?"

"What would you call yourself? A reformed rake? Or one who simply hasn't been naughty lately?"

Laughter burst out of him before he could hold it back. "I don't think I would call myself naughty, Minerva."

"No, but you were thought of as wicked." A more somber note crept into her voice. "Was it worth it?"

"Was what worth it?"

"The shame you felt at your behavior."

Did the woman have some kind of pathway into his brain?

"What about you, Minerva? What about your trouser skirts and your digging for artifacts? Did you never think people would call you wicked?"

"They would call me something," she said, "but I doubt it would be wicked. Foolish, perhaps. Or loony. I've heard that once or twice. It's as if people need someone about whom to talk. They like having a scapegoat in their midst, someone who is odd enough to attract attention. If there isn't anyone like that in a group, sometimes people turn on themselves."

"You're very wise for someone as young as you are."

"I'm not that young," she said. "I would dare say I'm the same age as you or thereabouts."

"That old?"

"Old enough to be considered on the shelf and nearly at spinster stage."

"Did you never want to marry?"

"I did, when I was younger. But then there was Neville to consider. Most of my energies went to raising him. Thankfully, there was no problem about money, so I didn't need an occupation in addition to being his sister and quasimother."

"But as Neville grew? Surely he didn't require all your hours. Wasn't there time to go to a social or a dance or even a meeting where you might have met some acceptable young men?"

She hesitated for so long, he wondered if he'd offended her.

"That's the question, isn't it?" she finally said. "Acceptable. You see, I had become interested in archaeology by then and it became a consuming passion. I wanted to do things more than I wanted to be married. No one with whom I spoke was the least bit interested."

"But you did have an offer or two, didn't you?" he asked, guessing. "Were the Covington sisters shocked when you turned down your suitors?"

"They approved of the first one. He was in banking and very respectable. Not so the second. He was one of Lady Terry's relatives who had developed a *tendre* for me on a dig. I'm afraid he wasn't suitable at all, according to them."

"What about you? Did the banker or the relative tempt you to marriage? Just a little bit?"

She sighed heavily. "No. Isn't that a terrible thing to admit? Shall we go on to the next packet?"

He was strangely loath to do so. Instead he wanted to know more about her.

"Which one initiated you into womanhood?" he asked. "The banker or the relative?"

"Neither," she said. "That was my driver."

"I BEG your pardon?"

She smiled, glad that he wasn't the only one who could be shocking. She had bent the rules of propriety as well. Perhaps not as publicly as he, but just as surely.

"I had reached a certain age," she said, more than willing to explain the situation to him. She wasn't ashamed of her actions, after all. They had seemed rational and reasonable at the time. "I knew I wasn't going to marry. And I had already felt a stirring of emotions."

"The need for release, I take it?"

Her smile broadened. "Exactly. I looked around, considered all my options, and selected Hugh. After all, he was the most attractive. He's very tall and he has broad shoulders and quite a handsome face."

"Did you pay him?"

"Of course not. I only offered myself to him with no guarantees of affection or future between us. I laid out the situation systematically and asked if he might be interested."

"I take it the man wasn't a fool and accepted your offer?"

"He did. It was quite enjoyable for a deflowering. Why ever do they call it that? I'm not a flower. I had the image of a bee buzzing around me, but of course, Hugh wasn't a bee."

When he didn't say anything, she looked up from the paper. He was staring in the direction of the sideboard.

"Would you like a whiskey?"

"Yes," he said. "More than anything in the world at the moment."

She stood.

"But I'm not going to have one."

She sat back down. "Why not?"

"Because whiskey has become my best friend of late. A crutch, if you will. I like how it feels when the world is a haze around me and I'm numb to my feelings. A warning, if nothing else, that it's a false friend or I'm on my way to becoming dependent on it. I credit my awakening to a certain woman of my acquaintance. She called me a drunkard, as I remember."

He turned his face in her direction again and she was once more startled at his appearance. She'd often thought Hugh was the most handsome man of her acquaintance, but compared to the Earl of Rathsmere, he was almost plain. What was it about Dalton that separated him from other men? An intensity, perhaps. A way of looking at her that seemed to spear through her, even though he had no sight in that eye.

"Are you still sleeping with your driver?"

"No," she said, surprised at the question. "There

were only a few occasions. I felt about passion the
same way you feel about whiskey. It can be just as ad-
dictive as spirits, I think. And I shouldn't have called
you a drunkard."

He ignored her apology for another question. "So
you enjoyed it?"

"Very much. I liked being touched. And kissed."

"I'm surprised your driver allowed you to call a halt
to the relationship."

"Why should you be? I went into the situation explaining that it was transient at best. There was no
promise of anything in the future."

"And he didn't protest?"

"He did," she said, admitting that reluctantly. "But
as much as I enjoyed passion, it frightened me a little."

"Because you could become lost in it," he said, nodding toward the sideboard.

"Because I could become lost in it."

"Did the Covington sisters know about your arrangement?"

"I can't imagine how they would know, unless they
could see into my bedroom. I was extremely discreet.
Much more so than you."

"Me?"

"Even I knew about your relationship with the
famous actress. Then there was that shocking duchess.
Then the dancer. I used to think you sought out the
most flamboyant women on purpose."

"And what would that be?" he asked, his voice
sharp enough to cut glass.

"The better to be shocking, perhaps. Or to encour-
age people to talk about you. You had nothing else to
do with your time."

He sat up straight, both forearms on the desk, hands
flat on the blotter. If he could see, she would have been
immolated with that glance.

"Are you implying that my behavior was because I was bored?"

"Of course. Weren't you? What a pity your brother didn't involve you with his work earlier. You're quite fair and you could have handled all of these problems easily, don't you think?"

Blind or not, he had a penetrating stare.

She smiled back at him, determined not to wilt in the face of the anger she could feel rolling off him.

"You are the most astounding woman," he said.

"Why, because I'm honest? I think you'll make a very good earl if you continue as you've started."

He didn't say anything, which was just as well. She had no intention of complimenting the Earl of Rathsmere.

Nor of liking the blasted man.

Chapter 20

$\mathcal{M}$inerva hadn't been able to sleep well, which she put at the feet of the Earl of Rathsmere. For some idiotic reason, she kept replaying their conversations in her mind.

If she looked at his left profile, she could hardly tell that he'd been injured at all. He had a habit of blinking and turning his head in the direction of the speaker, just as he might if he could still see. Occasionally, it was disconcerting to find herself the object of his blue-eyed stare.

From time to time she had to look away.

Sheer attractiveness might have once rendered the Earl of Rathsmere irresistible. She could easily see why endless women had tumbled onto his bed.

But beauty was in the eyes of the beholder, was it not? Therefore, there was something about her that found him irresistible as well. What was lacking in her character that could so easily ignore his flaws?

He had a temper and he didn't mind showing it. He was often unreasonable and argumentative. He gave her orders and he expected her to obey.

Yet when he spoke of his brother, there was a note in his voice that hadn't been there before: a fondness, sorrow, and perhaps a certain regret.

What was life like for Dalton now? He couldn't carouse and he couldn't shock society. What was he going to do with his life? What did former rakes do? Other than trying to find Neville, of course.

She must simply attempt to convince him of Neville's innocence.

Why on earth had she told him about the Covington sisters? Why had she given him a mental picture of herself racing down the street, petticoats bouncing in the wind? He was deceptively easy to talk to, and she'd felt a kinship to him, which was idiotic, of course. She had nothing in common with the Earl of Rathsmere. She was the exact opposite in all ways.

He had been society's scamp.

She had done everything she could to avoid society in every degree.

He had charmed countless women into shedding their clothes.

She'd only had one lover.

The Earl of Rathsmere indulged in passion whole-heartedly.

Passion was a drug, she discovered, an opiate of the senses. She could just as well do without it.

No, they had nothing in common. Not one scintilla of interest.

Yet something warm blossomed in her in Dalton's presence. A feeling that was idiotic at best and disloyal to Neville at worst.

This Dalton MacIain avoided society. Was it because of circumstance? Or was he truly changed? Had going to America altered his basic character?

The fact that she wanted to know was a danger sign.

She really shouldn't return this morning. She should send a note to him explaining that she had other, more important things to do.

None of the books she'd meant to read had been opened. In addition, she was behind in her correspondence and in answering several requests. Nor had she finished cataloging the newest finds from her last expedition.

She moved to her secretary to write the note only to discover that Mrs. Beauchamp had placed her incoming correspondence on the tray just for that purpose.

Picking up the first letter from Lady Terry, she opened it reluctantly.

The handwriting was shaky, so different from Lady Terry's elaborate script that she was startled.

My dearest Minerva, the letter began:

> *Time is marching on as time does. I have not felt well enough to explore the castle of late. In other years I might have left Scotland for sunny France, but even that seems beyond me now. I had hoped to see you soon. Is there a chance of that? I do understand about your dear brother. Please do not think I'm unaware of your fears, but you have proven to be such a joy in my life that I wanted to see you once more.*

Shame enveloped her, turned the back of her neck warm. She really should have found time to go to Scotland, but she'd been so worried about Neville.

The two had met when Minerva was exploring Partage Castle in Scotland. Lady Terry introduced herself, explaining that she was looking for property to purchase. The older woman had gone on to buy the castle along with acres of surrounding land.

When Lady Terry wrote and invited her to further explore Partage, she'd been thrilled.

She hadn't expected to develop a fondness for the septuagenarian. She enjoyed Lady Terry's company, sharing what she learned about Partage Castle as well as discoveries she'd made on other sites. Lady Terry's

questions had revealed a similar interest and a surprising sense of humor.

She really did need to write the dear woman. Even
more important, she needed to find a way to go to Scotland. Lady Terry's health was obviously failing. Besides, a visit to Scotland was a better occupation than
whiling away her time with the Earl of Rathsmere.

She'd go as soon as Neville was found.

Where was Neville? Not in London, she was beginning to suspect. She had the most terrible feeling he
was still in America. If he'd been hurt or killed, would
she ever know? Would word somehow come to her?

Turning, she stared out the window at the coming
day. The clouds were scuttling across the London sky,
promising fresh breezes and no hint of rain. A perfect
day to travel to Scotland. An ideal time to board the
train to Glasgow. She would need a few hours to as-
semble her equipment, but she could manage.

Yet Dalton would be expecting her.

She wanted to dismiss the memory of him sitting
at his desk, his hands clenched, his face carefully
stoic. His voice had trembled when he asked about his
brother's handwriting. His laughter had surprised her,
but she began to watch for it. Perhaps she even incited
it with her comments.

Their arrangement was casual, not one of employer
and employee. She could easily send him a note, something simple to explain that she was due in Scotland.

For the first time in her life the idea of an expedition
didn't fill her with excitement. She wasn't the least bit
eager to board the train.

THERE WAS a fifty-fifty chance Minerva wouldn't
return. Dalton bet himself that she'd come. This was
the woman, after all, who had broken into his home in
order to speak to him.

Curiosity would compel her, if nothing else.

Would she still be curious about him? Or would she be disgusted?

He'd told her too much of the truth yesterday. He'd let down his guard. He hadn't been the least bit charming.

Her blunt way of speaking fascinated him. She skewered him with words, thought nothing of his wealth or his new title, despised his reputation, and made him work for any crumb of acknowledgment.

She didn't hesitate to reveal herself, a frankness that startled and amazed him. Was it because she was plain?

Although her face had felt— His thoughts stumbled to a halt. He had put his hands on her face as he'd never done to another woman, at least one who hadn't yet shared his bed.

What had James said? What had a smile done to her face?

He raised his hand, splaying his fingers as if he could see them. He could still recall the softness of her skin, the contour of her cheeks. Her chin wasn't pointed as much as squared, her jaw firm. He'd felt her tension when he touched her. Had she clamped her teeth together rather than speak in that moment?

What had Minerva said? That he needed release? Maybe that was it. He was craving the company of a woman. That was why she occupied his thoughts. He didn't want to see any of his former acquaintances. The idea of a woman he'd once known feeling sorry for him was enough to make him celibate for the rest of his life. Nor did he want to pay for his pleasure. He had no intention of being blind *and* having the pox.

Would Minerva come today?

Benny had sent more cases, which meant decisions he had to make, things he needed to buy, investments he should consider. Even if Minerva didn't return, he'd find a way to continue the work, a way that didn't involve Howington.

Like it or not, he was the Earl of Rathsmere. He had a heritage he had to uphold and responsibilities that didn't feel as onerous as they might have once.

Would she come today?

Why did it matter so much?

A knock on the library door startled him.

"Your Lordship," Mrs. Thompson said, "Mr. Wilson is here to see you."

It wasn't yet nine. Nor had he expected to see James today. A leaden feeling settled in his stomach.

"Show him in, please, Mrs. Thompson."

"Very well, sir. I'll bring tea, shall I?"

He nodded, grateful when the gesture wasn't accompanied by a rolling feeling of nausea.

When James entered his library, he asked him to close the door. He didn't want anyone overhearing this meeting.

"You found something," he said in greeting.

"I don't know what I've found," James said. "The staff at Gledfield are loyal, Dalton. They love your family. To a man, they all think Arthur's death untimely, especially since no one was ever found to be responsible."

"No errant hunters on our property," he said.

"No."

He nodded again.

"One thing . . ." James said. He hesitated so long that Dalton knew it wasn't going to be good news. "Did you know Lewis was there when Arthur was killed?"

Dalton clasped his hands together, interlacing his fingers and gripping so tightly he was causing himself pain.

"No, I didn't know. Nor did Lewis say anything."

"He was," James said. "According to the staff, he left directly after Arthur's funeral."

"Do you think he had something to do with Arthur's death?"

There, he asked the question aloud.

He took a deep breath and felt something slide into place. He'd pushed away the thought each time it had come to him, not wanting to believe Lewis would have killed Arthur.

"I don't know," James said. "There's the question of why he was at Gledfield."

"Lewis went through his inheritance in record time. Maybe he went there to beg money from Arthur."

"Would Arthur have given it to him?"

He remembered what Lewis said. "I don't think so."

"Did he want the title that much?" James asked.

The question shocked him into silence.

"Aren't you forgetting me?" he finally asked. "There was one brother between Lewis and the title."

"Unless you consider the premise that Neville acted on Lewis's behalf. Maybe Neville was to make sure you died in America."

Had James considered that idea all the way back from Gledfield?

"Lewis didn't know my friends," he said.

"Are you sure that's true? He couldn't have met Neville anywhere?"

"Why would Neville do such a thing? For money? According to his sister, Neville had his own fortune."

"Are you siding with Miss Todd now in her determination that her brother is innocent?"

He wanted to, God help him, and that was such a startling thought that he put it away to examine later.

"I don't see how I can," he said. "I saw him raise his

pistol. I saw him fire at me. That's not something you can easily forget."

"It would be the perfect crime, Dalton. Lewis wouldn't be suspected, especially if your death happened with an ocean between the two of you. And, if God forbid, something happened to Neville, there would never be anyone to divulge Lewis's part in all this."

"Do you think he's behind Neville's disappearance?"

"I don't know," James said. "It's a thought to consider."

Dalton nodded again.

"What do you want me to do?" James asked.

"I don't know," Dalton said. "I haven't gotten that far in my thinking."

He didn't want to consider that Lewis might be responsible for Arthur's death or that his brother had somehow convinced Neville to kill him. Yet it made sense in a sickening way.

"Lewis is a damn good shot," he said. "Was he in the house when Arthur was killed?"

"No one saw him."

"Do they think he killed Arthur? Does the staff think that? Samuels, Mrs. MacNeal, and the others?" People who had cared for and loved his mother and felt the same about Arthur. "What about Alice?"

"I didn't come out and ask them who they think shot Arthur," James said. "Samuels looked at me oddly when I asked where Lewis was when Arthur was killed. I think he suspects something. As to Alice, I haven't talked to her yet."

"Then maybe I should hold back any judgment until you do."

"I would advise against confronting Lewis," James said. "Besides, such an accusation would destroy any future relationship with your brother. Not to mention trust."

"I could trust Arthur with my life," he said. "I wouldn't trust Lewis with a biscuit."

James was smart enough not to say a word in response.

Chapter 21

$\mathcal{M}$inerva arrived only minutes after James left. To his surprise, she was brusque and businesslike, insisting that she didn't want tea, thank you, and shall we begin immediately, Your Lordship?

When had he become Your Lordship again?

He didn't protest, merely retrieved the packets Benny had sent and began to work.

She didn't smell of cinnamon today. Had she changed scents deliberately? He could only detect that odd dusty odor. Where did she acquire that? Were her clothes hung in the attic?

Was she wearing her trousers skirt? He almost asked her, then decided it was better if they maintained this restrained, almost cold behavior.

Her words were clipped, each of them precise. Twice she stopped herself in mid-sentence as if she were monitoring her speech.

After the question of the egress to one of the farms was resolved, he heard her put the packet on the adjoining chair.

"You loved Arthur very much, didn't you?" she asked.

Coming on the heels of what he'd learned from James, the question threw him into the past.

No one had ever asked him how he felt about his brother. Most of his friends thought he considered Arthur a millstone, the elder brother, the earl, someone who would contain and constrain his lifestyle if he could. The truth was somewhat different.

"Yes," he said. "I loved him a great deal. I respected him. He was everything an older brother should be. I'm afraid I can't say the same about me in regards to my younger brother, Lewis."

"Perhaps you'll ease into the role," she said.

Did she only see the good in people? First Neville and now him. Neither of them was worthy of her good thoughts. Was her driver in the same category?

She readily admitted to being shocking, in such an artless way that he wanted to caution her not to do so with just anyone. Her story might be used as fodder to hurt her, cause tongues to wag, and hateful things to be said about her.

A man's worth was somehow enhanced by his disreputable character. A woman could be ruined by the same behavior.

He reached for a few more cases, placing them on the desk between them.

As they continued going through the packets, his admiration of her way of thinking, her practicality, grew. He'd never considered the women he knew as pragmatic. When he made the mistake of saying that to her, she responded with a pert comment.

"You've never met the right women."

"You might be right."

"There's no question I'm right. Just consider who you associated with, Dalton. They had fortunes or husbands. They didn't need to be practical. They didn't have anyone relying on them."

Until Arthur's death no one had depended on him, either, a comment he didn't voice.

He sat back in his chair and looked in her direction. Did she study him? Did she remark, mentally, upon his scars?

"Thank you for your assistance. You've made it much more pleasant than dealing with Howington."

"Why do you still employ him as your secretary when you dislike him?"

"When he first came to work for me, I didn't find anything wrong with him. He was very competent and he's probably still doing a good job. But something about the man grates on me. It's a feeling I have, like something you can't remember or a tune you can't stop humming." He shook his head, wondering if he could truly explain. "I can't put my finger on it and that's why I don't dismiss him."

"Because it doesn't seem fair?"

He nodded. "Before I dismiss him, I'd like to have a rational reason for doing so. Maybe I don't dislike Howington as much as envy him."

"Why envy Howington?"

"It could be any man, I suppose. Perhaps I envy him the ability to read. To write. To walk into a room and know whether it's day or night. To write a bank draft. To know how much money is in his pocket. To know if he's stained his shirt or cut himself shaving. To not frighten children with his appearance."

She didn't say anything for a moment. He was damned if he wanted her pity.

"Poor Howington," she finally said. "To have to bear the brunt of your being a grumbly bear."

"I am not a bear," he said. "As for grumbly, I suppose I am."

"I'm surprised that you're envious of anyone."

He inclined his head. "I confess to being beset with as many human emotions as anyone else, Minerva. What about you? Are you ever envious of another woman?"

"Sometimes the Covington sisters," she said, to his surprise. "They have each other. As obnoxious and annoying as they can be, they dote on each other. They're family. I don't have a sister and I've always wished for one."

And now she didn't have a brother.

He suddenly understood her in a way that surprised him. Family was vitally important to her. Family gave you protection. Family offered unconditional love.

Minerva wasn't a law unto herself. She wasn't alone and separate from others because she wished it. She had simply adapted to the circumstances that life gave her and made the best of them.

Neville was family.

In a perfect world, Neville would be the loyal little brother. Would she, in this perfect world he imagined for her, have married and had children? He could envision her as a mother. Part of her character would insist on pushing her babies out of the nest, inciting them to go and explore and find themselves, while at the same time guarding them with her life.

How did she see him? A despoiler of innocents, a man separated from his life of debauchery by a certain level of tragedy. A man so bored with life that he'd enlivened it by being a source of gossip.

He'd come to the same conclusion months before she had.

If his sight were magically restored tomorrow, if he woke and could see in his left eye, would he go back to the life he lived before America? A question he'd never before asked himself, and one that troubled him now.

How did he expunge those images he'd seen in America? How did he remove the scars incised on his soul? How did he forget the men he knew, some whom he'd admired, most he'd liked, fallen on the field of battle? Men from Rhode Island, Massachusetts, New York, some places he'd never heard of before going to America.

Each one of them seemed a reminder to him. Not of Dalton MacIain, pre-America, but of a Dalton who was like them, separated from family and those he loved, aching for home and a better time. Thinking that all he needed to be happy was a cessation of gunfire and the smell of flowers or baking bread instead of blood.

If, somehow, magic happened and he awoke with the ability to see the day, would one of his first acts be to go to a gaming hell or wander into one of the ton's innumerable entertainments and announce himself home again?

Would he seek out those sycophants who had yet to call on him, those widows and straying wives who had never sent him a note or card? Or would he be bound to a better nature, something that was growing inside of him now, a need, an urge, a wish to be more like Arthur and less like Lewis?

Would his blindness be an eternal reminder of who he had been? Or a goad to be something more?

He was not the Rake of London. He was only himself, mortal and humbled, the yoke of responsibility hung around his neck in the form of an earldom. A title for which his brother had probably killed.

What was he going to do about Lewis? Summon the authorities and give them his suspicions? Would that be enough? Would Lewis escape punishment for taking a life?

He brought himself back to the conversation.

"You wouldn't frighten people in the least, Dalton, if you ventured out into society more," Minerva said. "Especially since you started wearing an eye patch. You look quite dashing with it."

"Mrs. Thompson made it," he said, then wondered why he had. Was it so important that he give the woman credit? Yes, it was.

"She does like you," she said.

"How do you know that?"

"She always smiles when speaking of you. There's always a very maternal look in her eyes."

"Good God."

"You don't like people caring for you?"

How had this conversation been turned on its ear? Minerva had a way of doing exactly that.

"Why on earth would I want to venture out into society?" he asked.

"To be part of it again," she said.

He smiled. "I was one of them once. I lost my calling card on the battlefields of America, in places like Manassas and Leesburg."

"Is there nothing about society you miss?"

"Absolutely nothing," he said, realizing it was true.

"Nothing you want to experience again?"

"No."

"Then what will you do with the rest of your life? Act the part of recluse?"

"I'm finding that it has its pleasures."

"Have you always been able to dictate the terms of your life?"

"Once I obtained my majority, yes. Money brings with it a certain freedom, Minerva. Neville no doubt felt the same."

There, he needed to bring Neville back into the conversation. He needed to right himself, else he would capsize in a sea of words.

"Didn't you feel the same when you came into your fortune?" he asked.

"No," she said, "since it was obtained only after my parents died."

He wanted to call back the question and apologize, but she continued.

"Women are expected to adhere to a certain position in life. Your wayward duchesses and dance hall girls are the exceptions. The rest of us are exceedingly proper."

"There aren't that many of you who are exceedingly proper, Minerva. You would be surprised at how many women wish to be wicked."

"See? That comment alone makes me think you miss society. Or your hedonism, if nothing else."

"Ah, because men have needs, is that it? Because we all need release, I believe."

She didn't speak for so long he wondered if she was embarrassed. Were her cheeks red? What about the tips of her ears? Or was she simply staring at him narrow-eyed, her lips pursed in annoyance?

He evidently had the ability to annoy Minerva very quickly.

"Well, yes," she finally said. "But you have a mistress, don't you?"

He had never had a conversation about sex with any woman, let alone in his library, at his desk. That it was happening with Minerva Todd didn't surprise him, however.

"A mistress? I can assure you, Minerva, that I don't have a mistress."

"Perhaps not now, but once. Do you not think a man should provide for any offspring of an illicit union?"

"I do believe a man should provide for his offspring, however they were introduced into the world."

"Good," she said, in such a particularly officious tone that he was annoyed.

"I'm happy I meet with your approval. What about you? No more lovers among your staff? Have you a footman or two? Are you going through the servants one by one?"

"No, I haven't a footman, and no, I'm not going through the servants one by one." She sounded insulted. "Perhaps I have a gentleman caller."

"I doubt it."

"Why? You consider me so plain that I wouldn't attract any man? Perhaps they're hungry for my fortune."

"You're most definitely not plain. I've felt your face, remember? If you had a gentleman caller you would have told me about him already. You might have even bragged about the fact. You've told me everything else about your life."

"I have not."

"Then tell me what you haven't mentioned," he dared her. "Something that you've held back because it's too personal."

She didn't speak, but he heard her skirt brush against the desk as she stood. Had he truly insulted her this time?

"Forgive me. I shouldn't have said that."

"Neville," she said.

"I beg your pardon?"

"I'm afraid you might be right about Neville. If you are, I don't know what I'm going to do."

The door opened, then shut, and the room was curiously empty without her.

Chapter 22

$\mathcal{M}$inerva walked into her storeroom, closing the door behind her. This room was her sanctuary, more than any other place in her home, especially at this hour of the day. Here, the servants knew not to bother her, even to knock on the door to announce a visitor. As far as she was concerned, when she was in this room, visitors could go to perdition.

Right at the moment she felt that way about the entire world.

She loved the early morning. At this time of day the house was quiet. She could get a great deal of work done, but also be alone to think.

In the past, she'd looked at the storeroom as a place of solace. Today, however, she was so miserable she doubted even her work could take her mind from her troubles.

The room was large but made smaller by open shelving lining each wall. Shelves even obscured the lone window, and if there had been a fireplace in the room, she would've placed shelves in front of it as well. As it was, the room was cool during the summer, though almost frigid in the winter.

Scraps of fabric and pottery filled the boxes on each shelf, each carefully labeled with a string and tag.

Since she was a little girl, Minerva had been fasci-nated with the past. The people who lived five hundred years ago captured her attention more than the living. She wanted to know about their lives, their hopes, their daily routines. A year ago she'd found an intact bowl, a delicate piece of pottery with a design in blue and black squares around its lip. She'd held it in her hands for nearly an hour, wondering at the person who used it last.

The air in the room was musty, despite Mrs. Beauchamp's efforts at squirreling potpourri jars filled with cinnamon or lemon or something flowery in various places. She had tried to tell the housekeeper that the smell didn't bother her but knew that she was going to lose this domestic battle as she had lost countless others.

A scarred, gray wood table sat in the middle of the room, two chairs facing each other on either side it. In actuality, the second chair was rarely occupied. Neville sometimes followed her into the storeroom to argue a point. Or, before he was given his inheritance, to badger her about money.

A length of dark blue fabric was stretched out on the table. One of her recent finds at Partage Castle, it was a richly embroidered garment she thought was a ceremonial robe that had survived when other fabrics like linen and wool would have dissolved after the passage of years. Beside it was a tray of her tools containing delicate picks, soft boar's-hair brushes, an examining glass, and her journal. She needed to examine the garment, to make sketches of the pattern of the embroidery and consult her reference books in order to try and date it.

Until a few days ago she'd been excited at the prospect of sharing what she found. Now she sat and stared at the garment and only saw Dalton MacIain laughing.

There is no explanation that would induce me to forgive him.

What was she going to do?

She could go to her solicitor and ask if he'd heard from Neville, but the man didn't have a good opinion of her brother. Still, perhaps Neville had requested a bank draft or that a letter of credit be forwarded to him.

Whenever she mentioned Neville, she had to parse her words carefully. Mr. Pettibone did not like her to disagree with him. On those rare occasions when she did so, his fleshy nose turned bright pink and his cheeks a ruddy color. More than once she thought the poor man was going to explode.

The solicitor knew that Neville had gone to America. She'd had to endure an hour of lecture over that knowledge. If she told Mr. Pettibone that Neville was missing, he would probably move heaven and earth to freeze all of her brother's funds.

Why hadn't Neville returned home? Or had he come back to London and just not informed her? Had he resented her rules and instructions? He'd once accused her of conspiring with Mr. Pettibone to limit the amount of money he could withdraw in a month.

When she told him it was only a matter of prudence, he'd lost his temper.

"I'm a grown man, Minerva," he said. "I'm not still in short pants and you don't get to dictate how I live. Not anymore."

If Mr. Pettibone gave instructions to the bank not to pay any of Neville's drafts, it might bring him out in the open. Did she want to resort to such drastic measures?

She had promised her mother to care for her brother to the best of her ability. She'd never thought the vow would be so onerous.

Before Neville went to America, she hadn't seen him for months on end, even though they shared the same house. He had either been staying with friends, attending country house parties, or she was in Scotland.

How odd that she felt his absence so keenly now. Was that because she knew, somehow, that he needed her? If so, it would be the first time in years.

On the rare occasions they were together, she attempted not to treat him like a younger brother, but it was difficult, sometimes, to hold her tongue, especially when she saw him spending too much money in ways that would not benefit him one whit.

"You only have so much principal, Neville," she once told him. "I hope you're not spending any of that. Or, heaven forbid, gambling it away."

He had leveled a look on her that was almost hateful. No, she was just imagining that. He'd been annoyed, that was all.

"I didn't realize I had to get your approval before I spent a penny, sister."

"Of course you don't," she said. "But I do hope that you allow your natural common sense to come into play."

She had gilded the lily a bit with that comment. The problem was, Neville hadn't yet grown into his common sense. He had the strangest friends and he didn't seem to consider the pros and cons of a matter before jumping into a situation, such as going to America with the Earl of Rathsmere.

She knew Dalton had to be wrong. Neville would never have tried do something so terrible as try to kill him. Perhaps she should have shared with Dalton the last letter she'd received from America. In it, Neville apologized for his abrupt departure, which made her cry. He seemed, in those words, to have matured, to have become the man she'd always hoped he would be.

No one could have a better sister, Neville had written.

Or a more patient one. I'm certain I didn't deserve your patience, Minerva, but I'm grateful for it all the same. You and I are family and family matters more than anything else.

Were those the words of a would-be murderer? No.

She had the feeling that if Neville hadn't come home, it was for a reason. Was he afraid of something or someone?

Was he afraid of Rathsmere?

If Neville had truly tried to shoot him, there had to be a reason. What had Rathsmere done that was so evil? What had he done that he wasn't admitting?

She pushed away the memory of him sitting across from her in the carriage, adorned in his eye patch, his blue-green eye fixed on her as if he could see clearly. Or in his office, talking about his brother. Sometimes she caught him looking at her before glancing away. In those moments, she'd come very close to asking him what he saw. Did he still think her arrogant? Or ugly, for that matter?

"I beg your pardon, Miss Minerva."

She looked up to find that Mrs. Beauchamp had opened the door of the storeroom, a strict violation of her orders.

"The earl is here."

"You mean his carriage," she said.

"No, Miss Minerva. I mean the earl himself is here."

It was only a little after seven. He never sent his carriage before eight and he'd never come himself.

"I've put him in the family parlor, Miss Minerva. Shall I bring him refreshments?"

She nodded. "Please, Mrs. Beauchamp. And a few of your spice biscuits, I think."

Her housekeeper smiled and took herself off, no doubt to fawn over His Lordship.

What was he doing here?

She glanced down at herself. At least she hadn't

been going through boxes. Her dark blue dress was free of dust. Her hair was carefully arranged in a no-nonsense style, the snood at the nape of her neck covering the bun.

Was she pale? Did she need a little color? And why was her heart beating so fast? He couldn't see her, and if he did, could just as easily offered a scathing comment about her appearance as he had when they first met.

The parlor was large, stretching nearly the length of the house. When her parents were alive, they often entertained, the room filled with people laughing and talking, the sound of music, and the scents of her mother's bouillabaisse or chicken stew. She hadn't entertained in the intervening years. Nor had Neville ever brought his friends home.

Her mother had loved red, so the settee and chairs were upholstered in red. The white lace curtains were tied back with red ropes ending in tassels. The ferns once in front of the windows had been removed. Neither Mrs. Beauchamp nor anyone else on the staff had the ability to nurture the plants, and she herself didn't have the patience.

The settee was in front of the fireplace, while a chair sat on either end, each piece of furniture accompanied by a round tufted ottoman in red velvet. White lace runners sat on each of the mahogany tables, deftly dusted by the downstairs maids every few days.

Not a speck of dust could be seen on any of her mother's statuettes of dogs, shepherdesses, and tiny sheep. The lamps were perfectly polished, their wicks trimmed in expectation of a gathering in this room she so often ignored.

She walked into the parlor and stopped, staring at Dalton. He commanded the room. He was seated in a chair, his posture rigid, his chin at a perfect autocratic angle as he stared in the direction of the fireplace. His hand rested on top of the walking stick at his side as if it were a scepter. She could almost see him with a crown and robes of state. He had the demeanor to be a king.

"Are you going to take your place in the House of Lords?"

He turned his head toward her. "Good morning to you, Minerva. I haven't yet decided. What brought that question on?"

"You looked very regal sitting there."

"I was just trying to determine how many types of potpourri were in the room."

"Three," she said. "I think. My housekeeper is determined to make everything smell like flowers or oranges or lemons."

"Or cinnamon. But this morning you don't smell of cinnamon, but that curious dusty odor."

"I was in my storeroom," she said. "It's where I keep all of my finds. What you're smelling is probably age. Or the past."

"Perhaps one day you can show me this treasure trove."

With anyone else, she might have immediately demurred or said something like she didn't share the space with anyone. But she could see herself leading him into the room and explaining what each of the boxes held.

She pushed that disturbing thought away and sat on the settee opposite him. Sunlight crept into the room from the windows to her left, puddling around him like a yearning lover.

Had he come to tell her that her services were no longer needed?

She folded her hands, one atop the other, and tried to compose herself.

"I received a note last night," he said. "Something that jarred my memory. We have another place to go, another person who might have heard from Neville." Then he asked, "Are you wearing your trousers skirt?"

"No," she said. "A blue dress."

"Pity."

"Are we going somewhere disreputable?"

"You really shouldn't sound so delighted by the prospect. No. Besides, what would the Covington sisters say?"

"No doubt they've noticed your carriage and I'm already being discussed in horrified tones."

"Does that mean you won't come with me?"

"Of course not. Give me a moment," she said.

She passed Mrs. Beauchamp in the hall and apologized for the sudden change of plans.

"Are you going out this early, Miss Minerva?" the housekeeper asked, her words swimming in an ocean of disapproval.

"I am, Mrs. Beauchamp," she said brightly.

With that, she grabbed her reticule and her bonnet and prepared herself for another adventure with the Earl of Rathsmere.

Chapter 23

"*W*here are we going?" she asked when they were in the carriage. "And why so early?"

"To a woman I know. The time is early for us, but late for her. She normally goes to bed around nine."

"Who is she? Another member of the demimonde?"

"I would hesitate to call Lucille Grampton any name at all. She defies explanation and description."

His smile effectively stole her words. She stared at him, wishing her experience of his world was greater.

"You think she might know Neville."

"Yes."

"Why?"

"Because young men gravitate to Lucille like a child to candy. Neville wasn't an exception."

She hadn't eaten anything for breakfast, which she told herself was why her stomach clenched. She was most definitely not affected by his words or the hint of admiration in his voice.

Of course the Rake of London would admire a woman of ill repute.

"Why is it necessary for me to come with you?"

"You're my chaperone," he said.

"I beg your pardon?"

"Lucille is very . . ." His voice ground to a halt. His grin startled her.

She waited, curious.

"Insistent."

"Insistent?" Her eyes widened.

He wouldn't say another word until they arrived, the carriage halting before a town house in a prosperous square.

She left the carriage first, and when he extended his hand, she gripped it with one of hers, helping him leave the vehicle.

All the way to the front steps she was rethinking her decision to be here. But then, it hadn't been her decision, had it? Dalton simply waved his hand and here she was.

Who did he think he was? He acted the dilettante made a hermit by injury, a recluse because of circumstance. It wasn't as if he wished to reassess his life and change his direction. No, he hid from the world because he was no longer as perfectly handsome as he had once been.

What balderdash.

He was a charming wizard, capable of convincing any woman to do almost anything. Look at her. She was acting as his eyes and his secretary and neglecting her own work. No doubt experienced women gazed after him with longing. The unsophisticated girls of the world probably sighed after him, as if realizing that MacIain was not for them. Wait until they were matrons, bored with their husbands, and then he would be there to assuage any desires they might have.

She was not among that group.

No, she knew entirely too much about Dalton MacIain to fall victim to his sorcery. Nor did she pity him.

She'd never known a less pitiable man.

"We're at the front door," she said. "Would you like to knock, or shall I?"

"What's wrong?" he asked, turning his head in her direction.

"Nothing."

"I sincerely doubt that, Minerva. Your voice has a coating of frost that wasn't there when we were in the carriage. Are you annoyed because I said that Neville was fascinated with Lucille?"

She didn't answer, only lifted the knocker and let it fall.

When no one came to the door, she began to tap her foot.

"Is there a rope to the right of the door?" he asked. "About waist high, I think, emerging from a small hole?"

"Yes."

"If you'll pull on it, it will ring a bell inside the house. If no one answers, then I've miscalculated and Lucille has retired early. We'll simply have to return around midnight."

She yanked on the rope, hearing a bell peal from deep inside the house.

A moment later the door was pulled open by a thin scowling woman in full skirts and a white apron, a perky white cap on her crown of black hair.

"Yes?"

"Dalton MacIain here for Lucille. I hope she's still receiving."

The woman turned and disappeared into the house, leaving them standing on the stoop.

She'd never been so summarily dismissed, and in seconds. Before she could question Dalton, she heard squeals of excitement as footsteps raced down the hall. A flurry of red, perfumed silk enveloped Dalton, nearly knocking her over in an attempt to reach the man. Minerva heard his laughter, then the tinkling tones of a female as she rained kisses over his face.

"My darling Dalton. Where have you been? What have you been doing? What is this ugly patch for? Who wounded you so dreadfully? You must tell me. I'll set my dogs on him. Was it a duel? Did you fight for a woman? No, no, I do not want to know. I would be crushed. No woman must hold your heart more than Lucille. I will not hear of it."

Minerva moved farther to the left, the better to allow the reunion. What a pity Dalton couldn't see the woman. She was practically spilling out of her décolletage. Or perhaps eyes weren't necessary, the way Lucille was pressing herself up against him. She wouldn't be surprised if the woman took his hands and brought them to her bosom.

After a quick, dismissive glance in Minerva's direction, Lucille put her arm through Dalton's and pulled him forward.

"You must come inside. How bad of Pansy to leave you standing on the doorstep like a peddler. Come, my darling. Come."

Lucille was evidently French or affected a French accent. If she wasn't mistaken, the woman's perfume was also French. It followed her like a noxious cloud, providing an olfactory trail to follow.

Minerva entered the house behind them.

The parlor was lovely, decorated in restrained taste in pale blues. No gaudy crimson here, or abundance of tassels and fringe. Only a settee in silk upholstery in a shade so pale as to be almost white, and a matching chair and ottoman sitting at a right angle. Ferns sat on pots in front of the large bay window, and porcelain knickknacks with a French flair sat on the tables and mantel.

"If you wish," Lucille said, glancing at her, "you may go and take tea with Pansy in the kitchen." The other woman wiggled her fingers at her. "Go on now."

Go on now?

"Lucille, if I may, I'd prefer her to remain with me."

"But, my darling—" she began, only for Dalton to interrupt her.

"She's indispensable."

That was nothing more than a bald-faced lie. She was almost tempted to retreat to the kitchen, but she was too curious to leave the room.

Dalton had been led to the settee and was now joined by Lucille, whose red hair had fallen to her shoulders in a style more applicable to early rising than entertaining guests. But then, her attire was hardly acceptable, either, with the silk garment leaving little doubt that the woman was nearly naked underneath.

Sitting beside Dalton, Lucille wound herself, kitten-like, over him. Her right hand patted his chest, which made Minerva wonder what her left hand was doing. One leg stretched up, her calf beginning a slow rubbing motion on Dalton's right leg.

Insistent? Yes, the woman was definitely that.

Sitting in the adjoining chair, holding her reticule in front of her, Minerva felt rendered invisible by Lucille's cooing and stroking.

Dalton was clutching his walking stick in what looked to be a death grip.

Minerva's mood suddenly lightened and she began to smile. Now she understood why she was Dalton's chaperone.

"Lucille, my dear," he said, reaching up and slowly removing her hand from his chest.

"You have not called on me, my darling. You have not let Lucille know you were all right. I worried so about you. I wept many nights. Many, many nights."

Every time he moved Lucille's hand away from him, it crept back in place. Plus, the woman was kissing her way up his shoulder and would hit his ear any moment. He'd tried to stretch away from her, but her leg had trapped his.

"I'm sorry, Lucille. I've been a bit of a hermit."

"I could have soothed you in my way, Dalton. You know that. Give me a chance."

"Yes. Well. I've come to ask about some friends," he said. "Men you might know."

Lucille reared back. "Friends? Who are these friends of yours?"

He gave her five names, one of which was Neville's.

"Have you seen them lately?"

The question did what his hands had not been able to do. Lucille moved to the end of the settee, frowning at him.

"Why is this? Why do you wish to know?"

"Let's just say I'm renewing my acquaintances," he said.

Lucille suddenly looked at her, the green-eyed gaze like chips of glass.

"This involves you?"

"Yes," she said at the same time Dalton said, "No."

Lucille looked from one of them to the other.

Minerva could see Dalton's irritated look all too well. The trouble was, he couldn't see hers.

"It's no good, Your Lordship," she said, sitting forward. "My shame must be told."

She withdrew a handkerchief from inside her reticule, grateful her mother had insisted that all ladies carry one in case of unforeseen emergencies. She also had smelling salts, but thankfully had never needed them.

Blotting the handkerchief to the corner of one eye, she made a sound remarkably like a sob. Who knew she was that good an actress? For that matter, who knew that she would be in the presence of someone like Lucille and need acting skills?

"He doesn't know about the little one. I shall be banished from my home. But I think he would want to know. I know he would."

Lucille's frown deepened. If she didn't take care, those lines would become permanent. As it was, she had the distinct impression that the woman wasn't as young as she'd originally appeared.

"Who is this man you seek?" she asked.

"Neville Todd," Dalton said.

Lucille's considerable eyebrows arched northward. "This man? Isn't he too young for you?" she said to Minerva, who buried her face in her handkerchief and managed another credible sob.

"Do you know where we can find him, Lucille?" Dalton asked.

"My darling, was he not with you? One of those men you took to America? I have not seen him since. But he is not like you. If he were in London, he would come to see Lucille. I know this. He has not come."

A few minutes later, having declined refreshments, dried her nonexistent tears, and attempted to summon the last of her composure, she and Dalton made their way to the front door.

Their departure was delayed by Lucille's version of a farewell, consisting of numerous kisses rained over Dalton's face and one very long one on his lips. In addition, her hands roamed from his shoulders to his hips, with one grabbing his backside in a proprietary manner.

Lucille had all the promise of sticking to Dalton like an extra appendage or a barnacle.

Minerva separated them by beginning to cry again, the masquerade surprising her because she was strangely close to tears. Because Lucille had no news of Neville, she told herself. That's the only reason she was feeling weepy.

Once in the carriage, having made their escape,

she turned to Dalton as he wiped his mouth with his handkerchief.

"I thought you never paid for a woman."

"I haven't."

"Doesn't Lucille charge you?"

"Appearances to the contrary, I have never utilized Lucille's services."

"I'm not sure I believe you. She seems very . . ." Her words trailed off.

"Interested? She is. She nearly attacks me every time I see her, which is, blessedly, not often."

She narrowed her eyes and studied him.

"She's a madam."

"She is that," he said.

"You took me to a bordello," she said, amazed.

"I haven't taken you to a bordello. Lucille's establishment is run very differently. Her clientele requests companions for the evening and Lucille sends the girls to them. She bills them once a month for her services, and most of them pay immediately. Those who don't, well, let's just say that's the last time they use Lucille's services."

"And Neville did."

He nodded.

She stared out at the passing scenery.

"What, no outcries that your brother is a saint?"

"No."

He reached over and found her hand where it was resting on the seat.

"He's a man, Minerva. Men have needs."

"Do you?" she asked, turning to look at him. "How long has it been since you were with a woman?"

His laughter caught her off guard.

"I should have guessed that would be your response, but you never fail to surprise me, Minerva. What possessed you to claim to be a girl in trouble?"

"A more sympathetic ruse than being an older sister," she said wryly. "What happens now? Are we going somewhere else?"

"I've explored every single haunt your brother might visit. I've left my card. All we can do now is wait."

"Truly?"

"I know you're disappointed," he said.

"I merely want to find Neville."

"We will."

For the first time, he said it in such a way that she didn't feel as if her brother's life was in danger. He still held her hand, and as they drove back to his home, he gently squeezed her fingers.

She would not let him know how close she was to real tears this time.

Chapter 24

Dalton stood at the library door, listening to Minerva's footsteps in the corridor as she headed toward him. Even her steps were confident and assured, but of course she knew the way by now.

This was the third week of their arrangement, and he knew he had to end it soon. Otherwise his fascination with her would only grow, and nothing could come of that.

What woman would want a blind man?

He had a fortune, but she didn't need it. Any charm he might have once possessed had been drowned in the months he was mired in pity.

He couldn't even dance with her.

"I thought of an idea," he said when she reached the door.

She was wearing a new perfume, something that reminded him of lilies and other spring flowers. He sniffed audibly, smiling when she laughed.

"I decided to smell of something other than cinnamon," she said.

"What is it called?" he asked.

"Spring in Scotland," she said. "It's supposed to remind the wearer of thistles and heather, but I can't smell it myself."

"It doesn't smell like Scotland to me, but an English wood."

"Perhaps I'm a wood sprite come to visit."

He suspected she was smiling. He wanted to place his fingertips on her face and feel her smile.

"What's this idea?" she asked.

She took his hand as naturally as if she'd done it before, leading him to the two wing chairs in front of the fireplace. She sat and then he did, wishing he could see her.

"I have a cousin who recently returned from America. Her husband was with the British Legation. I know she must have contacts. There is every possibility that Neville never came back to England."

"Would they know if he was dead?"

Her voice was a careful monotone. Perhaps she thought it revealed nothing of her emotions, but he'd had days to listen to her, to study her inflections. He probably knew her better than anyone on his staff. Or anyone else, for that matter. Fear lingered in her tone along with a grief he hoped she'd have no cause to express.

He stretched out his hand, unsurprised when she placed hers on it. She could read gestures and moods better than anyone he'd ever known. Or perhaps she was just learning him, too.

"Let's not think that, but since we haven't found him, perhaps he hasn't returned to London."

Her hand gripped his firmly. "I didn't want to think that Neville would avoid me," she said. "The last time I saw him, we argued."

"People forget inconsequential things when they long for home. Arthur and I didn't part on the best of terms, but I didn't think about that when I wanted to come home."

He didn't tell her that one of the first greetings he'd received while still on board ship was the news that his brother was dead and he was now the Earl of

Rathsmere. No man had ever ascended to a title with as much regret.

"I think it's possible Neville's still in America. I telegraphed my cousin and asked if she could make use of some of her contacts. He might be trying to arrange passage back to England. He might be sailing home this minute. He might have even gone to the British authorities and asked for assistance. We need to investigate that angle as well."

He wanted to reassure her somehow, but what could he say to ease her mind? There was every possibility that Neville had died, but he wouldn't say that. Nor would he tell her about the conditions under which they'd lived for so many weeks and months. That wouldn't reassure her, either.

The wish to comfort her was new, yet this compassion he felt was not exclusively singled out for Minerva. Somehow, over the last year, he'd become more aware of his fellow human beings' welfare.

Before, he would never have noticed that Mrs. Thompson was always a little weepy after her half day off. Or that one of the upstairs maids had a lisp when she talked that evidently embarrassed her, enough that she mumbled when she spoke. Nor would he have been as acutely aware of Howington's displeasure. The man had a way of expressing himself without words. The atmosphere of any room immediately changed when Howington walked into it.

Had he been so immersed in his own pleasure back then, or the drive for it, that he hadn't been aware of the people around him? Had he been so surfeited by drink or exhausted from his adventures that he'd never seen what was before his eyes?

A strange and ironic twist of fate, that he saw more being blind than he had sighted.

"What will I do if he's dead, Dalton?"

He couldn't bear the sorrow in her voice.

Gripping her hand tightly, he pulled her toward him.

"Come here, Minerva."

He could hear her stand. When she moved in front of his chair, he didn't hesitate, reaching up and placing both hands around her waist. When she tumbled into his lap, he smiled.

"What are you doing? Let me go, Dalton."

He cupped her face with his hands.

"Kiss me, Minerva."

"I beg your pardon?"

"I have this dislike of looking ridiculous," he said. "If I lower my mouth to yours and hit your nose, it will bruise my consequence. I'll be an object of pity."

"I can't kiss you."

"Just a taste of passion," he said.

"Absolutely not."

"I have needs," he said with a smile.

"As if that's my concern."

"Are you afraid?"

"Of course not. I just don't want to kiss you."

"Not at all?"

"Not one little bit. Not an iota."

"No curiosity about what it might be like to kiss the man Queen Victoria said was most certainly the worst rake in all of London?"

"No."

"You're fibbing, Minerva."

"I'm not."

He lowered his head, brushed his lips over her heated cheek. To his surprise, she didn't move away. Slowly, he traced a path to her lips, breathing against them before placing his mouth on hers.

A kiss should be an appetizer. A kiss was a prelude, strings being tuned in an orchestra pit, dawn on an important day.

A kiss was not a feast. A kiss was not an explosion of the senses. But this one was.

He could smell her, that hint of earthiness mixed with her new perfume. Her skin was warm against his fingertips, her cheek heating as he inclined his head to deepen the kiss.

Her mouth opened slightly on a gasp.

He wanted to banish her sorrow, the pain Neville had caused her. He wanted to change the tenor of her thoughts, give her something to replace her dread.

He could give Minerva passion. That's the gift he could give her.

He'd been too long without kisses. Too much time had passed since he'd had a woman in his arms, pliant, female, soft and fragrant—a mystery and a delight.

He inhaled her breath and the small sound she made when one of his hands reached around to hold the back of her head.

Her lips were so soft, pillowy, and welcoming.

He'd been without color in his life for nearly a year yet he could swear he saw sparkles of blue, red, and yellow as Minerva's tongue darted out and touched his.

He'd never seduced anyone in his library, but he was giving thought to doing so.

Would the astounding Miss Todd be amenable to a little afternoon loving?

SHE ABRUPTLY stood, moving a few feet away.

When he smiled, she glanced toward the desk, not wanting to be charmed by him. That kiss was bad enough. She had succumbed, only too willingly. She had been swept up in passion again and it happened so suddenly that she hadn't thought to protect herself. If he'd seduced her, she would have allowed him. She had no defenses against a kiss—and more—from Dalton MacIain.

She didn't have any doubt whatsoever that a great many women would've tumbled into his bed for the sheer beauty of him. Then, added to his physical attractiveness was his charm, when he chose to use it, and his intelligence when it crept out.

She moved to the chair in front of the desk.

"Shall we begin?" she asked, wishing her voice didn't sound so tremulous. It wouldn't do to let him see how shaken she was by a kiss.

"I heard from Dorothy," he said, standing.

For a moment she stared at him, trying to remember the name. Then it came to her. The girl who'd known Neville.

"Did you?"

He made his way to the desk without faltering. Here, in his library, he didn't use a walking stick.

"She came to see me last night."

She was not going to feel a spike of jealousy. How utterly absurd.

"She smelled of turnips."

"I beg your pardon?"

"Turnips and a nauseatingly sweet perfume."

"Is my perfume nauseatingly sweet?" How foolish of her to ask.

"No, but I prefer you smelling of cinnamon and dust."

"Why did Dorothy smell of turnips?"

He shrugged. "I've no idea, but I earned her disfavor, I'm afraid. I suggested that less is more in the scent department. She left in a huff."

"Had she seen Neville? Please tell me you questioned her before you insulted her."

His bark of laughter might have made her smile at any other time, but she waited impatiently for him to tell her what Dorothy said.

"She has not seen Neville," he said. "And misses

him greatly. Evidently, your brother was quite generous in many ways. She offered to allow me to take his place in her affections."

"Of course, one could expect a woman of low repute to be fickle. After all, they survive by the whims of the gentleman they pleasure."

"It's not only the women of low repute who are fickle, Minerva."

She was not going to ask him to explain that comment. She didn't want to hear about a parade of titled women through his bedroom.

"If she hadn't smelled of turnips, would you have taken her to your bed?"

No, she really shouldn't have asked that question. The kiss had disturbed her. When he didn't answer, she retrieved one of the packets on his desk and began to feverishly read. This problem involved cattle, of all things.

"No," he said. "I wouldn't have."

He smiled again, and this time she studied him. He looked dangerous and charming at the same time, a warning to all young girls not to look too close or stare too long lest they be mesmerized.

She was no longer a young girl.

"At least you know you didn't frighten Dorothy."

"How reassuring," he said. "You mean, by that remark, that if I find myself desperate and lonely I can, at least, pay for pleasure."

"Did I say that? How shocking of me."

"You implied it."

"Perhaps it's true. If you need release that badly, you can always hire one of the women at the pleasure gardens. Or Lucille."

And not kiss me.

"I've never, as you say, *hired* one of those women in my life."

"Why did my brother?"

"I can't say."

"Or won't?" she asked.

"I find this conversation strange in the extreme, Minerva."

"Why, because I'm being frank? You're the one who's the Rake of London. Have you never had an honest conversation with a woman?"

"Not one in which she encouraged me to employ a prostitute, no."

"Oh, bother, you know very well I did nothing of the sort. Besides, I doubt you'd ever get that desperate or lonely."

"Let's pray you're right."

She studied him. His right hand was on the stack of paperwork, palm flat on the pages, fingers drawn up as if he wanted to make a fist. His other hand was out of sight. Was that clenched into a fist as well?

It was evident the kiss hadn't disturbed him like it had her. Her heart was still beating too fast. Her lips felt swollen and sensitive.

They worked for several hours and she was careful to keep the conversation on the task at hand and not anything personal. They solved the problem of the wandering cattle, the repairs to the ballroom floor, and a new roof on top of Gledfield's north wing.

He was adamant about approving the new stable design, and she had to describe it to him numerous times, making a notation of his comments and improvements. But he surprised her when he demanded that one of the maids be sacked.

"She stole something," he said. "That's grounds enough for dismissal."

"Doesn't the poor thing get another chance?"

"No," he said, then refused to say another word.

"Why not? Everyone makes mistakes."

"That wasn't a mistake, Minerva. That was a choice. A mistake is when you don't know the difference. Her choice was to steal. It's a rule at Gledfield. No one will remain on staff who's proved themselves to be a thief."

"So, you do adjudicate morals after all."

"Someone who makes the wrong choice should reap the consequences of that choice," he said, his voice brittle.

She studied him, realizing what he was saying. He believed his blindness was the payment for his choice to go to America. He was reaping the consequences of his idiocy.

Finally, it was time for her to go. She stood.

"Thank you for today," he said, as he did every day.

As she did every day, she said something innocuous in response and went to the door. She always said good-bye to him with a final look, as if to enshrine him in her memory.

Today, the sight of him disturbed her on an elemental level.

He'd kissed her, yet made no mention of it afterward, as if it were unimportant.

She'd never received a more important kiss.

The curtains were open at the window behind him, allowing the afternoon sun to stream into the room, bathing his shoulders and showering him with light.

His black hair and black eye patch gave him the appearance of Lucifer, God's beloved angel before his fall from grace. Had Dalton MacIain ever been that innocent? Or had he been a rake from the cradle, winking at his nurse and cozening the female servants?

"Who was your first conquest?" she asked.

"I beg your pardon?"

He did that when she'd startled him, retreated into faux propriety as if he couldn't believe her effrontery.

"It was a maid at Gledfield, wasn't it? Did your parents ever find out? Or Arthur?"

He didn't answer for a moment. Finally, he shook his head. "You're the most astounding creature, Minerva Todd. Yes, it was a maid, and no, my parents never discovered it."

"Did Arthur?"

"Yes, and he lectured me extensively on the merits of never taking advantage of the staff. I felt like a worm when he was done."

"What happened to the girl?"

"She married a miller, I believe, and had a great many little millers."

"None of them yours?"

"Good God, no. One thing I've been very careful about, Minerva, is not to sow my seed the length and breadth of England."

But he had one child, a little boy who looked exactly like him.

"And here? Are you never tempted to dabble with the staff?"

The tips of his ears were turning red. Was he angry or embarrassed?

"My staff is sacrosanct, Miss Todd. Even my acquaintances knew that. I would have cut them off without a word if they bothered one of them." He moved his hand, flexing his fingers.

"Am I not considered staff, then?"

He smiled. "You're speaking of the kiss? Shall I apologize?"

"No, perhaps not. You don't frighten me, either, Dalton," she said.

She didn't stay to see the effect of her announcement or turn around after leaving, to look back. She walked down the corridor as she had for the last three weeks.

If she turned right, she'd head toward the kitchen,

where Mrs. Thompson would greet her, as would Daniels, waiting to take her home.

The housekeeper always sent her on her way with some treat that annoyed Mrs. Beauchamp and made her frown. From the aroma in the air as she approached, it smelled like ginger biscuits.

Today, however, before moving on to the kitchen she stepped into the parlor, went to the window on the far right, and opened the lock.

Chapter 25

If the Covington sisters could see her, she'd be ruined. The elderly ladies were harmless most of the time, but when they saw something that truly disturbed them, they could carry tales far and wide. She'd often told Neville that if he must come in at dawn, to do so in a way their neighbors couldn't see.

She had to admit, though, that Neville did have a great deal of charm. Perhaps that's why the three sisters never gossiped about her brother, despite the fact that he sometimes staggered home at outrageous hours.

Neville made a point of taking some of Cook's pastries over to the sisters from time to time. He would sit and have tea with them, spending an hour or two at each session. No doubt he was the only male they allowed past the front door.

Of course, they'd seen him grow up. They'd been younger then and walked the neighborhood each morning and each evening, the better to note any changes or deleterious behavior. When Neville decided to climb one of the trees in the park and found himself stuck, it was one of the Covington sisters who brought the news to her. When Neville rescued one of their cats from a chasing dog, they conveyed that information to her as well, along with their gushing praise.

Neville had handled the Covington sisters a great deal better than she had. Perhaps she should have taken them some treat. Or commented about one of the kittens she'd seen sunning in the window. Something other than passively becoming the subject of their intense scrutiny.

She often studied the shards of an ancient pot with the same fixed determination, as if it held a secret she could decipher if she looked hard enough. In the case of the pot, there were facts to be ascertained. She couldn't say the same about her life.

Until tonight.

Tonight, the Covington sisters would have had a great deal of gossip to spread if they saw her surreptitiously making her way to the stable after her own staff had retired for the night.

She climbed the stairs to the room above the carriage bay where the stable boy slept. To her relief, Michael either wasn't yet asleep or roused easily. When she asked him the most important question, he nodded enthusiastically.

"Yes, Miss Minerva, I can drive the carriage," he said.

"Then you may drive me tonight on one condition."

He was still nodding.

"You mustn't tell Hugh, or anyone else for that matter. Do I have your word?"

Ever since their relationship, Hugh no longer slept above the stable. Instead, he'd taken lodgings elsewhere. She didn't think it was longing on his part as much as tact. If he wanted to bring another woman to his bed, she wouldn't know about it.

Nor, if the truth be told, would she care.

She had enjoyed Hugh. She had learned a great deal from him. He had instructed her in the ways of passion so that she wouldn't die a maiden. She would have at least known then the touch of a man and the joy that came from lovemaking.

She'd been quite willing to live for the rest of her life without duplicating the experience. Hugh had left her with enough lovely memories that it simply wasn't necessary.

Until she met the Rake of London.

She couldn't get the memory of Dalton touching her face out of her mind. Then he'd kissed her. How was she supposed to forget that? Or the yearning she felt the minute the kiss ended?

She wanted him. She wanted to touch Dalton the same way he'd touched her, stroking her hands and fingers over his skin, learning him so she could close her eyes and forever remember every contour of his body.

His rakish smile made her pulse dance. Deep inside, she hurt. Not with pain but something else. An emptiness, a need she'd never before felt. A feeling she knew only he could ease.

She most definitely did not consider him an ogre.

Would he consider her a harlot?

She tucked herself into the carriage, grateful that Michael hadn't lit the lamp on the outside. He was, bless him, quiet as he led the horses out of the stable and down the alley.

What sort of woman lusts after a man who wanted to do damage to her family? That question cut too close to the bone. She pushed it away as well as other thoughts that had nearly kept her in her room, a woman about whom the Covington sisters could find nothing to criticize.

Very well, she could be nearly perfect, but what good was that? She had attempted, for years, to be the perfect older sister for Neville, only for him to reject her training and turn his back on her.

She had tried to be a proper young woman, pushing back her interest in those things that were not considered feminine to pursue. She had made herself miserable for a goodly number of years until it occurred to her that no one truly cared if she was happy or not.

They only cared if she was obeying the rules.

Who decreed that women couldn't wear trousers?

Who decreed that women should wear corsets?

Who decreed that women couldn't be intellectually curious? That she shouldn't want to know about people who had gone before, women who had gone before? What had their lives been like? What had they thought or felt? How had they coped with the circumstances of their times?

Who decreed that every woman should marry? And if they didn't, that they were destined to huddle together like the Covington sisters, abandoned little chicks who'd grown up to be scrawny hens.

Who said that a woman shouldn't act on her feelings, even if that feeling was lust?

She could feel her cheeks warm, a heat to match the rest of her body.

Perhaps she should blame Dalton. After all, he had kissed her and started the fire burning. Or maybe it began the very first time she saw him, a magnificent specimen of man regardless of his scars.

She grabbed the strap above the window when Michael took a turn a little too sharply. With any luck, he'd be able to navigate the lane behind Dalton's town house.

To her relief, he didn't have any problems. Although stopping was something he needed to work on, she congratulated him when he opened the carriage door.

"This is the very first time you've ever driven a carriage, isn't it?"

He nodded.

"It's all right if you speak, Michael."

"Yes, ma'am, it is. But I knew I could do it. I watched Hugh enough years. And I knew I wanted to try."

She really couldn't fault the boy. After all, she was doing something novel as well.

"Remember our agreement," she said. "I won't tell anyone you drove if you don't tell anyone where you brought me."

He nodded again, and this time she didn't try to make him speak.

"Wait here. I might be a little while. I don't mind if you get inside the carriage and sleep for a bit."

Another nod. She patted him on the shoulder and left him without a word. Perhaps she intimidated him. After all, she paid his salary. Or perhaps he was just simply dumbstruck at her shocking actions. After all, a proper gentlewoman didn't go anywhere without a chaperone, let alone at midnight.

But she'd already been shocking, hadn't she? She had accompanied the Earl of Rathsmere all over London with no chaperone, only the two of them in the carriage. Also, she knew full well that it wasn't entirely proper to be acting as his secretary. If it was, Howington wouldn't have greeted her with a glare every morning.

She made her way around to the side of the town house. Tonight there was a full moon, bright enough to illuminate the hedges and the windows they guarded.

As she stood there, her conscience made itself known.

What on earth are you doing, Minerva? Going to a man's house in the middle of the night for the sole purpose of bedding him? Are you that desperate? Are you that lonely?

Not as lonely as curious. Should she have to bury her curiosity entirely?

Was it a terrible thing to want another kiss? And

more? Was she a horrid woman for indulging in hedonism, both in thought and act?

Granted, she was not as schooled in passion as he, but she knew it when she felt it. She knew it when she saw it. His cheeks had been bronzed. His breath had come as fast as hers.

Or perhaps he'd only kissed her because he was bored. He'd been without his companions. He'd willingly made himself a hermit. She might be a diversion, nothing more.

Very well, she'd treat him as a diversion as well. Someone to satisfy her curiosity. But she'd felt that same way about Hugh and look how terribly that had turned out.

She hated dithering. How much better to simply make a decision, to do something rather than worrying about it. She was not the type to hesitate once a course had been set. Evidently, her conscience was not prepared for such a vigorous debate because it suddenly went silent.

The unlocked window slid upward without a sound.

The maid had closed the draperies and Minerva had to fight them for a moment. She raised her leg, grateful for having had the foresight to wear her trousers skirt, and was entering the house when a hand clamped hard on her shoulder.

She screamed.

SOMETHING WOKE him.

For a moment Dalton lay there as he came to himself. As it happened every night, he blinked a half-dozen times, staring into the darkness before realizing it was permanent. One day he would awaken with knowledge of his loss of sight and these first few seconds wouldn't be so jarring.

What time was it? Since he rarely slept a whole night through, it had to be the middle of the night.

Dalton slid his pistol out from under his pillow, holding it in his right hand. He might be blind, but he was damned if he would be a passive target.

Slowly, he sat up, looking in the direction of the sitting room. He'd never thought to lock his door, but maybe it was a practice he should begin.

Had Dorothy known Neville's whereabouts after all? Had she told him that people were searching for him? Had Neville decided to finish him off tonight? Or was it Lewis, coming to prove his suspicions correct?

The knock on the sitting room door startled him. He doubted if anyone sinister would announce himself. He put the pistol on the bedside table and got up.

After grabbing his dressing gown and patting himself to make sure all the naked bits were covered, he strode through his sitting room.

"Your Lordship!"

It wasn't like his housekeeper to shout at him.

"Yes? What is it?" he asked as he pulled the door open.

"Oh, Your Lordship, it's a catastrophe for sure. We've the authorities at the door and he's nicked Miss Todd!"

He couldn't even begin to fathom what Mrs. Thompson was saying, so he wordlessly followed her to the staircase and made it down the steps.

The odor of garlic and onion wafted through the foyer. Cook had been in an exploratory mood tonight, producing an Italian dish even though she came from Devon.

"This is the Earl of Rathsmere himself, awakened by all this nonsense," Mrs. Thompson said, announcing him as if she were a majordomo and this a ball filled with notables.

A male voice greeted him. "Do you know this woman, Your Lordship?

"Oh, do let me go!"

"Minerva? What are you doing here?"

"I found her, Your Lordship, trying to get into your parlor by a window. You should keep those locked, sir."

"I assure you that I do. And who would you be?"

"My name is Robert, sir. Robert Hinnity. Mr. Wilson set me to watching your house. A good thing, too, or I wouldn't have caught this woman."

He could just imagine the scene. Mrs. Thompson standing there looking scandalized. Perhaps a maid or two observing the excitement with wide eyes. Minerva, flushed and embarrassed, if Minerva ever got embarrassed. And the righteous Robert Hinnity, looking proud at his capture.

"Thank you, Mr. Hinnity, I shall take care of the matter from this point onward."

"Sir? I should report her to the authorities."

"It's not necessary," he said. "I will handle the matter. Thank you for your diligence."

He heard the door close and turned to his housekeeper. "Thank you, Mrs. Thompson, that will be all."

"Will you be needing anything else, Your Lordship?" Mrs. Thompson asked.

"No, thank you. Go back to your room, Mrs. Thompson. I'm sorry you were disturbed."

"If you're sure, sir," she said, reluctance coating each word.

Was she afraid of leaving him alone with Minerva? Why, to protect Minerva's reputation? Or his?

"I am. Thank you, again."

He heard the sound of slippers on the steps and waited until the only noise in the foyer was the breathing of his companion.

"Is she gone?" he asked, extending his hand.

Minerva put her hand on his, no doubt believing he needed guidance.

"I think so," she said. How meek she sounded. Quite unlike her.

"Do you want to explain breaking into my home again?"

"Must I?"

"I'm afraid you must."

"I came to seduce you," she said.

He had expected a variety of explanations, but not that one. The woman had the ability to constantly startle him into silence. He turned and, still holding her hand, crossed the foyer and began to mount the steps.

She would have pulled away from him, but he kept a grip on her hand.

He had no intention of questioning her in the foyer. Or in the library, for that matter. He wasn't an idiot. If Minerva Todd had come to seduce him, who was he to protest?

Dalton heard the seventh step groan just as it had when he moved into the house ten years ago. He'd had two carpenters look it over, work on it with much banging and swearing and hammering, then proclaim the issue repaired. Only for the sound to come back days later.

He felt for the door to his suite, entered, and closed the door behind them.

"However do you do it, Dalton?" Minerva whispered. "It's black as pitch in here."

Her emotions came through her speech. He knew when she was sad, when she was irritated and trying not to show it. Amusement danced in her tone sometimes, as if the words themselves were smiling.

At the moment she was nervous.

Her hand was cold, and when he put his fingers on her wrist, her pulse was racing.

Placing his hand flat on the door, he allowed himself one last instant of rational thought. Did he really want Minerva in his bedroom? Hell, yes. Did he want to be seduced by Miss Todd? That might be an interesting experiment, one he was eager to try.

After their kiss, she'd been at the forefront of his mind. Evidently, she felt the same.

It was as if Providence, in partial reparation for his blindness, had plunked Minerva Todd down in his house.

"Shall we discuss this idea of you seducing me?"

"It's your fault. You kissed me. I quite enjoyed it."

"And that's why you're here? Because of a kiss?"

"Well, partially. It's the promise of the kiss. You kiss very well, Dalton. Better than I've ever been kissed, as a matter of fact. I wanted to know—strictly as an intellectual pursuit, you understand—if you loved as well as you kissed."

"Couldn't you just ask me?"

He leaned against the door and folded his arms. In the darkness, she probably couldn't see his smile.

"Very well, I'm asking. Do you make love as well as you kiss?"

"Better."

"You see, that will never do. Most men, I understand, are given to grandiose statements about their sexual prowess."

"They are?"

"They are."

"Who did you hear that from? The Covington sisters?"

"Does it matter? Anyway, I could take your word for it or I could experience it myself."

"In the interest of scientific exploration?"

"Of course," she said. "I have an excess of curiosity. At least that's what I've always been told."

"You would challenge scandal for the sake of curiosity?"

"There have already been enough tales about me," she said. "I'm not as feminine as I'm supposed to be. Or as ladylike. I am stubborn to a fault, intractable in several ways. I bray when I laugh. I slump when I walk."

"And you say things no other woman I've ever known would dare to say."

"See?"

He could hear her coming toward him.

"Ouch!"

"Minerva?"

"Just a moment. I'm nursing a broken foot. Really, do you need all this furniture in here?"

"Shall we discuss the placement of my furniture or seduction?"

"This isn't very easy," she said, surprising him. "I suppose you have a great deal of experience in seduction. I don't."

"I like your laugh," he said. "It isn't the least donkeylike."

"Truly?" she said.

"My honest opinion. How's your foot?"

"Better."

"Shall I massage it?"

"Please don't. I can't imagine anything worse. Why do people always want to touch an injury?"

He smiled. "I can assure you I won't touch your foot. Other places, perhaps."

She was close now, only a few feet away.

"You don't smell of cinnamon tonight," he said.

"I don't? Well, I didn't have scones before I came."

"Nor worked in your storeroom?"

"I couldn't concentrate."

"I had the same affliction, I'm afraid," he said.

"Truly? You were thinking of me?"

"I was. The kiss was memorable for me as well."

"You're the Rake of London. You've kissed thousands of women."

"Hardly thousands."

"Hundreds, then. At least hundreds, am I correct?"

"Perhaps," he said.

"But you haven't kissed anyone lately. Do you think that's why it's so memorable?"

"Perhaps, but it might just be you, Minerva."

"I think it's due to your lack of release."

His smile broadened. "I can only thank you, then, for your compassion in aiding me in seeking an end to my problem."

"You're ridiculing me."

"Minerva, I swear on my sainted mother that I'm doing no such thing. I've never been more serious."

"Oh."

"I don't think I've ever been seduced, however."

"Well, there's always a first time for that, isn't there?"

"I suppose there is," he said. "How shall we proceed?"

"Slowly, until my foot stops throbbing."

He'd never pictured a seduction that began with wanting to laugh.

Chapter 26

She wasn't reluctant to be led into his bedroom by the hand, but she still couldn't see. The sensation was disturbing, more than the time she'd blindfolded herself in the parlor.

"There's a full moon out tonight. Would you have any objections if I opened your curtains?"

"If you wish," he said. "Do you want me to light a lamp?"

"I've never made love in the light before," she said. "I should think moonlight would be enough."

He didn't say anything in response.

She turned. In the faint moonlight she could make out the bed, the bureau, and armoire. She could see his figure, suddenly startled to realize he was taking off his dressing gown.

Underneath, he was naked.

"Do you ever wear a nightshirt to bed?"

"Never. I detest them."

He didn't move to cover himself nor did he say anything, merely stood there letting her look her fill.

She could have studied him for hours, but she felt odd looking at him when he probably didn't know.

"I'm watching you," she said.

"Are you?"

"I thought Hugh was attractive, but you're even

more so. I think you're as beautiful as a statue and perfectly proportioned."

His legs were thickly muscled, as were his arms. Dressed as he was each day in a loose white shirt and black trousers, she'd only a hint of his physique. She knew his chest was broad and that he was tall, but who would have guessed he was so perfectly formed?

"I've never been called a statue. Hopefully, you'll find me warmer than that."

"Can I come closer?"

"Who am I to deny you?" he asked, smiling.

A lock of hair fell down on his brow, giving him an even more wicked look, as if he'd just roused from a bed of debauchery. Or as if a satisfied woman had reached up and threaded her fingers through his hair.

She walked toward him, stopping a few feet away, her hands fisted in her trousers skirt.

"Will you turn?"

"Turn?"

"I have an intense desire to see your backside," she said.

His laughter made her smile.

Moonlight was his friend. Or maybe his lover, caressing the planes and valleys of his body with a gentle touch, casting him in a pale light that only accentuated the magnificence of his body.

"Oh my," she said.

"Do I meet with your approval?"

To answer him, she reached out and palmed one smooth buttock. It flexed at her touch.

"Oh yes, you do. But you must know how truly striking you are. Surely other women have told you."

He turned to face her.

"Not in so many words. Nor as directly, Minerva. What are you wearing? Your trouser skirt?"

"I am," she said. "That way I had no need for a crinoline or a hoop. I'm not wearing undergarments, though," she said, feeling her face warm.

"No corset?"

"No. Or corset cover, I'm afraid."

"So there is just one layer of clothing between you and nakedness, is that it?" he asked.

"Yes."

"And you traveled through London nearly naked to come to me?"

"It's not all that far from my house, but yes."

Before he could say anything further, she narrowed the gap between them, reaching out and touching his face much as he had hers. Her left hand trailed gently over the scars near his right eye, fingers dancing over the closed lid. Whoever had done this terrible thing to him should be punished, but it wasn't Neville.

Her brother, however, had no part in this moment or this night.

"Shall I take off my clothes?" she asked.

He smiled, the expression so sweet it made her heart swell.

"I wish you would. A little description would be welcome, too."

"Why should I describe myself? In a few minutes you'll feel me. Wouldn't your hands be your eyes?"

"Then by all that's holy, Minerva, would you please hurry?"

"I'm supposed to be seducing you, Dalton," she said, smiling.

Stepping back, she pulled her bodice out of the waistband of her skirt and began to unfasten the buttons.

"My breasts are quite large, too large for my frame, probably. You'll find that out in a moment. They're also very sensitive."

He grabbed one of the four posters and swung himself up into the bed, sitting on the edge of the mattress. She wanted to reach out and stroke his leg, her fingers dancing along the hair there or through the dusting of hair on his chest.

"I'm removing my bodice now," she said.

"Slowly," he said. "Too damn slowly."

Her smile widened.

"I have two buttons at my waist. I'm unfastening these now."

"Thank God for progress." He patted the mattress beside him. "Once you're naked, Minerva, would you join me here?"

She stepped out of her trousers skirt and left it on the floor.

"You sound as proper as if we're having tea," he said.

"But I don't feel the least bit proper."

Nor did he look that way.

She took two steps to the bed and reached out her hand, her fingers trailing up his erection.

"You have an obelisk," she said.

His bark of laughter sparked her own smile.

"An obelisk?"

"Or a fertility statue. Or even a learning aid. The better to acquaint young maidens with what might happen on their wedding night. If they're fortunate."

"You have the most unfettered imagination,"

"Oh," she said bending her head. "I don't think it's imagination at all. Anticipation, perhaps."

She bestowed a soft kiss on the tip of his erection.

He jerked, startled.

"Bloody hell, Minerva," he said.

"I'm not a virgin. If you wish me to have had absolutely no experience in the act, I can pretend, I suppose."

He reached out and grabbed her arm and before she could say anything else he had somehow lifted her and placed her on the mattress. Now he knelt over her, a study of shadows in the pale moonlight.

"You're going to call me astounding again, aren't you?" she said. "I do wish you wouldn't."

"Why not?"

"Because it makes me sound like I'm doing something terrible. Like I'm odd. There goes astounding Minerva Todd, with her trousers skirt and her yen to dig in the dirt."

"There goes astounding Minerva Todd, with her ability to kiss like a demon and her surprising sensuality. Who would have guessed it, with her being all proper and proud?"

"Sensuality? I've never been called sensual."

He moved so he was straddling her.

"There," he said. "I have you trapped. You can't disappear like a dream in the night."

"Did you dream of me?"

"I envisioned you here," he said, surprising her. "But the reality is so much better than what I imagined."

"I have to say the same," she said, reaching up and placing her hand against his chest.

His muscles flexed as if to welcome her touch. She stroked upward to his shoulders, feeling the power of his arms and marveling at how muscled he was.

"Aren't you going to kiss me?"

"And lose my mind again? I think I'd rather touch you first, learn you."

A thrill raced through her at his words.

"Only if I can touch you in return."

"Not right now," he said, bending and placing a kiss between her breasts. "Your breasts are sensitive?"

"Yes," she said, and the sound came out a sibilant whisper.

He trailed a path with his lips to the tip of one breast. First, a gentle, acquainting kiss. Then, the touch of his tongue on her nipple.

A sound escaped her. Not quite a moan, but more an approving acknowledgment of what he was doing, of his teasing touch and the smile she felt against her breast.

"I quite like large breasts," he said. "And the more sensitive, the better."

"How very fortunate for both of us," she said, the breath leaving her as he placed his mouth over her nipple and softly began to suck.

Her lower body wanted to move—hips to arch, feet to plant themselves firmly on the bed, the better to offer her entire body to him. She stroked her hands up and down his arms, her short nails gently scratching at his skin.

He was spending entirely too much time on her breasts when there were other parts that wanted to be touched or kissed.

She felt molten inside as if her entire body was heating to welcome him.

Come into me. Were those words too shocking to utter? But, oh, how she wished he would.

She reached down between them and grabbed his erection with both hands, stroking it, measuring it with her fingers. It was at least nine fingers long and so wide around that her thumb and forefinger didn't meet when she extended them around it.

How very much she wanted to experience him. Each time he drew a nipple into his mouth or grazed it gently with his teeth, the ache grew.

"Kiss me, please."

He lifted his head from her breasts. "I am, Minerva."

"On my mouth. I want your kisses."

He raised his head again. "Are you a demanding lover, Minerva?"

"I suppose I am. Tonight, especially."

He raised up, kissed her gently on the cheek and then on the chin. Once more on the nose.

"What about tonight is special?"

"You. You're driving me daft."

"I haven't even begun, Minerva," he whispered.

Softly, he placed his mouth on hers. Then his tongue was there, touching the tip of hers, dancing along her teeth, exploring and dominating, causing lights to flicker behind her eyelids.

She congratulated herself on her courage. Somehow, she had known what it would be like to make love with him. Somehow, her body had recognized that he was a master of all things carnal, that he could bring her pleasure with the stroke of a hand, now teasing the hair at the juncture of her thighs.

"You're very receptive, Minerva."

"It's you," she said against his lips.

"Do you want me?"

With that, he gently inserted a finger into her, his thumb still stroking, maddening her.

She nearly bit his lips.

"Yes."

Her arms went around his neck to hold him tight.

She widened her legs for even easier access. He stroked his fingers against her while crooning soft words in her ear. Words of praise, seduction, teasing words that accompanied his middle finger gently stroking her. She shuddered, her breath uneven. Her heart thundered in her chest, her pulse racing.

This wasn't just passion, but something more. Something earthy and elemental, as ancient as the universe.

She was, at that moment, any woman, every woman.

The urge to mate, to be taken, to reach satisfaction was dominant. If she couldn't have him, she knew she would die.

She reached one hand between them again, grabbed him like he was a club and pulled him to her. His gentle laughter taunted her.

"It isn't a handle, Minerva."

"Then give it to me," she said. "Now."

"Minerva Todd, do you always get your way in all things?"

"Please. Dalton, please."

Her hips rose. She was shaking.

"Please."

He bent down and kissed her as he slid inside. Her hips arched, her feet planted flat on the mattress as she surged upward to meet him.

The pleasure was so acute she nearly fainted.

He filled her completely, banishing any thoughts of emptiness or longing. She would remember this moment, these seconds, the feel of him, forever.

His mouth left hers and she moaned as he drew back. But then he surged forward again, their hip bones bumping.

"Put your legs around mine," he said.

She did. She would've done anything at that point. Her nails gripped his back and held on, awash in pleasure and need and the sharpness of something she'd never before felt.

He pushed up against her, each gentle press encouragement for the pleasure to ripen, to deepen, to spread throughout her body until her fingertips tingled.

She pulled his head down for a kiss. She sobbed his name, had the sudden horrifying thought that Mrs. Thompson or any of the servants might hear.

Then she didn't care.

Her body exploded from the inside out. She became

a sparkling star and he was the only solid thing in her world.

HE WANTED her. He needed Minerva in a way that startled him. She was brazen and shocking, yet so essentially good and whole that to be near her purified him.

Their bodies met and merged in a perfect union even though their minds occasionally clashed. Spirit? If he were to consider spirit—an odd thought, since he wasn't so inclined—he thought they might have similar spirits. They were each daring, not easily cowed, determined to stand apart from society since they didn't fit well inside it.

He drew back.

She pulled him forward, insistent in passion.

He smiled and let Minerva seduce him.

Bliss filled him and he kissed her rather than startle all the neighbors with his shout of joy.

SHE HELD him in her arms, wondering which of them was trembling the most.

She could hardly draw a breath, her heart was beating so hard. She'd never known that passion could be violent, so elemental that she wouldn't have cared if the world saw them mating.

His arms were around her, pulling her close.

"I'm here," she said, feeling the inexplicable need to offer him comfort. She wrapped her arms around his shoulders, her cheek against his chest.

"So long," he said. "So long."

"So long for what?"

"Someone touched me."

She almost spoke then, to offer up a dozen instances when people had put their hand on his sleeve or taken his arm.

But that's not what he meant. He needed to be considered a man. A lover who experienced passion and pleasure. He needed to be held as she was holding him now as if she couldn't bear to be parted from him as her heart gradually slowed and her breath returned.

"I'm here," she said again, reaching up and kissing his cheek. Her heart expanded in that moment, widened to include him. She'd never been precognitive before, or even believed in it, but she knew he'd always have a spot there for as long as he wanted it, and perhaps longer.

Chapter 27

"*H*ave I given good service, sir?"

Dalton looked toward the doorway. "For God's sake, man, announce yourself. I know I've asked you more than once."

"I'm sorry, Your Lordship. But have I given good service in all other ways?"

"If you'd quit sneaking up on me, I could say yes."

"Then may I ask a question, sir?"

"Isn't that a question, Howington?"

"Very droll, sir," his secretary said.

He wasn't trying to be amusing.

"What is it?"

The quicker Howington spit out what was on his mind, the quicker he could be left alone. He wanted to think about Minerva, surprising Minerva, enchanting Minerva, astounding Minerva, even though she disliked the label.

Since it was the Friday to Monday, he didn't expect her at his house. But he should have made arrangements regardless. He missed her.

Somewhere, a warning bell clanged in his mind.

"May I ask why Miss Todd assists you in matters that would normally be my province?"

Because I lust after Minerva Todd, and I've never experienced a similar feeling for you.

What would Howington say to the truth?

He decided not to test the man.

"There are plenty of other duties for you, Howington. Don't feel as if Miss Todd is trying to usurp your place."

"Begging your pardon, sir, but what else am I to think? Everything I've seen her do are duties I could execute as well, if not better."

He doubted that, since Minerva challenged his mind, amused him, and interested him more than any other woman he'd ever met.

"Perhaps you would be happier somewhere else, Howington."

"Sir," his secretary said, sounding shocked. "On no account, Your Lordship."

The man grated on his nerves, irritated him when they did work together, and was a colossal pain in the arse. In addition, there was that feeling he had, the one that hadn't gone away. Something was wrong about Howington and he couldn't figure out what it was.

"I think you need an employer with two good eyes. That way, you wouldn't have to keep announcing yourself."

"Your Lordship, you can't be serious."

He disliked being told, in so many words, that he was an idiot, especially in his own home.

"I find that I'm completely serious, Howington. Not only that, but it's a situation I should have acted on months ago."

"But everything I've done for you—"

The man's voice halted when Dalton held up a hand.

"For which you've been amply compensated, Howington. I'd venture to guess that you might even be the highest paid secretary in all of London."

Howington cleared his throat. "Are you implying that I've stolen from you?"

He hadn't been, but it might be a good idea to have Benny assign one of his staff to look over his accounts. Or did Minerva have a head for numbers? He trusted her.

The warning bell clanged again.

"I came to tell you a telegraph came for you," Howington said.

He heard the man step toward the desk. A moment later a piece of paper drifted down to rest on his hand.

"Perhaps Miss Todd can read it for you."

With that, Howington announced his departure, the first time he'd ever done so. It was a relief to Dalton, knowing this time it was permanent, that he wouldn't see Howington again.

Mrs. Thompson was kind and gracious enough to read the telegraph to him.

He only had a vague recollection of Glynis, his female cousin from Scotland. He knew she'd married at their London house, with his mother making the arrangements. She'd truly liked the woman, often saying that if she had a daughter, she'd like her to be just like Glynis.

Perhaps he needed to hold a reunion of sorts for the entire clan. Or maybe he should wait until after the war was over and invite his American cousins as well. After all, they sprang from the same family.

Glynis's words surprised him enough that he asked Mrs. Thompson to reread the telegraph.

"And that's all she said?"

"Yes, Your Lordship. 'Have located Neville. Letter to follow.'"

"She might've told me where he was."

"I'm sure it will only be a few days until we receive the letter, Your Lordship. It might come in tomorrow's post."

"I hope you're right, Mrs. Thompson."

"It's sorry I am that Stanley left your employ," she said. "I always liked the young man. But he disappointed me greatly in his actions."

He had to take a minute before he matched Stanley with Howington. Odd, that he never thought of the man by any other than his surname.

Stanley didn't fit him, and when he said as much to Mrs. Thompson, she laughed, a tinkling laugh that made her sound twenty years younger.

"I used to say that about my dear Fred," she said. "The name never fit him, either. He needed something more adventurous."

"Has it been very long since you lost him?"

She reached over and patted his hand.

"Bless you for asking, Your Lordship, but it has been quite long. I've been a widow longer than I was married, but that doesn't stop the memories. Nor does it stop the wondering. I wonder what he would have been like if he lived. I wonder what it would have been like if we'd had children."

"All I can say, Mrs. Thompson, is that I'm grateful for your presence in my home and all the help you've given me since I returned from America."

He didn't add that he was a little ashamed to admit he could barely remember her in the days before he'd left London. Days in which he was more occupied with his own pleasure than the presence of the people who lived in his home and whose sole purpose had been his comfort.

Hardly an improvement, to go from being a rake to a recluse.

Did Minerva think the same? And when had her opinion begun to matter?

"I'M SORRY, Miss Minerva, but I can't go. Not with my mam being sick and all."

"Thank you, Charlotte," Minerva managed to say, although she didn't believe a word of it.

This was the first she'd heard of Charlotte's mother being ill. She sent her best wishes to the woman and watched as the maid left her sitting room.

Nora had refused to accompany her to Scotland as well. The reason was her fear of trains, of all things, which came about suddenly.

Betty had claimed she was afflicted with a sickness of the bowels, explaining every symptom in such graphic detail that she'd waved her hand in front of her to stop the girl.

Each one of the maids who had gone to Scotland with her in previous expeditions was refusing to accompany her now.

Fine, she would simply go by herself, although traveling with only Hugh as her companion wasn't the wisest choice she could make, especially after their confrontation this morning.

When she informed him she wanted to go to Scotland, he only nodded, his face bland.

"Are you angry with me for some reason?"

"On no account, Miss Todd. It's not my carriage. If you want to take it somewhere or allow someone else to drive it, it's not my say."

She had a sinking feeling in the pit of her stomach. "Michael told you."

He gave her a sideways look.

"Michael didn't have to tell me, Miss Todd. The carriage hadn't been put up the way I do it."

"You mustn't blame him, Hugh, or punish him in any way. What he did was at my direction."

"Yes, Miss Todd."

"Are you going to be like this all the way to Scotland?"

"I don't know what you mean, Miss Todd."

"Oh, bother, Hugh. You know very well what I mean. If you're angry with me, go ahead and say it now and let's get it out in the open. Otherwise, stop calling me 'Miss Todd' in that tone of voice."

"Why did you go to him?"

She almost stomped her foot in frustration. She'd made a terrible mistake by having a relationship with Hugh. He hadn't understood why it had to end, and now he wanted to bring the past into the present.

"I really don't have to explain, Hugh," she said.

"You wear on a man, Minerva. You settle in like a hook and hang there."

"Is that how you feel?" she asked, startled by his description.

"I'd be your lover still, if you'd allow it."

How did she tell Hugh that she'd never felt for him what she felt for Dalton, damn the man?

"It's better if we don't discuss it," she said.

"I know what's happening between you and your earl. I can't blame you for aiming higher."

"Aiming higher? The man drives me insane."

"But you can't forget him. He's your flame, just like you're mine. Moths, Minerva. We're all moths."

He turned and left the bay, leaving her standing there staring after him.

She was going to have to make the decision about Hugh. Perhaps it would be wiser to simply release him to go and find another position.

Was she going to be endlessly bedeviled by her mistakes? First Hugh, and now Dalton. What had she done? Stupid, stupid woman, she'd gotten herself enmeshed with a man who interested her too much.

He crooked his little finger and she sprang to his side like a trained dog. Even her seduction of him hadn't been hers after all. She had walked into his net and been trapped.

She was starting to feel entirely too much for the Earl of Rathsmere. She would not be just one more of his conquests. Poor plain Minerva Todd, drawn to the spider's web like a drunken fly. Or a moth, like Hugh said.

She remembered every moment of that night. When dawn broke over the eastern sky, she didn't want to leave, but she had, donning her clothes amidst laughter and kisses.

He'd walked her to the garden gate in his dressing gown. The Earl of Rathsmere stood there nearly naked to ensure she got to her carriage without incident.

She watched him until a sleepy Michael had pulled away and driven her home. The hour was still early enough that she crept to her bed without any of the servants seeing her.

Only to be unable to sleep, thinking of him.

No, she was not going to be imprisoned by emotions. She was not going to become one of those foolish women who couldn't do anything except pine for their beloved.

She had work that interested her, a sponsor she admired, and several hundred miles to put between her and Dalton MacIain.

She was going to Scotland.

After sending a telegram to Lady Terry that she was on her way, she packed her trunk with all her equipment and cooking utensils. She had Cook load the carriage with another trunk of foodstuffs that would last a few weeks, jars of pickled things and dried meat. Her aprons were next, each full-length and equipped with pockets for pencils, notebooks, measuring devices, and small glass jars.

Hugh would load the heavier tools into another trunk, everything from small shovels and picks to brushes for removing the dirt from more delicate objects. It might have made more sense to take a carriage to Scotland, but the journey would have lasted days. Instead, they would take a train to Glasgow and hire a carriage there.

The preparations for the trip to Scotland calmed her mind and eased her emotions. She couldn't go back to work for Dalton. She couldn't sit across the desk from him and study his face day after day, acting like a lovesick woman. She couldn't sit next to him in the wing chair and not reach over and touch him. Just her fingertips on the top of his hand, or her palm on his sleeve. She would want to graze her knuckles across his cheek in the afternoon, feeling the growth of his beard. Or bend to kiss his eye patch, as if doing so might grant him the gift of sight.

What would she do if he wanted to touch her in turn? Could she push away his hand if he cupped her face? What would she do if he whispered to her, "Join me in my room, Minerva"?

What would she do if he kissed her again as they sat alone in the library?

No, she was much better off going to Scotland. Out of sight, out of mind, wasn't that the saying? All she had to do was occupy herself with her work and visit with Lady Terry.

Dalton MacIain would no longer be at the forefront of her thoughts. Nor would she continue to chastise herself. She would excuse her actions in the spirit of curiosity. She had wanted to know what it would be like to bed the Rake of London.

Wonderful. Glorious. Divine. Unbelievable.

Now that she knew, she would endeavor, somehow, to forget the episode.

She would have left for Scotland without another thought had not Mrs. Beauchamp waylaid her.

"Miss Todd," the housekeeper said, "I hope you realize that I know my place. I've never said much when you wear your trousers skirt or fiddle with things from a grave all day long."

"Yes, Mrs. Beauchamp?" she asked, pulling on her gloves.

"But I feel I have to tell you that I think you're making a mistake, going to Scotland with only Hugh as company."

"I'll be fine, Mrs. Beauchamp."

"It's not that he'd do anything, Miss Todd. I've faith enough in Hugh, but it's what other people would say. It's not done, Miss Todd, you being a single lady and all."

"I'm not exactly a maiden in the schoolroom, Mrs. Beauchamp."

"No, Miss Todd, but you're not a widow, either. You've never gone to Scotland without a maid or two with you."

"None of them wish to accompany me, Mrs. Beauchamp, and I can't force them."

"Well, for them, it's sleeping in a tent, Miss Todd, with no accommodations and the like. It's always raining and they're always wet."

"I didn't know that's how they felt," she said.

"Nor should you. They didn't tell you, Miss Minerva, but they did share their feelings with me."

She'd taken pleasure in her expeditions, while it was now quite obvious that her servants hadn't.

"Thank you for your concern, Mrs. Beauchamp, but I'll stay with Lady Terry on this trip. That should silence the gossips."

Mrs. Beauchamp didn't look mollified.

"What am I to do," she asked, "if no one wishes to accompany me?"

"Don't go, Miss Minerva."

She stared at her housekeeper, wishing she could

make the woman understand. She had to leave, as quickly as possible, before she did something even more foolish.

"AND WHY on earth do you think I want to employ you?" Lewis asked.

Stanley Howington didn't rise when Lewis MacIain entered the parlor. Or what should have been the parlor had it been cleaned. Newspapers were scattered on several surfaces along with a selection of dirty dishes.

"Don't you employ a maid?" he asked.

"I don't have the funds to employ anyone," Lewis said. "There's a caretaker of sorts for the house, but he doesn't do anything but mumble when he sees me."

He didn't enter the room fully, but leaned against the door frame, folding his arms. "If I did have the money, I certainly wouldn't be hiring a secretary. Why ever for?"

"Because I provided you with information," Howington said. "That deserves some loyalty, does it not? Not to mention the funds I advanced you when Dalton was in America."

Lewis didn't say anything for a moment, merely regarded him with an impassive expression.

Howington had seen that look many times before from Dalton. The man had no idea of all of the services he performed since he'd been hired. He was the one who ensured the servants and the tradesmen were paid and looked over Mrs. Thompson's expenditures. He'd kept the man supplied in liquor.

What did he get for his loyalty? To be treated with disdain when Dalton noticed him. More often than not, the man barely knew he was there. Everything had changed after America. The earl's disdain had transformed into ridicule and active dislike.

At first he thought that Dalton must know what

he'd done. But there was no way he could have. No, the man's antipathy rose from another reason entirely, one that was a mystery. The new Earl of Rathsmere had developed an intense dislike to him, and Stanley had known his days were numbered.

But to be pushed out because of a woman? Especially a woman like Minerva Todd? No, he wasn't going to accept that insult.

Howington's face felt stiff when he attempted to smile. If he had any other recourse, he would turn his back on the MacIains and have nothing to do with them. But his pride had gotten the better of him. By walking away from the Earl of Rathsmere, he'd effectively damaged his chances of being employed by another peer. Without a letter of introduction, without references, he might as well be one of the walking poor of London.

"Very well," he said, his voice composed. "Perhaps I should throw myself on your brother's mercy. Tell him what I did and beg his forgiveness."

"Go ahead," Lewis said. "It's your word against mine."

"Not entirely," Howington said. "I keep very good records, Lewis. I never throw anything away. I have a copy of the letter I sent you. The one recommending William Harris to do your bidding."

If he hadn't been studying Lewis so carefully, he might not have seen the subtle change of expression. The man was in a bind and knew it.

"You can begin by cleaning up this room," Lewis said, stepping away from the door. "And your next task will be to figure out how I get some money."

"Without killing your brother this time?" Stanley asked, smiling.

Chapter 28

$\mathcal{M}$inerva was late. She was late when she'd always been punctual, arriving at nine. Perhaps he needed to finalize their employment agreement. She would always appear when he expected her. In return, he would pay her double what he'd paid Howington.

Would she agree to come to his house on a Saturday or Sunday? The past two days had been miserable without her. Could he convince her?

How on earth was he to work with her all day and not kiss her? Or clasp her hand in his, just to feel her touch?

"I hate like hell to make that smile disappear," James said.

Dalton turned toward the door, just able to make out the shape standing there. But it was more than he'd been able to see a few weeks ago.

He motioned toward one of the chairs in front of his desk.

"Then don't," he said to his old friend. "I take it you've interviewed Alice."

"I have."

He turned his head, staring at the window, startled at the brightness that greeted him. He blinked and turned away.

"What kind of day is it?"

"It looks to rain," James said. "But I haven't come

here to discuss the weather. We have to talk about Arthur's death."

He knew that. He'd known from the moment James entered the room. But he was stalling for time, hoping against hope that James had brought him some other news than what he expected. How did he cope with the realization that Lewis was motivated by greed? That he'd allowed it to drive him to murder? How did he accept the fact that Lewis killed Arthur?

"Alice is a lovely woman," James said.

"I haven't seen her since I returned to London," Dalton said. "She's made no effort to get in touch with me."

"You've been such a recluse, do you blame her?"

"Yes," he said. "She was Arthur's wife, but she married someone only months after his death. I doubt it was my reclusiveness that prevented her from seeing me. No doubt it was embarrassment."

"If it makes any difference," James said, "she seems very happy. Her husband was present during our interview. He's very protective of her. They held hands the whole time."

Why was he so irritated on Arthur's behalf? Had he forgotten about Sarah? The very woman who had led him to question Arthur's death?

"What did Alice say?"

"Lewis and Arthur had a fight the night before. About money, she said. To quote her, 'It was always about money with Lewis.'"

He nodded, unsurprised.

"She saw him coming into the house about two o'clock. She got word of the accident a few minutes later."

The feeling in his stomach was reminiscent of those months in America, when he'd been so hungry that he'd eaten something suspicious, only for it to make him ill.

"Even suspecting what we do," James was saying, "there isn't enough proof to go to the authorities. No one actually saw Lewis shoot Arthur."

"Then what the hell do we do? Forget it? Pretend it didn't happen? Let him get away with it?"

"There's one way," James said, "but it means making you a target."

"How?"

"We flush him out," James said. "We give him news that inspires him to act quickly, hopefully carelessly."

"I have no objection to being a target, James, but what news are you considering?"

"What's the one thing Lewis wouldn't want to happen, the one thing he wouldn't want you to do?"

"I'm not sure I understand."

"If Lewis was behind Arthur's death, and also at the root of what happened to you in America, then he wants the earldom."

"And the fortune that goes along with it," Dalton said. "He's already gone through his inheritance." Before James could say anything further, he understood. "My marriage. He wouldn't want me to marry and father children."

"Exactly."

"I doubt he would believe I'm getting married, James. I've been a recluse."

"Not with Miss Todd."

His ears felt hot.

Had Hinnity reported Minerva's arrival the other night? James probably knew the exact moment Minerva entered his home and how long she remained.

"I don't mind being a target, James," he said. "But not Minerva."

"I can assure you, Dalton, that she won't be in any danger. I'll put my best operative on guarding her."

His mind didn't shy away from marrying Minerva. The bell that would've otherwise clanged at the idea was somehow silent.

"Would Miss Todd agree to the deception?"

"Is there any reason she should know?" Dalton asked. "I could communicate the news to Lewis in a note."

"It would be better if he read the announcement in the newspaper."

"Then I'd better inform Minerva we're engaged."

If the engagement were publicized, he would have to make sure that the world knew she broke it off, so she wasn't affected by the ruse. If anything, society would understand. Poor girl, trapped in marriage to the monster.

Damn it, he wasn't an ogre. At least she'd never considered him one.

Ten minutes after James left, their plan agreed upon, Mrs. Thompson appeared at the door.

"Sir, the post has come," she said.

Normally, the mail was Howington's duty. At least he was spared the man's slinking into the room.

"The letter from your cousin is here."

"So soon?" Glynis must have mailed it before telegraphing him.

"Would you like me to read it?"

No. The answer was instantaneous. He didn't want to hear another bit of bad news, this about Minerva's brother.

"Yes, if you don't mind, Mrs. Thompson."

She settled into the chair in front of him, opened the letter and began to read.

The news was as bad as he feared.

Minerva needed to know, but he dreaded telling her. How could he bring her pain?

"Begging your pardon, sir," Daniels said.

Every single member of his household knew to announce himself except for that fool, Howington. Once again he was grateful he wouldn't have to deal with the man again.

If Daniels was here, then where was Minerva?

"I've a note, sir," his driver said.

"A note?"

"Yes, sir."

"Miss Todd isn't with you?"

"No sir. She just sent a note."

"Shall I read it, sir?" Mrs. Thompson asked.

When she finished reading the one-sentence note, he said, "That's all? 'I will be unable to assist you in your endeavors'?"

"Yes, Your Lordship."

"Thank you, Mrs. Thompson."

"Is there anything I can get you, Your Lordship?"

"No, Mrs. Thompson. Thank you."

He was extraordinarily calm at the moment, a fact he noted even as he turned to Daniels.

She'd sent him a note. She was not going to get away with sending him a note. Bloody hell.

"I need you to take me to Miss Todd's house."

He'd taken extra care with his appearance this morning, in preparation for seeing the annoying woman. His shoes had been shined by one of the maids, his shirt ironed by another. He'd managed not to cut himself too much while shaving. If he had any mishaps, it was because his mind hadn't been on his task.

Instead, he'd been thinking about Minerva, the most irritating woman in the world.

"Do I look presentable, Mrs. Thompson?"

"You look perfect, sir."

He smiled his thanks for her loyalty.

A few moments later he and Daniels were in the

lane behind his house and his driver was opening the carriage door.

"It looks to rain, sir, and the air feels funny the way it does just before a storm."

At least he wasn't out in a field somewhere, waiting for the Confederate army to come over the hill, a comment he didn't make to his driver.

"A little spot of rain won't hurt us, will it, Daniels?"

"Not at all, Your Lordship."

At Minerva's house, Daniels acted as his guide.

"There are two steps now, then a walk a little farther to the main steps. There are five of those."

He really didn't need Minerva to escort him through London, did he? If he hadn't asked for her help, though, he wouldn't have employed her to be his secretary. Things wouldn't have progressed as far as they had and he wouldn't be on her doorstep, annoyed and irritated that she was playing coy.

He'd never chased a woman in his life, didn't she know that? But he was evidently chasing Minerva Todd, because here he was. No, that wasn't right. He had a damn good reason for being here: Glynis's letter about Neville.

He knew, from Daniels's description the last time he was here, that the house was dark red brick with white framed windows. The front door, like his own, was black. The steps were framed by a black wrought-iron railing on either side, and a gas lamp with the same wrought-iron pattern sat at the curb before each house.

"The house next door, sir. There are two ladies in the parlor windows downstairs, and one standing in an upstairs window."

"The Covington sisters," he said, smiling.

"Do you know them, sir?"

"I know of them. A pity we didn't bring Arthur's

carriage, the fancy one. I might have given them a thrill. Where are they, Daniels?"

"Slightly to the right, sir, in the town house next door."

He raised his hand and waved.

A moment later he was at the door and Daniels was trotting back down the steps to stand at the carriage and be stared at by the Covington sisters.

Only a plain knocker adorned the door, something that felt shiny like polished brass.

The door opened and the smell of cinnamon washed over him.

"Yes? May I help you?"

Was she the cook of the house, the woman responsible for cinnamon scones each morning?

He introduced himself. "May I speak with Miss Todd?"

"Oh, Your Lordship, I'm sorry. She's not at home."

Where the blazes was she? That question was answered before he could ask it.

"She's gone to Scotland, sir."

"Scotland?"

"Yes, sir."

He tried to command his features to remain expressionless. The less he revealed, the less vulnerable he felt.

"Thank you."

He stepped back and turned, wishing he knew where the hell the railing was. He didn't trust his balance enough to sail down the steps without holding onto something. He heard the door close softly behind him and released the breath he hadn't known he was holding.

He waved at Daniels, hoped the man knew it was a cry for help, and stood there feeling exposed and foolish.

She'd gone to Scotland, damn it. She'd traipsed off to Scotland in her trousers skirt and her full lips.

Why?

Why had she left him so precipitously?

No doubt she was tired of being a nursemaid to a blind man. Had she felt the same when she'd come to his house, to his bedroom, to his bed?

He was damned if he was going to be an object of pity.

"Are you the earl?"

The female voice was directly below him.

He jerked, startled, not expecting to be confronted by a stranger. He grabbed the gold top of his walking stick tighter.

"You have me at a disadvantage, madam."

The odor of mothballs and soap came closer.

"I'm Amelia Covington."

One of the Covington sisters. Did they interview all of Minerva's guests or had he somehow incited their curiosity by waving at them?

"Are you the earl?" she asked again.

He bowed slightly. "Dalton MacIain, the Earl of Rathsmere," he said, thinking of Arthur when he did so. Would he ever grow comfortable with the title? Or would he continually remember Arthur, who was, he suspected, a much better earl than he'd ever be?

If Miss Amelia Covington expected more courtliness from him, she wasn't going to get it. He'd done all he could do.

"Are your sisters here?" he asked again.

"No, they're at home. They chose me to come and speak with you."

"May I ask why?"

"Minerva's gone off to Scotland, Your Lordship."

"So I've been told."

"Can you not go and fetch her?"

"I beg your pardon?"

"She's the sweetest girl, but sometimes we think she needs someone looking after her. Just imagine, going off to Scotland on her own, with no maid and only that driver of hers."

"Hugh," he said.

She came to his side and grabbed his arm, startling him again. "Come to tea, please, and we'll tell you why we think she's in danger."

"Danger, Miss Covington?"

"Danger, Your Lordship."

AT THE bottom of the steps Daniels greeted him, grabbing his right arm as if to pull him away from Miss Covington.

The woman, however, was relentless.

A moment later he was going up an identical set of steps, Daniels on his right side and Miss Abigail Covington clinging to his left arm.

At the top of the steps, Daniels whispered, "Sir, do you want that I should go inside?"

"There's no need," Miss Covington said brightly.

She grabbed Dalton's hand as if he were a child, holding onto it with the grip of a paranoid mother.

"His Lordship will be fine with us."

Heaven help him.

"If you'll remain here, Daniels, I'd appreciate it. I won't be long."

That last sentence was both for his driver and Miss Covington. This wasn't going to be an extended visit. He would remain long enough to understand what she was saying about danger and then leave.

The minute the door was open he smelled more mothballs and something thick and rich like marmalade.

"There's a table here, Your Lordship," she said, but not quickly enough for him to avoid it.

He stumbled, righted himself, and pasted an appropriate social smile on his face. They walked down a long hall and then into another room, one almost uncomfortably warm.

Someone pulled his walking stick away from him and grabbed his arm. Maybe he should have made Daniels accompany him.

The room felt suffocatingly small. He enlarged it in his imagination, had the Covington sisters looking somewhere else other than at him. But he didn't doubt they were staring directly at him, probably measuring every twitch and muscle flex.

"This is my sister Gladys," Abigail Covington said. "And my sister Helen. This is the Earl of Rathsmere," she continued, obviously addressing them. "The man Minerva's been going to see each day."

"Do you have a spy in Miss Todd's household?" he asked.

"A spy?"

A different voice spoke, one without the sweetness, but with a more acerbic tone. He didn't know if it was Helen or Gladys.

"That makes us sound very nefarious."

"Instead of simply interested. It's Minerva, after all."

"We knew her mother and father."

"And Neville as well."

Instead of three women, he felt like he was surrounded by thirty.

Abigail—at least he thought it was Abigail—directed him to a chair. He sank down into it gratefully.

"Here's your walking stick, Your Lordship," one of the sisters said. Helen?

"Of course," Abigail said, "we are very close friends with Mrs. Beauchamp."

"Mrs. Beauchamp?"

"Minerva's housekeeper. The most sturdy and reliable woman that ever was. Why, she could give lessons to our own housekeeper."

"And has, on many occasions," one of the other sisters said.

"Very generous in her training."

And her information, evidently.

"What's this about danger?" he asked, trying to steer the conversation back on course.

"Because of Hugh, of course."

"We tried to tell her—through Mrs. Beauchamp, of course—that it was not the proper thing to do."

"Gladys has made pumpkin bread, Your Lordship. Would you like some? I'd be more than happy to feed you."

Good God, no.

"Thank you, Miss Covington, but that's not necessary."

"But you will partake, won't you? Gladys will be offended if you don't."

The Covington sisters were gentle tyrants. He didn't want anything to eat or drink. He was here because Abigail had whispered of danger to him.

He put a polite smile on his face, one that reminded him of his childhood and lessons in manners. Arthur was much better at events like this, always knowing when to say the proper thing.

"Here's your tea, then, Your Lordship," Abigail said with a hint of disapproval in her voice.

If she was annoyed at him, she wasn't going to share what she knew.

"I do apologize, Miss Covington," he said. "I'd love some pumpkin bread."

He took the plate she gave him and wondered if he could get away with simply holding it.

"You were mentioning danger?"

He was having a difficult time wading through this marsh of words, a clear sign that he'd been a recluse for too long. Strange, that he didn't have any difficulty verbally sparring with Minerva.

"Why ever would she go to Scotland alone with only her driver?" one of the women asked.

"I believe Miss Todd has an interest in archaeology," he said, wondering if he was giving away any secrets. If so, Minerva would not be pleased with him.

"Of course she does. But are there not enough places in England to interest her?"

Dear God, had he found himself in a nest of anti-Scottish women? Perhaps he should tell them his family name, and inform them he was descended from Highlanders, Scottish Highlanders.

"Is there nothing you can do, Your Lordship?"

"What would you have me do, Miss Covington?"

"Go after her, Your Lordship. Keep her in England where she belongs."

"She is not my ward, Miss Covington. She merely acts as my secretary from time to time." He had planned on asking her to perform the task full-time, at least until he replaced Howington.

"Is there nothing that can be done to protect her reputation, Your Lordship?"

The irony of someone asking the former Rake of London how to protect a woman's reputation was not lost on him. Especially since he'd done everything he could to ruin her himself. Granted, he had not instigated the affair, but he hadn't gently guided Minerva back home when she'd come to him, either. Instead, he'd taken advantage of the situation—and her.

"Minerva is a force to herself," one of the Covington sisters said. "She is the epitome of a modern woman, an example for any young woman to follow. Why, her escapades keep us entertained for hours at a time."

"You admire her, Miss Covington?"

"Indeed, Your Lordship. She is someone to emulate for her fashion sense alone."

"Her fashion sense?"

Was he stuck with asking questions?

"She wears trousers, Your Lordship. I'm not sure if you were aware."

"Yes, Miss Todd informed me."

"See? Does that not explain how courageous she is?"

He couldn't wait to tell Minerva that the Covington sisters were fascinated by her, that they weren't nosy as much as filled with admiration.

"But we know full well that while we might be forward thinking women, the rest of the world is not so forgiving. Why, people might even think things about Minerva's work for you each day. But to go off with only her driver to Scotland, to an abandoned castle, well that's just asking rumors to fly, don't you think?"

Evidently, they thought so.

"Someone will believe the worst."

"That she's involved with her driver."

"He is a magnificent specimen of man."

"Like the prince of Persia in that new novel."

"Or the count of Montrose."

He was adrift in a sea of words. Or imaginations.

"I'll go to Scotland," he said, forcing himself to take a bite of bread. The second bite was easier, since the bread was more a pastry and delicious.

"Is that entirely necessary, Your Lordship?"

"I'm sorry," he said. "I don't understand. Don't you wish for me to rescue Miss Todd?"

"Of course, Your Lordship, but Minerva's taken the train, and we know for a fact that it doesn't leave for another two hours."

"The Caledonian Railway," another of the sisters said.

He was beginning to tell them apart. The acerbic one was Helen, while the one with the sweet voice and the cooking skills was Gladys.

"Quite a marvelous thing. Did you know that you could travel to Scotland without stopping?"

He held out his plate, and thankfully one of the sisters took it.

"If you'll excuse me, then, ladies, I will be about the business of rescuing Miss Todd."

He heard whispering.

"We most definitely approve," Abigail Covington said.

Did they realize that he didn't give a flying farthing for their approval? Evidently not. Besides, he had an excuse for plucking Minerva from the train: Neville's whereabouts.

A much better reason than the truth: *I missed you. I thought of you endlessly. You can't leave me.*

Chapter 29

King's Cross Station was only ten years old and awe-inspiring in size with its two arched roofs. No doubt the design of the building was responsible for the noise: echoes of clicking machinery, the hiss of steam, and the humming drone of conversation.

Minerva sat on a bench not far from the departure platform, wishing Hugh wasn't pacing a few feet away.

The journey to Glasgow took nearly thirteen hours, and she was prepared to nap during some of it. However, waiting for the train was always the most onerous part of the entire trip.

She couldn't wait to get to Scotland. She liked everything about the Scots: their language, their way of speaking, their hospitality, and their humor. Most of all, she admired their independence.

How strange that Dalton MacIain's heritage was Scottish.

Three times she'd gone to Partage Castle, and each time Lady Terry had invited her to stay in the house she'd built not far from the ruins.

The stately manor house with its white brick and blue painted shutters would have been at home in any English county, but in that area of Scotland it looked too large, too square, and too, well, foreign. In addition, the trees planted on either side of the drive from the white stone gate were too manicured. The rest of the land around the castle was wild, untamed, and more Scottish.

She preferred to remain at the site in order to begin work at dawn, but she would stay with Lady Terry this time to assuage Mrs. Beauchamp's concerns. Besides, she really didn't want to be alone with a sullen Hugh.

She had begun the journey this morning attired in a proper dark blue dress with white cuffs and collar. She couldn't wait to change into her trousers skirt and a dark blouse and begin work.

By tomorrow she'd be at Partage Castle.

The rain, now beating on the arched roof above, added to the cacophony around her.

Hugh refused to share her first-class accommodations, insisting on riding in the second class compartment. She'd given up arguing with him; during their expeditions to Scotland, he wasn't just her carriage driver. He was her assistant. She couldn't do what she did without his help.

What did he mean, she wore on a man? She was most definitely not a moth.

Dalton MacIain was not her flame. No, it was better if she didn't think about the man. Easier said than done, however.

He had proven surprisingly intelligent and thoughtful. She didn't know who he'd been before his experiences in America, but from the rumors, she suspected she wouldn't have liked him very much. But this man? This man with his black eye patch and his defiance toward the world held too much fascination.

How was he doing without her?

Did he miss her?

She should have sent him a note that said more than it had, but she couldn't bear the idea of Howington reading it to him. Or even sweet Mrs. Thompson. Besides, what could she have said?

That night was a terrible mistake.

I'm too attracted to you. If you crooked your finger, I'd bound across the room like a faithful puppy to be at your side. I think about you entirely too much. I have even dreamed about you, isn't that the most foolish thing? Dreaming of a Scotsman who was an English earl.

I can't see you anymore. I can't be with you. I can't bear it. You're tearing me in two, making me think that Neville might have done something monstrous and then kissing and loving me.

No, she was simply not going to allow herself to think about the man. He was a danger, an attraction she couldn't afford, and an addiction she didn't want.

She was not going to think of how he held her and kissed every inch of her skin. She was not going to remember the bliss she'd felt. But most of all, she wasn't going to remember holding him in her arms when he trembled.

She would think of Partage instead.

Dark and brooding on the landscape, the castle sat black against the sky. The Clyde ran swift beneath the cliff, while long grasses flourished in the ruins, waving at her in greeting.

Sometimes, she felt like she could hear the past if she stood still long enough. If she did, the voices of those who lived there four hundred years ago might speak to a curious English woman.

Lady Terry had shared with her information that Partage was supposed to have been the site of the castle of the Bishops of Glasgow. She hadn't discovered any evidence that such a site existed, but then, she wasn't in Scotland more than a month at a time. Perhaps she should spend more time there.

Anywhere but in London where a certain earl lived.

THANK PROVIDENCE and all the angels that there was only one departure platform at King's Cross. The station was located at the northern edge of central London, a half hour from Minerva's home.

Daniels was a good enough driver that he navigated the rainy London traffic with ease.

"I'm not supposed to leave the carriage, Your Lordship," Daniels said once they were at the station.

"Bugger the carriage," he said. "I don't care if the damn thing's nicked." He pulled some money from his pocket and stretched out his hand. "Give it to someone to watch the carriage, then."

Daniels took a few bills, then pressed the rest back into his hand. "That's enough, sir."

"Then let's be off," Dalton said. On a quest to rescue a woman from her own folly. To protect Minerva Todd, not that she would thank him for it.

She was too opinionated, too stubborn, too much an individual. She pushed against the mold of society, bent its restraints, and was in the process of making herself a source of endless gossip.

His need to protect her startled him. She was, on the face of it, not the type of woman who engendered protective impulses. But that was the problem, wasn't it? People didn't see the true Minerva. They didn't realize her loneliness or that she was easily wounded despite her crusty exterior. They didn't know her capacity for affection or her sense of loyalty and duty.

She wasn't plain; she was beautiful in a way that was completely Minerva's.

He loved her voice, loved her way of speaking. Loved her mind and her wit. He might be coming too damn close to loving her, a frightening enough thought that it occupied him as they entered King's Cross Station.

SHE LOOKED up to find Hugh approaching her.

"I've been thinking, Minerva," he abruptly said. "I think it would be a good idea if I started looking for another position."

She didn't know what to say. He was right. She had bent the boundaries of propriety with Hugh and he was the one to have suffered for it. She expected him to go back to the role he had maintained for years and that was impossible.

"If you think that's wise, Hugh."

He nodded.

"It is, what with you being involved with the earl and all."

She was certainly not going to justify her relationship with Dalton. Not when she was certain she'd made another mistake there, too.

"You're in love with him, aren't you?"

Oh, good heavens, no. She could not be in love with the Earl of Rathsmere. What a ridiculous idea that would be, feeling something for the Rake of London.

No, she was not that foolish.

She was most definitely not in love with him.

"Of course not," she said. "Nor am I a moth, Hugh."

"He'll hurt you, Minerva. Men like that do. He'll toss you aside like yesterday's handkerchief. I'd be surprised if he remembered your name the same time next year."

She felt each word like it was an arrow tipped in poison. Hugh might be right about everything. Just one reason why she was leaving for Scotland and not sitting in the Earl of Rathmere's library.

"Speaking of the earl," Hugh said, staring behind her.

She turned and looked.

The Earl of Rathsmere was headed toward her, his hand on Daniels's arm.

Dalton's mouth was thinned. His jaw was hardened and he was frowning. He hated to be the object of attention and he was most definitely that. The sight of a devastatingly handsome man in an eye patch striding through the station was enough to capture anyone's notice.

Whatever was he doing here? For that matter, what was her heart doing jumping up and down in her chest?

SHE WAS on her way to Scotland to escape him. He wasn't that much of a fool. He knew only too well that she was going to Scotland rather than coming to grips with what she'd—what they'd—done.

She was entirely too bohemian, shocking, unafraid to bend rules or ignore them altogether. She startled him continuously, amused him endlessly, forced him to reassess himself, and made him want to be a better man.

No woman should have that power.

The noise of the station was overwhelming, like a wave of sound coming toward him. He'd never felt as isolated as he did in that moment.

Or as afraid.

How idiotic. He'd faced fear in America as he stood there outflanked by the enemy. One day, all he'd seen was a continuous line of gray soldiers with guns pointed in his direction. He'd thought, at the time, that they looked like a monstrous porcupine, one with death on its mind. If he could force himself to remain calm then, a little noise in a cavernous station wasn't going to make him turn tail and run.

The urge was there, though, to find a quiet place, a small and cozy corner where he could identify by touch everything around him.

He was here to find Minerva. Pushing his discomfort to the back of his mind, he strode forward with his driver as his companion.

"Do you see her, Daniels?"

"Not yet, sir, but we aren't at the departures platform yet."

He nodded, damning his need to be guided like an infant in a pram.

Daniels suddenly said, "Good afternoon, Miss Todd."

"Is she there?" he asked.

"She is," Minerva said. "And she would appreciate being addressed correctly. What are you doing here?"

"I've come to save you," he said.

"I beg your pardon?"

"The Covington sisters sent me. They fear you will destroy your reputation if you continue on to Scotland with only your driver in attendance."

"Oh, bother, you have to be jesting."

"I assure you, Miss Todd, that I am not. I spent a good thirty minutes being utterly confused in their company. All I am certain of is one thing: they fear for your reputation. Evidently, they have doubts about Hugh's honor."

"And you're better? They evidently don't know to whom they entrusted my virtue."

No one could infuse a statement with as much disgust as Minerva Todd.

"I've given my word to rescue you."

He dropped his hand from Daniels's arm and strode forward, reaching the bench where she sat.

"Dalton," she said softly, "can you see me?"

"Only light and shadow, Minerva. I guessed that the shadow in blue was you."

"I'm going to Scotland, Your Lordship. Nothing will stop me."

"I have news of Neville," he said.

"What?"

He turned and walked back in Daniels's direction, hoping his driver had the sense to catch him if he strayed too far. Bless the man, he reached out and grabbed his sleeve.

"You can't mean to keep the information to yourself," she called after him.

He glanced back in her direction. "You can't mean to travel to Scotland with only your driver as a companion."

"I've already given notice," Hugh said.

He didn't give a flying farthing if Hugh quit on the spot. He didn't like the man very much at the moment, if ever. Not only had Hugh abetted Minerva in her idiotic choices: the night she broke into his home and the day she'd invaded his garden. Hugh was also Minerva's first lover, and there was no way he was going to forget that.

"How convenient. Are you going to leave Miss Todd's employ after the expedition to Scotland or now?"

"Afterward," she said. "Not that it's any of your concern. Where's Neville?"

"I'm not going to tell you here, Minerva."

"I do not like you very much at the moment, Your Lordship."

"That's not a matter of importance. If you want to know what I know, you'll come with me."

"I can't," she said. "All of my equipment and my trunks are loaded on the train. I can't do without them. Not my journals or my aprons, my pens, my notes."

"Send Hugh to retrieve them. Have him take the trunks back to your house."

"Tell me where my brother is, Dalton."

How sweet her voice could seem sometimes. How seductive.

"No," he said.

"Hugh, will you get our trunks?"

The words were tantamount to a capitulation, but he knew he'd only won the first round.

Perhaps it was a good thing he was blind. He didn't doubt they were the object of speculation from dozens of people. A Punch and Judy show at King's Cross. One thing about rumors, though, he'd learned in the last year. You had to know people to hear them. Minerva didn't talk about other people and neither did his staff. If he was the stuff of rumors, he was blissfully unaware.

"Tell me where he is," she said, once they were in Dalton's carriage.

"Once we're home."

"I won't go back to your house."

"I'll send for Mrs. Thompson. You'll have a chaperone, which is a damn sight better than you'd have in Scotland."

"You can be the most arrogant, autocratic, rude creature it has ever been my experience to meet."

"While you, on the other hand, are impulsive, rash, and given to outlandish behavior with no thought to the consequences."

"You drove me to it."

He inclined his head in her direction.

"I beg your pardon?" he said.

"Never mind."

"Are you blaming me for your sudden decision to leave for Scotland with only your driver in attendance? A man who was once your lover?"

"You needn't shout at me, Dalton."

He hadn't realized he was yelling.

He'd never yelled at anyone in his entire life. He was the master of a look, a raised eyebrow, a sardonic quip.

Minerva Todd was making him insane.

Chapter 30

*H*e thanked Daniels when the man stopped the carriage in front of his house. Holding his hand out for Minerva, he unerringly walked across the wet cobbles to the steps leading to his door. With a little more practice he wouldn't have any hesitation at all. Of course, it would be easier if he wasn't being pummeled by rain.

"I apologize for not having an umbrella," he said, dropping her hand.

He reached for the banister with his right hand, his left clutching the top of his walking stick.

She didn't speak until they reached the top of the steps.

"Why do you have a mushroom as a door knocker?" she asked.

"A mushroom?" He tried to envision the door knocker, then smiled. "It's not a mushroom. It's a thistle. A reminder of my Scottish heritage."

"When I think of you as Scottish," she said, "I envision you as a Highlander. I understand they were arrogant, too."

He glanced in her direction.

Despite the rain marring what had promised to be a bright, fair day, he could almost make out details of her shape as she stood beside him.

Perhaps he should make another appointment with that fool, Marshall.

The rain was coming in a torrent now. Both of them were getting soaked.

He wasn't surprised when the door was locked. James had instilled security in all his servants. He let the knocker fall twice, and when it was opened, Mrs. Thompson spoke.

"Oh, Your Lordship, I am sorry. Here I am making scones in the kitchen while you both are standing on the doorstep wet as two cats."

"It's nothing, Mrs. Thompson. I assure you."

"I'll go and get some towels for you."

Her voice changed slightly. Dalton took that to mean she'd stepped aside. He motioned for Minerva to proceed him, and counted the steps once he entered his house. He reached out with a hand after he'd reached a dozen, turning toward his library.

"Are you going to tell me now, Dalton?"

How easily she vacillated between his given name and *Your Lordship*. She used *Your Lordship* when she was annoyed with him. He did the same when he called her Miss Todd.

In public, they were almost proper. Here in his home, they reverted to what they were: a man and a woman teetering on the brink of some kind of relationship. He wanted to be around her. He liked having her in his life. She challenged him.

No woman had ever challenged him before. No one—save his mother—had ever made him want to make her proud.

He stopped abruptly at the door to his library and turned to her.

"Will you be my friend, Minerva Todd?"

"Your friend?"

"I find I have a dearth of them lately. But I don't want just anyone as a friend. I've become rather selective. I want someone I can trust. Someone who will tell me the truth. Someone I genuinely like and admire."

He turned and headed into his office.

She didn't speak. What the hell was she thinking?

"Should I rescind the invitation?" he said.

He went to stand in front of the cold fireplace. Again, he did so almost without thought. Familiarity made navigating easier. So, too, the fact that he could almost see the wall, the bookcases beyond, and the table between the two chairs.

Yes, he needed to make an appointment with the physician as soon as possible.

"You think all those things about me?"

"I'm not given to saying things I don't mean, Minerva."

"I'm Neville's sister. How can you trust me?"

"I trust you because you're Minerva Todd. I don't care who you're related to."

Mrs. Thompson bustled into the room.

"Here I am, Your Lordship, with your scones and tea and towels."

She handed him a towel and he hoped she'd done the same for Minerva. He began to dry his face and hair. In a moment he'd excuse himself to change, an option Minerva didn't have.

"I'll just put the tray here, shall I?"

"That looks absolutely wonderful, Mrs. Thompson," Minerva said. Her voice sounded thin, as if worry were eating away at it.

The best thing he could do for her was to tell her the news now.

"If you'll ring, Your Lordship, if you need anything else," Mrs. Thompson was saying.

He nodded.

A moment later he heard the door softly close. Did his housekeeper think anything about leaving them alone together? Did she remember those years of licentiousness? Or did he simply pay her enough not to question what he did?

He stood beside the chair, wishing Minerva would sit first. He hadn't completely forgotten his manners. He heard a whoosh of fabric and then sat. He stretched out his hand toward the other chair, palm up. A moment later she placed her hand on it.

"I would be very honored to be your friend, Your Lordship."

And now she called him *Your Lordship* in a soft and sweet tone, playing hell with his earlier assumption.

"I don't want to hurt you, Minerva."

"Why would you say such a thing?"

He pulled out the letter he had tucked into his pocket.

"I've news of Neville from my cousin."

"The one who'd been in the diplomatic corps," she said.

He nodded.

"Neville is a prisoner of war," he said. "They're not sure which prison he's at. They've narrowed it down to two."

He handed her Glynis's letter.

He knew when she got to the part that would trouble her the most.

I'm hoping it's not Andersonville, Dalton, because I haven't heard good things about that place. If a man doesn't die of disease, there's every chance he will starve. I'll try to find out exactly where he is. I know that he's been transferred once, perhaps twice. As soon as I know, I'll write you.

He didn't tell her what he'd heard about those places. Both the Union and Confederate prisons were renowned for their hideous treatment of prisoners. He suspected more men died than were ever released.

Minerva didn't say anything. A moment later he heard the chink of china.

"Tea, Dalton?" she asked.

"Thank you. And a scone, if you don't mind."

Sometimes, hearing bad news was like that. It hit you all at once, but you tucked it away to examine it in bits, later. A corner here, another bite there. Little by little, so it didn't destroy you.

He suddenly wanted to equalize their positions, give her a hint of the pain he felt so she would know she wasn't alone.

"Did I tell you about Arthur? How he died?"

"No." Her voice was lifeless, empty of that certain spark that made her Minerva.

"He was killed in a hunting accident. Only he hadn't been hunting. I suspect that he was killed deliberately. I suspect that my brother, Lewis, killed him."

Now that he said it aloud, it sounded even more terrible.

"What are you going to do?"

"I haven't the slightest idea," he said. He would tell her about James's idea later. For now, it was enough that he had shared the mystery of Arthur's death with her.

She startled him by beginning to cry.

He'd never known what to do when a woman cried, but this was different. This was Minerva.

He couldn't bear to hear her sudden soft weeping. He expected violence in her grief, but this restrained, almost ladylike sorrow was a knife through his chest.

"That's why I wanted to tell you here," he said. "Not in public."

Her weeping only increased.

"Minerva." He reached out again, but this time she didn't put her hand in his.

He fumbled for the tray, returning his uneaten scone and full cup. Standing, he made his way to Minerva's side.

He reached down and pulled her up into his arms.

For a moment she resisted, then she stood, wrapped her arms around his waist and placed her cheek against his jacket.

Even preparing to travel on a train she hadn't worn a hoop. His smile was a rueful admission of her iconoclastic nature. Yet as singular as Minerva was, she was not unlike any other human being. She loved, and because of that love she was in pain.

"Minerva, please don't cry."

Her crying terrified him. Not because he'd never seen a woman weep, but because he'd never been so affected by a woman's tears.

"I'll find him, Minerva. I promise. I've agreed to finance my cousin's trip to America," he said. "He has this idea of becoming a blockade runner. He needs cotton for his mill."

She didn't ask any questions and that surprised him. Minerva was invariably curious.

"He'll be heading for the southern states," he said. "Once we find out where Neville is, I'll ask him to see what he can do. After all, Neville's a British citizen. He should be exchanged or released. Hell, if nothing else, Duncan can help him escape."

"You would do that?" she asked, her voice laden with tears. "For Neville?"

Not for Neville, but for her.

He held her close, content to do so for as long as she needed to be comforted. Until after her tears had passed. Until the day turned to night. Until her heart was eased.

The feel of her in his arms was somehow reassuring. She was a warm, pliant woman, a female who encapsulated all that was right about this new sight-less world of his. He was no longer trapped in a black bubble because of Minerva. She brought him light. She made it possible for him to view what he'd ignored for so many years: how he, accorded privilege and wealth, had chosen to waste his blessings.

Or had that been why he'd gone to America? To make something of himself? To have his life count for something more than being the Rake of London?

For whatever reason, he was no longer Dalton Mac-Iain, who'd won the round for drinking the most whiskey in a quarter hour. Nor was he the man who had charmed the Ice Duchess into his bed. Or the host of countless parties where debauchery ruled and licentiousness was the behavior of the day.

He was simply himself, stripped of everything but the essential man, capable of experiencing uncertainty and tasting fear.

This mortal man, this newly made earl, was some-how a better man with all his failures than the one who had ridden high on the crest of rumor and gossip.

HE WAS holding her, and for the first time in a very long time she felt safe. What kind of woman was she to feel comforted by the Rake of London?

"You aren't who you're supposed to be," she said, pulling back.

She needed to step away from him, but she didn't.

"What does that mean?"

"You're supposed to be a rakehell, a wastrel, a de-generate. Instead, you're kind and intelligent, caring and generous. Just when I think I've figured you out, you change."

"You make me sound as boring as a minister."

"You're not boring at all."

He confused her, startled her, made her lose her

thoughts, stumble through words, but he'd never bored her.

She stood on tiptoe and kissed him. At first it was a simple gesture of thanks for being so kind when she was crying. Of acknowledgment that he'd thought of her feelings in telling her about Neville. All too soon the kiss changed character, became less friendly and more passionate.

Several minutes were lost to the kiss, and no time could have been better spent. When she wrapped her arms around his neck, he broke off the kiss.

"I'm no saint, Minerva. Kissing you will lead to more."

A warning, couched in a whisper.

She only reached up and kissed him again.

"I promised to seduce you," she said a moment later. "I never got the chance."

"And you would do so now? Here?"

She should ask him to take her home. She should retreat to her house, chastened by the Covington sisters and their fears for her reputation. She should do a great many things right at the moment.

Perhaps it was rebellion. Perhaps it was need. Perhaps it was simply that she wanted to touch him for however long she could.

"We need to get out of these wet clothes, Dalton."

"Ah, that's the reason, then. You're concerned for our health," he said, amusement coloring his words.

She couldn't help but smile. "Lock the door, Dalton."

He released her, went to the door and did as she asked, then returned to her side on the carpet in front of the cold fireplace.

"Have you ever loved anyone in your library?" she asked, her voice sounding husky.

"Never," he said, concentrating on the buttons of her dress.

"No dalliances with bored wives or expectant virgins here?"

He hesitated at the third button.

"No bored wives. I never sought out a wife for dalliance, Minerva. Nor encouraged a woman to break her marital vows."

"But you never refused them, either. And expectant virgins?"

"Frankly, the idea of schooling a virgin in passion is, well, tedious."

"Then you're glad I came to you experienced as I was?"

"You aren't all that experienced," he said. "You have a great deal more to learn."

"Do I?"

He nodded.

He bent and kissed the tip of one breast through her bodice.

"You're wearing a corset."

"Loosely laced," she said. "And a corset cover as well as a shift."

"You're impenetrable. You're an ironclad vessel against which I'm a mere dinghy."

She laughed, then reached out and unfastened his trousers with unerring fingers. When she placed her cool hand around him, he drew in a sharp breath.

"Does that hurt?"

"Good God, no."

"Shall I remove my hand?"

"Absolutely not," he said, bending to kiss her.

He trailed a hand around her waistband until he found the buttons.

"You don't smell of your perfume today."

"What do I smell of?" she asked.

"The far off scent of cinnamon. I'll have to ask Cook to bake cinnamon scones every morning. That way, the spice will always perfume the air, reminding me of you."

She didn't need scent to think of him. Perhaps it would be wiser not to confess that.

He opened her bodice, separated the fabric and kissed his way from her throat to the lace of her corset cover. His tongue darted out, lightly touching and tasting her skin.

"I love how soft your skin is," he said.

She reached up and placed her palm against his cheek in wordless thanks. He made her feel beautiful.

"How do we get rid of this?" he asked, pulling at the corset cover.

She abruptly sat up, pulling off the top of her dress, then making short work of the corset cover. He didn't wait for her to unfasten the busk of her corset but did it himself until she was half naked.

She should have felt embarrassed. Or ashamed for her wantonness. Instead, she felt odd, unlike herself. Lighter than air yet weighted with worry. For a few minutes she wasn't going to think. She wasn't going to agonize. She wasn't going to grieve.

While she was sitting up, she wiggled out of her skirt and removed her two petticoats.

His palms found her breasts, his fingers curving around them. He brushed his bristly cheek against her skin, smiling when she made a sound.

"Is that uncomfortable?"

"No," she said, reaching up. Her fingertips trailed across his face. "Do you have to shave more than once a day? Do you do it yourself or does Howington help you?"

"Howington is no longer in my employ," he said. "As for shaving, the first few weeks I was bloodied but unbowed."

"Such a stubborn man," she said softly.

"Says the woman who is just as stubborn. Or is it more proper to call you obstinate?"

"Either one will do," she said. "But let's not talk of character now. Touch my breasts again, please."

"You're nearly as ribald as a duchess as I once knew," he said.

"Should you really be talking about a former conquest when you're bedding me?"

"I seem to remember your remarking on a certain driver of yours when I was standing naked in front of you."

"Turnabout is fair play, I suppose. Shall we make an agreement between us, then?"

"I shall never bring up another conquest."

"Neither shall I," she agreed.

"Good, because every time you mention Hugh, I want to punch the man in the face."

"Truly? Why?"

He didn't answer her, bending to nuzzle at her neck. Her soft sound became a moan.

"Do you really think I'm ribald?" she asked a few minutes later.

He raised up on his forearms and stared at her.

"If you'll give me an exemption from the rule we just made, I'll tell you that you're unlike any other woman I've ever known."

"Truly?"

"I like that you're honest. I love that you're direct. You startle me sometimes, but that's not necessarily a bad thing. I never know what you're going to say."

"That's not necessarily a bad thing, either. Forewarned is forearmed. If you surprise people, they normally give you the truth in return."

"So that's your strategy."

"Actually, it isn't. I don't seem to have a strategy when it comes to you, Dalton."

"I feel the same about you, Minerva. I don't behave as myself around you. But there are people who might say I haven't been myself ever since returning to London."

She placed a hand on the back of his head, pulling him down for a kiss.

"Must we be so profound?"

"On no account," he murmured against her lips.

He spent the next quarter hour kissing her everywhere. His fingers led the way over the curve of her shoulder and down to her arm. He hesitated at the inside of her elbow then traveled down her arm to the palm of her hand.

His fingers trailed to the end of each fingertip.

"You have calluses," he said.

Her hand immediately clenched into a fist. He pulled her fingers free.

"They're fascinating," he said. "There an indication of how different you are."

"Different is not necessarily better."

"In this case, you're wrong," he said. "Different is most definitely better."

Her heart was going to break, she was sure of it.

"DALTON," SHE said, her voice catching on a sigh.

"Patience," he said.

He didn't need his eyes as he kissed his way from her waist to her concave abdomen. She jerked when he kissed her navel and touched his tongue there.

He smiled in response.

She had beautiful legs. He traced a path from her ankles to her knees, and then up her shapely thighs to the nest of hair.

He kissed the crease at the top of her thigh, then did the same to the other leg.

She whispered his name again, her fingers grabbing at his shirt.

He raised up and kissed her on the lips.

"Patience, dear Minerva."

He had never wanted to extend his loving for hours and hours. He'd always been determined to find pleasure more than give it. But this was Minerva, and he wanted to erase the sting of her tears and bring her joy.

He tasted her, teasing her with his fingers and then his tongue. She widened her legs and implored him with a moan. For long moments he indulged himself in pleasing Minerva.

Her breath grew shallow, her moans louder. She reached down and pulled his hand up to cover her left breast. For a moment he abandoned his teasing to raise up, draw a nipple into his mouth, gently grazing it with his teeth.

When he returned to her intimate folds, his tongue and fingers flicking against her, she widened her legs, lifting her hips up to offer herself to him.

Her hand played in his hair; he could feel her fingers tremble.

The sound of her climax opened up something inside him, more elemental and less selfish than passion.

Raising up on his forearms, his hands clenched into fists, he entered her, surging into her heat with too much speed and need. An apology trembled on his lips as she raised her hips to meet him. He steadied himself, breathing hard, and remained motionless, the hardest task he'd given himself in a very long while.

He spoke against her ear. "I should have been slower, gentler," he said. "Forgive me."

"Oh, bloody hell, Dalton. I was just going to tell you to move. Harder, please."

Her words surprised a laugh from him.

"What an astounding woman you are."

She answered him by lifting herself up and then grabbing both his buttocks and pulling him down. He had never been coached so ably.

He laughed again, surging into her. The top of his head was about to blow off. His heart was beating like a stallion. His breath was stripped from him. All he knew was that he ceased to be himself but was part of her. Or she was part of him.

Then she was shattering in his arms and this time he accompanied her, a journey of a thousand breaths and a dozen lifetimes at least.

Chapter 31

$\mathcal{D}$alton wanted, in a way that was alien to him, to ask if he was a better lover than Hugh. He wanted her praise. It was a sign of his vulnerability around her. If nothing else, he should have heeded the warning in that thought.

Instead, he rolled to the side, pulling her with him so they faced each other on the Aubusson carpet.

He wanted to give her more of himself, a feeling he'd never had before this moment.

"I think you must be magic," he said. "I think you must have been directed to my life for a reason. First, to charm me out of my dour mood. Second, to enchant me completely."

"I enchant you?" she asked in a breathless voice.

He leaned over and kissed her, smiling against her lips.

"Oh, you do, Minerva. You most certainly do."

"A minister wouldn't have bedded me on the floor of your library," she said. "See? You're hardly boring."

"You have a heretical mind," he said.

"I do?"

"You should sound disturbed by that, not delighted."

Making love had either been a lark in the past or something fervently desired. Neither situation had involved his mind, only his loins. He'd forgotten the woman as quickly as the deed was done or he awoke wishing himself home.

He'd never felt anything but a certain fondness for the women in his bed.

Now? Not fondness at all. Something more. Something that rumbled through his life with the force of a wave or thunder. Something elemental, like nature itself.

He rolled to his back, staring upward, seeing the ceiling as a patch of white. Was it his imagination or could he see the plasterwork?

"You have a mistress."

He turned his head. "I beg your pardon?"

"I saw her, Dalton. Your mistress. She's very beautiful."

"You have me at a disadvantage, Minerva. I don't know what you're talking about."

"Will you say that about me tomorrow? 'You have me at a disadvantage.'"

"I really don't know what you're talking about. I don't have a mistress."

"I might be considered your mistress," she said.

She was more than a mistress, and he'd never said that about another woman. Nor had he ever thought to contemplate the future at the side of one particular female.

What would life be like with Minerva?

Each day would be an adventure. There would be something about someone or something in each day that would be special to her, and consequently to him. She would find something amazing or amusing, something that challenged her and in turn him. She would argue with him. She would ridicule his beliefs. She would attempt to convince him of some point or another. She would praise him and challenge him in the same breath.

She would occupy his bed and his heart.

"You have a son."

He suddenly realized who it was she was talking about.

"He looks just like you."

"Does he? Arthur and I looked a great deal alike. People sometimes wondered if we were twins. You're talking about Sarah, and she's not my mistress. She was Arthur's."

He felt her raise up. Was she staring at him to see the truth of his comment?

"She's really not your mistress?"

"No, she's not. But I would like her to be part of my family. The boy, too. I'm his uncle and I've never been an uncle before."

"Is that normal, making a by-blow a part of your family? And isn't that a ghastly label for anyone to wear?"

"I think you choose what's normal for yourself in your life, don't you? If you're wise you do."

He was beginning to understand that, just as he knew that he hadn't chosen wisely before. But he didn't have to continue making the same mistakes.

"When did you find out about Neville?" she asked a few minutes later.

"This morning. I went to your house straight away."

"Was that when the Covington sisters waylaid you?"

"I found them to be very pleasant, all in all. Except for the part about being entirely too interested in your life. They look to you as some sort of heroine."

"What?"

"I think they live vicariously through you, Minerva."

"Oh dear. I wonder what they would think to see me now?"

"Marry me."

She didn't say anything for so long that he thought she hadn't heard.

"Marry me," he said again. "I've never asked another woman to be my wife. Does it normally make a woman mute?"

She sat up.

"I've never been asked to marry in that fashion," she said, "so I can't answer that. I would imagine it does, however. It's certainly had that effect on me."

He sat up as well, wanting to reach for her but thinking it was perhaps better if he didn't.

"I would tell you I'm quite wealthy, except money doesn't seem to interest you. I could expound about all my family's various interests, but you know most of them since you've been working with me."

"Are you certain you don't just want a permanent secretary? Someone who could put up with your grumbling without quitting?"

"Only if she was also my countess and slept in my bed. Oh, you might have to guide me from time to time. I feel it only necessary to add that as part of your wifely duties."

"You can't be serious, Dalton."

"Is it my face?" he asked.

"Your face? What about your face?"

"I know I'm scarred," he said, wishing she would either just say yes or no quickly. No sense dragging this out.

"Oh, bother. You're as handsome as sin and you know it."

He felt something in his chest loosen. "You've never thought I was ugly, have you?"

"Only because you're not," she said, her voice tinged with irritation.

"Marry me."

She began to put her clothes back on. Since she wasn't

speaking, wasn't giving him a chance to marshal his counterpoints to her arguments, he did the same.

He'd never felt as supremely awkward in his life.

Standing, he made his way to the chair, fumbled for his cup and drank his cold tea, wishing he knew what to say.

The knock on the door was a welcome relief.

"Are you decent?" he asked her.

"Yes," she said, her voice curiously without expression.

He hesitated at the door. No doubt anyone would be able to tell what they'd been doing in his library. At the moment, he wasn't certain he could face down his housekeeper with the equanimity one needed for a circumstance such as this.

He opened the door, forcing a smile on his face. "Yes?"

"Mr. Wilson is here, Your Lordship."

Good God, that's all he needed.

"Give me a moment, Mrs. Thompson," he said. "I'll come and meet with him in the parlor."

"Very well, Your Lordship."

He felt an uncharacteristic flush warm the back of his neck. Once he closed the door, he turned to Minerva.

"Will you be all right here for a little while?"

"Yes," she said again. No other comment, just that single word.

Is that what a marriage proposal did to Minerva, reduce her to one-syllable words?

He left the room, feeling as if there was something more he should have said or done.

SHE COULDN'T become the Countess of Rathsmere. Had he lost his mind? The world would think them both insane.

He had to be jesting. In a moment he'd say something like: "You thought I was serious, Minerva? What kind of fool do you take me for?"

No, he wouldn't say that, but he had to have temporarily misplaced his judgment.

He couldn't be serious. He couldn't mean it.

Her fingers were trembling. No, her whole body was trembling. Perhaps some of it was due to pleasure, but most of it was because of shock.

How dare he ask her to marry him? How dare he throw her into confusion like that?

She didn't know what to think.

She wanted to go home.

She needed to go home.

Hugh had taken her carriage. Still, she had to get home, one way or another, and she was more than willing to make her way on foot.

Darkness had fallen in the last hour, however, and she wasn't fool enough to walk the London streets in the dark.

She would simply have to appeal to Mrs. Thompson, and through her, to Daniels.

She had to leave. Now, before Dalton returned and catapulted her into more confusion. She wanted to be home, in her own room. Where she could think, rationally and logically, about what he'd said.

Marry me.

He hadn't said anything about emotions. He'd only mentioned his wealth. He would probably have started enumerating the number of horses, cattle, houses, and carriages he possessed, plus the number of servants who worked for him, had they not been interrupted.

She had to leave.

After straightening her clothing, she wished she had a mirror to see how mussed her hair was. Her chin felt abraded. Did she look well-kissed?

She opened the door, looked both ways, and left the library. She headed toward the foyer and the hallway to the back of the house.

"The announcement appeared in the papers this evening," James Wilson was saying. "If Lewis is innocent, then he'll no doubt send his congratulations about your forthcoming marriage."

She halted in the middle of the corridor, turned and stared beyond the library door to the parlor.

"And if he isn't?" Dalton asked. "He'll make an attempt on my life?"

"I would be willing to bet on it, Dalton. I've made arrangements to protect you, so you shouldn't worry."

She continued toward the foyer, walking quicker until she was almost running through Dalton's home.

She had to get out, now. If Daniels wouldn't take her home, she'd walk, anything to leave.

He hadn't meant it after all. He hadn't been serious. This was just some sort of ruse he and Mr. Wilson had devised. Where was the relief she should feel? If nothing else, she should feel a little amusement at her own gullibility.

Instead, she was crying again. Silly, silly tears that proved she was better off home.

THANK HEAVENS for Mrs. Thompson's kindness. The dear lady took a look at her face and bustled to the doorway, leaving Minerva no choice but to follow her.

They crossed the garden, eerily beautiful in the rainy dusk. Time had gotten away from her and she'd be returning home after dark, a fact that would no doubt scandalize the Covington sisters.

They couldn't possibly admire her. From this moment on she wouldn't believe anything Dalton MacIain said. But she wouldn't be seeing him again, so that would be enormously easy to do.

"Daniels," Mrs. Thompson said when they reached the stables, "I want you to take Miss Todd home, straightaway."

To her relief the driver didn't say another word, but he did glance at her, then back at Mrs. Thompson. Did she have a sign on her forehead? Fornicator. Foolish Woman. Idiot.

When he opened the door for her, she turned to Mrs. Thompson.

"Thank you," she said. "For everything."

She doubted she'd see the woman again.

Mrs. Thompson only nodded, the kindness in her eyes almost Minerva's undoing. She would not weep in front of the two of them. Somehow, she had to wait until she reached her bedroom. Then she would release all the tears that were building up. Between the situation with Neville and Dalton, she might cry for weeks.

"Will you take me to the back of my house, Daniels?"

She didn't want the Covington sisters to see her come home, alone and hours after she should have arrived.

"WHAT DO you mean, she's gone?"

Dalton had thought, on returning to his library, that Minerva might have gone upstairs to refresh herself. But when she hadn't returned, he summoned Mrs. Thompson, only for his housekeeper to answer him in a sullen voice he'd never heard her use.

"Crying she was, poor thing. Upset as much as I've ever seen a body upset. All she wanted was to go home, and who was I to tell her no?"

"How long ago?"

"I'm sure I don't know."

He pushed past her, walked at a fast clip to the front door and down the steps.

"James!"

Damn the darkness. Damn his eternal darkness. Damn the man. Damn the situation.

Had James already left? With any luck he hadn't. With any luck he could commandeer the man's carriage since Minerva had taken his.

Why had she left?

"What's wrong, Dalton?"

"Take me to Minerva's house," he said. "Where's your carriage?" He gripped James's sleeve. "Now."

He didn't have a good feeling about this.

Chapter 32

*T*hankfully, the journey home didn't take long. Long enough, however, that Minerva managed to thoroughly berate herself for her stupidity and was beginning to turn her anger on others.

How dare Dalton stop her from traveling to Scotland?

How dare the Covington sisters involve themselves in her business?

How dare Hugh take on a sanctimonious tone?

How dare Dalton ask her to marry him when it was all only a tactic to trap Lewis? That was unkind as well as unfair. Thank heavens she hadn't revealed what she was feeling.

She'd taken Hugh as her lover because of curiosity. She had discontinued their association the instant she realized he cared more for her than she did for him. It seemed to her that any relationship should be evenly matched, neither caring more than the other.

Yet here she was, in the exact same circumstance. She was longing for the Rake of London, Dalton MacIain. She was a lovesick fool, someone staring out the window and wondering what to do.

She loved him.

How very odd to find herself in love with someone she hadn't liked for a long while.

Of course, she hadn't known him then. Now she

wondered if many people knew Dalton at all. He might well be known as reclusive, but he was also very protective of himself, guarding his emotions with such care that it had taken her a while to realize he wasn't the debauched soul she thought him.

He cared for those in his employ. He had a streak of altruism. He was kind when there was no reason to be kind, with no one looking on to judge and no one to impress.

He had a sense of humor that revealed itself slowly.

He wasn't unaware of his own sins. She suspected he judged himself too harshly, as severely as he judged Neville. Yet, even so, he was honest and fair to her. He'd kept his word and revealed everything he'd found out about her brother.

Now, somehow, she had to save Neville from the prison camp in America.

But, first, she had to face the facts. She was in love with the Earl of Rathsmere. What an utter fool she was.

Could you kill love? She was going to attempt to do so.

When he'd uttered those two words, she'd been speechless. She'd been incapable of saying a word, suffused as she was by disbelief. The most handsome man she'd ever seen, a man who'd just loved her and brought her exquisite pleasure, asked her to marry him.

Marry me.

He hadn't intended for her to be his bride. All he'd wanted was to fool his brother into thinking he was getting married.

Marry me. The words had been a game, a subterfuge, nothing more than that.

From this point on she would ignore the Earl of Rathsmere, wish him well, but have nothing further to do with him. She pressed her hands to her stomach.

Please God, don't let her suffer the consequences of her actions with Dalton. She'd used a vinegar-soaked sponge in all her previous episodes, but not today. She'd never thought to be suffused with grief and worry, then cozened out of it by passion.

She should have told him no, but that word had been as far from her vocabulary this afternoon as *marriage* was now. She was going to have to practice using it. No, she would not see Dalton again. No, she would not participate in his ruse. No, she wouldn't welcome his help in rescuing Neville. No, she never wanted to see him again. No, she wouldn't welcome his touch. Ever.

She ignored the yawning chasm in her chest, the one where tears were rising. She ached with sadness.

Because of the rain the night seemed even darker when Daniels pulled into the wide alley that separated the stables from her house. Nor had any streetlamps been erected here, no doubt on the theory that no self-respecting homeowner would be traveling through the alley after dark.

Normally, a lantern was lit and hung from the outside of the stable, but tonight it was extinguished. Had Hugh returned and just as quickly left?

She would have to draft a letter of recommendation for him. There, she should concentrate on her tasks rather than how she felt. She was still too close to tears. A strange sensation to want to weep and kick something at the same time.

There weren't any lights on in the rear of the Covington house, but that didn't mean the sisters retired early. They might be keeping watch at the front, eyeing the square.

The carriage slowed, then stopped.

Before she could open the door, Daniels had dismounted and was opening it for her.

"If you don't mind, Miss Todd, I'll see you to your house."

"That's not necessary, Daniels."

"Still and all, I'd feel better about it."

He'd always been kind to her, and exceedingly polite. She wasn't angry at the driver, but at his employer.

"Thank you, Daniels."

There, if the Covington sisters saw her, they'd witness her being properly escorted to the door.

She dismounted, holding onto the frame of the carriage for balance until her foot touched the street. She fluffed her skirts, straightened her shoulders, and pasted a smile on her face for Daniels's benefit.

The rain had stopped for the moment, but the riffling clouds overhead, gray against the black night, were a future promise of it. She was in the mood for a storm, a thunderous ovation from nature itself. Rain washed the world clean, gave the air clarity and swept away the old odors.

Suddenly, she wanted winter. Not the crisp weather of autumn, but ice and snow, dreary days and chilled nights. That would match her mood.

As she rounded the back of the carriage, Daniels followed her. A moment later she heard an oath, then nothing.

Suddenly, a man's arm tightened around her waist while his hand clamped over her mouth. She screamed, but the sound was muffled as he dragged her backward.

She was being attacked. Lurid stories she'd read in the newspaper filled her mind as she kicked out. She struggled in the man's grip, reached up with both hands behind her and pinched what she could find.

"Bitch!"

She kicked at him again. His arm reached around

her neck and tightened, cutting off her air. She bit at his hand and tasted blood.

"Damn bitch!"

"Shut up! Somebody'll hear you."

"Like I bloody care," the first voice said. "She bit me!"

"Take her to the carriage."

She knew that voice. Howington? What was Howington doing here?

"You sure he'll come for her?"

"I'm sure," Howington said. "For some reason he's taken a fancy to the bitch."

She bit at the hand covering her mouth again. Her attacker swore, loosening his grip long enough for her to scream. She didn't see the blow before he struck her. The side of her face was suddenly on fire. Even her teeth felt loose. She stumbled several steps before she was grabbed again and a cloth stuffed into her mouth.

She could hardly breathe. Tears welled in her eyes.

"Get her to the carriage."

She knew that if they put her in a carriage, she'd never live through it. She kicked out again, managed to get one arm free and turned to face her attacker. Fear gave her strength as she slammed her fist into his face. He retaliated by punching her again, the blow coming hard and fast. Blood spurted from her nose as he grabbed her by one arm, dragging her to another carriage.

"What the hell?"

Minerva blinked her eyes open, tried to focus, then wondered if she was hallucinating.

Abigail Covington was standing there holding a lantern and a fireplace poker. Her sister, Gladys, the cook in the group, was pressing a long handled fork to Howington's throat. Helen was, surprisingly, pointing a rifle at the head of the man who was dragging her.

"Let her go," Helen said. "I'm quite a good shot. I haven't had any target practice in a while and I'm looking forward to it."

She was abruptly released and fell to the street.

"Get over there with your friend," Helen said, pointing to Howington.

Abigail came to Minerva's side, stretched out a hand and helped her to stand. Pulling the cloth from her mouth, she used it to stem the blood from Minerva's nose.

To her shock, Helen raised the rifle, pointed it skyward and shot. The explosion deafened her for a moment.

"There, that should summon help, I think," Helen said, then whipped out a pistol from the pocket of her skirt and kept it leveled on the two men.

Every window on the street was lighting up. Soon the alley would be filled with neighbors, all wondering at the commotion and hungry for scandal.

A man came running down the street, attired in a dark blue suit and looking as proper as a banker except for his mussed hair and sweaty face. A carriage entered the alley, blocked from pulling closer by the other vehicle. As she watched, Dalton and James emerged, each man looking capable of pummeling Howington and his companion. In fact, she didn't doubt that those men were in grave danger right at the moment.

She hugged Abigail, said a little prayer of thanks, and wished she could just slip away.

Chapter 33

The parlor was filled with people.

The three Covington sisters sat on the settee. Mrs. Beauchamp had already served tea and refreshments to the women. She'd been startled when Helen Covington requested a shot of whiskey. Mrs. Beauchamp didn't look the least perturbed, however, as she poured a measure into the woman's cup.

George, the man who had been assigned the duty of watching out for her by James Wilson, was seated on the chair at one end of the settee. He, too, was enjoying a bit of tea and a jot of whiskey.

Minerva was sitting on the chair at the other end of the settee drinking tea. She could have done without the tea and taken the whiskey straight up.

Mrs. Beauchamp had tsked over her in the kitchen while she placed a salve on her face and a plaster on her nose.

"You'll have black eyes in the morning," Helen Covington announced, looking enormously pleased at the idea. "You acquitted yourself well, though, Minerva. He'll need that hand of his looked after."

Her nose still hurt and her face felt like it was swelling, and she wanted to escape to her room. Her visitors, however, didn't look like they were going anywhere without answers.

Dalton was standing beside the fireplace, staring in

her direction as if he could see her. James was beside him. She had the feeling that Dalton was angry at James, but he didn't bother to convey that to her. In fact, he hadn't said a word.

Dalton and James had conferred for a few moments with the authorities before they'd taken Howington and his accomplice away. They hadn't deigned to tell her what that was about, either, a fact that annoyed her the longer time passed.

All she knew for certain was that the entire neighborhood was awake, the Covington sisters looked delighted to be in her mother's parlor, and she was hurting, still wanting a good cry and then an opportunity to pummel something.

"Why did you set a guard on me?" she asked, glancing from George to James.

All three sisters looked at James.

"He was quite noticeable," Helen said. "We saw him right away."

It would have been nice if they had told her about George.

James looked down at the floor. Dalton looked as if he wanted to hit something.

Very well, she'd try another question.

"Why did Howington want to kidnap me?"

Helen and her two sisters nodded in approval.

"To lure Dalton somewhere," James said. "That's only a guess, but an educated one."

"Why?"

"To kill him," James said. "Just like Arthur was killed. I expected him to act against Dalton directly. I didn't think he would involve you."

"You let him know we were going to be married," she said, speaking to Dalton.

"The notice is in tonight's paper, my dear, which is why we were awake, waiting to celebrate with you."

She glanced at Helen, Abigail, and Gladys. They looked so happy, their eyes sparkling, their cheeks pink with excitement.

"I hate to disappoint you," she said, "but it was all a ruse. He only pretended to want to marry me to set a trap."

"Is that what you think?" Dalton asked.

"It's what happened, isn't it?"

"It wasn't," Dalton said. "James thought it would be a good way to force Lewis to act. If I announced I was getting married, possibly fathering a brood of children, there went the possibility of Lewis inheriting the earldom. I didn't know that James had placed the announcement for tonight's paper when I asked you to marry me."

She was not going to believe a word he said.

"When I asked you to marry me it was because I wanted you to be my wife."

She could have slapped him silly. Didn't he know the Covington sisters were sitting right there listening to every word? Didn't he know that tomorrow the story would be all over London?

"Will you marry me, Minerva?"

She glared at him, but since he couldn't see her, the expression was wasted.

"I don't really want to talk to you right now, Dalton."

"It's the only thing to do," he said. "Besides, there's a possibility you may be with child."

All three Covington sisters opened their eyes wider. The pink of their cheeks deepened. James's eyes were twinkling. George turned his head a little as if he wanted to escape the room as quickly as possible. Mrs. Beauchamp, bless her heart, turned bright red, said something about cinnamon scones and retreated in a flurry of petticoats.

Minerva closed her eyes for a moment, took a deep

breath, exhaled, and finally opened her eyes again and looked at Dalton.

"You think my brother is a would-be murderer. What kind of family would that create?"

"I know my brother is a murderer, so I would say a slightly abnormal one. I apologize for that. But I wouldn't be a normal husband, either. You would have to be my guide from time to time, tell me if I'm presentable, and if I've cut myself shaving."

She was not going to allow her heart to melt. He hadn't mentioned anything about affection. He wanted a friend and she wanted so much more. Granted, they were physically compatible, but they couldn't spend their lives in a bed.

Although it might be fun to try.

"We aren't suited," she said, wishing it didn't hurt to speak. "I don't care a whit about being a countess."

"That just shows how well we're suited," he countered. "I don't care a whit about being an earl."

She frowned at him.

He still hadn't said anything about his feelings. Was she supposed to marry the man just because he asked?

"No," she said.

All three Covington sisters gasped.

She glanced at them. Each woman had a look of incredulity on her face. She could read their thoughts well enough. Who was she, Minerva Todd, to deny the Earl of Rathsmere?

"I don't want a friend," she said. "Yes, I wouldn't mind being your friend, but I want more. Not in being an earl more, Dalton. But in emotions. Besides, I know quite well why you want to marry me."

"Why is that?"

The sisters turned their heads in an identical motion to stare at Dalton while she looked in the other direction.

"You're lonely and you think yourself ugly, and I'm the only woman you've been around for nearly a year."

"Are you insane, Minerva?"

As a declaration of love, it was lacking something.

"*NOT INSANE*, Dalton, merely truthful."

He advanced on her, hoping like hell there weren't any cute footstools or ornamental ottomans in the way. Her parlor didn't seem to be overly stuffed with furniture, as was the fashion.

He heard something being moved.

"There you go, Your Lordship," Helen said.

He smiled his thanks.

"You're not being truthful," he said to Minerva. "You're just being disparaging. It's a common trait of yours when you're feeling out of place."

"How did you come up with that idea?"

"I've observed you, Minerva, in a manner of speaking."

He'd almost reached her. He could tell by the sound of her sigh. He stopped.

"Am I in front of you?"

"Yes," she said.

"Close enough to shake you?"

"Well, yes, if you want to. I must confess that I wouldn't like being shaken."

"Then listen to me, Minerva Todd. I've never talked to another woman like I have you. I've never been amused by anyone as much or been skewered so well and so ably. I've never thought a woman's intellect was fascinating. I've never damn well chased across London after a woman. I've never spent hours and hours remembering everything a woman said, or hearing the sound of her laughter in my head. I've never thought to myself, 'What would Minerva say to this?' I've not once, in all my days of drunken celebration, ever wanted to take a woman home to Gledfield and wish I could see her expression when she sees it for the first time. I hate my blindness because I can't see you laugh, Minerva. Or your face after we've made love."

When she didn't speak, he shook his head. "Say something."

"You really mean all those things?" she asked.

Her voice didn't sound normal, almost as if she were trying not to weep. Hell, he hadn't meant to upset her.

"I really mean all those things. Will you marry me?"

"What happens when Neville comes home? What will you do, Dalton?"

Because of her, because she was so certain that Neville would never have done what he'd witnessed Neville doing, he was willing to suspend his disbelief.

"I won't make any judgments until I talk to your brother."

"That's fair enough, Dalton." She sighed. "Once you hear Neville's explanation, it will make sense, I know it."

Had he ever had anyone believe in him the way Minerva believed in Neville? His mother, perhaps. And Arthur, a point at the root of all the arguments between them. His older brother wanted more from him than the dissolute life he'd led. An irony, that Arthur's death had been one of the components of his change.

"What do you want?" he asked.

"What do you mean?"

"You don't want my wealth. I doubt you want jewelry. You ignore my praise or appreciation. What can convince you to marry me?"

"I need to go to Scotland," she said.

"Now?"

"If not now, then quickly. Will we be married soon?"

"Does that mean yes, you'll marry me?" He didn't give her a chance to decline. "As soon as I can arrange it, if that's what you wish." He spoke to the room. "I think Minerva means that it will be a small affair, but would you be our guests?"

Helen spoke for the sisters. "We would be honored, Your Lordship. But that means you won't be our neighbor, won't it, Minerva?"

"Unless there's a nice house near where you live, Your Lordship."

He felt a frisson of panic. "We might be living in Scotland a good portion of the year," he said.

Suddenly, arms wrapped around his waist and Minerva kissed him softly. He cupped her face and felt her wince, wishing he'd been able to punch Howington before the man had been led away.

He'd set the authorities on Lewis, and that situation would have to be addressed in a matter of hours. Minerva, however, was his first priority.

"I realize I'm not that great a catch. I've gotten some of the sight back in my left eye, but I've no guarantee that it will get better."

"Oh, piffle, Dalton. I don't care. You're still the most astounding man I've ever met."

He felt something open up in his chest.

"I adore you, Minerva."

"Oh, Dalton, I feel the same. I think I have from the very beginning."

He began to smile, remembering how she'd angrily skewered him to the spot in the garden.

"Very well," she said, rightly interpreting his smile, "maybe not from the beginning, but certainly now."

He would take *now*. *Now* was a very good place to start.

He didn't have any trouble finding her mouth. She was still talking when he kissed her.

Epilogue

January, 1863

$\mathcal{D}$alton was seated at his office chair in front of the library window, enduring another examination.

"How long has it been, Your Lordship," the physician asked now, "since you noticed the new changes in your vision?"

"About two weeks. I can see a little sharper in my left eye. Not to the point of being able to read, of course, but shapes seem to have more shape, if that makes any sense."

Dr. Marshall smelled of licorice. Did the man notice that his home was pleasantly scented with cinnamon? His cook had become an expert at making Minerva's favorite scones in the last six months.

The physician leaned so close that he could feel the other man's breath on his face. Any second now Marshall would stick his nose in his eye and there would go any recovered vision he had.

He was required to look into a bright mirror reflecting the sun, then another instrument that made his eye water.

Finally, the physician reared back. "I'm holding up my hand, Your Lordship. How many fingers am I showing?"

"I'm ecstatic to be able to see that it's a hand, Dr. Marshall, but I have no idea how many fingers are showing."

"But at least you can tell it's a hand, Your Lordship. That is an improvement."

"I can see my wife's face," he said. "I haven't been able to do that before."

"Truly, Your Lordship?"

There was a strange note in the physician's voice, making Dalton wonder exactly what the man was thinking. That he was odd for marrying when he didn't know what his wife looked like? Or that he was imagining things?

This morning he'd awakened beside Minerva, the dawn light illuminating her face in that flash of a second. Sleeping, she'd been beautiful, even more arresting than James had said. In that next instant the image of her had blurred, as if Providence had granted him sight for only that perfect moment.

He hadn't said anything to anyone, but he'd called for the physician.

"Will my vision get better?"

"Only time will tell, Your Lordship. It's conceivable. It's a very good sign that you've improved and not gotten worse."

"Is that possible?" he asked. "That it would get worse?"

The physician straightened. "If you'd asked me that question a few months ago, I would have had to prepare you for the fact that it would probably become much worse. But now?"

"Yes? Now?"

"Now I think we can safely say that you will continue to improve. Perhaps one day you might be able to read. But I do want to be notified the minute anything changes."

"Of course."

Minerva would be the first one he told, and then Dr. Marshall.

Even her name made him smile. Minerva Todd MacIain. It was fitting that a woman who was so interested in Scotland have a Scottish name.

He would tell her what the physician said the minute they returned home. First, however, she was all for showing him a surprise at her old house.

Minerva's surprises came in many different styles. Like when she presented him with Florie, a mare new to the stables at Gledfield. She had a tender mouth and a gentle gallop, the perfect horse for a one-eyed equestrian.

Another surprise was the day she announced that Lady Terry had left her Partage Castle. The poor woman had died before Minerva could visit with her in Scotland, but she'd made Minerva an heiress.

"Now you're a countess with her own castle."

"I'll gladly share it with you," she said. "I'll make you my assistant."

He smiled, remembering a few of their adventures in Scotland.

But the greatest surprise Minerva Todd MacIain had given him was news only a month old.

He was to be a father. She was to be a mother. The two of them were to be parents, a miracle that kept him awake some nights, worrying about whether he would be an acceptable father. He suspected their first child would be a girl. She was adamant it was a boy.

Life was full and rich, in a way he'd never contemplated in his hedonistic days. He did things he'd never thought he'd do, silly things that would have garnered his disdain only years earlier. Last night, for example, he'd arranged for a dance in their garden.

"Come," he said to her. "It's a romantic time of evening, Minerva. What the Scots call gloaming."

"It is," she said. "There's a haze in the air like Scotland, but I can still hear the carriages in the square."

"You can also smell the honeysuckle and the roses my mother planted. She would have liked you."

"Would she?"

He nodded. "I think she would have heartily approved of you. In fact, I can almost hear her say, 'Dalton, Minerva is just the woman for you.'"

She laughed and he felt his heart expand. Who knew that Minerva had such an infectious laugh? She sounded like a young girl only days away from childhood, carefree and delighted.

He turned and lifted his left arm. Suddenly, the sounds of violins flooded the garden.

"Have you hired an entire orchestra?"

"Only a quartet. Come and dance with me, Minerva." He held out his arms. "My dearest Minerva, my wife, the most astounding woman in the world, will you dance with me?"

"Here, Dalton?"

"Here," he said, "in our own private garden."

She walked into his arms and allowed him to lead her into a waltz. A little more decorous, probably, than one performed on a ballroom floor. Down the paths and around the garden they whirled and laughed. If some of the servants watched through the windows, they hadn't minded.

Now his wife had another surprise for him and he couldn't imagine what it might be.

As they entered the town house, he waved to the Covington sisters, no doubt peering from one of the windows. The three of them had been guests at their wedding and they'd entertained the women at dinner twice in the last few months. He would always be grateful to them for saving Minerva the night she was kidnapped.

Lewis would go to prison if convicted of Arthur's death and most certainly for arranging Minerva's abduction. His feelings about that were complex. He felt a measure of guilt that he hadn't been a better influence over Lewis, and sorrow that Lewis had destroyed his life because of greed. Added to that was relief that his brother's plans, aided by Howington, who was also incarcerated, hadn't succeeded.

An audit of his finances had proven what he suspected. Howington had helped himself to thousands of pounds while he was in America.

"Now, as to my surprise," she said, once she'd handed over her coat and bonnet to the maid.

He did the same, thanking the young girl.

"It's Neville."

"We'll find him," he said, injecting more hope into the words than he felt.

He'd already sent a sizable sum to the British Legation to finance Neville's release from the prison camp where he was being held. The delay, he'd been told, was due to the press of war and the fact that negotiations had broken down numerous times.

"No. You don't understand. He's here, Dalton," she said.

She put her hands on his chest, lifting her face. Why had he ever thought her plain? Even a blind man could see her beauty.

"He's home."

He stared down at her, a dozen emotions all vying to be victor in that moment. He finally settled on patience, assuming a calm he didn't feel.

"He's finally home."

Was he supposed to sing hosannas? Evidently, if the beatific smile Minerva gave him was any judge.

His willingness to bring Neville home was born from his love for her, not his belief in the man's innocence.

"Will you talk with him? Will you hear him out?"

He'd promised her that, hadn't he?

Taking his hand, she led him down the hall and into the parlor.

"I love you," Minerva said once they'd entered the room. "But I also love my brother. So I'm going to leave the two of you alone to talk in hopes that you will remember that, both of you."

He stared at the door she closed.

"Dammit, Minerva."

"I've often felt the same way," Neville said. "She puts you on a pedestal and you can't help but fall off it."

Neville was seated in one of the wing chairs in front of the fireplace.

He turned and went to stand in front of his brother-in-law, staring at the man. Even with only one eye, he could see the changes the year had made in Neville.

"You look like hell."

The other man shifted in his chair, and when he did, the loose fabric of his trousers pressed against his legs, revealing limbs like twigs.

Dalton had never seen anyone as thin. His wrists stuck out of his jacket. His Adam's apple was prominent and his face was barely more than a skull covered in skin.

"The voice of honesty, finally," Neville said, smiling. "You would be surprised by all the people who have told me how good I'm looking when I know I'm a ghost. Oh, I'm a ghost with a little meat on its bones, but some days I feel so transparent that I'm sure people can see through me."

He was surprised Neville had survived the voyage home.

"I understand I have you to thank for rescuing me."

"It wasn't me, but my cousin."

Neville inclined his head slightly. "My thanks to him, then."

"He's a she, actually. Glynis's first husband was with the British Legation in Washington. I knew they were trying to arrange a trade. I didn't know they'd been successful."

"Just in time, I understand," Neville said. "They're no longer trading prisoners. So I'm doubly grateful."

Dalton sat on the adjoining chair, considering his words. He loved his wife. He admired her. He wanted to be around her for the rest of his days, but in this he had to obey his own counsel.

"Why the hell did you try to kill me?"

"Minerva said you thought that." He shook his head. "I didn't."

"I saw you aiming at me."

"I wasn't aiming at you, but at Harris. He'd been saying some things I thought were odd for days. I wondered what he had planned. The moment we rounded the curve on the path, I knew what it was. He had his pistol trained on you. My only choice was to shoot him."

"Did you?"

Neville shook his head. "His aim was better. We thought you dead at first, you know."

Neville rested his head back against the chair as if the conversation tired him.

"If you'll remember, he was slightly ahead of us and to the left. I was riding beside you until the trail became too narrow and I moved back."

The shooting was a blur to him. He hadn't been able to remember much of what happened just before he was shot and nothing afterward. The image of Neville raising his pistol was the clearest memory he'd had.

"Why? Why was he trying to kill me?"

"You need to talk to your brother," Neville said.

"Is that what he said, that Lewis had paid him?"

Neville nodded.

"Dying men confess all manner of sins. They wish to go to their maker with a clean conscience. At least that's what happened in prison camp. More than once when I thought I was dying I told anyone who listened about my regrets."

"Your sister always believed you would come home."

Neville smiled, the expression more sad than amused.

"One of my sins, Dalton. That I was never as good a brother as she was a sister."

He knew a great deal about regret.

"We were damn fools, Neville. I was the biggest one of all."

"Minerva doesn't think so, or she would never have married you. My sister is a damn good judge of character. At first I couldn't see how you would suit. Then I realized the two of you are very much alike."

A knock on the door signaled the end of their privacy. A moment later Minerva entered, followed by Mrs. Beauchamp with a tray. From the looks of the pastries piled high, they were trying to fatten Neville up in a day.

"Are you done?" Minerva asked after the housekeeper left the room. "Or do I have to hide all the pokers and knives?"

He exchanged a look with Neville.

"We're done," he said.

He had made peace with his past in order to savor his future. Neville's appearance was the last part of that past. He didn't know if his story was the truth, but he suspected it was, especially if Lewis featured in it.

A strange thing about love, he thought as Minerva stretched up to kiss him. It blunted all the aggressive emotions. One couldn't hate or distrust in the presence of love.

In the future, if rumors were told of him and his role as the once infamous Rake of London, people might nod at each other and exchange stories. Hopefully, they'd say that he'd taken to being quite a good earl. They would probably talk about Minerva as well, telling tales of how she loved to dig in the soil of Scotland and wear something too much like trousers to be entirely proper.

Those same people might say that two such shocking creatures deserved each other.

Indeed, they did, and he, for one, was damn thankful.

Author's Notes

John Godfrey Saxe's poem, "The Blind Men and the Elephant," was actually written in 1872. I've utilized a little literary license by allowing Minerva to quote it ten years earlier.

I was reading about George Alfred Lawrence—the author of Guy Livingstone, a novel published in 1857 featuring a handsome Guards officer. Mr. Lawrence decided, in December of 1862, to leave England and volunteer to serve General Lee as a staff officer. This led to my discovery that other men had also left England with the express purpose of participating in the Civil War. Ergo—Dalton MacIain was born.

The incident Dalton relates, with he and his men flipping a coin to decide who would go to the North and who would go to the South, was taken from recollections of Field Marshal Viscount Wolseley as related in James A. Rawley (ed.), *The American Civil War: An English View* (Mechanicsburg, Pa., 2002), p. xiii.—and *A World on Fire: Britain's Crucial Role in the American Civil War*, Random House Publishing Group.

Welcome to the World of
Karen Ranney.
Turn the page to find out what other
wonderful romances Karen Ranney
has in store for you.

In Your Wildest Scottish Dreams

Seven years have passed since Glynis MacIain made the foolish mistake of declaring her love to Lennox Cameron only to have him stare at her dumbfounded. Heartbroken, she accepted the proposal of a diplomat and moved to America, where she played the role of a dutiful wife among Washington's elite. Now a widow, Glynis is back in Scotland. Though Lennox can still unravel her with just one glance, Glynis is no longer the naive girl Lennox knew, and she vows to resist him.

With the American Civil War raging on, shipbuilder Lennox Cameron must complete a sleek new blockade runner for the Confederate navy. He cannot afford any distractions, especially the one woman he's always loved. Glynis's cool demeanor tempts him to prove to her what a terrible mistake she made seven years ago.

As the war casts its long shadow across the ocean, will a secret from Glynis's past destroy any chance for a future between the two star-crossed lovers?

Return to Clan Sinclair

A Novella

When Ceana Sinclair Mead married the youngest son of an Irish duke, she never dreamed that seven years later her beloved Peter would die. Her three brothers-in-law think she should be grateful to remain a proper widow. But after three years of this, she's ready to scream. She escapes to Scotland, only to discover she's so much more than just the Widow Mead.

In Scotland, Ceana crosses paths with Bruce Preston, an American tasked with a dangerous mission by her brother, Macrath. Bruce is too attractive for her peace of mind, but she still finds him fascinating. Their one night together is more wonderful than Ceana could have imagined, and she has never felt more alive.

But when the past reaches out in the form of an old foe, Ceana's life is in danger. Now Bruce must fight to become her savior—and more—if she'll let him.

The Virgin of Clan Sinclair

Ellice Traylor has a secret. Beneath her innocent exterior beats an incredibly passionate and imaginative heart. She has been pouring all of her frustrated virginal fantasies into a scandalous manuscript. But when her plans for her future are about to be derailed by her mother's matrimonial designs, she takes matters into her own hands.

Ross Forster, the Earl of Gladsden, has spent his life creating order out of chaos. He expects discipline and calm from those around him. What he does not expect is a beautiful, thoroughly maddening stowaway in his carriage.

But when Ross discovers Ellice's secret book, he finds he can't stop thinking about what other fantasies the disarming virgin can dream up. He has the chance to learn when a compromising position forces them to wed. But can the uptight Earl survive a life with his surprising new wife? And how will the hero of Ellice's fantasies compare to the husband of her reality?

The Witch of Clan Sinclair

Logan Harrison is looking for a wife. As the Lord Provost of Edinburgh, he needs a conventional and diplomatic woman who will stand by his side and help further his political ambitions. He most certainly does not need Mairi Sinclair, the fiery, passionate, fiercely beautiful woman who tries to thwart him at every turn. But if she's so wrong for him, why can't he stop kissing her? He's completely bewitched.

Mairi Sinclair has never met anyone like Logan Harrison, the perfect example of everything she finds wrong with the world. He's also incredibly handsome, immensely popular, and impossible to resist. His kisses inflame her and awaken a passion she can barely control.

Can two people who are at such odds admit to a love that would bind them together for life?

The Devil of Clan Sinclair

To Dance with the Devil . . .

For Virginia Traylor, Countess of Barrett, marriage was merely the vehicle to buy her father a title. Widowhood, however, brings a host of problems. For her husband deliberately spent the money intended for Virginia and her in-laws, leaving them penniless—unless she produces an heir. Desperate and confused, Virginia embarks on a fateful journey that brings her to the doorstep of the only man she's ever loved . . .

He's known as the Devil, but Macrath Sinclair doesn't care. He moved to a tiny Scottish village in hopes of continuing his work as an inventor and starting a family of his own. He bought the house; he chose the woman. Unfortunately, Virginia didn't choose him. Macrath knows he should turn her away now, but she needs him, and he wants her more than ever. Macrath intends to win—one wickedly seductive deed at a time.

The Lass Wore Black

Third in line for an important earldom, Mark Thorburn is expected to idly wait to take up his position. Instead, he devotes himself to medicine, a life's work that leads him to the door of famous beauty Catriona Cameron.

The victim of a terrible accident, Catriona has refused to admit even the most illustrious physicians to her lush Edinburgh apartments. But what if a doctor were to pose as a mere footman, pretending to serve her every need . . . would she see through such a ruse?

Entwined in the masquerade, Mark manages to gain Catriona's trust, only to find that somehow she has captured his heart at the same time. But when their passion becomes the target of a madman bent on revenge, Mark will have to do more than heal her body and win her love . . . he'll have to save her life as well.

A Scandalous Scot

One scandal was never enough . . .

After four long years Morgan MacCraig has finally returned to the Highlands of his birth . . . with his honor in shreds. After a scandal, all he wants now is solace—yet peace is impossible to find with the castle's outspoken new maid trying his patience, challenging his manhood . . . and winning his love, body and soul.

Jean MacDonald wants to leave her past behind and start anew, but Ballindair Castle, a Scottish estate rumored to be haunted, hasn't been the safe haven she envisioned. Ballindair's ancestral ghosts aren't as fascinating as Morgan, the most magnificent man she's ever seen. Though their passion triggers a fresh scandal that could force them to wed, Jean must first share the secrets of her own past—secrets that could force them apart, or be the beginning of a love and redemption unlike anything they've ever known.

A Scottish Love

Shona Imrie should have agreed to Gordon MacDermond's proposal of marriage seven years ago—before he went off to war and returned a national hero—but the proud Scottish lass would accept no man's charity. The dashing soldier would never truly share her love and the passion that left her weak and breathless—or so she believed—so instead she gave herself to another. Now she faces disgrace, poverty, and a life spent alone for her steadfast refusal to follow her heart.

Honored with a baronetcy for his courage under fire, Gordon has everything he could ever want—except for the one thing he most fervently desires: the headstrong beauty he foolishly let slip through his fingers. Conquering Shona's stubborn pride, however, will prove his most difficult battle—though it is the one for which he is most willing to risk his life, his heart, and his soul.

A Borrowed Scot

Who is Montgomery Fairfax?

Though she possesses remarkable talents and astonishing insight, Veronica MacLeod knows nothing about the man who appears from nowhere to prevent her from committing the most foolish and desperate act of her life. Recently named Lord Fairfax of Doncaster Hall, the breathtaking, secretive stranger agrees to perform the one act of kindness that can rescue the Scottish beauty from scandal and disgrace—by taking Veronica as his bride.

Journeying with Montgomery Fairfax to his magnificent estate in the Highlands, Veronica knows deep in her heart that this is a man she can truly love—a noble soul, a caring and passionate lover whose touch awakens feelings she's never before known. Yet there are ghosts in Montgomery's shuttered past that haunt him still. Unless Veronica can somehow unlock the enigma that is her new husband, their powerful passion could be undone by the sins and sorrows of yesterday.

A Highland Duchess

The beautiful but haughty Duchess of Herridge is known to all the ton as the "Ice Queen." But to Ian McNair, the exquisite Emma is nothing like the rumors. Sensual and passionate, she moves him as no other woman has before. If only she were his wife and not his captive . . .

Little does Emma know that the dark and mysterious stranger who bursts into her bedroom to kidnap her is the powerful Earl of Buchane, and the only man who has been able to see past her proper facade. As the Ice Queen's defenses melt under the powerful passion she finds with her handsome captor, she begins to believe that love may be possible. Yet fate has decreed that the dream can never be—for pursuing it means sacrificing everything they hold dear: their honor, their futures . . . and perhaps their lives.

Sold to a Laird

Lady Sarah Baines was devoted to her mother and her family home, Chavensworth. Douglas Eston was devoted to making a fortune and inventing. The two of them are married when Lady Sarah's father proposes the match and threatens to send Lady Sarah's ill mother to Scotland if she protests.

Douglas finds himself the victim of love at first sight, while Sarah thinks her husband is much too, well, earthy for her tastes. Marriage is simply something she had to do to ensure her mother's well-being, and even when her mother dies in the next week, it's not a sacrifice she regrets.

She cannot, however, simply write her mother's relatives and inform them of her death. She convinces Douglas—an expat Scot—to return to Scotland with her, to a place called Kilmarin. At Kilmarin, she is given the Tulloch Sgàthán, the Tulloch mirror. Legend stated that a woman who looked into the mirror saw her true fate.

Douglas and Sarah begin to appreciate the other, and through passion, Douglas is able to express his true feelings for his wife. But once they return to England and Douglas disappears and is presumed dead, Sarah has to face her own feelings for the man she's come to respect and admire.

A Scotsman in Love

Running from their pasts . . .

Margaret Dalrousie was once willing to sacrifice all for her calling. The talented artist would let no man interfere with her gift. But now, living in a small Scottish cottage on the estate of Glengarrow, she has not painted a portrait in ages. For not even the calming haven in the remote woods can erase the memories that darken Margaret's days and nights. And now, with the return of the Earl of Linnet to his ancestral home, her hopes of peace have disappeared.

From the first moment he encountered Margaret on his land, the Earl of Linnet was nothing but annoyed. The grieving nobleman has his own secrets, which have lured him to the solitude of the Highlands, and his own reasons for wanting to be alone. Yet he is intrigued by his hauntingly beautiful neighbor. Could she be the spark that will draw him out of bittersweet sorrow—the woman who could transform him from a Scotsman in sadness to a Scotsman in love?

The Devil Wears Tartan

A Man in the Shadows

Some say he is dangerous. Others say he is mad. None of them knows the truth about Marshall Ross, the Devil of Ambrose. He shuns proper society, sworn to let no one discover his terrible secret. Including the beautiful woman he has chosen to be his wife.

A Fallen Woman

Only desperation could bring Davina McLaren to the legendary Edinburgh castle to become the bride of a man she has never met. Plagued by scandal, left with no choices, she has made her bargain with the devil. And now she must share his bed.

A Fire Unlike Any They've Ever Known

From the moment they meet, Davina and Marshall are rocked by an unexpected desire that leaves them only yearning for more. But the pleasures of the marriage bed cannot protect them from the sins of the past. With an enemy of Marshall's drawing ever closer and everything they now cherish most at stake, he and Davina must fight to protect the passion they cannot deny.

The Scottish Companion

Haunted by the mysterious deaths of his two brothers, Grant Roberson, tenth Earl of Straithern, fears
for his life. Determined to produce an heir before it's
too late, Grant has promised to wed a woman he has
never met. But instead of being enticed by his bride-
to-be, Grant can't fight his attraction to the understated
beauty and wit of her paid companion.

Gillian Cameron long ago learned the danger of
falling in love. Now, as the companion to a spoiled
bluestocking, she has learned to keep a firm hold on
her emotions. But from the moment she meets him, she
is powerless to resist the alluring and handsome earl.

Fighting their attraction, Gillian and Grant must
band together to stop an unknown enemy from striking. Will the threat of danger be enough to make them
realize their true feelings?

Autumn in Scotland

Abandoned by a Rogue

Betrothed to an earl she had never met, Charlotte Haversham arrived at Balfurin, hoping to find love at the legendary Scottish castle. Instead she found decaying towers and no husband among the ruins. So Charlotte worked a miracle, transforming the rotting fortress into a prestigious girls' school. And now, five years later, her life is filled with purpose—until . . .

Seduced by a Stranger

A man storms Charlotte's castle—and he is *not* the reprehensible Earl of Marne, the one who stole her dowry and dignity, but rather the absent lord's handsome, worldly cousin Dixon MacKinnon. Mesmerized by the fiery Charlotte, Dixon is reluctant to correct her mistake. And though she's determined not to play the fool again, Charlotte finds herself strangely thrilled by the scoundrel's amorous attentions. But a dangerous intrigue has drawn Dixon to Balfurin. And if his ruse is prematurely revealed, a passionate, blossoming love affair could crumble into ruin.

An Unlikely Governess

She had no recourse but to accept the position . . . and no choice but to fall in love.

Impoverished and untitled, with no marital prospects or so much as a single suitor, Beatrice Sinclair is forced to accept employment as governess to a frightened, lonely child from a noble family—ignoring rumors of dark intrigues to do so. Surely, no future could be as dark as the past she wishes to leave behind. And she admits fascination with the young duke's adult cousin, Devlen Gordan, a seductive rogue who excites her from the first charged moment they meet. But she dares not trust him—even after he spirits them to isolation and safety when the life of her young charge is threatened.

Devlen is charming, mysterious, powerful—and Beatrice cannot refuse him. He is opening new worlds for her, filling her life with passion . . . and peril. But what are Devlen's secrets? Is he her lover or her enemy? Will following her heart be foolishness or a path to lasting happiness?

Till Next We Meet

In a departure from her nationally best-selling Highland Lord series, Karen Ranney brings us another emotionally intense and passionate story that will speak to her fans.

When Adam Moncrief, colonel of the Highland Scots Fusiliers, agrees to write a letter to Catherine Dunnan, one of his officers' wives, a forbidden correspondence develops and he soon becomes fascinated with her even though Catherine thinks the letters come from her husband, Harry Dunnan.

Although Adam stops writing after Harry is killed, a year after his last letter he still can't forget her. Then, when he unexpectedly inherits the title of the Duke of Lymond, Adam decides the timing is perfect to pay a visit to the now single and available Catherine. What he finds, however, is not the charming, spunky woman he knew from her letters, but a woman stricken by grief, drugged by laudanum, and in fear for her life.

In order to protect her, Adam marries Catherine, hoping that despite her seemingly fragile state he will once again discover the woman he fell in love with.

So in Love

The Highland Lords: Book 5

Jeanne du Marchand adored her dashing young Scotsman, Douglas MacRae, and every moment in his arms was pure rapture. But when her father, the Comte du Marchand, learned she was carrying Douglas's child, Jeanne was torn from the proud youth without a word of farewell—and separated not long after from her newborn baby daughter. Jeanne feared her life was over, for all she truly cared about was lost to her. Can the power of love prevail?

Once Douglas believed his lady's loving words— until her betrayal turned his ardor to contempt. He cannot forget even now, ten years later, when destiny brings her to his native Scotland, broken in spirit but as beautiful as before. His pride will not let him play the fool again, although memories of a past—secret, innocent, and fragile—tempt him. Can passion lead to love and forgiveness?

To Love a Scottish Lord

The Highland Lords: Book 4

A Lord Not Meant to Marry

Hamish MacRae, a changed man, returned to his beloved Scotland intending to turn his back on the world. The proud, brooding lord wants nothing more than to be left alone, but an unwanted visitor to his lonely castle has defied his wishes. While it is true that this healer, Mary Gilly, is a beauty beyond compare, it will take more than her miraculous potions to soothe his wounded spirit. But Mary's tender heart is slowly melting Hamish's frozen one . . . awakening a burning need to keep her with him—forever.

A Lady Who Dares Not Love

Never before has Mary felt such an attraction to a man! The mysterious Hamish MacRae is strong and commanding, with a face and form so handsome it makes Mary tremble with wanting him. Already shadowy forces are coming closer, heartless whispers and cruel rumors abound, and it will take a love more pure and powerful than any other to divine the truth—and promise a future neither had dreamed possible.

The Irresistible MacRae

The Highland Lords: Book 3

To avoid a scandal that would devastate her family, Riona McKinsey has agreed to marry the wrong man—though the one she yearns for is James MacRae. Had she not been maneuvered into a compromising position by a man of Edinburgh—who covets her family's wealth more than Riona's love—the dutiful Highland miss could have followed her heart into MacRae's strong and loving arms. But alas, it is not to be.

A man of the wild, tempest-tossed ocean, James MacRae never dreamed he'd find his greatest temptation on land. Yet from the instant the dashing adventurer first gazed deeply into Riona's haunting gray eyes, he knew there was no lass in all of Scotland he'd ever want more. The matchless lady is betrothed to another—and unwilling to break off her engagement or share the reason why she will marry her intended. But how can MacRae ignore the passion that burns like fire inside, drawing him relentlessly toward a love that could ruin them both?

When the Laird Returns

The Highland Lords: Book 2

A Marriage He Never Wanted

Though a descendant of proud Scottish lairds, Alisdair MacRae had never seen his ancestral Highland estate—nor imagined that he'd have to marry to reclaim it! But the unscrupulous neighboring laird Magnus Drummond has assumed control of the property—and he will relinquish it only for a king's ransom . . . and a groom for his daughter Iseabal! Alisdair never thought to give up the unfettered life he loves—not even for a bride with the face of an angel and the sensuous grace that would inflame the desire of any male.

A Passion They Never Dreamed

Is Iseabal to be a bride without benefit of a courtship? Though she yearns for a love match, the determined lass will gladly bind herself to Alisdair if he offers her an escape from her father's cruelty. This proud, surprisingly tender stranger awakens a new fire inside her, releasing a spirit as brave and adventurous as his own. Alisdair feels the heat also, but can Iseabal win his trust as well as his passion—ensuring that both their dreams come true . . . now that the laird has returned?

One Man's Love

The Highland Lords: Book 1

She swore to hate him . . . but he knew her heart was his.
He was her enemy, a British colonel in war-torn
Scotland. But as a youth, Alec Landers, Earl of Sher-
bourne, had spent his summers known as Ian, running free on the Scottish Highlands—and falling in
love with the tempting Leitis MacRae. With her fiery
spirit and vibrant beauty, she is still the woman who
holds his heart, but revealing his heritage now would
condemn them both. Yet as the mysterious Raven, an
outlaw who defies the English and protects the people,
Alec could be Leitis's noble hero again—even as he
risks a traitor's death.

Leitis MacRae thought the English could do nothing more to her clan, but that was before Colonel
Alec Landers came to reside where the MacRaes once
ruled. Now, to save the only family she has left, Leitis
agrees to be a prisoner in her uncle's place, willing to
face even an English colonel to save his life. But Alec,
with his soldier's strength and strange compassion, is
an unwelcome surprise. Soon Leitis cannot help the
traitorous feelings she has when he's near . . . nor the
strange sensation that she's known him once before.
And as danger and passion lead them to love, will
their bond survive Alec's unmasking? Or will Leitis
decide to scorn her beloved enemy?

After the Kiss

The promise of a single kiss . . .

Margaret Esterly is desperate—and desperation can lead to shocking behavior! Beautiful and gently bred, she was the essence of prim, proper English womanhood—until fate widowed her and thrust her into poverty overnight. Now she finds herself at a dazzling masked ball, determined to sell a volume of scandalous memoirs to the gala's noble host. But amid the heated fantasy of the evening, Margaret boldly, impetuously, shares a moment of passion with a darkly handsome gentleman . . . and then flees into the night.

Who was this exquisite creature who swept into Michael Hawthorne's arms and then vanished? The startled yet pleasingly stimulated Earl of Montraine is not about to forget the intoxicating woman of mystery so easily—especially since Michael's heart soon tells him that he has at last found his perfect bride. But once he locates her again, will he be able to convince the reticent lady that their moment of ecstasy was no mere accident . . . and that just one kiss can lead to paradise?

My True Love

Anne Sinclair has been haunted by visions of a handsome black-haired warrior all her life. His face invades her dreams and fills her nights with passionate longing. So the beautiful laird's daughter leaves her remote Scottish castle, telling no one, to search for the man called Stephen—a man she does not know but who fights in war-torn England, a place she has never seen.

Stephen Harrington, Earl of Langlinais, never expected to rescue this unexplained beauty from the hands of his enemy. And yet, when their eyes first meet, he feels from the depths of his soul that he should know her . . . that he needs to touch her, and keep her by his side forever. For unknown to both of them, they are in the center of a centuries-old love . . . a love that is about to surpass their wildest dreams.

My Beloved

They call her the Langlinais Bride—though she's seen her husband only one time . . . on their wedding day, twelve years ago.

For years, naive, convent-bred Juliana dreaded being summoned to the side of the man she wed as a child so long ago. Now her husband, Sebastian, Earl of Langlinais, has become ensnared in his villainous brother's wicked plots—and has no choice but to turn to his virgin bride for help.

Juliana now finds herself face-to-face with a man so virile and so powerful that she's fascinated by him—just as he asks her to go against everything she holds true. Sebastian never counted on being enchanted by the beauty of this innocent angel he intended to keep as wife in name only—and he dares not reveal to her the secret reason why their love can never be . . .

The Glenlyon Bride
from the Scottish Brides Anthology

A Novella

A land of legend and wild beauty—of clans, lairds, honour, and passion—Scotland forever stirs the soul of romance.

Now, in one incomparable volume, four of Avon Romance's bestselling authors present stirring tales of hearts won and weddings to be, featuring a quartet of unforgettable heroines about to discover the rapture of love in a world as untamed as the men they will one day marry.

Upon a Wicked Time

He was her ideal husband, and she should have been his perfect bride . . .

Tessa Astley is everything a duke should want in a wife. A breathtaking beauty with a reputation that is positively above reproach, she desires noting more than the love of her husband, the man she's long pined for.

Only Jered Mandville doesn't want a soul mate, just a proper duchess hidden away on his country estate to beget heirs. He certainly doesn't see a place for his bride in his decadent life in London.

Tessa won't let her fairy tale slip through her fingers. She'd do anything to win Jered's heart. So Tessa starts a campaign to win him by invading his home, his reckless adventures, and his bed—all to prove to her cynical duke that even a happy ending can be delightfully wicked . . .

My Wicked Fantasy

An Explosive Encounter
Mary Kate Bennett was married too early, widowed too young, and left to fend for herself without a penny. Her path was never meant to cross with Archer St. John's, except for a terrible carriage accident with the wickedly handsome Earl of Sanderhurst. Mary Kate awakens in a mysterious lord's bed to a life more luxurious than she could have ever imagined, facing a man she's never met before but instinctively knows . . .

A Heart Held Hostage
The whispers about Archer follow him wherever he goes. Had the reclusive nobleman murdered his unhappy countess? When Mary Kate enters his life so unexpectedly, the bold earl is convinced that she has all the answers he has been searching for. So why can't he think of anything else besides her decadently red hair, her luminescent skin, and the feelings this vibrant, spirited beauty evokes within his masculine soul?

A Wicked Fantasy
Their love can be a fantasy, or it can be strong enough to entwine their destinies forever.